M... ...
silence her guests. In a clear, sweet voice she said,
"This is my dear sister, Miss Glorianna Kendell, who
has come to visit me." He didn't even know a sister
existed.

Glori sensed the stares she was getting and would
have fled if she could have found the door. When
she agreed to Daphne's plan, she'd had no thought
of being displayed like a curiosity in a cage. She
detested being the center of attention, and now she
could feel her face getting red to the roots of her
hair.

"I know I can depend upon you all to make my
sister feel welcome," Daphne continued, glancing at
Maxwell. Then inspiration struck—there would be a
slight change in her scheme. The arrogant Mr. Rutherford would hate her for it, but it really didn't matter.

Still smiling sweetly, Daphne faced her audience
and said, "I am also most pleased to announce that
in three days' time, on Saturday morning at eleven,
dearest Glorianna will become the bride of Mr. Maxwell Rutherford."

A deafening silence erupted from the assembled
throng . . .

THE GOLDEN SWAN

AILEEN HUMPHREY

DIAMOND BOOKS, NEW YORK

THE GOLDEN SWAN

A Diamond Book/published by arrangement with
the author

PRINTING HISTORY
Diamond edition/January 1991

ISBN: 1-55773-448-8

Diamond Books are published by The Berkley Publishing
Group, 200 Madison Avenue, New York, New York 10016.
The name "DIAMOND" and its logo are trademarks
belonging to Charter Communications, Inc.

PRINTED IN THE UNITED STATES OF AMERICA

10 9 8 7 6 5 4 3 2 1

THE GOLDEN SWAN
comes to you through
the courtesy of:

Marianne Willman, Laura Halford,
Barbara Faith, Carol Yavruian, Barb Johnson,
and Carol Katz;

Jim Posante and his window shade;

Editors Damaris Roland and Melinda Metz;

Romance Writers of America, Inc.;

Dr. Alex Halliday,
Department of Geology,
University of Michigan;

Dr. Daniel Fisher,
Department of Paleontology,
University of Michigan;

Bev Pooley and things British;

Mylanta.

CHAPTER ONE

S HE couldn't get anywhere near the chain on his leg without making him angry, so she quickly pulled her hand away.

Then "Kissy kissy kiss" in a distinctly female voice was followed by an indignant squawk. One brilliant blue feather drifted to the floor. The parrot flapped his wings and made a halfhearted swipe with his hooked beak, causing the thin young woman in front of him to step back.

"Come now, Shakespeare," she coaxed, adding little clicking sounds she hoped would calm him. "I'm only trying to clean your bowl. Like it or not, we must learn to cooperate for the time I shall be confined here." Glori's voice remained softly melodious while she slowly reached for the bowl again, but the bird grabbed it with one scaly taloned foot and glared at her. "Oh, my, you *are* unhappy. Would you like me to scratch your neck?" But the bird would not be soothed and had thus far kept Glori away from the food container on his perch.

From outside she could hear a lone carriage rattling along the cobbles toward the house across the street. With the cream of society gathered there, a reception was under way to honor the most popular new poet for

1

this spring of 1866. There would be many such events
during the Season, which blossomed from April to July,
and again during the Little Season, which commenced
in September and ended before Christmas.

Placing her wire-rimmed spectacles on the bridge of
her nose, Glori abandoned the bird and hurried across
the room to push aside the snowy lace curtains. Below, a
hackney splashed to a stop on the wet street. She waited
to see who would emerge into the afternoon drizzle—not
that she'd actually know anyone she saw. Even so, she
had found it interesting to observe the other carriages
when they arrived, with ladies in fine dresses and gentlemen who looked so dashing in their regimentals or black
morning coats and striped trousers.

Glori supposed such people attended all the plays and
operas. They probably went to the museums, too. Those
were the places she wanted to go before returning to the
village where she had been born and raised, so isolated
from the exciting things in the world.

A little while ago she had been speculating upon what
the people she saw might be like at home. She guessed
that a particularly rotund gentleman ate vast quantities
of kippers for breakfast. If she were closer, she supposed
she would have been able to hear his corset creak. Glori
had also noticed that the plump lady with him, probably
his wife, walked as though her shoes were far too small.
From this she concluded that the woman was grumpy,
which severely affected her digestion.

The straggler who had just arrived was hidden from
Glori's view until the cab pulled away. Then she saw
the back of a man, dressed much like the others. Yet
this man's coat seemed to fit more smoothly, his trousers
straighter, and he certainly wouldn't need a corset. Quite
tall and broad of shoulder, he climbed the stairs confidently. The black enameled door opened to admit him
before he even touched the brass knocker. Fascinated,
Glori saw that in the lighted entry hall he removed his

gloves, then his hat. His hair was dark. She thought his movements had an easy elegance. Here was a man who undoubtedly smiled a great deal and didn't care for kippers at all.

The door closed.

Glori wondered why he had come alone. Surely he would have no trouble finding female company. She supposed his features would be clean-cut, with a strong jaw. His eyes might be sapphire blue. Men would trust his firm handshake, and women would find his touch . . . enchanting.

Chiding herself, Glori reined in her imagination before it went any further. She thought she'd be better off wondering why such an elegant man had arrived in a hired hack instead of his own carriage. With a sigh, she let the lace curtain fall back into place and tugged here and there at her own decidedly inelegant dress. It made her feel as if she were wearing a baggy blue tent spread over a crinoline. Belted at her smaller-than-ever waist, it had no tucks, no ribbons, no ruffles. It was a practical muslin dress with a prim white collar, a dress she had worn at home in the country while tending to domestic matters or marketing. The reason Glori wore it here in the city was that it had long sleeves and a high neckline to cover her thinness.

Slipping her spectacles back into her pocket, she turned away from the window to renew her housekeeping efforts with the hostile bird. If someone had asked, Glori would have explained that she didn't care to be at the gathering across the street. No one, however, had asked. An invitation to that reception would certainly have been declined had she received one, even though her sister and brother-in-law were there.

Glori and Shakespeare eyed each other in speculative silence as she poked at a few limp strands of hair, smoothing them into the tight bun that had been drawn to the back of her head. Thus prepared to resume her battle with the bird, she was finally able to distract him with a slice of apple and spirit away his seed cup for washing and refilling.

Intending to read for a while now that the bird was happily eating, Glori hiked up her hooped skirts so that she could curl her five-feet-seven-inch self into the large velvet chair, where her skirts covered the arms and fell to the floor. As gas lighting had not been extended to this portion of the house, a paraffin lamp sat on the table next to her. She turned up the wick, and the flame glowed more brightly inside the painted glass shade, pushing back the gloom. Surrounded by a score of daguerreotypes, the lamp seemed to fight for standing room on the tabletop. After checking to make sure the wick wasn't smoking, Glori settled back and unfolded the London *Times*, blessing those unknown people across the street for entertaining her sister today.

Daphne's determined lessons in deportment were driving Glori mad. Still, it was easier to humor her and try to listen than waste more time and energy arguing. They did enough of that as it was. But Daphne would insist that Glori learn how things were done in the highest circles of society.

With the increased lamplight the ornate mahogany furniture glistened, some two dozen gold-framed paintings and drawings claimed greater importance, robed figures on a collection of Chinese vases became recognizable, and Shakespeare's feathers showed an even brighter blue and yellow against the striped maroon wallpaper. Noting the change in his surroundings, the bird perked up and mimicked the sound of carriage wheels on the street. A hodgepodge of word sounds and two piercing whistles followed.

"Well done!" cried Glori. "You may soon stand for Parliament with statements of that sort. Tell me, what is your opinion of the Austro-Prussian situation—do you think it means war? What are your thoughts on the industrial problems? I see. Well, then, how do you stand on the Reform Bill? Have you been following Garibaldi's activities?"

In reply the bird yawned, stood on one leg, and picked at his foot, then whistled again. As a closing gesture, he made an elaborate production of scattering seeds.

"Yes, you seem to have the rudiments of campaigning down rather well," she informed him. "You've made a great show of generosity, but I haven't the foggiest notion of what you've said."

Conversation with a bird being of limited interest, no matter what his political inclinations, Glori began to read aloud from the newspaper. Her pauses were occasionally punctuated by Shakespeare's rattling wheels and kissy kisses, with an especially fine barking dog inserted here and there.

When the bird failed to render an editorial comment on the volume of exotic feathers being imported for the millinery trade, Glori put her spectacles in place to see that he had tucked his head beneath his wing and gone to sleep. The soft, steady ticking of the wall clock kept her company.

Presently the door swung open and Glori's sister burst in, her mood as fiery as the color of her hair.

"The entire afternoon has been a waste of my time!" Daphne announced irritably. She dropped herself gracefully into the chair across from Glori, a beautiful doll in a cloud of pale pink, and tapped her foot impatiently. That's when she noticed how her sister was curled up in the chair. "Good heavens, Glori! Must you sit in such an unladylike way? How often do I have to remind you of such things!"

Without moving from behind the paper, Glori said, "What has sent you off like a skyrocket? I thought you were looking forward to the poetry reading."

"I don't care a fig for poetry, and you know it! Henry is so much older that he understands it. I was trying to

find out what Bella Saunders will be wearing tomorrow
night. She'll try to outshine me if she can."

"May I assume that you didn't find out?"

"I didn't have an opportunity to wheedle it from her.
I left because I'd been insulted!"

At last Glori lowered the paper and looked at her sister
over the top. "Did Sir Henry come home with you?"

"No."

"How odd that you were insulted, yet your husband
remained there."

"Actually, Henry doesn't know a thing about it."

"Now we're getting closer to the truth," said Glori. "I
suspect you've returned to exercise your spleen in private. Did you finally fail to entice some man into your
web?"

"I don't have to *entice* anyone!" Daphne snapped as
she fussed with the folds of her skirt. "I can't help it if
some people are attentive to me."

"Except *this* man, it would seem."

"I didn't say a word about a man."

"You didn't have to." Glori returned to her reading.

These two had grown up together and knew each other
well. Daphne simply ignored Glori and continued to tap
her foot, though such limited activity was hardly enough
to vent her frustration. Maxwell Rutherford had pointedly ignored her, and it made her angry. He always managed to spark her temper. She didn't know why she even
bothered to talk to him, especially when she disliked his
cousin so much. She spent the next few minutes devising disagreeable tortures for the unobliging Mr. Rutherford.

Restlessly Daphne pushed herself free of the chair and
wandered about the room, looking for dust. Then she
paused before a rococo mirror to inspect her carefully
arranged hair. Parted down the middle it was gathered
in bright coppery curls that framed her small face. She
wrapped one less than perfect tendril around her finger to

return her image to a state of perfection, taking care not
to hide her gold filigree earrings set with jade. They had
been a gift from a gentleman friend, though, of course,
her husband didn't know it. Something moved, and she
noticed that beside her own reflection was that of her
sister, turning a page of the newspaper.

Ever since this sister had arrived a fortnight ago,
Daphne had not ceased to wonder how they could have
had the same parents, how they could be the only children
of the Kendells of East Wallow. Glori was such a pale,
gangly thing, who looked as though she'd been kept in
a dark dungeon and fed on nothing but crusts and water.
Coming so near death from an inflammation of the lung
often did that, she'd been told. Sir Henry kept saying to
be patient, that the poor girl wasn't back to health, but
Daphne saw no hope of improvement at all. Medical
men weren't magicians, so she couldn't see what a
London doctor could do for her sister. Their parents,
however, had insisted upon sending Glori to London for
that purpose. Sir Henry had encouraged them to do so,
assuring them that their daughter would be well cared
for in his home.

Poor Glorianna. Who would ever have thought that the
name she'd been given at birth would prove to be such
a misnomer. Daphne recalled that her sister had been a
nice-looking child, but she'd grown up to be as appealing
as a wet dog. And, Daphne suddenly realized with a sly
smile, the absolutely perfect revenge on the disagreeable
Maxwell Rutherford.

Knowing that Maxwell had accepted her husband's
personal invitation to attend their ball tomorrow night,
Daphne decided to have her husband ask the wretch to
take Glori in to supper. He couldn't very well refuse.
After all, Sir Henry was the new ambassador to Italy,
and Maxwell was climbing the diplomatic ladder.

Yes, Maxwell will be livid when he's left with Glori
for the evening, and it will serve him right! Daphne

thought smugly. But she would tell her husband that
she was doing it to provide a bit of happiness for her
poor dear sister. And she would insist that Glori enjoy
herself, whether she liked it or not.

"Glori, do pay attention," Daphne said with new purpose to her day. "I believe it's time for us to think about
what you'll be wearing tomorrow night."

From behind her paper Glori said, "I suppose I'll look
much as I do now. One hardly needs fine clothes to sit
with your bird for a few hours."

With her grand new plan in mind, Daphne simply
headed for the door, pausing to pat the bird on the back,
which resulted in a muffled squawk. "Kissy kissy kiss!"
she sang to the wing that covered his little head with its
tiny ear, then withdrew from the cozy room.

Lowering her paper, Glori watched her sister's departure. She had almost asked about the tall gentleman who
arrived late to the poetry reading, but thought better of it.
In all likelihood such an inquiry would have earned her
another lecture. Still, she only wanted to know who he
was and what he might be doing when he wasn't attending afternoon teas. It seemed to Glori that he wasn't a
man who would be content with such tame sport for long.
His whole body shouted out for a more active life, with
muscles like the ancient Greek athletes whose statues she
had seen in an illustrated magazine—statues with drapes
drawn over them for the sake of decency.

The news events of the world slipped from Glori's
mind when she supposed that the man she had seen
getting out of the cab might even be an athlete. He
could surely perform some deed of great strength. Yet
she was just as certain that he could be gentle as well
as fierce, and wondered what it would feel like to be
held in the arms of such a man. He might crush her
to his chest . . . but perhaps not. She didn't think she
would like being crushed, actually, unless he was terribly
careful how he went about it. But he'd be consumed with

passion, of course, with smoldering eyes and—

One resonant *bong* from the clock marked the half hour as abruptly as it knocked Glori back into the world of reality. Giving the sagging paper a snap, she resumed her reading, or a fine imitation of it.

Just when she and Shakespeare thought their afternoon had become quiet again, Daphne returned with a jewelry box in one hand and a ball gown of frothy peach tulle over her arm.

"Come now, do stand up," she urged Glori, holding the dress out. "This isn't new, but it will do nicely. Besides, I don't wear it any more. I had it copied from one that Queen Victoria is said to have admired, though she has worn only those awful black clothes these five years since Prince Albert died. This dress is so sweet and innocent. As you sew very well, I have no doubt that you can do wonders with alterations."

Daphne didn't seem to notice that Glori had stopped reading—almost stopped breathing, too. Heedless, Daphne tossed the dress onto her sister's lap, over the newspaper.

"Have you taken leave of your senses?" Glori demanded of Daphne, who had put the jewel box on a chair to search through it. "Though improving, I have yet to manage a single day without taking to my bed to rest. A party is out of the question!"

"I hardly expect you to spend the evening dancing, Glori. You can join us for a while, then leave. Stay in bed all afternoon if you like." Daphne untied a small quilted bag, then removed a single strand of matched pearls. "These will suit you wonderfully," she bubbled. "So correct for such a *young* lady."

"Count again, and you'll find that I'm really not as young as—"

"Glori, no one *cares* how old you are," Daphne interrupted impatiently while searching through her jewelry once more.

"Listen to me!" Glori shouted, throwing the dress aside. "What you ask will be dreadfully embarrassing! Everyone will look at me as if I've escaped from Bedlam or the zoo!"

"I can't imagine anyone thinking such a thing! If it bothers you, don't wear your spectacles. Then you'll never know whether they're looking at you or not."

Glori returned to the newspaper, with no idea where she'd left off. "I won't do it," she said. "There is nothing more to say on the subject. I look like a scarecrow."

"Yes, perhaps you do, but your teeth are good," Daphne said absently. Then she chirruped, "Here they are!" and produced the earrings that matched the necklace. Pushing aside the newspaper, Daphne held the pearls next to Glori's thin face. She shook her head and said, "How could mother have been such a goose as to send you here in your condition? One cannot ignore the fact that London had an outbreak of cholera last month, though it has passed. Even so, you would have been better off staying in East Wallow."

"I only wish I were back there right now!"

"Do you really? Do you truly *want* to go back to that poky village? I distinctly remember you saying that East Wallow offered little to enrich your soul. As dear as father is, I will never understand why mother ever married an impoverished younger son who chose to hide away in such a place to dig up strange things and study snails. *Snails*, for heaven's sake! You'll never be able to cultivate suitable friends with a father like ours. Word gets about, you know. I was very lucky to have Aunt Alyce introduce me to society. If she hadn't gone on to her great reward so long ago, she would have done the same for you."

"I've begun to have an appreciation for snails that I didn't have before." Glori made no effort to conceal her irritation.

A little cat smile slowly shaped Daphne's delicate

mouth. "Glori," she began smoothly, "perhaps we can strike a bargain. If you'll oblige me by attending my ball tomorrow night, and behaving nicely while you're about it, I'll pack you off to East Wallow as soon as I possibly can." She was gratified that her sister seemed to be giving the idea serious consideration. "After all, it's unlikely that you'll ever see any of these people again, so it won't matter in the least if they find you . . . a little on the thin side."

"Why are you doing this?" Glori asked skeptically. "As I recall from our less than enjoyable childhood years, any time you did something for me, I ended up wishing you hadn't."

"My only hope is that you might have an hour or two of happiness added to your quiet, empty life," Daphne intoned piously.

"What humbug! You always were one to find *some* way to get what you wanted, no matter how unreasonable."

"Well, do you want to go home or not?" Daphne demanded, arms akimbo.

A great sigh escaped the frail occupant of the big chair. "There seems to be little choice. At least I'll be able to do something nicer with my hair for the occasion."

"Oh, my, that you cannot do!" Daphne stated emphatically. "You know your hair is sapping your strength. My physician distinctly said that you must cut it off and not crimp or curl it if you want to get well again."

"Your physician, madam, is an idiot, and you are amazingly silly!"

The shocked expression on Daphne's face reminded Glori that her sister was probably trying to do the best she could for her, and she berated herself for not trying harder to get along. She told herself that it was time to make a greater effort to improve things between them now that they were grown.

"Perhaps you're right, though I cannot quite

agree," Glori said, attempting to calm troubled waters. The placement of her spectacles upon her nose was done automatically before she scooped up the bouffant gown and left the room. She had been up for so long that she had begun to feel light-headed. It was time to lie down.

"Girls," her sister harrumphed, "have no refinement these days. This is what comes of encouraging young ladies to read newspapers!"

Knees up, Glori lay for the longest while on her bed. When at last her head cleared, she sat up slowly and looked unhappily around the room. Great pink cabbage roses covered the papered walls. Yards and yards of pink silk had gone into the draperies that trimmed both windows. She was glad that this room didn't have as much furniture as most of the others. They seemed cluttered to her, though it was the highest style to decorate in such a way. Her parents' house in the country contained less ornate Queen Anne furnishings. A house that was clearly out of fashion, plainly comfortable, and she liked it.

Turning around, she studied still more flowers that spilled across the thick Oriental carpet that covered much of the floor. Her idle inspection followed the pattern to the side of the room, where a dressing table stood between the two windows. Further to the right was the washstand. Heaped on the floor in front of the washstand was a pile of peach tulle. Queen Victoria may well have admired such a dress, but Glori found the prospect of appearing in it depressing. Though she had never sought to be a lady of fashion, she had no desire to appear an object of ridicule, and that's exactly what the dress would make of her.

I shall remain in my room and send word at the last possible moment that I'm too exhausted to attend Daphne's extravaganza, she thought. It isn't as though I actually promised to present myself! After a few delicious moments of reveling in her rebellious plan, Glori considered what that act would cost her. If she didn't materialize tomorrow night, there would be no transport back to East Wallow. She didn't have enough money to leave on her own, and Daphne knew it. Any anticipatory pleasure she had had, even for so brief a moment, evaporated.

The objective, she told herself, must be kept in mind: to quit this house, along with her sister and the lessons in deportment she was determined to teach.

Bone-tired, Glori tried to figure out what to do about *that dress*. With the household in an uproar over preparations for the ball, it was impossible to find anyone to help move the gilt-framed pier glass from another bed-chamber into her own so that she could see herself to make the necessary alterations. After considerable pushing and pulling, Glori managed it alone, though the task proved exhausting.

After removing her own dress, she dropped her sister's gown over her head. It settled unevenly upon her out-of-date round hoop, which wasn't full enough or even the right shape. This dress was flatter at the front and wider at the sides, with an extended back of long trailing skirt.

That the waistline of the gown was much too high was only one more problem. She grasped handfuls of surplus fabric across the bosom, tucking and folding it here and there, and scowled. Even if the top could be stitched in and persuaded not to bag, she knew she would still look peculiar. Above the daring neckline that didn't come anywhere near her neck, her collarbones and the ribs beneath them stood out like the carcass of yesterday's chicken. Attempting to spread the tulle puffs more modestly over her chest, Glori quickly decided that there wasn't enough tulle in the country to cover her well enough.

The problems with the top of the dress were no worse than those at the bottom. Shaking the skirt out, she was rudely reminded that the garment had been made for a much shorter woman. Anyone could see what she saw: The dress was too short, which was no surprise. Glori took after their father's side of the family and stood a good ten inches above her diminutive sister, who was no taller than their petite maternal grandmother.

Glori's spirits sank further when she found the hem of the dress insufficient to let down. Not only did the dress look ridiculous, her feet showed all the way to the tops of her button-up shoes. These serviceable black high-tops were the best—and only—ones she had with her. Aghast at the sight of herself, Glori lifted the skirt and removed her hoops. Thus deflated, the hem of the skirt settled to the floor.

Discouraged, Glori studied her reflection. The effort expended in moving the pier glass had hardly been worthwhile. It failed to assist with the improvement of her appearance at all. She could not be favorably impressed by any aspect of what she saw. Even the most skilled alterations couldn't help the fact that the color was wrong for her. If given a vast selection to choose from, peach would have to be the worst. By contrast her hair appeared neither light nor dark, but simply awful, her complexion sicklier. Her eyes became dark depressions in her head. Knowing this was the impression she made and that she could do nothing more about it, Glori's spirits sank even further. Bad as it was, she must resign herself to the situation.

Changing into her own clothes again, Glori removed to the small sitting room to sew on the gown until dinner was served. Shakespeare proved to be as much company for her as she was for him. Chatting away in a manner that seemed to appeal to the bird, she tried to hold back the tears so she could see her stitches. She remembered the growing-up years and the thoughtless neighbor boy who had called Daphne the pretty little one and herself the plain big one. At the time Glori hadn't thought it could be any worse. She'd been quite mistaken.

* * *

The hour of the ball crept relentlessly closer, with a foreboding of impending doom that slithered right along with it. Sitting at her dressing table, making futile efforts to do something with her hair, Glori felt worse than ever. Beneath her eyes the gray circles had become a little darker, and her lips looked rather blue. When Daphne brought in the pearls and a corsage of white rosebuds, even she was struck by how extraordinarily pale her sister had become.

"Good heavens, you *have* upset yourself," Daphne remarked as she carefully pinned the flowers to Glori's dress. Next she fastened the strand of pearls around her sister's slender neck. She placed the earrings on the dressing table so she could poke here and there at the peach tulle covering Glori's chest.

"People will think you're someone's servant if you cover yourself up that way. A lady may dress with less restraint." With a dainty thumb and forefinger Daphne lowered the bits of net that Glori had arranged over her exposed flesh. Glori pushed the fabric back into place and kept her hands on top of it.

Patting the top of her sister's head solicitously, Daphne said, "I suppose you'll do as you like no matter what I say. Just rest quietly until our friends have arrived. I'll send word when I want you to join us."

Alone, Glori laid her ugly-duckling self down on her bed, taking care not to crush the flowers. Resting the back of her hand across her eyes did nothing to block out what she saw in store for the evening. One fat tear rolled into her ear. A loud sniff broke the silence. The price of her ticket back to East Wallow was dear indeed.

As she lay there contemplating the events of the past thirty-odd hours, it hadn't slipped her mind that if she had accepted the proposal of marriage from John Cleveland the apothecary's son or Alexander Holden, the soft-spoken, prosperous farmer, she wouldn't be in this situa-

tion. Rubbing her temples with her fingertips, she wondered if things would have been any better. They were
both fine, honest, nice-looking men, but that was all. No
great spark ever lit their thoughts. Though her parents had
been encouraging her to marry, she was grateful that they
hadn't been inclined to insist upon it.

Still, both men had always treated her with consideration, and Glori supposed she could have loved either one
of them well enough after a time. And she would have
produced a collection of little apothecaries or farmers as
appropriate, while managing her home with cheerful efficiency. But surely there had to be more than that. Where
was that special undefinable *something* that a man and
woman shared? It was more than simply *getting along*.
There was something that made her parents touch each
other in passing—something that made them smile when
no one else knew why.

No, Glori reasoned, either of those safe but dull mat-
ings would have lasted a lifetime. Her present predica-
ment, disagreeable as it was, would be resolved in a matter of hours. By tomorrow or the day after she expected
to be on her way back home. The thought provided a
temporary peace.

Mounds of white roses and carnations delighted the
eye and filled every heavenly breath. The ladies' evening
gowns in clear colors of spring were outlined by the black
of the gentlemen's formal evening wear. Hundreds of
candles burned in crystal chandeliers and wall sconces
throughout the house. Such light lent a flattering glow
to each lady's complexion and softened the telltale signs
of dissipation that carved haggard furrows into many a
man's face.

A sliding wall between the large drawing room and the
music room had been opened to form a spacious, glittering ballroom. An orchestra played at one end before a
bank of potted palms. Dancers turned to the lively music

of a Strauss polka that all but drowned out thought, let alone conversation. There were, however, two women who succeeded at both.

One of them was a young widow named Bella Saunders, a voluptuous beauty gowned in two shades of shimmering blue taffeta. Her sultry eyes followed the movements of a dark-haired man of impressive height and breadth, who stood at the edge of the dance floor with several other people. She thought that at thirty years of age he was at his prime and nicely ripened.

Maxwell Rutherford had been singled out again.

"I declare, he makes me limp when he simply looks into my eyes," Bella cooed. "I expect he has a most agreeable manner, though his mustache must tickle so."

The direction of her attention was not lost on the tiny, dazzling redhead standing next to her, who smiled wistfully, then said, "Personally, I've never found the least objection to his mustache."

With that parting scratch, accompanied by a green-eyed feline smile, Daphne Mountrockham turned and seemed to float away in her snowy billowing gown toward the group of people that included her husband.

"My lovely wife," announced stately gray-haired Sir Henry, bowing slightly as he lifted Daphne's fingers to his lips. "We'll be much better company now that you've arrived to keep us all from turning this into an evening of nothing but politics."

Patting his whiskered cheek, Daphne said, "Henry, you are so sweet to me, though I confess I have danced precious little with you tonight. In spite of that, I positively *adore* you." There was only the slightest trace of a provocative pout on her petal-soft lips.

Did Sir Henry seem to stand a mite straighter? On their wedding day he had thought the sun rose and set in his beautiful young bride.

"I was just telling these gentlemen that I'm considering the addition of Maxwell Rutherford to my staff—if he'll accept, that is. It seems the ambassador to Sweden has the same thought. Rutherford's with the foreign office, you know."

Catching that younger man's eye, Sir Henry indicated that he would like Maxwell to join them. In response to that signal both Maxwell and his friend Elgin Farley arrived. "I believe you two know everyone, so I can omit the introductions."

"Yes, we're all acquainted," Maxwell replied, nodding to the assemblage, who smiled and nodded in return. Elgin nodded, too.

Then Sir Henry said, "Maxwell, I seem to be neglecting my wife shamefully. Will you be good enough to save me from her wrath by twirling her around the floor?"

"Of course," Maxwell replied politely. "If you'll excuse us?" He escorted Lady Mountrockham to the edge of the dance floor, where he took her into his arms and fitted their steps to a waltz. It was like dancing with an exquisite porcelain figurine.

"How very sweet you are to rescue me from a chair among the dowagers," she said.

"I doubt it would ever come to that. You're far too lovely to be left stranded." He deftly guided them around the other couples on the floor.

Looking past the dancers, Daphne saw that Bella Saunders watched every move they made. She did enjoy seeing Bella turn inside-out with envy. Yes, Lady Mountrockham was immensely pleased with herself. When she'd left the shapely widow Saunders such a little while ago, she hadn't the slightest idea of how she would arrange to speak privately with Maxwell. Then, while she was running plots through her mind like sand through her fingers, the specimen in question had been laid at her feet, so to speak, by none other than her own husband! Quite sure of herself, Daphne made her next move.

"You are simply amazing, Maxwell."

One eyebrow rose in question, his head tilted slightly.

"I do believe you're as manly on a ballroom floor as you would be . . . anywhere else." She seemed to study his lapel for a moment, then looked up seductively from beneath long auburn eyelashes. "But enough about dancing," she said softly. "Tell me of your diplomatic aspirations. If there's any possibility of helping you to advance, you may feel confident that I'll do whatever I can. . . . " Her words drifted away like thistledown, with the listener never knowing quite where they might land.

Once more her glance sought his, her fantastic green eyes no less hypnotic than she correctly judged them. She usually found it sufficient to provide an opening and then let human nature take its course. She was certain that Maxwell would soon be eager for an occasional afternoon of pleasure—when it suited her, of course.

Maxwell recognized the glint in Daphne's eyes and found a safer topic. He said, "I've hardly thought about much besides the weather lately. This rain makes a devilish mess of planning anything."

"Yes, it has been horrid," Daphne agreed. Then, without missing a step, she slid her delicate hand from Maxwell's shoulder and drew it along her ivory throat while she told him of the dreadful cold she'd caught after a rainstorm last fall. "I was soaked right through to my underthings," she told him in a giggling whisper. Then she laid slender fingers upon her creamy bosom and told him of the fright she'd taken when it had thundered so.

Through the scent of jasmine that wafted around her, Maxwell was well aware of the message Daphne was sending and tried once again to change the subject. Clearing his throat, he said, "I understand that you and your husband will soon leave for Italy. Do you speak the language?"

She was quick to take up any subject Maxwell preferred—for now. After all, she'd played this game before. She knew he found her attractive. The rest was only a matter of time.

"No, I don't speak Italian," she told him sadly. "To correct this flaw I'm having lessons two days a week and hope for some proficiency before we take up residence there." Actually, her desire to learn a foreign language had no attraction other than the rumor that Italians were remarkable lovers. She hadn't been disappointed with her instructor.

"I'm looking forward to your company in Italy, Maxwell. People from home are of such tremendous importance when one is so far away, don't you agree?"

"I suppose they are, though I've not accepted an offer for a post in Italy. Truth to tell, one hasn't been offered."

"But it *could* be. I assure you that *anything* you desire is within your grasp if you wish it." Her voice had fallen to a husky whisper. She had almost decided to forgive him his previous slights and not saddle him with Glori after all.

So far Maxwell had managed to get by without giving insult, but he didn't know how long he could keep it up. While maintaining his cordial facade, he desperately wished he were somewhere else at this moment. The wilds of America would do nicely. The last thing he wanted was to be in Italy, or anywhere else, with Daphne Mountrockham.

"Realizing your interest, I'm having an intimate little tea tomorrow afternoon at three. May I expect you?" Her limpid green eyes turned invitingly up to him.

"I'm so sorry," he told her. "I have appointments scheduled for tomorrow, though you can be sure that your husband will pass along any other invitations to me."

A beat later the music ended, and another partner appeared to draw Daphne away. Maxwell bowed to her, his expression bland. In that instant he lost every shred of clemency she might have extended to him. She'd make certain that he would have to take poor Glori to supper—or worse—if she had to tie them together.

CHAPTER TWO

H E thought it was over.

Breathing remarkably easier now that Daphne had twirled away in the arms of some other man, Maxwell returned to the company of Elgin Farley, who stood alone, looking through the crowd for familiar faces. The cluster of people that had included Sir Henry had drifted apart. Making a slight adjustment to the white bow tie that seemed to be choking him, Maxwell said, "I'd appreciate it if you would stick to me like a bloody leech until we're out of here, my friend. As long as we stay together, nothing can go wrong."

"I wasn't aware that there was a problem, but I'll stick to you like a limpet, if you like, and settle for a detailed explanation later. Just tell me what it is that I'm supposed to protect you from."

"I'll tell you later. I don't want to send up any alarms by making it obvious. All we have to do is put in a respectable amount of time, greet the right people, and we can be gone. For now it's enough to know that I'm comforted by your exalted presence."

"Thank you, I suppose," replied Elgin, "but you might at least tell me what sort of attack you're expecting: boiling oil, cannons, big spoons . . . " Then he glanced around surreptitiously and asked, "Is it permissible to head for the card room to see who's about? Almost anyone will do, as I've been away for so long. Though rest assured," he said, holding up his right hand, "I'll watch over you the way you haven't been watched since your nanny had you in leading strings."

"That's exactly what I had in mind." With Elgin at his side, Maxwell aimed for the table-filled card room that had yet to cloud with smoke.

Circulating slowly, they received many invitations to join a game, though all were declined. One group gave cause for prolonged conversation as the ambassador to Sweden sat among the card players. Yet even for his company, Maxwell was unwilling to make himself a stationary target, a sitting duck for the sporting woman.

By the time they circled the room, the air had become thick, and Maxwell noticed how much time had elapsed. "I suppose we must put in a brief appearance in the ballroom before we leave. Have to say good night to our host. Polite is polite, but let's not be too long at it, if you please."

"Good God, Max! I'll hardly get a look at the flock of sweet young things that've been flushed out for the Season. That's why I came back to town!"

"Sorry to keep you from the floor with the lady of your choice, old boy, but the three of us would look as mad as hatters dancing together."

"My, my, we are serious about this, are we not? It's a wonder you came at all, when you're in such a pucker to be gone."

"Just keep an eye out for Sir Henry, if you please, so we can say farewell and be on our way."

After entering the ballroom again, they took up positions well off to one side of the double doors. It was an out-of-the-way spot from which Maxwell could observe those around him. He would be able to locate Sir Henry, or see Daphne before she could reach him, affording him time for a discreet but swift departure. So Maxwell kept a sharp watch, and Elgin simply looked around.

It was then that the ample form of Bella Saunders leapt into prominent view. Her suspiciously blond hair, styled as it was in ringlets, would have attracted considerable attention even if the display of her other astonishing features had not. Her breasts quivered like great mounds of rising bread dough. When she shifted ever so slightly to speak to the distracted man next to her, it was in flagrant defiance of the laws of gravity. The architectural achievements of her corsetmaker were remarkable. Watching, Elgin Farley appeared to be in a trancelike state.

"My God, Farley, have you been away for so long that you forgot it's most impolite to stare so at a lady's . . ." Maxwell gestured toward the area of his waistcoat.

"It's only because of good manners that I do it," Elgin insisted without amending the direction of his undivided attention. "No personal interest at all, I assure you. Pure self-sacrifice. She might need me if an emergency arises. Have you ever known me to allow an animal to suffer?"

Maxwell slanted a look at his friend. "Until this moment I thought you'd been referring to your farm stock."

"Until I noticed Mrs. Saunders I *had* been referring to my farm stock," Elgin readily admitted, grinning.

"And, of course, you are merely a humble humanitarian. If the lady should strain herself and need your assistance, you'll be ready," Maxwell said in low tones. "It's plain to see that it would be shabby indeed if you failed to help out in her hour of need—or however long it might take for her to regain her equilibrium."

"Think of it this way, Max. The woman has gone to a great deal of trouble for a jolly good show. What if no one paid the slightest interest after all that? How frightfully disappointing it would be for her."

As much truth as anything else went into that observation, and Maxwell turned his face away, hiding a broad smile behind the hand he used to smooth his mustache. Then he made an unnecessary adjustment to his neatly knotted tie and ran a hand down the pleats of his shirt. When he'd regained his composure, he said, "Farley, if you were a noble fellow, you'd have a care for the widow Saunders's best interests and warn her not to bend over so. She might hurt herself or even some innocent bystander. A nasty business *that* would be."

"Ah, well, I suppose I've too great a care for my own welfare ever to be so brave," Elgin lamented. "I fear that even if I missed being crushed by the initial accident, I would certainly be trampled by the pure of heart who rushed to her rescue. Perhaps the field should be left to those men who are more courageous than I."

"A wise move, I believe, because we'll be tossed out on our dignified backsides if anyone hears us."

"True, so true," Elgin replied with another easy grin, lacking the smallest speck of remorse.

Once again Maxwell found it necessary to hide a grin behind the hand that smoothed his mustache. Then he went on to relate bits and pieces of news. Following a lengthy explanation of how a pig came to be sleeping in the bed of a mutual friend, Elgin exclaimed:

"What is that apparition?"

"I beg your pardon?"

"It just this minute sat down in the farthest chair, wearing a peculiar orangish dress."

"If it's wearing a dress, it must be a woman. Surely you haven't forgotten that much while you were in the country."

"Who is it, that's what I want to know. Looks like she's escaped from Bedlam or the zoo. Not at all the thing for someone to bring her here. You can see that she's not liking it a bit. Good thing the poor girl's not sitting too close to the Incredible Widow Saunders. Would make her look even worse."

"Haven't the slightest notion who she is," Maxwell admitted. "Don't believe I've ever seen her before, judging from the top of her head. She doesn't seem inclined to show her face."

Though her face couldn't be seen, Maxwell could see her sharp collarbones well enough, along with her skinny arms and the way her fingers were knotted together on her lap. Feeling terribly sorry for the girl, he thought the kindest thing would be to ignore her, as she was trying so hard to be invisible.

"She doesn't seem to be in the way of knowing how a lady dresses in town. Must be very green, indeed," Elgin decided. "You'd think someone would have put her wise before bringing her out like this. Can't understand it."

Daphne had waited for the right moment. It was to appear as though she had just thought of having Maxwell take Glori in to supper. Now she wanted Sir Henry to arrange it, but he had disappeared. Time was flying by, and she must do something. Glori was here, Maxwell and Elgin had returned from the card room. Together, those men made the most handsome pair of wallflowers she'd ever laid eyes on.

Issuing a martyred sigh, she reminded herself that her first duty this evening was to her sister, a responsibility that she took quite seriously—in her own way. Since dancing with Maxwell, she had convinced herself that this idea of hers had nothing to do with spite and everything to do with family devotion, and she must get on with it.

In fact, her immediate intervention was called for. It was apparent that her fine plan stood at great risk if Maxwell was left unsecured much longer. At any moment he might approach one of a dozen ladies and receive an eager acceptance to dine in his company. One of those ladies was Bella Saunders, dangerously close at hand. Searching the crowd, Lady Mountrockham was still unable to locate her husband and decided that this was no time for the weak-spirited. She would have to arrange things herself.

After weaving her way through the crowd, Daphne reached Glori's side and said, "It's time to come with me. I want to introduce you to my friends."

"Can't I just sit here to meet them? I'm not feeling quite the thing, you see."

"I see no such thing. We made a bargain, don't you remember?" Daphne snapped.

"If I hadn't remembered, I wouldn't be here at all!" Glori whispered fiercely.

"Well, then, come along." She untangled her sister's hands and tugged her in the direction of the potted palms where the orchestra played.

"Daphne, without my spectacles I can't see anyone," came Glori's protest, more to the purpose of having an excuse to leave the room to look for her eyeglasses than to have the pleasure of focusing on the people she would be meeting.

"Never mind. Seeing them will make no difference at all," Glori was told as she was led past beautiful blurs of color that became people at about arm's length.

Stepping up to the conductor and placing a gloved index finger across her lips, Daphne waited for the music to subside. As soon as it was quiet, she would introduce her sister to everyone, then say that Maxwell could now come forward to claim her as his supper partner. It was certainly a more awkward way to manage it than to have Sir Henry do it, but an ambassador's wife learned to deal with these inconveniences.

Raising a dainty hand toward the dancers, she called, "Your attention, please . . . " and waited another moment for the crowd to hush. During that pause, she made it her business to be certain she had Maxwell Rutherford's attention. Her smile turned soft enough to melt London Bridge, while her spring-steel hoops dug into the cellist's shin and the ribbons on her dress caught at his bow.

What Maxwell saw, from his position of security, was his fragile hostess, who appeared as though she'd been graced by a halo. Satin ribbons of emerald green looped from the shoulder to the hem of her white organdy dress. Tiny pink flowers, fashioned from silk, caught the ribbon across her billowing skirt. The same flowers, tied with the same ribbons, were tucked among the curls of her flaming hair. Vivid green eyes framed by dark lashes gazed at Maxwell. The ribbons matched Daphne's eyes, the flowers copied the pink of her flushed cheeks. Surely, here was an angel, a tiny spirit come to earth to bring beauty into their desolate lives.

Feeling safe now, Maxwell's conscience pricked him for having thought so contemptuously of Daphne. Perhaps he had misunderstood her behavior tonight. She might not have known how the situation had appeared to him. He supposed he'd learned so much of what society was truly like behind its moral facade that he'd begun to mistrust everyone. Feeling rather ashamed of himself, he turned his attention to the person who stood at Daphne's side.

It was the same Unfortunate that Elgin had pointed out to him. His heart went out to the pathetic girl who stood there, blushing furiously. Her hair was in a tight unattractive bun, and she wore an awful dress that just hung on her. She reminded him of a withered orange peel. The assemblage was silent now, trying to appear as though they were simply waiting, not staring. Impossible, of course.

He watched Daphne raise her hand again. In a clear, sweet voice she said, "This is my dear sister, Miss Glorianna Kendell, who has come to visit me."

The few who had known had forgotten that a sister existed. None of them, however, would have expected Daphne Mountrockham to have a sister who looked like *this* one.

"She must be on loan from Bedlam or the Zoological Garden," snorted a wrinkled matron behind her fan to the elderly gallant at her side. Long past a prime she never had, she took perverse delight in pointing out someone, *anyone*, less attractive than herself. It hadn't been easy until tonight.

Glori could feel rather than see the stares she was getting and would have fled if she could have found the door. When she agreed to Daphne's plan, she'd had no thought of being displayed like a curiosity in a cage. Just sitting as inconspicuously as possible had been bad enough. She knew how she looked to these people and had felt the heat when her face went red to the roots of her hair.

"I know I can depend upon you all to make my sister feel welcome," Daphne continued.

When she glanced at Maxwell again, inspiration struck. Her eyelids lowered a fraction in quick calculated study. There would be a slight change in her scheme. The thought that followed was more wicked than ever because she knew a secret that would force the arrogant Mr. Rutherford to do anything she wanted him to, though he'd absolutely hate her for it. It didn't really matter.

Still smiling sweetly, Daphne faced her audience and said, "I am also most pleased to announce that in three days' time, on Saturday morning at eleven, dearest Glorianna will become the bride of Mr. Maxwell Rutherford."

A deafening silence erupted from the assembled throng. The supposed bride-to-be would have run, had her feet been capable of doing so. The red drained from her face, leaving it sheet-white. Darkness rimmed her vision. The bump and shuffle of orchestra instruments faded away to an echo in the distance, then came no more as she fainted at her sister's feet.

Everyone's eyes were on the great pile of peach-colored fluff into which Glori had disappeared. Everyone's eyes except Daphne's, that is. Her interest was riveted upon Maxwell Rutherford. The vivid coloring that had deserted her sister seemed to have traversed the room to rise in that esteemed gentleman's face. Daphne was more annoyed than alarmed by the fact that Glori had crumpled to the floor. After all, she had seen the girl faint before, and it hadn't appeared to hurt her in the least.

"Oh, Mr. Rutherford!" exclaimed Daphne in a musical trill. "Impetuous men are commonly unnerved at a time like this." Tittering rippled through the audience of this unscheduled farce. "Shouldn't you be bearing your beloved off to someplace more comfortable than the floor? Young ladies of . . . of sixteen years often swoon thus, I warn you."

Perhaps Moses had parted the Red Sea much the way Maxwell's approach separated the crowd, but Moses undoubtedly enjoyed that passage considerably more than Maxwell did his. At the moment there was absolutely nothing he could do except comply unless he wanted to make a fool of himself.

True to his word, faithful Farley was right behind as they made their way to the stricken girl. The ladies in attendance had pulled off Glori's gloves to slap her hands. They fanned their fans and waved vials of hartshorn until the sharp smell of ammonia pinched their own noses, too. Excusing himself, Maxwell replaced these women to kneel beside Glori.

From across the room he'd seen that she was thin, but he hadn't realized just *how* thin until he lifted her. He concluded that most of her weight must be the dress. Maybe she hadn't fainted at all. Maybe she had simply starved to death on the spot.

Daphne lead the way out of the ballroom and into the wide hall, then held open the door to a small sitting room with striped maroon wallpaper. Before entering, she said, "Mr. Farley, will you find someone to bring water for dear Glori? Please make certain that it's cold."

Elgin hurried away. Daphne stepped into the room behind Maxwell and closed the door.

Still holding Glori in his arms, Maxwell stood angrily before his hostess and said, "The game is over. Someone may come to a wedding on Saturday, but don't expect me!"

He crossed the room to gently lay his unconscious burden on the carved sofa, managing not to knock any pictures or bric-a-brac off the table as he passed. The heavy scent of Daphne's jasmine perfume rose from the dress Glori wore.

"Oh, you'll be here," Daphne assured him. "You see, I know the family scandal. I'll ruin the Rutherfords, every last one, if you don't show up to marry my sister."

Maxwell's head snapped around. "You're bluffing."

"I'm honestly not. Randy, that nasty cousin of yours, is a thief, though he's not a very good one. I caught him at it in February, at the Fitzholdens'. I didn't tell anyone at the time, however—"

"This is blackmail!"

"Indeed, it is. And so very effective."

At that moment Elgin entered, ahead of a footman who carried a tray with glasses, a pitcher of water, and a decanter with something substantially stronger. With nothing more required of him, the servant left.

"Don't concern yourself with the license," Daphne told Maxwell. "As you'll probably have a great deal on your mind during the next few days, I'll see to it myself." A wave of her slender hand said more than any additional words possibly could. Then she was gone, closing the door firmly to block the way to those whose curiosity she did not intend to satisfy.

Elgin stood helplessly by, fists jammed into his pockets, distorting the fit of his trim-fitting trousers. Evening clothes weren't tailored for such abuse. Maxwell's coat strained at the seams when he folded his arms tightly across his chest and stared at the door through which

Daphne had just passed. Near the door he noticed a scruffy-looking stuffed parrot attached to a perch. Feathers littered the floor. Very likely moth-infested, he concluded.

Casting an eye to Glori, Maxwell became rather alarmed to find that she was still deathly pale and hadn't moved at all. Placing two fingers to her throat to be certain a pulse still beat there, he encountered cold waxy skin before he felt the slight yet reassuring cadence he sought. Then he could only stare at the inert female.

"For crissakes, I don't want a wife. *Any* wife. What in hell am I supposed to *do* with her?"

"A doorstop, perhaps?"

"Try again."

"Is this a joke of some sort, Max?"

"Do you see me laughing?"

"Then I assume that the individual from whom you needed the protection was none other than Lady Mountrockham herself."

"It has become quite obvious, has it not? She isn't nearly as angelic as she appears to be."

"I didn't protect you very well. Sorry about that. Hadn't expected an attack from that quarter. Not the thing at all. Perhaps we can call in one of those ladies with a fan to see to this poor girl, and we'll slip out of here."

"It wouldn't help. I'm expected back on Saturday."

"So you are. Sticky wicket you've got set up. Of course, I'm eager to know how you managed to be so lucky, but at the moment I'm more interested in what you're going to do about *her*." He nodded toward Glori.

"Oh, hell! Wait around and talk to her, I suppose. I got the impression that she had no more advance warning of the proposed nuptials than I did."

"Maybe she's strange in the head and you can respectably quit this thing," Elgin offered.

Maxwell shook his head and looked with mixed pity and disgust at Glori. "I doubt that our ingenious hostess would leave me an avenue of escape that easy to follow."

"Why did Daphne do this to you? I thought you were a favorite of hers." Elgin's remark was followed by a rascally wink.

"We've had a difference of opinion, on several occasions."

Elgin laughed ruefully. "Yes, I recall some of them."

Maxwell just didn't know what to say to this dismal little creature who would soon awaken to the company of two strange men. He didn't want to frighten her, yet he had to find a way to derail this disaster.

Glori stirred, her brow pulled into papery pleats.

"Poor thing, she must be feeling like warmed-over gruel."

"Sorry, I didn't quite hear you," Elgin said.

"It was nothing of importance. I was merely saying that she must be feeling awful."

This observation reminded Maxwell that a friend had said his wife sometimes fainted when she was breeding. He studied Glori's supine form with this possibility to mull over. Could it be that she was in just such a dilemma and her sister was trying to marry her off? It wouldn't be the first time such a condition had inspired drastic measures to find a husband.

He wondered if Glori was one of those unfortunates, used by some callow fellow and abandoned to her fate. His protective instincts stirred. If he were her brother, the cad would have hell to pay.

Glori turned her head. Maxwell leaned closer in case she spoke.

"Kissy kissy kiss!" shrieked Shakespeare in Daphne's voice.

Maxwell straightened up and spun around so fast that he nearly unbalanced Elgin. While Maxwell's eyes stabbed the corners for the enemy that went with the disembodied voice, Elgin stared at Shakespeare. With nothing more to say at the moment, the bird picked idly at his toes.

"My God, Daphne's turned herself into a parrot!" Elgin exclaimed.

"I thought she was stuffed!"

"Stuffed? Not Daphne. You must be thinking of Bella Saunders."

"Not either one of 'em. I meant the bird. I thought the damn thing was stuffed!"

Shakespeare stretched his neck as far as he could in an unsuccessful attempt to sink his sharp beak into any part of Maxwell that he could reach.

"Well, you can clearly see that she's not stuffed, though she probably should be. Imagine going through life with Daphne's voice popping out at you from every nook and cranny. It's enough to put you off your feed!"

"Shakespeare is a *he,* not a *she,*" came faintly from the sofa.

"Beg pardon?" Elgin said as he bent down, trying to catch Glori's words.

A bit of color had returned to her face, and her eyelids fluttered open. Gazing out from shadowed sockets, she focused on the man attending her.

"Mr. Rothford?"

"You mean Rutherford. But no, I'm not. The name's Elgin Farley, at your service. Max is over there."

"Where?" she asked, rising up on one elbow to squint. She looked like an owl disturbed in a dark barn.

Maxwell winced and positioned himself beside Elgin, towering over Glori. Rigidly polite he said, "I'm right here beside you, Miss Kendell."

Glori sagged against the sofa and closed her eyes in an attempt to keep the room from spinning.

Hazy. His silhouette had been hazy, but she knew it, she was sure of it, and knew the way his body moved when he climbed the stairs and the angle of his hat. Knew that he removed his right glove first. Little things. Almost . . . intimate things. And now she knew his mellow voice, too. Here was the man she had watched from the window yesterday, the same man who had lifted her from the floor with such care. The man who had held her safely in his arms and spoken softly through the cold fog to comfort her.

Now he stood tense and guarded. Which, she wondered, was the true Rutherford; the gentle giant or this stiff stranger? It amazed her that in spite of the horrible trick that had been played on him, his reaction to her had been one of kindness. Without further contemplation, Glori knew the answer to her own question. Blinking slowly, she found that the room had stopped revolving.

"Please sit down and excuse my dramatics, gentlemen. I'm afraid I rose rather quickly and began to feel dizzy again."

They took seats while Maxwell assured her, "There's no need to apologize, Miss Kendell. Shall I send for a physician?"

"Heavens, no! There's nothing wrong with me that a little time and a few more potatoes won't cure."

Maxwell began to sweat. Time? How much time? he wondered. Was she speaking of the months until an equally scrawny child arrived? "Miss Kendell—"

"Glori," she corrected. "Please call me Glori. I think with the fix we are in, we may all consider ourselves well enough known to one another to use first names, even though we have never actually been introduced."

"Glori, then. And yes, we do indeed find ourselves in a fix."

"We shall get ourselves out of it, of course."

"You have no desire at all for this match?" Maxwell asked hopefully.

"None, though I don't mean to offend you."

Offend him? God, if she only knew! He was just glad

that she didn't seem to be in a family way and in need of a husband to go with the condition.

"You're not to worry about offending me, Miss Kendell. Glori, that is. But tell me, just how do you propose we get ourselves out of this? A gentleman can't respectably end this thing. It must be left to the lady. Can you apply to Sir Henry for help?"

Glori shook her head. "Sir Henry is truly a love, but a bit . . . vague. In all likelihood he would think the marriage perfect. He's a romantic, I'm afraid. And my parents are too far away to know what's happening here. I think it will be best if I simply leave. You may as well know that my sister will never retract her edict, now that she has made it. She'll probably manage to put the announcement in tomorrow's *Times*," Glori said woefully.

Maxwell gave her a sympathetic smile. "You speak of leaving, but you don't look as though you could walk away—let alone run away."

"I shall need your help, if you don't object. You see, I haven't enough money to buy pins, not to mention a train ticket. As much as I dread asking you for funds, I must."

"You'll go back home?"

"Yes, to East Wallow."

"When will you make this great escape?" As he spoke he fished his wallet from an inside coat pocket, removing several notes that he pressed into Glori's hand.

"Tomorrow," she said, rolling the bills into a tight wad. "I'll go tomorrow night after I've rested, when there's no one about to notice. If I felt more the thing, I'd be gone tonight." Then her bravado cracked, and she said, "Mr. Rutherford—"

"Maxwell," he corrected.

"Maxwell. Will you mind terribly being jilted? It isn't the thing to do to a gentleman. You have had so much forced upon you that I'm loath to heap more on your plate."

He only chuckled at her choice of words and supposed that back in East Wallow there was a swaggering sixteen-year-old boy from whom she had learned such cant. "Don't let it bother you, Glori. I'll come about. You, on the other hand, cannot simply leave here and go wondering until you find a train. Tomorrow night I'll have a hackney waiting in the lane behind the carriage house, with a maid to go along with you. The driver will be instructed to wait from, oh, say . . . around dusk to almost dawn. Does that match your plans?"

"Yes, quite well."

"Good, then it's settled. But don't go with anyone who can't tell you who has sent the cab."

"My God, Max!" groaned Elgin. "It sounds as if you're planning a kidnapping. Can't you just leave town?"

"If I did, you can be sure I'd be a ruined man. Daphne would see to it. Or make certain that someone else did the dirty work for her. She has a tremendous amount of influence at the moment."

"What does that matter? Your uncle is more powerful than an ambassador's wife."

"Not this time. I can't do much else, nor can my uncle. The only hope is for Miss Kendell to end the matter with a timely vanishing act." There was a grim note to Maxwell's voice that neither of his companions missed.

"The fat will be in the fire if you're caught helping her get away."

"I have to weigh one risk against another. Consider the alternative to this plan, my friend. What do you see?"

Elgin frowned. "A frightful bit of business on Saturday at eleven."

"Exactly. So the plan stands, though we'll have to use great caution so no one might guess what we're up to. At the end of it I'll manage to appear tragically jilted. Perhaps I'll even take myself off to the country until I can face the world again."

"Well, that's all there is to that," Glori concluded from

her horizontal vantage point. "I will be gone, and you
will be properly heartbroken." When the gentlemen prepared to rise from their chairs for departure, she blurted,
"Wait, please, Mr. Rutherford . . . Maxwell. It's obvious that you and my sister are anything but strangers to
each other. Why did she do this? Did it have anything
to do with the temper she was in yesterday afternoon?"

Maxwell took a deep breath and expelled it slowly. "I
wish I could answer that, but I can't. Though I can say
that this isn't your fault, Glori. None of it. Sometimes
things simply happen."

"Engagements like this do not *simply happen!*"

All Maxwell could do was shrug. He couldn't very
well say that her sister wanted to have an affair, but he
did not. Couldn't say that her sister thought her ghastly
enough to be the ideal form of revenge. That wasn't the
sort of thing one discussed with a young lady of sixteen
years—or any other lady, for that matter.

While Maxwell struggled with his thoughts, Glori
knew she couldn't expect him to say much more than
he had. Couldn't very well expect him to admit that he
and her sister were lovers, that they had quarreled and
this was the result.

Glori was the first to look away, saying, "If you don't
mind, I think I'd like to be alone now, so that I may
climb off my pillory in some amount of privacy."

"May I call someone to help you?" Maxwell asked.

"No, I'd rather you didn't."

"Well, then, good night. I shall look forward to meeting you again one day under less demanding circumstances. Your servant, ma'am."

Shakespeare watched through beady black eyes as
Maxwell and Elgin prepared to take their leave. The
bird quickly side-stepped to the end of the perch that
was nearest the door and lunged at Maxwell as he passed.
Once again it was unsuccessful, but he'd been closer,
which gave him hope.

After the men left, Glori made another attempt to sit up. She hadn't wanted to risk becoming dizzy again while they were watching her. Nor did she want them to see her cry. She should have guessed that Daphne would have known a man like Maxwell Rutherford.

Shakespeare did well to keep his fowl mouth shut.

As the carriage horse plodded along, Maxwell and Elgin grew more and more somber. And though they hadn't spoken since leaving Glori, their thoughts were closely aligned.

Finally Elgin said, "Do you think she'll be able to do it? Leave, I mean. She isn't very strong."

"I expect she'll manage. It doesn't sound too complicated."

"Max, I've never seen you backed against a wall before. Are you going to tell me what Daphne has up her sleeve? Surely, your Uncle Neville can—"

"No!" A muscle jumped along Max's jaw.

"That's all? Just no?"

"That's all."

"Sounds serious."

"It is."

"And if you can't get out of it?"

Maxwell took a deep breath, held it, puffing his cheeks as he exhaled. "I'll be a married man." He leaned back into the corner of his seat, top hat pushed down over his brow, arms folded tightly across his chest. "In that event I suppose I could leave the girl with my aunt and uncle to incubate for a few years. Who knows what might hatch. She can hardly be an asset as she is. My God, she wore galoshes with the ugliest dress I've ever seen!" He shifted his weight on the lumpy seat and crossed his long legs, mindful not to kick Elgin. "Fortunately, it shouldn't be that difficult for her to slip away. I expect this will all come to nothing in the end."

In silence Elgin stared out the window, thinking about

the supper he'd missed until a change of attitude suggested he'd bit into something sour. He said, "Max, there is one other thing, though I hate like the devil to bring it up."

"Hmm?"

"I was just wondering . . . What if she can't make a go of it and you end up married? Do you suppose that damn bird will come along with her?"

Shuddering, Maxwell slumped further into the corner and said, "Farley, go to hell!"

CHAPTER THREE

HEAVENLY cool.

Her ears had almost stopped ringing. Glori had all but forgotten how wonderful a damp cloth could feel on one's forehead. Annie, the worried little maid, turned the cloth over, clucking around her like a hen with one cracked egg. When Daphne arrived, she wanted privacy and sent the girl away. Looking rather pleased with herself, she said, "It's good to see a bit of color back in your cheeks, Glori. We all had quite a start."

"Yes, especially Maxwell Rutherford," Glori replied without disturbing her cool cloth.

"Despite your overreaction, it really did go rather well, don't you think?"

"No, I don't think it went well at all! Did Mr. Rutherford provoke you somehow? Is that why you've done this?"

"Glori, I don't know what you're talking about!"

"Then I shall have to speak more plainly. Were you having an affair with him? Was there an argument, and you've done this to get even?"

"Glori, how can you say such a thing!"

"I'm not stupid, and I *know* you. I have eyes in my head, and I can see that you're up to something, or you

41

wouldn't be doing this to either one of us."

"I haven't done this *to* you, I've done it *for* you."

"What rot!"

"Such horrid language for a lady. It's a good thing Maxwell can't hear you, or he would take serious exception to it, I promise you."

"He has cause enough to take serious exception to a great many things. I doubt he would even care about one small vulgarity! How could you do this?"

"I saw the chance to arrange a match, and I did it. How else do you think you'd ever be able to catch someone like him? Besides, it's time to think about a husband, so why not Maxwell?"

"Because this isn't what either one of us wants! Can't you understand that? Yesterday you said you would send me back to East Wallow if I went to your party. You've done this instead. Did you plan it all along?"

"No, it simply came to me as we stood there. It was a stroke of genius, was it not?"

Glori didn't seem to appreciate her sister's mental dexterity.

"Actually, I had first planned to have him take you in to supper. Then I realized that this would be the perfect time to announce an engagement, if you were only engaged, but you weren't. That's when I decided it was as good a time as any to engage you."

"And that's the only reason you did it?"

"Of course. Didn't I just say so?"

"Then you will have to set about *dis*engaging us. We don't care for it, thank you."

"Glori, give yourself time to get used to the idea. Come," she coaxed, "tell me what you and Maxwell talked about in the sitting room."

"Oh, the usual things for those about to be married—how do you do, my name is Glori. Have we met before?"

"You are so tedious!" Daphne yelled.

"I went to your party, but I will not go through with this!" Glori shouted back.

There was a moment of silence before that little cat smile thinned Daphne's lips. Turning away, she collected the strand of pearls that lay on the dressing table, along with the earrings Glori had never put on. Then she patted her sister's foot through the covers and said, "Go to sleep—things always look better in the morning. I must return to my guests now. Good night, Glori."

When the door closed there was the unmistakable sound of a key turning in the lock. A mutinous Glori snatched the wet cloth from her forehead and sent it *splat* against the door.

So this is how it is. I'm to be a prisoner. What a miserable jest. This is the sister who constantly lectured me on proper conduct. Criticized my speech, my posture, my very thoughts. The very same sister I had been trying to get along with! Glori fought back the tears of frustration that stung her eyes and burned her throat. Something akin to hysterical laughter threatened to engulf her, and she struggled to subdue it. She had the feeling that if she laughed or cried now, she might never be able to stop.

Yet it was only last week that Glori had laughed merrily over Daphne's lecture against any undue displays of intelligence that might frighten possible suitors away. "If the men of England want stupid wives, they deserve them!" Glori had said. Her sister had been dismayed by such an opinion and warned of unnamed but dire calamities that were certain to befall her, should she let her tongue run away with her in public. Though Glori had scoffed, it hadn't stopped the flow of instruction concerning the proper and—heaven forbid—improper subjects for conversation among genteel company.

Now, locked up in her room, Glori wondered when she would have an opportunity to make those vague references to politics that were so right for a lady's conversation. Of course, she reminded herself, the raising of flowers was an acceptable topic, while the raising of cattle was absolutely not. That's because cattle *did things* that flowers did not do. Neither should she be so crass as to speak publicly of a gentleman's trousers or, even worse, anyone's legs. If that portion of one's anatomy must be mentioned at all, they were referred to as one's *limbs*. A person's legs were shocking to the sensibilities, or *should* be.

Daphne had pointed out that in the refined homes of America, where so much that was British was imitated, even the pianos were draped to cover the legs. The very idea made Glori laugh. Daphne then admitted that the pantalettes which adorned the legs of one such piano might have been put there to twit a British gentleman who was present. Still, she had not been amused when Glori asked what mad passions a man might be driven to by a glimpse of piano ankle.

On one point, however, the sisters did agree. Prince Albert's attitudes about society (including its legs) had been quite prudish, considering he and the queen had parented a swarm of children. It made Glori wonder if they had ever noticed each other's legs during the process. Still in all, he had been a remarkable designer and engineer—for a prince.

"Modesty in all things must be the byword of an unmarried lady," Glori was repeatedly told. And one must *never* become the object of gossip. Gossip could absolutely ruin a person, and society was unforgiving.

Though she hadn't seen any more of London than what was visible from the windows of her sister's house, Glori was well on her way to being heartily sick of its *society*. Once she had longed to see the fabled sights the city had to offer, having read so much about Westminster Abbey, the Houses of Parliament, the Tower of London, the parks and canals, even the tramway. Now she just wanted to go home—home to East Wallow, which was on the outer edge of nowhere, with every likelihood of remaining so. There were no remarkable estates, no hot mineral water baths. Not even the site of a minor miracle.

Glori would be the first to admit that the hamlet lacked any attraction for the fashionable. In fact, the fashionable seemed to go out of their way to avoid it. Few traveling coaches stopped at the inn, though the food was fine and the beds clean. The village did, however, boast an ancient rune stone that scholars of antiquities found to be immensely fascinating—primarily because no one had ever been able to make head or tail of it. Glori knew a real kinship with that stone. She felt old and worn down, without anyone who understood anything about her—except, perhaps, for Mr. Rutherford.

Forcibly controlling her emotions to overcome her scrambled thoughts, Glori reminded herself of what she had to do: escape. Someone might unlock the door and forget to lock it again, or she might be able to force it. Perhaps one of the servants would help her. Disagreeable as it would be, she would sleep in her clothes, just in case. Whenever an opportunity presented itself, she would be ready. With the same needle and thread she had used to alter that awful ball gown, she would sew the money Maxwell had given her to her corset cover.

While stitching away Glori wondered what it might have been like if she, not Daphne, had met Maxwell Rutherford first. They might have become friends and even attended the Mountrockham's ball together. A dress of pale mauve gauze would have shown her exquisite sloping shoulders, if she'd only had exquisite sloping shoulders. Then she decided that the dress wouldn't be mauve. It would be a rich amethyst shot with silver, and Maxwell would hold her in his arms as they whirled around the dance floor, swept along by a tide of beautiful music—though she couldn't quite decide what that music should be. But his hand would be warm and firm against her back, and when he smiled at her, his blue eyes would flash in anticipation of a rapturous meeting behind a screen of potted palms.

Glori finished the last stitch and made a knot, snipping the thread with her teeth. It hadn't mattered that she knew only country dances, not the waltz that was done in London, or that her thin shoulders were best hidden from the world. She'd only been supposing how things *might* have been. What she had to do was get back to East Wallow.

After telling Glori good night and locking her chamber door, Daphne returned to the ballroom. Her nemesis was there waiting for her, languidly swishing the blue taffeta fan that matched her dress.

"Imagine that," the bountiful Bella drawled. "Your sister has brought the elusive Maxwell Rutherford up to scratch. How strange that you didn't mention it before."

"It was a secret."

"Oh, really? I do hope she's feeling better. I could go to her now and keep her company."

"I'm so sorry, Glori is resting, poor dear. Too much excitement—she doesn't want to see anyone. In fact, she's just told me that she intends to stay in her room until the wedding to conserve her strength. I suspect it's really because she's so very shy."

"Seeing the two of you side by side, I wouldn't have guessed she was your sister."

"I know. I would *never* have worn those pearls without the earrings."

Unless someone was out in the passage near Glori's door, he wouldn't have heard the soft scratching sound she made while trying to open the lock. A bent nail file and an assortment of twisted hairpins later, she was still as much a captive as she had been when Daphne had shut her in a few hours before. If determination had been a consideration, Glori would have been out long ago. That quality, however, had scant bearing on the fine art of lock picking.

Close to dawn the music in the ballroom ended. The great fuss that followed was unavoidable when so many people all wanted their carriages at the same time. By then, however, Glori was asleep, so she didn't hear any of it, or the key that turned when Daphne looked in to make sure her sister was still there. Hours later the sun shone brightly across her bed, but Glori still slept. She didn't move an eyelash until she heard her name called.

"Good morning, Miss Glorianna." It was Annie. "Would you like your breakfast while it's hot, or do you want me to leave the tray for you?"

Glori rolled over and groped for her spectacles on the bedside table. "Just pour the chocolate and leave the tray, Annie." Sliding out from under the covers, still wearing her dress and sturdy high-button shoes, she inched toward the door as quietly as possible. Pulling it open, Glori found herself face to chest with a burly young coachman who effectively blocked her exit.

"Kindly move aside!" she ordered.

"I'm sorry, miss," Annie said, twisting her apron uneasily. "His orders are to see that you don't leave this room while the door is unlocked. He's got the key and must return it to Lady Mountrockham as soon as I'm done here. She said you're in a nervous state because of your wedding coming up so soon and can't be left to wander about."

"That's ridiculous!" Glori shut the door on her smirking guard.

"I expect so, miss, but those are his orders." Lacking a proper table, Annie moved aside the bottles and jars and laid breakfast on the dressing table.

"Yes, I see how it is. I know you can't help it."

"Thank you, miss. I'll bring you anything else I can. Best that you eat now. Goodness knows you need it.

Going hungry will only make things worse."

After the maid was gone, Glori ate her meal in angry silence before looking for another escape route. She soon learned that it was an awfully long way down from her third-story window with not so much as a handy drainpipe to cling to, and decided she would need a different plan.

Sometime after her second cup of chocolate, she thought of the fireplace chimney. If a chimney sweep could pass through it, surely she could, too, as thin as she was. Bending over, she twisted around to look up into that sooty passage and instantly gave up the idea. Even if she could get up onto the roof, how would she get off the roof?

When Annie brought her next meal, Glori asked quietly if she might be able to find another key that would fit the lock on her door. A few hours later Annie returned with a pot of hot tea, fresh biscuits, and four keys wrapped in a large serviette.

It took great self-control for Glori not to try the keys as soon as the door was closed. Good sense dictated that she wait until her dutiful watchman was well away from his post. Then each key was fitted carefully into the lock, jiggled and turned, wiggled and twisted, without result. She tried them all a second time, then a third, making adjustments in pressure and position, again without success.

Not one of the keys fit her door.

When Annie brought her supper tray, Glori asked for a screwdriver. She had it in mind to go to work on the brass lock plate. Inside the serviette that arrived with her evening tea was that tool. Unfortunately, it wasn't large enough to turn even one of the screws. What she gained was a blister on the palm of her right hand and a new respect for locksmiths and carpenters. She prayed that Annie would somehow be able to get the correct key away from her sister.

Evening turned slowly into night, and Glori gave up her grand plan of sprinting away into the dark. Unable to concentrate on a book, she traded her wrinkled clothes for a more comfortable nightgown. Blowing out the flame in her lamp, she longed for escape into sleep. It was a long way off.

A sound sharpened her attention, or had she been dreaming? It came again. Someone was throwing something at her window. Spectacles in place, Glori left her bed and raised the window sash to search the mews. The yard looked so different bathed in silvery light and moon shadows.

"Glori! Down here!" came the harsh urgent whisper.

"Mr. Rutherford? What are you doing down there?"

"Trying to find out why you're still here. The cab has been waiting. Why aren't you in it?"

"Be quiet, someone will hear you!"

"The Mountrockhams left hours ago," he answered as softly as he could and still be heard. "If our luck holds, we won't wake the servants. What are you waiting for?"

"How did you know which window was mine?"

"For crissakes, Glori, not now! Let's get going!"

"I can't get going. I've been locked in."

He muttered something uncivil and tossed aside the remaining pebbles. Thinking for a moment, he said, "Tie your sheets together and use them to come out the window. Just remember to fasten your end to something sturdy."

"I . . . I don't think I can do it," she answered, her eyes on the distant ground.

"Yes, you can. Give it a try."

Without saying anything else, Glori turned from the window, lit a lamp, and set upon her bedding. When the sheets, draperies, and a light blanket were tied corner to corner into a rope, she fastened one end to the side rail of her bed and dropped the other end out the window. It didn't reach the ground.

Maxwell stepped from the shadows. "Don't worry, I'll catch you. Just be careful!"

That was when she realized she was still in her night-gown but decided it didn't matter. If she took the time to dress, she might miss her chance to get away.

Driven equally by desperation and the thrill of escape, Glori took a deep breath and lifted the hem of her night-gown so she could swing one leg over the windowsill. Taking hold of a sheet, she looked down and wasn't able to move at all. Cold fear froze her there.

"Go back inside, Glori," came Maxwell's firm voice. His heart contracted painfully as he watched and sensed the fright that had stilled her. "Go back inside," he repeated as calmly as he could, afraid she would fall, cursing himself for being so consumed with his own freedom that he had risked Glori's safety. "Look back into the room and go inside. I'll come up and see what I can do about getting you out." Finally following those directions, she disappeared from his view, one slim bare foot the last thing he saw.

Removing his coat and tossing it next to the house, Maxwell studied the wall for a moment before he hoisted himself onto a windowsill on the ground floor. He balanced there by gripping the window trim, and, standing on tiptoe, managed to get one hand on the tip of the blanket that hung just within his reach. Arms bulging, he began to climb hand over hand.

What happened next went so fast that Glori hardly had a chance to react. The bed began to slide, and she lunged for it. As she leaned her weight against it, the improvised rope went slack, and she heard a thud. Panic gripped her as she dashed to the window to see Maxwell sprawled on the ground. A knot had come undone and the blanket was still in his hand. He looked dead.

"Maxwell!" she cried, heedless of who might hear. "Can you hear me? Please, get up!"

Slowly rolling to his side, he pulled himself to a sitting

position. He gripped his left ankle, shoulders hunched in pain.

Tears of misery filled Glori's eyes, and she slid a fingertip beneath her spectacles to wipe them away. She berated herself for allowing anyone else to attempt something she was too frightened to do. Now Maxwell had been hurt, perhaps severely, just because she wanted to go home.

The back door banged opened. Glori recognized the butler's voice shouting, "Who's out there? Begone or I'll set the dog on you!"

Maxwell looked up and stabbed a finger toward the useless but incriminating rope. Glori hauled it back inside. By the time it lay in a pile on the floor, Maxwell was gone, along with his coat and the blanket. Sinking down among the mess of twisted fabric, she fought back tears until her throat hurt, then began to untie the knots and put the room in order. While rehanging the wrinkled draperies, it occurred to her that they didn't even have a dog.

In the morning the supercilious housekeeper, Mrs. Granger, brought in breakfast, prompting Glori to ask, "Where is Annie?"

"Annie has been set to work in the scullery until she learns not to interfere in the business of her betters!" came the icy reply. Mrs. Granger made her indignation quite obvious, feeling that the menial task of serving Glori was beneath her. Without explanation, the woman then took a dark dress from over her shoulder and dropped it onto the bed before departing with her nose in the air.

Glori was relieved to be alone again, though the news of Annie's banishment to the scullery worried her more than a little. She hoped the girl wasn't in any serious trouble. But she was most distressed by Maxwell's injury and wondered how badly he had been hurt. Then she told herself that she would have to think more clearly if she ever wanted to get away. There was still today and tonight to make good her escape and she intended to do so. She'd just have to manage it without help from anyone else.

After dressing she went about the process of pushing, turning, and poking at every bit of molding and trim in the room in search of the latch to a secret panel. Her aunt Alyce's house was rumored to have such a thing in the study, with a stairway to the master bedchamber, where there was another hidden door. The trick was to find the mechanism that opened it.

Eventually Glori placed a chair on top of her dressing table to reach the raised plasterwork near the ceiling, running her fingers over every inch. Before she completed her quest the formidable housekeeper arrived with the midday meal. Encumbering clothes prevented Glori's prompt decent from her lofty perch. She could only look down in horror, uncertain of what that woman might do.

Huffing and puffing, Mrs. Granger deposited the tray on a chair, pointedly ignoring Glori. She didn't really care what *that young person* did as long as she stayed in her room to do it. She sailed out with as much self-righteous indignation as she had steamed in with.

Standing on the floor again, with dusty hands and straggling hair, the intrepid detective totaled her discoveries at several dried-up flies and two buttons that didn't match. Another survey of the room brought the fireplace tools to her attention. Using these heavy instruments, Glori thought she could surely pry the lock from the door and be done with it. Wondering why she hadn't thought of it sooner, she waited until after dinner to do the deed, when there would be less chance of being interrupted.

The day went on longer than Glori could have believed possible. Finally the evening meal was over, and the household quiet. Servants were no longer treading the hall outside her door, and it was unlikely that Mrs. Granger would pop in with hot tea. Glori selected an iron poker as the most likely of the fireplace implements. She brandished it like a sword and felt like Joan of Arc. Tonight she would set herself free, board a train, and be on her way.

Lower lip firmly between her teeth, Glori carefully fitted the tip of the poker into the keyhole, took a deep breath, and leaned her weight against it. The brass plate began to bend. Freedom was so close she could taste it.

Moments passed before it became obvious that all she had managed to do was ruin the lock plate. Then she wondered if she had damaged the lock so that no one would be able to open the door from the outside, either. Initial concern turned to morbid amusement when Glori thought of the house filled with wedding guests while that mountain of a coachman took an axe to the door to get her out.

Friday evening came to a close with nothing else to lighten her mood, certainly not the sight of the dress Mrs. Granger had left, which was apparently intended for her wedding. Still, she thought she might be able to slip away during the confusion that tomorrow morning would surely bring.

Though it had been ten years since Daphne left East Wallow, Glori couldn't think of anything that had happened before or since the separation that would have inspired any affection between them. But in all her twenty-one years she had never disliked her sister quite as much as she did right now.

On Saturday morning at ten forty-five Maxwell and Elgin entered the Mountrockham residence. This time their steps weren't quite as brisk as they had been a few days before. Maxwell was limping slightly. Sir Henry, hand outstretched in a congratulatory greeting, was the first to welcome the two men when they arrived in the drawing room.

"Maxwell, I should have known you'd recognize a diamond in the rough. I didn't even know you had come to call on our Glorianna," Sir Henry confided with a hearty chuckle. "My wife says I never pay any attention to what's going on around me, but I do. Did you know that I had planned to introduce you to Glori when she felt more the thing? Well, I did. She's not at her best now, you know. Inflammation of the lung almost killed her. Would you care for a drink? Something for you, Elgin? No? I can see that you're both a bundle of nerves. Best get yourselves over there by the potted palms." Thumping the silent Maxwell on the shoulder with a well-manicured hand, Sir Henry consigned him to Elgin's care and went off to restore his own empty glass.

Others replaced Sir Henry with their good wishes before Maxwell and Elgin had moved very far. No one asked awkward questions. It simply wasn't done. At least not here and now.

"Have you invited any of these people?" Elgin asked when there was a pause in traffic.

"Not one. I'd been hoping *I* wouldn't even be here."

"What about your aunt and uncle? Have you told them anything?"

"I sent a telegraph message to let them know when I'd be arriving. I didn't say anything about the possibility of having someone with me."

"What about Miss Kendell's parents?"

"I have no idea." Maxwell then surveyed the wedding guests and said, "This is quite a collection the Mountrockhams have put together on such short notice."

A casual perusal of those people was impressive, even if one didn't know exactly who they were. The ladies and gentlemen wore dresses, boots, coats, hats, all by notable designers. Bella Saunders was there in another Worth gown from Paris. This wasn't a gathering of the simple folk.

If there had ever been a time when Maxwell doubted

the force Daphne could exert, the group assembled here corrected that misconception. The place fairly reeked of money and power. Public disgrace would only be compounded by what any one of these people could do if Daphne chose to tell all. Maxwell couldn't begin to guess who among them his cousin may have victimized. Industrialists, politicians, a royal, the church, bankers . . . He knew these people. Their methods ranged from subtle to ruthless in dealing with their problems. They could be valuable friends or dangerous enemies.

With only himself to think about, Maxwell would have thumbed his nose at Daphne's threat of blackmail and made a new life in Canada or even Australia. Of course, if there had been only himself, the problem would never have arisen in the first place. But there were others to consider, and the weight of family honor rested heavily upon him. As a Rutherford, he would rise to the occasion, do what must be done, and keep a stiff upper lip in the process. It was inconceivable that a British gentleman would do anything less.

Yet, even at this late hour, Maxwell hoped against hope that Glori wouldn't show up. He had fantasies of the wedding being postponed indefinitely because the bride couldn't be found. That was still a dream when he took his position before the familiar potted palms, with Elgin at his side. Silently he cursed Daphne Mountrockham. At least he thought it had been silent.

"Careful," Elgin warned. "As I recall, you said the same thing about the same woman years ago."

And so he had. Back then she'd been Miss Daphne Kendell, staying in town with her aunt for her coming out.

In his rutting youth, when passions were stronger and judgment weaker, Maxwell had often been in the company of the beautiful Daphne. They were part of a lively set that went sightseeing, rode in the park, and planned outings. Daphne had had a good many admirers, but she favored Maxwell Rutherford above them all. She made a point of being with him as often as she could. Though girls of good families were not to be tampered with, she made it very difficult for him to adhere to that code of behavior. Before she discovered that she could catch a wealthy husband, even though she lacked a dowry, Daphne tried everything she could think of to get Maxwell to the altar.

During one tearful meeting she demanded that he marry her. She said she was in a delicate condition because of what he'd done. Maxwell pointed out that he hadn't yet had the opportunity to do anything at all—though until then he'd been looking forward to it. In addition to her physical condition it seemed she had mistaken her gentlemen friends.

Angry? Yes, Maxwell had been angry. Not because of the ruse Daphne had tried to pull, but because she couldn't even remember whether or not she'd ever been in bed with him—or whatever secluded glade they might have substituted for a bed. *That* was more than his manly pride could take lying down. He avoided her as best he could after that. He hadn't always succeeded, but he had managed to dodge any monumental problems for a while.

Then, about two years ago, he'd been at a house party in Surrey. Daphne was there without her husband. The first night Maxwell was told by a maid that a certain red-haired lady had paid quite handsomely to be shown to his room and that she was waiting for him in her nightclothes. Maxwell promptly set off for the nearest inn with an empty bed.

Now it seemed his luck had run out. He was finally at Daphne's mercy. Still, Glori hadn't arrived, so all was not yet lost. He would try to look surprised if she didn't show up. He'd volunteer to search the stable and cellar. He'd suggest they head for the river—but never mention King's Cross Station.

His hopes crumbled when Glori appeared, with red
puffy eyes, in another of her sister's awful dresses.
This one was navy blue, with a fold mark around the
bottom where the hem had been let down. The top
bagged, and the sleeves were too short. She also wore
a matching hat trimmed with blue feathers and beads.
The hat fit better than the dress, but that didn't say
much, though he thought one of the feathers could be
tied into a decent trout fly. At least the dark color made
this ensemble less conspicuous than the ball gown had
been, though the smell of Daphne's perfume clung to
everything Glori wore.

Daphne arrived, too, as beautiful as ever, letting Maxwell know with the slightest nod that her resolve was as
firm as ever. Then her calculating gaze fell on the man
next to him. Elgin Farley was lighter in coloring and
clean shaven—an unusual state, as most men had facial
hair of some sort. Though rather glum at the moment,
he was roguishly good looking, with a lusty reputation.
Definitely worth inviting to tea.

Sir Henry stood there looking quite official, while
beaming approvingly upon them all.

Without her glasses Glori had to move closer to see
the face of her intended. Maxwell's eyes weren't blue
as she'd thought they might be, but an earthy brown
threaded with bronze. And he had a mustache. Dark
brown, almost black, like his hair. Soft and silky looking. His hair grew wavy and longish over his collar.
She noticed a small mole on his left cheek. His features
were clean-cut and strong, much as she thought they
would be.

She looked so worried when she whispered, "Maxwell, your ankle, how is it? When I saw you there on
the ground, I—"

"It's only twisted, it's nothing," he assured her hurriedly, somehow uncomfortable with her concern. "One
more night and I would have been able to get you out,

you know. I had difficulty locating a specialist from the less respectable part of town."

"A specialist?"

"A burglar. A man I heard of who gets into big houses and steals things." A tired half smile formed when he continued the hushed explanation. "As he isn't incarcerated at the moment, I was going to have him steal you. Actually, I got the kidnapping idea from Farley."

Farley produced a tight smile.

Glori was unable to stifle a nervous giggle and pressed her fingers to her mouth. After everything they'd gone through over the past few days, being carried off by a burglar struck her as outrageously funny. "Oh, I *am* sorry," she said, trying not to look amused. "I do, however, have a plan of my own."

Maxwell's weary expression hardened as he shook his head over the futility of it all. "It's too late."

"No, it isn't," she whispered. "I simply won't go through with it. I'll say I've changed my mind."

"It's too late," Maxwell insisted. "Your sister will be certain that I've put you up to it."

"It doesn't matter. What can she do?"

"A great deal, I'm afraid, and I've got to think of my family."

"The gossip, is that it? I assure you that I won't mind if you won't."

"Believe me, it's too late. I've got to go through with this!"

Visions of a Rutherford being dragged before the courts nearly choked Maxwell. The public disgrace of any member of the family would make chances of his own continued employment unlikely, and he was not an independently wealthy man. Even worse than that was what his aunt and uncle would suffer. They might even be obliged to leave the country.

"Glori, I swear I'll take care of you, and I'll make this up to you somehow," he whispered urgently.

Bella Saunders saw Maxwell's earnest appeal and assumed it to be caused by sappy adoration. Looking at Glori, she simply couldn't understand it.

As for the bride herself, the scrambled pieces had slowly fallen into place until she saw her situation clearly. Everything had changed since that dreadful engagement announcement that Daphne made—changed since she had been locked in her room. She had been virtually helpless then, but she wasn't anymore. There was nothing to stop her from taking her eyeglasses from her pocket, putting them on, and walking away. She still had Maxwell's money attached to her corset cover. No one in East Wallow would blame her if she left here. After all, they remembered Daphne.

Glori's mouth curved into an almost fiendish smile when she pictured herself sauntering down the stairs and out the front door. The scandal Daphne hated would be heaped upon her doorstep like hot coals.

But when Maxwell took hold of her hand, she couldn't forget that this was the man who had held her in his arms and murmured gentle words when her world had crashed around her. The magistrate stepped before the potted palms. The ceremony began. She glanced in the direction of the door, or where she thought it would be. There was only a moment to make up her mind, and a moment was all she needed to be free.

Still, this was Maxwell, kind and considerate, despite the fact that he'd been badly used by her sister. Outrageous Maxwell who would have had her kidnapped by a burglar. She had to admit that her life had been anything but dull since he had come into it. But how could she be a wife to a man who had been her sister's lover? Would he feel trapped and hate her for it? Yet, if she married him, she wouldn't be stuck in East Wallow for the rest of her life.

"Glori, please," Maxwell prompted, squeezing her hand.

With a last glance toward the door she took a deep breath and made the proper replies. The grip on her hand relaxed as Maxwell followed suit. Elgin held out a ring, Maxwell took it from him and slid it on to her finger. Too big. She curled her fingers into a fist to keep it there. It was done. They were married. She wondered who bought the ring.

It had all happened so swiftly, with numbing efficiency. That's exactly the way Daphne had planned it.

The Mountrockhams joined the newly wedded to introduce each of the guests. When the last one passed, Maxwell asked, "How are you doing, Glori? Do you think you can hold up a bit longer?" Pulling out his pocket watch, he said, "We don't have much time to catch the train. I didn't think you'd want to stay for the reception."

He was right; she didn't want to stay.

Elgin hurried them toward the door, taking careful note that the few pieces of luggage being loaded into the Mountrockham carriage didn't include a birdcage.

Feeling rather dazed, Glori wondered if it could have truly been only days since she'd looked out the sitting room window and watched Maxwell enter the house across the street. He had arrived long after the portly man who ate so many kippers.

She said, "Maxwell . . ."

"Hmm?"

"Do you like kippers?"

"*Kippers*? Can't abide the things. Does it matter?"

"No, I just didn't think you would like them." But she looked rather pleased that this early impression of him had been accurate, insignificant as it was.

Not quite sure if he had heard right, Maxwell looked quizzically at Glori. Her thin face was turned trustingly to his, an amused smile on her faded lips. Beaded fringe trembled on her borrowed hat. Yes, he must have heard her correctly. Kippers. Neither one of them really *wanted* to be married, she had nearly died and looked it, had been locked up for days, didn't seem to have any clothes of her own, he was being blackmailed, his ankle hurt like roaring hell, his career tottered on the edge of ruin, and she was glad that he didn't like kippers!

Perhaps Elgin's early suspicion hadn't been too far from the mark. Glori might have an empty room in her attic. Still, Maxwell figured that being such a frail young thing, she couldn't *possibly* affect the established structure of his life all *that* much.

CHAPTER FOUR

"MAXWELL, this marriage of yours was rather sudden, so let's not beat about the bush. Have the two of you been, ahh . . . " Neville James Randolph Garfield Rutherford, sixth duke of Westbourne, tugged at a corner of his walrus mustache and began again. "Is the young lady . . . That is to say, is she . . . "

"Is she what?" Maxwell finally asked, looking up from the toes of his shoes with maddening innocence. He had hardly slept since the night of the Mountrockham's gala and was nearly punch-drunk from fatigue. Though bright flames sizzled and danced along glowing logs in the cavernous marble fireplace, he was far too weary to absorb any warmth from them.

"Maxwell, it's perfectly clear that your uncle wants to know whether your bride is already with child," his aunt Maud stated matter-of-factly. "These things do happen sometimes, even in the best of families and—"

Lifting one hand to halt the flow, Maxwell said, "Rest easy, Auntie, I haven't compromised the girl and intend to leave her as chaste as I found her. She's been kept unbelievably secure, locked away in London with her sister and brother-in-law. Perhaps you know the Mountrockhams, or know of them."

Still an attractive woman despite her years, Maud paused thoughtfully over the tiny yellow knots she was adding to the center of a neatly stitched zinnia. "Oh, yes, that would be Daphne. Red-haired, isn't she? And positively mad for you at one time. Mountrockham is an ambassador, I believe. But let's not stray from the path," she said sternly. "You must know that my curiosity has been killing me since you arrived with Glorianna in tow. If you mean to explain yourself kindly, do it. If not just say so, and I'll leave you to yourself for as long as I can stand it. Just don't try to tell *me* that you've been swept away by some grand passion."

Some grand passion. Maxwell would have laughed had he not been too exhausted to do so, though his aunt hadn't intended any humor in her remark. Slumped into a tapestry-covered armchair, his long legs were stretched out before him, crossed gingerly at the ankles. Tired eyes at half-mast, he resumed the study of his shoes and noted that they had become badly scuffed since he'd put them on that morning to attend his own wedding. Obviously lost to propriety, he still wore his morning clothes well into evening. Changing out of them would have meant a delay in London.

Earlier that day on the train, while Glori had still been able to take an interest in the passing scenery, Maxwell prepared for this meeting with his family. His energies had been focused upon finding the best way to explain everything, without really explaining anything. That's what diplomats did best. He knew he'd have to tread cautiously, staying well away from any mention of his cousin and the blackmail business, yet sticking as close as he could to the truth. Maxwell commenced his narrative with:

"In a way it was a marriage of convenience. I decided that it would be most convenient if Daphne didn't ruin me." He glanced at his aunt and uncle; they were listening intently. "You see, I was one of many guests in the Mountrockham home the night Glori and I were sort of . . . *thrown together*. It was made to appear as though we had planned something of a clandestine nature. Daphne engineered the entire affair." Maxwell's audience looked properly appalled so he went on in the same vein.

"After a brief confrontation that I'd rather not describe, my lovely hostess pulled an ace from her sleeve. She threatened to make a nasty scene before some of the most influential people in the country if I didn't agree to marry her sister." He hurried past that part, hoping detailed questions wouldn't be asked.

"It would seem that Daphne has never quite forgiven me for not being more receptive to her attentions all those years ago and decided to get her pound of flesh. I can't begin to describe what the scandal would have been like, but rather than be mauled in the teeth of it, I chose matrimony."

Shaking a finger at the ceiling, Neville became alarmingly red-faced. After regaining his power of speech he blustered, "Let us understand exactly what is going on here! Do you mean to say that the young woman who is now asleep upstairs was a party to such a dastardly plot?"

"Lord, no! Glori is absolutely blameless," Maxwell said. "In fact, she even tried to talk me out of the whole business—said she could hide away in the country and ignore the gossip indefinitely. I, on the other hand, couldn't manage such a thing. I practically had to get down on my knees and beg her to marry me, just to silence Daphne."

"You don't say!" Neville couldn't fathom Maxwell begging anyone for anything.

"Of course, I'm telling you this trusting that you'll never quiz Glori about any of it. It would be distressing for her. And I try not to mention anything too personal, either. She's been quite ill and is sensitive about her looks."

Irritably Maud pushed aside her embroidery, saying, "I commend your concern for the poor girl, but this is unthinkable! I'm sure your uncle could have prevented it, had he but known. How does the rest of her family feel about this preposterous union?"

"I have no idea, they weren't at the wedding. I'm not even sure they knew it was taking place, as there had been only a few days' notice. Her parents live a rather remote, quiet life in Yorkshire. Her father is a scholar of the natural sciences, Glori tells me, and her mother paints."

Frowning beneath the great mustache that matched his salt and pepper hair, Neville drew himself up to a height that equaled Maxwell's. Then he locked his hands behind his back and rocked to and fro, which strained the waistcoat buttons over his ample middle. "Most irregular. Most irregular indeed! It won't do for a Rutherford to have such a hole-in-the-wall wedding, I can tell you that!" With a hopeful gleam he looked hard at his nephew and said, "Are you sure it was legal?"

Maxwell nodded. "Daphne made the arrangements and Daphne is thorough. The license was genuine enough, as was the magistrate who came with it."

"Ah, well, that's the way of it then," grumbled the old man.

"Over the past few days I've made inquiries about positions in other fields. Not only have I lost my appetite for London, I've lost my affection for the diplomatic service as well."

"Good heavens, you wouldn't actually consider going into *trade*!" exclaimed his uncle distastefully.

"Better trade then dodging Daphne Mountrockham at every turn," Maxwell retorted. "Besides, there are things other than politics that interest me. Though I do appreciate the home and education you've provided, we all know that I must make a future for myself. As for Glori . . . well, you've seen her. She needs rest and good country air. I'm hoping you'll keep her here. I can't very well cart her about to parts unknown and expect impossible things from her. I'll stay on for a day or two, until she's settled in, then return to my rooms in London. I've told Simms"—he meant his valet and jack-of-all-trades—"to have everything ready to go on short notice. I haven't any fixed plans past that."

After assuring Maxwell that Glori was welcome at Westbourne Hall, his aunt urged him to go to bed before he fell asleep in his chair. He didn't argue, but he wanted to talk to Glori first. The thing was he didn't know quite where to find her, though he had an uncomfortable idea as to where she might be. Soon after their arrival Glori had been whisked away by Mrs. Finney, their little bird of a housekeeper. That's the last he'd seen of the girl. Now he wondered if she might have been put into his room and consequently his bed, as advance preparations hadn't been made for her.

Having reached the first floor, candle in hand, Maxwell cautiously opened the door to his private domain. With considerable relief he found it unoccupied. The next logical place for Glori was the room next to his. Opening the door that connected the two rooms, he found a lamp burning low on a chest, leaving everything in dim light and shadows. It was here that he found Glori, sound asleep in her petticoats. Partly hidden by the crewelwork curtains of a Tudor bed, she was all curled up on the counterpane, with a quilt draped haphazardly over her.

From the open door of an empty armoire hung her hoopskirt, the graduated steel bands transforming it into a corpulent ghost. One of two trunks lay open. A dress had been draped neatly over a chair, apparently ready to be put on—obviously not one of Daphne's. For a moment Maxwell felt like a Peeping Tom, even though he knew he had every right to be there.

Reaching the foot of her bed, he softly called, "Glori, wake up. We need to talk."

No response.

"Glori!" he repeated a little louder. "Wake up!"

She stirred, then held very still, confused by the sound of a man's voice. "Maxwell?" she whispered.

"Yes. I just want to talk to you for a moment." He moved around to the side of the bed.

Easing one slender hand from beneath the quilt she stifled a yawn. "I only meant to rest for a little while," she was finally able to say. "I thought you might need some time alone with your family—they must have been full to bursting with questions."

Maxwell mustered a grin. "So they were, and rather blunt questions at that. You missed a jolly good show." He became a shadow that loomed across her when he tugged on the quilt to cover her more completely. She nestled into it. He said, "We need to talk tonight because there might not be much privacy in the morning."

Without giving it a thought, Glori moved over to make room for him at the end of her bed.

Without giving it a thought, Maxwell sat down. The bed sagged beneath his weight. He was far enough away that Glori didn't slide into the depression he made. Fingers woven, thumbs tapping, Maxwell geared up for what could be a touchy conversation.

"First," he said, "I want you to know that you're welcome here. Aunt Maud will be pleased to have you, though I must offer a word of advice; she isn't given to any unnecessary display of the grins, so you mustn't think she's gone sour because she's not smiling. When she turned sixty and five, she decided that smiling was giving her wrinkles. Actually, smiles or not, she's a game old girl."

"And your uncle?"

"Oh, he smiles all the time—says he doesn't give a damn if he gets to look like a hound." Maxwell didn't seem to notice his slip into rough language, and Glori, accustomed to her father's habits of speech, didn't seem

to care. "And don't worry about missing tea tonight,"
he added. "Mrs. Finney popped in to tell us you had
dropped off. I told her not to disturb you." Leaving one
foot planted on the floor, Maxwell bent the other knee
and shifted farther onto the bed.

"Next, there's no need to explain anything about the
wedding and all that. Essentially, I've said that we were
discovered alone together, and though innocent of any
impure designs upon my person, you married me to salvage my sterling reputation. If anyone becomes insistent,
you might say that we met at your sister's, that I admired
your great good sense, and thought it was time I settled
down."

Glori's soft sleepy laugh hardly allowed him to finish. She remembered all too well the conversation she'd
overheard through a chink in the chatter after the wedding. One guest wondered why Maxwell had hurried into
marriage to such an odd-looking female. The reply was
a bawdy one, suggesting that the bride might have hidden talents that no one else had yet sampled. Using a
flippant tone to mask the embarrassment she still felt,
Glori quipped, "How do you know I've got any sense
at all? Perhaps I'll just tell everyone that I made you my
love-slave and you couldn't help yourself."

Maxwell laughed softly into the velvety night. "That's
a better story than my own—tell it to anyone you
choose." Then he groaned. "Oh, for crissakes, what am I
saying!" He leaned back against the bedpost, resting his
head there. When he blinked, his eyes stung, so he left
them closed, completely forgetting that he had planned
to stay for only a moment. Then, not really expecting
an answer, he asked, "Have you ever been so tired you
felt drunk?"

"Once," Glori replied after giving it some thought,
stretching out warm and lazy beneath the quilt Maxwell
had spread over her. She took great care not to bump
his leg on the other side of the cover that separated

them. "It was back when East Wallow was struck by the chicken pox and I helped one of the families who had sick children."

"Aha! Then you've been drunk, too, or you wouldn't even know what I'm talking about!" He'd felt Glori's legs slide alongside his thigh and considered the joke fate had played. Very clearly he remembered the sight of her bare foot swung over the Mountrockham's windowsill. He didn't know of one other gentleman who had ever seen his intended's bare foot before they were married. Then he amended the view he'd had to include a good deal more than Glori's foot. It had been her leg, bare to her knee! It was the kind of thing he'd have to keep to himself lest malicious tongues hear of it and wag unmercifully.

"You'll have to mend your wicked ways, my girl, so as not to shock my aunt and uncle," Maxwell said. An instant later his head jerked forward. "Good Lord! You haven't *actually* been *drunk,* have you?"

"Alas, I have." Glori giggled. "It was a beastly cold. Christmas Eve, you see, and I'm afraid I enjoyed far more of the hot mulled wine than I should have. Much to my father's amusement—and the minister's dismay—I sang the most undignified sea shanties that night. Daphne sang hymns." The thought of Daphne singing hymns gave Maxwell cause to choke up. "Regrettably," Glori went on, "I had a throbbing head on Christmas morning." After a pause she added, "In my own defense I must say that I was but eight years old at the time, so perhaps I was only *modestly* wicked."

"Have you continued to indulge? I've a mind to hear your undignified songs." And Maxwell wondered why he'd never noticed what a haunting voice Glori had—half whisper and half tease, all shadow and no form, hinting at things she probably didn't even understand. A girl her age had no business sounding like that.

"I've hardly been able to look at mulled wine since,"

she said. "And considering recent events, I probably shouldn't sing for you until next week. You've had shocks enough of late."

"It can't wait that long. I'll be leaving soon."

"Where are you going?"

"Back to London to tie up a few loose ends. You'll be staying here, for now anyway."

"Oh . . . I see," she replied, the sparkle gone from her voice.

Maxwell found that he felt rather flat himself as soon as he'd mentioned his intended departure.

"Well, it's awfully late," he announced abruptly. "Time we said good night."

Glori's good night was little more than a whisper.

Yet, despite what he'd said, Maxwell didn't make any attempt to leave his comfortable spot. He stayed right there on the end of Glori's bed, exercising his muddled, scattered thoughts.

He'd been in such a rage over the past several days that he thought he could have killed Daphne with his bare hands, if there had been any chance of getting away with it. He now wondered if Glori had been in a similar state and that's why Daphne had locked her in her room. The fact that he and Glori had managed to survive the day together without turning on each other astonished him.

It now occurred to Maxwell that all the while the conversation downstairs had rolled on about how this one or that one felt about the marriage, no one had asked how Glori felt. Even he hadn't asked her when he had the chance. He had wondered about it, along with an assortment of other things, but he hadn't asked.

He said, "Glori, tell me what you're thinking. Have you been as angry as I have?"

There was no reply—she had fallen asleep.

Hauling himself off the bed, Maxwell looked down at his silent companion. Her hair had come loose from its pins and lay in darker swirls across a lighter pillow. The quilt was tucked up under her chin. Grinning, he murmured, "Modestly wicked, indeed," and gently stroked his knuckles along her smooth cheek. She was toasty warm—she'd always felt so cold before.

Never leaving her dreamy sleep, Glori sighed and rolled over, sliding a warm hand into his, curling her fingers around his thumb.

Maxwell stood there in the darkness with Glori's hand in his, wondering what he would ever do with this provoking child-wife he'd acquired. Admittedly, he was as responsible as Daphne for Glori being here. After all, he'd wanted her to go through with the wedding, when she was all set to march straight back to East Wallow. He still found it surprising that she hadn't known of his family connections until they'd left the train and found a carriage emblazoned with the Westbourne coat of arms waiting for them. It had seemed strange to be explaining that crest to someone he'd just married. But then, it seemed strange to be married at all.

He felt the ring he'd placed on Glori's finger hours before and realized that it wasn't loose now. With his finger he found the ribbon she'd wrapped around the underside to keep it from slipping off. It made him smile, and he didn't even know why. Tucking Glori's hand back under the covers, he gave a pull to the bell cord. When the maid arrived, she would undo whatever needed undoing so that Glori could get a proper night's rest.

Honeysuckle scented the bathwater. Glori dropped her flannel nightgown onto the rug and stepped into the polished copper high-backed tub. Crushed flower petals swirled around her ankles. Easing down, she melted into the warm infusion, and the petals clung to her raised knees. Lucy, a housemaid of middle years who had been assigned to act as lady's maid, handed Glori a cup of sweet tea before she turned her own attention to the trunks.

It had been almost noon when Lucy arrived to open the bedroom draperies, allowing buttery sunshine to pour across the floral carpet and over the dark oak furniture. Seeing that Glori was awake, she cheerfully announced that luncheon would be served late today, at two. Then the sturdy woman laid down a soft blue rug and explained that a bath was on the way. Glori hadn't wasted any time getting out of bed.

Now, sipping her tea, Glori leaned back, wiggled her toes, and relaxed. The tub, along with countless cans of hot water that filled it, had been carried up the back stairs by a compliment of footmen. They went no farther than the passage outside Glori's door. From there a pair of maids intervened to bring the bathing equipment into her room.

To Glori's way of thinking it was an impractical method of doing things. At home in East Wallow her father had added a nicely appointed bathroom to the rear of their house. That's where their tub, with its attached showerbath, was kept. It wasn't perambulated about by a regiment of servants. The water had only to be carried from the nearby kitchen, or the rain barrel outside the kitchen door.

There were also plans to add a pump to the bathroom. It already had a cast-iron stove to heat the water and warm the bather. To empty the tub, an attached waste pipe took the water out through an opening in the wall and into the garden. The soapy solution, her father maintained, was good for the plants but hell on the snails. (Glori had observed those wee gastropods after one such sudsing and saw for herself that they hadn't cared for it in the least.)

Of course, the bathroom at the Kendell home in East Wallow was nowhere as elaborate as the one Daphne had in Grosvenor Square. Daphne insisted that anyone who was anyone would have no less, and made a great to-do over her modern conveniences, including the flush lavatory shaped like a dolphin. Glori had agreed that they were fine.

While Glori luxuriated in the tub, Lucy hung up a number of things from the trunks, pausing to make a critical inspection of the day dress Glori would be wearing. It was badly creased. "If you can spare me, Mrs. Rutherford, I'll take this down for pressing, then come back and wash your hair." Glori agreed. With the dress filling both arms, Lucy hurried away to the kitchen, where she left the dress and collected the thick turkish towels that were waiting in a clean roasting pan in the warming oven.

Sitting quietly, Glori couldn't hear any activity in Maxwell's room, though she doubted he would still be asleep. She'd been startled to find him at the foot of her bed last night, especially after the speech he'd made on the train. He had taken great care to explain his honorable intentions, using the most delicate language possible. Nicely put, he said she need not fear that he would attempt to assert his—what had he called them—his *conjugal rights,* just because she had been a jolly good chap and gone through with the wedding.

Smiling into her tea, Glori couldn't recall another single instance when anyone had called her a *jolly good chap.* Still, it had been a comfortable enough conversation. Last night, however, had not been merely comfortable. It had been wonderfully shameless. She supposed the reason was fatigue on both their parts, intensified by the intimacy that darkness encouraged. Whatever the reason, she had enjoyed it tremendously.

Those thoughts went no further once Lucy returned with the warm towels, which she stacked on a chair near the porcelain stove. The teacup was put aside when the friendly maid brought out a pot of soft soap and began to work mountains of lather through Glori's hair, relating little snips of this and that about the household. Of course, the biggest news was the litter of puppies that had been born that morning. Lucy confided that the master and mistress were in a dither over the new babies. Then, after several rainwater rinsings, she towel-dried Glori's hair and anchored it with combs on top of her head. As nothing else was required of her at the moment, Lucy departed to hurry along the ironing of Glori's dress.

Picking up the washcloth and a cake of scented soap, Glori surveyed one leg, then the other. Her conclusion was that a stork might well envy such limbs. She, however, was glad to have skirts with which to cover them. Sometime during the lathering process, her thoughts drifted back to the previous night and the moment she'd heard Maxwell laugh—a low, throaty rumble that tickled her insides. It was something she'd like to hear again, though it wouldn't do to dwell on such things.

She thought, instead, about writing to her parents. Daphne had said she would tell them about the wedding, but Glori knew they would be anxious to receive some personal word from her, too. She supposed she could tell them that her new husband was . . . amiable. Amiable, with a mellow, earthy laugh. Then she remembered that Maxwell would be returning to London soon, and she wished he wasn't. And she wondered if he really would like to hear her sea songs. Adjusting the comb that kept her hair from dangling into the bathwater, Glori began to quietly sing:

"She had a black and a rolling a-a-eye, and her hair hung down in ring-a-lets. She was a nice girl, a proper girl, but one of the modestly wicked kind . . . "

Grinning, Glori hugged her soapy knees and vowed that before Maxwell left for London, she would hear him laugh again—that same deep rolling laugh that told her she had a friend.

Lucy returned with the dress and laid it carefully across the bed. Then she held up a huge warm towel, and Glori left the tub to be wrapped in it. After pulling on her pink cotton stockings, Lucy fastened them with India rubber garters above the knees. Next came long drawers with an open crotch for the convenience of attending the call of nature. Then a chemise that came down to her knees, a corset and lacy corset cover, to be followed by a flannel petticoat before the crinoline was added. Another petticoat went over the crinoline.

"I can tell you about one lady I tended," Lucy said while she managed Glori's dressing. "She insisted her laces be so tight that it took both me and Lizzy to do them up, and me with my knee on madam's back to get them snug enough! Goodness' sake, she had to wrap her arms around the bedpost so as not to be pulled clear across the room. In less than an hour she was a sight to behold, with that tiny little waist and full bust, and such generous hips!"

In the end Glori's corseting procedure had taken comparatively little time. That's because Glori had comparatively little to fit into her corset. There was no need to squeeze her in by lacing her up. The laces had already been adjusted to accommodate her thin self, and the wire hooks and eyes down the front were now used to harness her in.

Sliding her feet into her high-topped black shoes again, Glori dearly longed for her gray kid slippers with the little heels. Unfortunately, they were in the trunk that had been left behind in East Wallow when she decided that she wouldn't need quite so many things in London, at her sister's. While Lucy deftly manipulated the button hook to do up her shoes, Glori wondered how anyone's corset managed to survive an assault by those kindly but hamlike hands.

Of dove-gray muslin, Glori's dress had full pagoda sleeves and separate white undersleeves with elastic at the elbows and wrists. The undersleeves matched the small white collar. Rows of magenta braid trimmed both the hem of the skirt and the wide cuffs of the dress. Small buttons of the same color closed the front. Though the dress hung loose, as did all her clothes of late, this one had been a favorite. When Glori selected the pattern and fabric a few seasons ago, her mother remarked that the color was especially flattering. Now Glori could see that the color hardly mattered. She looked as bad in this dress as she did in anything else. No, she corrected, not as bad as she had looked in Daphne's clothes.

"There's a woman who does sewing for Her Grace," said Lucy. "She works quickly at her sewing machine, so you might want to have her make up a few things, just to fill in until others come from a proper dressmaker."

"Yes, that might be a good idea," Glori said, noting the tact Lucy used to say that her wardrobe was sadly lacking.

They moved to the dressing table, and Lucy lifted Glori's vast skirts to push a small stool underneath. Taking care not to land on the floor Glori sat down, her steel hoops and freshly ironed dress out of the way.

"Tell me, Mrs. Rutherford, how would you like to have your hair arranged? I'm afraid it will never be completely dry before you go down to join the others."

"Something simple, I think. I'll leave it up to you." Outwardly Glori studied her hair. Inwardly she winced every time she was called Mrs. Rutherford. She felt like an impostor.

Carefully Lucy plied an ivory-backed brush to undo the tangles from Glori's long hair. That left nothing for Glori to do. Nothing to do except think, that is. And it was Maxwell of whom she thought.

She was ridiculously pleased that he had come to see her last night—that they were on such easy terms now. But she wished she had been able to stay awake longer. And she wished she hadn't told him about the mulled wine on Christmas Eve, because he might think she was a secret drinker, a candidate for blue ruin. She supposed it might be best if she didn't allude to last night's visit at all, just in case he'd forgotten about the wine.

Yet, if she didn't mention something about his visit, he might think she found fault with his actions. Then he might feel compelled to apologize. The last thing Glori wanted was to have Maxwell apologize for something she had enjoyed. Still, he might see it as humorously as she did.

Then again, she supposed he might dislike being reminded of his lapse of decorum after he had prosed on and on about what a gentleman he intended to be.

"Will this do?"

"Hmm? Oh, yes," Glori replied when the question sunk in. Lucy was asking about her hair. "It's quite nice. Thank you."

A ribbon net held Glori's hair in a tidy roll at the back of her neck. Though charmingly styled, it didn't keep her from looking pathetically thin. At least the warm bath had given her cheeks a rosy bloom, and her dress wasn't wrinkled. Seeing that things were as good as they were going to get, Glori was prepared to see Maxwell again.

Shoulder to the window embrasure, Maxwell lifted his face to the warm afternoon sun and felt revived. Returning to Westbourne Hall and the familiar rolling countryside did that to him. The Cotswolds were magnetic, drawing him back to this big old stone house to gather his strength and renew his soul. Now he'd need that strength to sort out his life. His life and Glori's.

He'd collapsed onto his bed last night thinking of delightful, outrageous Glori. Glori, whose seductive essence had floated along with him when he'd left her bed, and was still hovering over him when he awoke this morning. Glori, whom he had pressured into marriage to save the Rutherfords. Maxwell heaped another generous serving of guilt on his plate to commemorate the event.

He knew very well that so far the cost of that rescue weighed heavily on Glori's side, while the benefits tilted toward his family—an obviously unjust division. He'd spent most of the morning trying to figure out how to even things up, to find something that would make Glori happy. He didn't think she'd want to return to London—God knows he didn't care for that himself. And now that Glori was married, she couldn't very well return alone to her parent's home, either. Such a move, so fast on the heels of a hasty marriage, would certainly be grist for the village gossip mill.

If Glori didn't want to stay here at Westbourne Hall, Maxwell thought he might set her up somewhere. Perhaps a cottage in a nice little town, with a refined lady companion for respectability.

"That would *never* work," Maxwell muttered.

"What's that you say?" called his uncle Neville from a wingback library chair, where he sat with a huge book on his lap.

"Nothing at all, Uncle. I just remembered something I'd left undone."

Crossing his arms over his chest, Maxwell tapped one long finger against his sleeve and continued his ruminations. It was clear to him that leaving Glori in some quaint little cottage forebode disaster. He could imagine the result if some timid, genteel companion should stand bravely between her and the hot mulled wine. The vision left him with an amused grin, but absolutely no confidence in the cottage idea. The trouble was, he couldn't think of anything else. He finally decided that, when the time came, he would simply ask Glori what she wanted to do, then consider whether it was advisable to let her do it. She was, after all, quite young to be out on her own. Somewhat mollified, he put that problem back on the shelf.

Now the other scene that had skipped so blithely through Maxwell's mind reappeared for one more go-round, and his amused grin broadened into a crooked smile. Never before had he spent any time in bed like he had with Glori—and he'd seen his share of feather ticks and leafy glades. He thought it was just as well that he hadn't lusted after her body, as he'd been too tired to oblige. Salome with her seven veils wouldn't have caught more than a passing glance. With a silent chuckle Maxwell consigned last night to the list of the most ridiculous wedding nights ever enjoyed by civilized man.

And he wondered how he could go about telling Glori that he'd like to do it all over again tonight, with a few of her sea shanties tossed in. He might even find out where she learned such songs. An earlier perusal of a map confirmed that East Wallow wasn't on the sea. How *did* a grown man explain all this to a virtual stranger to whom he happened to be lawfully fused? A stranger whose enticing whisper had heated his blood like warm brandy on a cold night, sending reason flying. . . .

A latch clicked and the library door swung open, interrupting Maxwell's reverie. Glori entered, her skirts sweeping quietly across the parquet floor as she moved into the sunlit room. Thin gray Glori had arrived, and Maxwell came back to earth with a disillusioned bump.

He stood confoundedly silent for a moment before he said, "Good afternoon, did you sleep well?"

"Quite well, thank you. How . . . how did *you* sleep?" Glori had come close to asking how he'd managed to find his bed last night, but his blighted expression told her that levity might not be quite the thing. In fact, his unexpected reserve made everything terribly awkward, and she added inanely, "I, umm, just thought you seemed to be tired . . . or something. . . . "

"Ah, hello there, Glori!" boomed Uncle Neville from the confines of his chair. He struggled to stand with the big book on his lap. When Glori made the appropriate curtsy for a duke, he waved the gesture aside saying, "We don't stand on ceremony at home, among the family. Do come over here and see this book of mine. We'll soon be listing the new litter in it. My wife will be joining us at table; she's still out in the barn with the pups. I suppose we'll be building a new kennel now," he rattled on. "Do you know anything about raising dogs?" Glori said she didn't. "Ah, well, you can learn. Capital little things, those pups. Now, come look at this."

With a hesitant smile for Maxwell, Glori went to stand beside the old gentleman's chair.

Maxwell watched and listened as his uncle explained breeding lines to the skinny girl who stood at his side. One thin finger pointed to something she questioned.

Yes, *this* is Glori, Maxwell reminded himself. The Glori who had saved the Rutherfords. Glori, who had looked rather dead when he'd lifted her from the ballroom floor. The same frail Glori with the same spectacles who had sat with him in the rocking train. For a while he'd been afraid she was going to be sick on him, but it had passed.

Seeing Glori again he thought it was nice that she had a dress that hadn't belonged to Daphne. And it was nice that she was of a pinkish tint today—she had been rather green around the gills at this time yesterday. And he was glad that she didn't look as though she'd been crying. He was truly and genuinely *glad*. But any thought that this tongue-tied waif in baggy gray could be related to the sophisticated witty woman who occupied last night's bed was impossible. That meeting had obviously given way to something his tired mind had conjured up.

Maxwell had heard stories about soldiers hallucinating when they'd gone days without sleep. The hungry ones saw and even smelled food, he'd been told. It followed that because it had been his wedding night, he had fancied that Glori was some delectably amusing creature from his own imagination. And in that fatigued half-dream he'd forgotten that he had sworn to take care of her. Unconventional conversations in dark bedrooms in the middle of the night did not constitute taking care of her.

Besides, he'd promised that he wouldn't, well, *do* anything, even if he wanted to, which he didn't. At least, not anymore. Oh, well, thought Maxwell, it's marriages like this that keep mistresses in business.

"Maxwell, is something wrong?" Glori asked.

"Wrong? Why do you ask that?"

"You appear as though you don't feel very well."

"Sorry. Wool-gathering, you know. Thinking about the pups. The old mum is a great pal of mine."

"Oh, yes, the puppies. I'm glad it's nothing serious."

They were both relieved when luncheon was announced.

Neville put aside the book to offer his escort to Glori. Maxwell followed pensively, giving the leather-covered globe a snapping spin as he passed. He was hardly limping at all.

Glori was thoughtful, too. She didn't believe for a moment that a beloved pet gnawed at Maxwell. The problem, she was certain, lay in their rendezvous of last night. Once again she regretted ever mentioning the mulled wine, but it was done and she would deal with it however she could.

Life, she decided, is very much like juggling frogs.

CHAPTER FIVE

NEVILLE and Maud, bless them, carried the luncheon conversation with lively descriptions of Daisy's previous litters. Whether it was from pure exuberance or because they had sensed the tension in the air, Glori couldn't tell. After luncheon, instead of accepting Maxwell's painfully polite offer of companionship, Glori said she must write a letter to her parents, who would surely become alarmed if they didn't hear from her soon. Maxwell said he understood completely, to please include his best wishes and say that he looked forward to making their acquaintance. He then disappeared until the evening meal.

During supper Maud asked all that was proper of her new niece, inquiring after her family in East Wallow and her pastimes there. She took considerable interest in the fact that Glori, who had been educated at home by her parents, taught at the village school. Adjusting and readjusting the position of her wineglass, Glori was relieved when everyone's attention turned from herself to the clean water pumping system in London. It was finally in use after seven years of construction, but there were doubts as to how well it was really working.

Unable to solve the difficulties with the pumps in

London while having his supper in the Cotswolds, Neville labored, instead, over identities for the new pups. He had decided against naming them after the Royal Family on general principle, and not after politicians, either, lest it affect their market value. During dessert Maxwell noticed how drawn Glori had become and suggested she might retire early, if she wished, without fear of offending. She did so.

Though she had sought her pillow prematurely, Glori was still awake when Maxwell entered his room. She heard a chair scrape the floor, his shoes thump onto a rug. An hour passed before it became obvious that there wasn't going to be another late-night visit. No hushed voices would be joined in soft laughter to redefine the silent shadows that draped her bed.

During the empty time that followed, Glori considered what might have happened if Maxwell had come to her room again. She had enjoyed the cozy merriment of the night before and assumed it would be repeated . . . wouldn't it? Which made her wonder if Maxwell might expect the same things she did. She couldn't imagine him thinking of her as a temptress. The very idea was laughable. He hardly even saw her as a female. Besides, they barely knew each other. But her last thought before sleep overtook her was regret that Maxwell didn't find her the least bit attractive—for all that she could do about it.

Maxwell's prelude to sleep was even more disordered than Glori's. Eschewing his bed for the upholstered chair that the marmalade cat loved to scratch, he simply stared at the door connecting his room to hers. He was having tremendous difficulty adjusting to this *arrangement* they had. For as legal as it was, it was no marriage, as far as he was concerned.

It wasn't as though he hadn't been well acquainted with arranged marriages, or marriages of conveniences of one sort or another. Some were good enough, others were more like divine retribution. In fact, he and Elgin had shared a good laugh when Nipper Yarmouth—that pompous strutting braggart with an eye for wealthy debutantes and court circles—ended up married to a pudding-faced shrew. After the knot was firmly tied, her father used the profits from his shoelace manufactory to pay off old Nipper's debts and keep him out of jail.

Thumb counting on fingers, Maxwell reckoned the impoverished young beauties spliced to rich old men. There weren't as many of them as he'd thought, but there were enough. And he couldn't forget the penniless young fellow who had wed a rich widow a dozen years his senior. That marriage had gained attention for how remarkably well it had turned out. Even so, Maxwell knew that the most common union of all was a man and woman paired according to similar social situations, with financial considerations involved. Sometimes they even cared deeply for each other. But common or not, it was far from the kind of life he had pictured for himself.

For all that being *in love* was considered a distraction from making a suitable alliance, his own parents had truly loved each other. He remembered them holding hands, whispering, smiling. As a child he'd been included in the joy that enveloped them. Then there was his uncle Neville and aunt Maud, who had been on their honeymoon for better than forty years, though when they did have a dustup it was a dilly. Still, Maxwell had always thought he'd have that kind of marriage if he ever took the step. Now . . . he could only shrug. It was all spilt milk, water under the bridge, so many snowballs in hell—and life went on.

And there was Glori.

Stoically he resolved to come to grips with the situation as it was, not as he had imagined it to be last night when he was so far off kilter from fatigue. He wondered if Glori thought he had run mad after the way he had invaded her bed. Tomorrow he would have to correct any unfortunate impressions. He would start out by being all

that was congenial and respectable. He'd try to smile
more. Smiling reassured people. There only remained
the task of devising some way to amuse the girl for a
few days until he returned to London.

Like the answer to a prayer the image of his cousin
Jane popped out of the gloom. He hadn't thought of her
in ages. They had got on famously that summer, years
ago, when she stayed at the Hall. She couldn't have been
much younger than Glori at the time. A great gun, Jane.
His aunt and uncle never did find out that he'd taught
her to play poker. Now he had the ticket because Glori
seemed to be a great deal like Jane in some ways—a jolly
good sport and not one to whine and whimper about silly
things. Tomorrow he'd take Glori to see the pups. Jane
would have loved it. Logic is what the problem calls
for, Maxwell declared to himself. Cool, clear logic—not
rampant, idiotic emotionalism!

When he finally blew out the candle and went to bed,
he expected sleep to follow, but once again his convo-
luted thoughts kept Morpheus at bay.

Though she heard the rooster crow before the sun came
up, she'd gone back to sleep for a few hours more. Still,
Glori was up and about much earlier than she had been
the day before and was as ready as she could be to face
her new world. Once downstairs she was directed to the
room where Her Ladyship was to be found. The door
stood open, and Glori looked inside.

The morning room, with its decorative plaster ceiling
and tall windows, was pleasing. She supposed it always
looked cheery because of the flowered paper on the walls
and the variety of plants and ferns that had been placed
around the room on tall stands. Like the rest of the house,
this room held a haphazard mixture of furniture. Pieces
from different periods were mixed together as another
chair was needed here or a table there, until each room
had a sampling of everything that had been stylish at one
time or another. So it was that a sofa with crocodile legs

crouched beside a William and Mary table, which held a modern glass-globed paraffin lamp. Maxwell's aunt Maud sat on the crocodile sofa trying to see what she could salvage of the embroidery thread that the cat had played with and chewed on.

"Good morning, Your Grace. I hope I'm not intruding," Glori said when she entered the room.

"Good morning, Glorianna," Maud replied, blue eyes twinkling when she looked up from the tangled rainbow on her lap. The lacy white cap that covered her chestnut hair had gone slightly askew. "Do call me Aunt Maud, if you like, and come sit next to me—there's plenty of room."

Indeed, there was room enough for them both on the sofa because Maud wore a rather small crinoline beneath her dress. Though her frock was stylishly cut, it lacked the very full skirt that was a fashion essential. Made of finely woven, dark green merino wool, her dress had a deep V yoke and tapered sleeves. The high collar and small cuffs were of Brussels lace. At her throat she wore a cameo broach. Peeping from beneath her hem were green morocco-leather half boots. Glori was wearing the plain blue muslin dress that concealed her thinness. Beneath her hem were serviceable black button-up shoes. She felt positively dowdy as she took her place beside the older woman.

"It doesn't injure my vanity in the least to admit that I find the exaggerated crinoline impossible to live with," Maud explained companionably, pulling at a length of red thread. "The first time I wore one, I knocked over a small tea table and a smoking stand. Dear Neville agreed that both the furnishings and I would be better off without the extravagant underpinnings." She then described the afternoon some ten years before when the inflatable rubber hoops she had just acquired began to sag quite badly when the air leaked out. As one simply couldn't take the bellows to one's undergarment to inflate it in public, she went straight home and never wore the thing again.

No matter what was holding them out, skirts were so expansive that they sometimes caught fire when the ladies wearing them stood too close to an open fire or hot stove. Severe injury or even death was not unheard of. People still talked of the crowded ballroom where one woman's skirt caught fire and the flames spread from dress to dress until scores of women were burned, along with the men who went to their aid.

Never a martyr to fashion, Maud insisted that she would gladly take to bloomers if her husband would only refrain from an attack of apoplexy at the mention of them. According to Maud, Neville had never forgiven Amelia Bloomer for inventing them or the Americans for exporting the ghastly things.

Glori could easily believe that, as her own father held similar feelings about the same garment.

"Your husband didn't think you would be awake this early," said Maud. "He has gone with his uncle to look at a neighbor's sheep. Have you any plans for today?"

"None at all, though I'm sure I can find something to keep myself occupied. I know that Maxwell must have a great deal to do now that he's home again."

"Well, then, would you like to see some of the house?"

"I would, indeed, thank you."

"Good heavens, Glorianna, there's no need to thank me. I shall enjoy showing it to you, though we don't want to see it all at once."

What Maud did want to see all at once was her nephew. She thought it would be too bad of him if he left Glori alone for another day. She didn't know what had gotten into him. He was usually so sensible, even under trying circumstances. Yet now . . .

Putting aside the lump of knotted threads, Maud said, "We'll begin in the long gallery, I should think. It gives one such a sense of history." Moving at an easy pace the two women ascended the stairs to the first-floor picture gallery where Maud made herself comfortable on the padded bench before her favorite painting.

"That must be Maxwell when he was a boy!" Glori exclaimed as she took the place next to Maud.

Maud's expression softened. "Yes, that's young Maxwell, with a devastating smile even then."

"And the toddler leaning against his knee?"

"My son, Randolph, though one is as dear to me as the other."

Indicating another picture Maud explained that it was the wedding portrait of Maxwell's parents. His father had the look of the Rutherfords. His mother appeared almost ethereal in a full-sleeved gown of wispy blue silk. Glori studied the picture for a while before she said, "I've been wondering why we came here instead of going to the home of Maxwell's parents. He hasn't mentioned them, you see, and I've been cautious about asking. Has there been some estrangement?"

"Good heavens! Hasn't he told you anything? His parents died in Ceylon when he was quite young. He has lived with us since they left England for the last time."

"Were they missionaries?"

"They were on holiday," Maud replied, wondering what else Maxwell might have neglected to explain to his wife. She then pointed out other pictures, introducing Glori to Rutherfords in shortcoats, in tall powdered wigs, and Elizabethan ruffs. Rutherfords in court gowns, in riding habits, and in armor. Rutherfords hawking and Rutherfords hunting. There was Sebastian Rutherford, Neville's father, who, Glori was told, had been an improvident gambler. A likeness of Neville was there with his sheepdogs. In the frame beside his was a much younger, classically beautiful Maud, wearing the Westbourne emeralds.

Glori did her best to acquaint herself with three hundred years of the Rutherford family—the ones Maxwell felt obligated to protect from any petty scandal that might come down upon their painted heads. There certainly were a lot of them. So many, in fact, that Glori began to wonder where the portraits of future generations would go—those Rutherfords who had yet to arrive and learn of their perfidious predecessor. She didn't think those future Rutherfords would care any more about Daphne's threats of scandalous ruination than the painted Rutherfords. A beringed hand patted Glori's arm and interrupted her thoughts.

"Glorianna, do look at that painting on the other side of the room. There, that fierce-looking fellow with the flashing sword. His name is Giles. We didn't have any dukes of Westbourne then—the first of them wasn't made until 1699—but, as I was saying, the story is that Giles stole away the lovely Sibyl and locked her in a tower until she agreed to marry him."

"Did he love her so very much?"

"Heavens, no! He only wanted her property, the very ground upon which this house is built. Giles was determined to have the land, and in the end that's all he got. The first chance Sibyl had she ran off to the Continent with a traveling troubadour. Because his wife was no longer at hand to produce his heir, the younger brother of Giles the Greedy inherited. Isn't it just *too* delicious?" Maud chortled.

Glori agreed that it was, thoroughly enjoying the company of this delightful woman. That's when she realized just who it was that Maxwell was trying to protect from scandal. Not some vast family line that lived on in gilt frames, but his aunt and uncle, very real people. With that in mind she could understand him a little better.

"I believe I recall hearing that you are an artist, Glorianna. Do you paint?"

"It is my mother who paints. I enjoy drawing, but I do it with more zest than talent, I'm afraid."

"Then you must see the sewing room, Glorianna.

Painting and drawing lessons have often been given there. Come, let's look at it together. You may want to use it as a studio."

When she saw it, Glori agreed that the third-floor sewing room would be a fine place to draw, especially in poor weather when she couldn't go outside. It was also apparent that the northern exposure with its diffused light was valued by the seamstress as well as the artist. Near the windows were comfortable chairs that had probably seen better days in the rooms downstairs, with small tables close at hand for sewing supplies. A large table for cutting fabric occupied the center of the floor.

Maud threw open the cupboard doors at the far end of the room and surveyed the fabric on the shelves, lifting the folded edge of one piece of cloth after another. "I haven't sorted through any of this in a very long time," she said, and pulled out a length of fine white cotton lawn, slipping a blue veined hand beneath a frayed corner. "I had intended to have something made up from it, but I don't think it suits me. Take it, Glorianna, and make something pretty for yourself."

Glori didn't know if she would ever wear anything so sheer, being as thin as she was, but gave her thanks and put the cloth aside on the cutting table.

Poking about in the cupboard, Maud came upon a box of buttons and sat down to sort through them. She didn't want to make it obvious that she was taking time for Glori to rest after all the stairs they had climbed. Maud said she was going to make something special and invited the younger woman to help find buttons that matched, then put them together on a piece of string. They picked through the odds and ends of everyday life that had been tossed into the handy tin button box and separated out the broken jewelry and lead soldiers and hooks with no eyes. As they worked they discussed everything from the stage production of *East Lynne* to the intrigues within the Prussian court.

As it would happen in a sewing room, the subject turned to summer clothes and a particular cotton fabric that Glori was no longer able to find. Maud said, "That civil war in America raised havoc on both sides of the Atlantic. I'm afraid that sources for raw materials for British industries as well as markets for our finished goods have simply vanished. It is sad to say, but I fear our cotton mills will never recover." She started another string with different buttons. "I'm so glad that Maxwell didn't go to America, though it was before the war that he'd spoken of it. He had it in mind to go into the wilderness and learn the languages of the aboriginal populations. I trust the desire for that sort of adventuring is behind him now."

Glori hoped so, too. In fact, the thought of it made her too restless to sit still and sort buttons, so she looked for something else to do.

On the way home from seeing the neighbor's sheep, Maxwell silently rehearsed the friendly speeches and reassuring smiles he would bestow upon Glori and tried to remember what he and his cousin Jane had talked about so long ago. Neville didn't interrupt him. When they reached the Hall, Neville continued on to the barns. Maxwell left his boots on the back steps to be cleaned and made his way up the back stairs in his stocking feet. In his room he washed and changed clothes and made plans to take Glori to see the pups.

Thinking that Glori might still be abed, he knocked on the connecting door before opening it. Her room, however, was empty, the bed made, nothing out of place. Maxwell was vaguely disappointed that she wasn't there when he wanted to talk to her, though he spent little time wondering why he felt as he did. Once again presentable, he tracked the ladies to the sewing room.

When he crossed the threshold, his aunt greeted him with, "Maxwell, what a surprise to see you here!" and turned up a remarkably smooth cheek to be kissed. "I trust the neighbor's sheep are well?"

Maxwell delivered the salute and said, "The animals are remarkably well." Then he turned toward the big table, where Glori stood over a piece of cloth, and produced one of his reassuring smiles. "Good morning," he said.

Glori smiled, too, though not with the same remarkable enthusiasm. She said hello and suggested that he sit down. He chose the chair nearest his aunt and returned his attention to Glori.

She was unfolding a long piece of fine white cloth, which looked even whiter against the soft blue of her dress. When she was satisfied with the arrangement of the fabric, she laid one of Maud's hand-drawn tissue-paper waist patterns upon it, one that the lady had copied herself from *The English Countrywoman's Domestic Magazine*. It was of a style that Glori thought she could adapt to fit herself by taking more tucks across the front.

All this while Maud had been watching her nephew with well-concealed delight. She said, "Maxwell, surely you wouldn't have come all the way up here unless you had something of importance to tell us."

Maxwell's only answer was a crooked smile.

That's when Maud remembered that she wanted to speak with the cook. Her nephew was on his feet before she was. Maud was every inch the duchess when she looked back at him from the doorway and said, "Maxwell, do behave yourself."

Maxwell thought he was behaving himself quite well when he ambled over to lean a hip against the table where Glori, scissors in hand, studied the goods before her. She had intended to ask him what was so special about the neighbor's sheep, but said:

"You have a button falling off."

"Where?"

"Here," and gave the dangling cuff button a tug. It came free in her hand. Setting the scissors aside, she

said, "Give me your jacket and I'll sew it back on."
While Glori plied her needle, Maxwell spoke of Daisy's
new puppies and offered to take her to see them.

"Oh, Maxwell, I am sorry. I'd love to see them, truly
I would, but it's impossible today. I've promised your
aunt that I would go along to take tea with the squire's
sister. We're going to see her pressed flower pictures."

Glori looked so disappointed that Maxwell said, "It's
quite all right, truly it is. Puppies don't grow so fast that
we can't see them another time. It's good of Auntie to
take you about."

Actually, Maxwell had managed to make it appear as
though it didn't really matter all that much. He didn't
know why it should matter at all, but it did. Yesterday
he'd been vexed because he didn't know what he was
supposed to do with Glori. Today he was just as irritated because she was too busy to include him in her
plans. He supposed it was because he had laid awake
last night wondering how to entertain this female he'd
been encumbered with, only to find that she wasn't in
need of his entertainments.

Apologizing again, Glori returned Maxwell's jacket and left to change her dress before calling on the
neighbor. Maxwell watched her go, then watched the
empty doorway. He slung the jacket over his shoulder,
hanging it from his thumb, but he didn't leave. It had
been years since he'd been up here, not since he'd
convinced his governess that he needed a bug-catching
net, which she then made out of an old curtain. That
was back when the Hall was a much livelier place and
had a live-in seamstress.

While wandering around the place, Maxwell paused
to look at the fabric Glori had left uncut. Lifting an edge
of the sheer stuff, he let it slide over his fingers, unable
to imagine her in anything fashioned from it. Then he
shrugged, for whatever she made had nothing to do with
him.

The open landau moved through a tranquil watercolor scene in sepia and greens when it pulled away from the broad stone porch of Westbourne Hall. Glori raised her gloved hand while Maud waved sedately to Maxwell, who now stood in the drive watching without waving back. As they rolled along, Maud explained that the Hall wasn't their principal seat, but it was the house they liked the best and where they spent most of their time. And she pointed out the peacocks that dragged their beautiful tail feathers across the lawn, and told where the peahens nested.

Though Glori looked where she was supposed to look, Maud didn't think the girl was really paying attention. She also found it curious that Maxwell had joined them in the sewing room when he probably hadn't been up there in twenty years. Maud reveled in the certainty that great things were about to happen, because the air fairly crackled when those two were together. It was *almost* enough to make her smile.

Not quite, but almost.

The next morning, propped against the chocolate pot on Glori's breakfast tray, was a note from Maxwell. After reading it she penciled a reply saying that, yes, she could be ready to venture out to see Daisy and her puppies at ten o'clock.

Though she hadn't a ball gown to her name, she did have a walking dress with a hem that cleared the floor by a hand span, and it fit nicely over her old round hoop. Though considered by some to be too short for decency, the style made popular by Princess Alexandria was just the thing for dusty country lanes. Glori had packed the dress in anticipation of excursions around London when she felt a little better mended. It was a two-piece creation of lightweight wool, with a deep rose skirt and a pink bodice trimmed with deep rose piping. Once again Lucy caught Glori's hair in a woven ribbon net and tied it up by narrow ribbons. A small black straw hat with pink bows was set fashionably forward on Glori's head. After tightening the combs that held it in place she picked up her gloves and went downstairs. Lucy followed behind with her black cloak.

Maxwell was waiting in the hall when Glori descended the wide oaken stairs. He executed a determinedly re-assuring smile, striding across the polished slate floor with his hand extended as Glori neared the bottom steps. His expression was as jaunty as his brown tweed jack-et and knickerbockers. Well-muscled calves gave shape to the tan and white argyle stockings that he wore with brown shoes. A brown necktie hung down the front of a white shirt with a turned-down collar. Proper country clothes for a proper country gentleman.

Glori looked openly upon Maxwell, for the sight of him was quite agreeable to her. She liked the way his smile was a little off center, and his mustache looked as silky as ever. Tempting as it was, she knew very well that it would never do to reach out and touch it. There were prescribed conventions that held the fiber of civi-lization together, and those canons did not include mus-tache petting as a form of welcome. Men did not greet each other on the street by chucking each other under the nose. Ladies didn't tweak the upper lips of the gentlemen to whom they were introduced.

So, once again, Glori thought it best to avoid thinking too intimately about Maxwell, or his silky mustache, or his satin smile. She would concentrate, again, on a letter to her mother. The correspondence threatened to become prodigious.

Maxwell smoothed a finger and thumb over his mus-tache and the corners of his mouth before he said, "Glori, what are you looking at? Do I have my breakfast stuck on my face?"

"Goodness no! I was just thinking about . . . writing home."

"I thought you had already done that."

"Yes, I did, though I might need to do it again today."

One manly eyebrow arched in speculation. "I see," he said, deciding not to ask for an explanation. "Would you like to have a cart brought around to take us to the barn?"

"Oh, that won't be necessary. I'm sure the walk will be invigorating."

After a moment's thought he said, "I suppose you're right. You've made it safe and sound all the way from London, so you can surely manage to go as far as the barn and back without mishap. Just tell me if you become tired."

Glori gave him a friendly smile. Maxwell assumed it meant agreement. He took the cloak from Lucy and draped it around Glori's shoulders. She pulled on her gloves and nodded politely to the footman who opened the front door for them. That young man, whom Maxwell had addressed as Graham, was so handsomely dignified in his neatly tailored black suit that Glori suspected the hearts of all the girls employed at Westbourne Hall went pitty-pat when they saw him.

Stepping out onto the broad front porch, they were almost blinded by the sunshine. Glori knew she should have brought a parasol to protect her complexion, but the sun felt so awfully good after being inside for so long. Maxwell put on his bowler hat and pulled the brim low to shade his eyes, then tucked Glori's hand inside the bend of his elbow before they descended the steps.

Feeling more alive than she had in months, Glori took a slow deep breath. It was a smashing day to be out walking, with mild temperatures and fleecy clouds that drifted through a bright blue sky, though it darkened far behind them to the west. To make the sunny day complete the grass was strewn with brilliant yellow dandelions.

They walked leisurely down the drive that curved past the rear of the house, where a man was planting

mounds of things in the kitchen garden. An aproned
woman came out the back door to spread wet towels
over a bush to dry. A fat orange cat lay squinting in
the sun. Maxwell pointed to a distant field of blood-red
gilly flowers and explained that they would be left for
a seed crop of the dye-producing plants. In the field
beyond that two plowmen guided a team of massive
shire horses. Harnessed in tandem, the four animals
pulled a plow through the stubborn clay soil of the
Cotswolds, with one man at the plow and the other
guiding the lead horse.

Glori and Maxwell followed a path toward the barns.
Glori asked how many sheep they had, where they all
were, and how many men it took to to shear them. She
asked what kinds of fruit trees and berry bushes there
were and wondered if the dovecote and greenhouse were
much used. She wanted to know important things and
minor things and things that had become so commonplace
that Maxwell hardly thought about them any longer. It
occurred to him that no matter what she asked, no matter
how obscure, he always knew the answer and felt rather
pleased with himself.

He explained that all the outbuildings were, like the
Hall itself, constructed of the local limestone, with roofs
of split limestone. Then he amended that statement by
saying that the roof of the Hall was of Welsh slate. Built
during the last century in the Georgian style, it was a
practical design draped with impractical ivy. Maxwell
thought there were twenty some rooms. Glori saw at least
a dozen chimneys, plus lead gutters and down spouts that
were all in fine repair. Sparkling windows mirrored the
heavens.

The next thing Glori wanted to know was how far the
quarried stone had been hauled when the structures were
built. Again, Maxwell was able to tell her.

Ahead and to their right, beyond a hedgerow, waited a
line of huge old elms that wore the small leaves of early

spring. In the stone-fenced field beyond the elms new lambs nuzzled their woolly mothers. A flock of rooks rowed across the sky. Shading his eyes against the sun, Maxwell watched the birds swoop into the elm trees, where they squabbled loudly and jostled one another for front-row seats on the sagging branches. Glori tugged at Maxwell's arm and pointed out the stragglers that would soon add to the racket. He just grinned, took hold of her hands, and put them over her ears. Then, holding one elbow, he steered her down the path.

Much to his surprise Maxwell found he truly enjoyed showing Glori about the place. She was easy to be with, and he felt confident that when the time came for them to go their separate ways, they could do it amiably. Whatever physical attributes the girl might lack, she was still jolly good company, and that's all that mattered for what little time they would be together. Of course, he hoped they would always be friends, just like they were now. A man and woman didn't have to be married to be friends, and that thought stopped him in his tracks.

"By jove, that's it!" he cried.

Glori looked around to see what it was.

"Sorry," he said, "I've just thought of something I've got to do. I'll take care of it later." He gave her a nudge that started them walking again.

Maxwell told himself that he certainly would take care of it later. Much later, when people had forgotten about their hasty wedding and were talking about something or someone else, and when he had Glori settled in a little place of her own with a companion and an allowance. He wondered why he hadn't thought of it before. He would have their marriage very quietly annulled because it had never been consummated! As soon as they returned to the house, he'd write a letter to a friend of his in London, a barrister, who could look into the matter and arrange things.

Yes, that thought left Maxwell a happy man. He suddenly noticed that the grass looked even greener and the sky a brighter blue.

And he noticed that behind those spectacles Glori had the longest, thickest eyelashes he'd ever seen.

CHAPTER SIX

⟨⟨❦⟩⟩

THE place had a low-beamed ceiling, whitewashed walls, and smelled of cows. A steel shovel scraped against the rough stone floor. The man with the shovel looked up and touched his cap, then went back to filling his wheelbarrow. In a far corner, past a row of empty stalls and beside a bin of maize, was a crate of dogs. Daisy had ignored the place that had been prepared for her, though she had carried over the old coat that had been put down for bedding when she chose her own nursery for the black and white babies that looked so like herself. Most of the pups were asleep, though the largest of them stumbled about on unsteady legs before collapsing into the puppy pile again. The fat orange cat strolled over to peer into the box, then wandered away looking bored.

Avoiding any quick movements, Glori knelt by the crate and talked softly to Daisy, who watched her through apprehensive, liquid-brown eyes, thumping her tail. Glori petted her head, scratched her ears, stroked her nearest paw. When Daisy licked the back of her hand, Glori rubbed her muzzle. Only then did she venture to stroke one puppy with one finger, drawing her hand away before the new mother became anxious.

Maxwell had been standing nearby, pleased to see how

careful Glori was with the little animals—with his Daisy-dog. Now he said, "I hate like the devil to spoil the party, but I'm certain that I heard thunder, and the wind is coming up. We'd better start back."

Reaching the open barn doors, Maxwell scanned the darkening sky and led Glori along the uphill grade toward the house, but the more he hurried the slower she went. They were still a long way from home when a few raindrops spotted their clothes. Then the drops became a deluge, and Maxwell quickly retraced their steps to the barn they had just passed.

"We could have run for it!" Glori panted when they were inside.

Closing the door against the blowing rain, Maxwell said, "I suppose we could have run for it, but my ankle would rather walk for it when the weather lets up."

"I *am* sorry! I was thoughtless to forget your injury."

"Glori, there's really no need to be so concerned. Though, if you have no objection, we'll wait out the storm in here."

She had no objection.

Hands on hips, hair dripping, Maxwell studied the hazy interior of their sanctuary, with its sturdy queen-post beams and thick stone walls. Two ventilators, set high on each end wall of the barn, allowed them weak dusty sunlight. "There isn't much to sit on," he observed.

To allow Glori to catch her breath Maxwell provided casual conversation that didn't require her to respond. "Lambing was over a few weeks ago, about the first of April," he said. "The floor in here was covered with straw, and those hurdles were used to section the place into separate cubicles for the ewes." He pointed out the woven willow fencing that was stored at the far end of the barn. "Sheep will be brought in next month for shearing. In the fall we'll store apples in here."

Glori was still propped up against the door, breathing hard, when Maxwell turned his attention to the loft,

where he and his cousins had piled uncountable bundles
of straw so long ago. The ladder they had used to get
up there still hung on the far wall. Removing it from its
pegs, Maxwell determined that the wood was still sound,
so he leaned it against the edge of the loft. He jiggled it,
made an adjustment in its position, then jiggled it again,
pronouncing it fit for use.

"Glori, did you do much climbing in East Wallow?"

Glori made a quick study of the ladder and said, "If
you're suggesting that I should climb up there, I prefer
the floor, thank you."

"I'd be a shabby host indeed if I allowed you to occupy
the floor. It's cold bare stone. I'll carry you up."

"You forget that my skirts would topple both of us
from that ladder."

"Well, then, you can remove whatever it is that's in
the way."

"Maxwell!"

"Hell's bells, Glori! You've already stood up before
half of London without your damned hoops!"

"Someone might come in and see us!"

"I beg your pardon?"

"I won't do it!" she told him indignantly.

Lips pursed, arms folded, Maxwell paced the distance
to the stack of hurdles and back. Stopping before Glori,
he said, "Am I to take that as your final word?"

"You are, sir, with hell's bells on!"

Primly, chin up, Glori drew her cloak more securely
around herself while the wet ribbons from her hat hung
over her face and destroyed what dignity she might otherwise have had.

Maxwell swiftly caught two handfuls of Glori's long
cloak and pulled the heavy fabric tightly around everything that billowed. Before she could object too loudly,
he had her slung over his shoulder. Emitting a peculiar
gasping squeak, she slapped one hand against her spectacles while the other clutched the back of Maxwell's

jacket. There was no way she could save her hat, which tumbled to the dirty floor.

"Are those damned hoops cutting you to shreds?" he asked gleefully.

Glori didn't really give him an answer, consumed as she was with trying to stay in place.

"Don't wiggle about, if you please, as I won't be able to hang on to you at all while I'm climbing." Shifting his load for better balance, Maxwell strode to the ladder and started up the rungs.

Wide-eyed, holding her breath, Glori dangled there watching the diamond pattern of Maxwell's argyle stockings flex over his calf muscles. With each jolting step the floor receded, and she wished she were still standing on it.

When they reached the loft, his steps were muffled thuds as he kicked a bunch of old straw into a deeper pile and half laid, half dropped Glori onto it. Her skirts erupted like dandelion fluff. Scrambling beneath the yards of cloth that imprisoned her, she provided Maxwell with an obstreperous outpouring to qualify the service he had just rendered.

Seemingly immune to it all, the object of Glori's displeasure sat down next to her on the straw pallet, drew the bulk of her dress to one side, and pinioned that rampaging, bulbous garment with his leg. And, gentleman that he was, he discreetly pretended not to have seen her display of ruffled petticoats and drawers.

When Glori managed to gain a sitting position, she accepted Maxwell's capture of her skirts as a necessary part of their mutual survival. Slapping the dust from her gloved hands, she put her spectacles into her pocket and removed the net from which half her wet hair had already escaped.

Watching her, Maxwell asked, "How is it that you've been able to avoid having your hair cropped? It's been my understanding that such a trimming is among the first acts performed to preserve the life of one seriously ill."

"It was my father's doing," Glori explained, now brushing straw from herself. "The doctor said my hair must be cut if I was to survive. My father said it must not be, nor any further bloodletting, either. He pointed out that he'd never noticed that men survived illness in any greater numbers for having shorter hair to begin with, and if bloodletting did any good, there would be soldiers leaving the battlefield in better health than when they arrived."

Maxwell couldn't help but smile. "How did the doctor receive such an opinion?"

"It was a jolly good row before it was over. I heard the shouting all the way upstairs in my bed. The doctor said that he'd given what medication he could, and if my father was determined to be pigheaded about cutting my hair, there was nothing else medical science could do for me. He pronounced my parent an unnatural father and said that my hair would probably all fall out, even if I did survive, though I've been lucky because not too much of it has come out."

"And your mother, Glori? Where did she stand in this great debate?"

"Though interested in the findings of the scientific world, she sided with my father on this piece of business. The doctor, you see, had terribly dirty fingernails, and Mum simply could not have faith in a man like that. After I began to improve, however, they feared I wasn't improving fast enough and sent me to London for another doctor's opinion." She sounded rather forlorn when she added, "They packed me off to Daphne's on April second, the day after Easter."

"Have you seen any London doctors?"

"Only one, and he was much like the other who came to see me in East Wallow. How has your ankle withstood the climb?"

"Umm? Oh, my ankle. It's remarkably well, thank you."

A knowing smile curved Glori's lips. "I'm relieved to hear it."

Still smiling, she laid back in the straw. Maxwell did the same. Side by side in the quiet, dim loft, they listened to the rain beating a tattoo on the roof. Worried mice abandoned their nests in the straw and scurried to safety in far corners. Thunder rolled over them. Somewhere out there a wet cow mooed forlornly.

Glori said, "You haven't fooled me, you know."

"Fooled you?"

"About your ankle. You didn't come in here to spare *your* weary body, but *my* weary body."

"Now that you've brought it up, old girl, why didn't you tell me how tired you were before we left Daisy and the pups? You could have stayed dry with a bench to sit on," he told her impatiently.

"Well, I didn't think I was quite so done in, and there's no need for you to be irritable."

"I'm not irritable, I'm worried about you."

"And I'm tired of being lectured." She pushed up the straw between them. He sneezed.

"Bless you."

"It's the dust. It always happened when I came up here, but that was a long time ago."

"Was this your hideaway?"

"It was a retreat for the lot of cousins one summer. We spent a great deal of time up here, wool-gathering and bragging."

"And smoking?"

"Heaven forbid! Uncle Neville would overlook a great deal, but anyone who lit a fire in a barn would have been paddled no matter how big they were."

Inside her flattened cage of hoops, Glori rolled to her side to face Maxwell. Sliding a gloved hand beneath her cheek, she said, "You've never mentioned your parents, even when I spoke of mine while we were on the train. May I ask why?"

"I've lived here at the Hall for so long that I had all but forgotten that my history isn't common knowledge." His gaze wandered to the massive beams above them before he said, "I was seven when my mother and father went off to Ceylon on an extended holiday. They'd gone the route of the Grand Tour years before on their wedding trip and wanted something a bit more adventurous. Westbourne Hall was to be my home for only a year until they returned, but they never came back." Maxwell stopped talking while he piled more straw beneath him, then shifted his shoulders from side to side to level the lumps.

"When word reached us that my parents had disappeared, Uncle Neville sent an agent to investigate. All the fellow could discover was that they had gone on a day excursion to observe monkeys in their natural habitat. The horse and carriage were never found; neither were my parents or the guide."

"I'm sorry." Glori didn't know what else to say. Maxwell offered nothing more. To fill the void she said, "Tell me about the rest of your family. Besides your aunt and uncle, I mean."

"There's my cousin Randy," he answered with little enthusiasm. "He's at university in Cambridge for advanced studies in ancient languages. He's Uncle Neville and Aunt Maud's only child, a changeling who arrived on a winter's day twenty-four years ago." That's all Maxwell could say without grinding his teeth.

"Is there anyone else?"

"No more uncles, two more aunts, and an assortment of cousins. Jane, the only girl cousin, is a great goer. You remind me of her, actually. She's Aunt Flo's only daughter, who married a missionary and went to India to save the heathen masses and buy enormous quantities of native jewelry. Jane has four brothers named after peaceful apostles—they're all in the military. Then there's Aunt Sally, who has three more boys who are quite a bit younger than the rest of us. There are second and third cousins, too, but that's enough family for you to soak up right now."

Glori subdued a particularly annoying piece of straw that had been poking her in the neck. Without mentioning her sister, she said, "I have family I rarely see. It's all because Papa is the black sheep of the family and fell from parental grace. His father had a well-dowered young lady selected for him, but he eloped with Mum instead. It wasn't at all the match Papa's family wanted for him, being the youngest son of an earl. So you see, I've come to you with little more than what I stand up in. My dowry wouldn't support a weevil."

"I daresay I'm able do a mite better than that," Maxwell told her. "To shield us from the cruel world, I have Uncle Neville's generosity, my situation with the foreign office—for now, anyway—and the income from a place north of here, near Stratford-on-Avon, where I once lived with my parents. It's been rented out all these years and rather takes care of itself."

"Does it have a thatched roof like the picture I saw of Anne Hathaway's cottage?"

"I fervently hope so. I paid the rethatching bill last summer, so it should be good for another fifty years."

A comfortable quiet descended. When Glori's wandering thoughts had gone full circle, she asked, "Were you really worried about me?"

"I still am."

"That's sweet of you."

"Oh, for crissakes!"

Glori's laugh came soft and shadowy.

Dust motes floated in the meager shaft of light that burrowed through the air above them. After watching the tiny specks for a while, Maxwell took a breath and blew a mighty gust that sent the particles spinning wildly. "I can breath fire, too," he said. "I'd show you how it's done, but I wouldn't be so foolish as to light up in a barn."

"Never mind the fire. Can you spin this straw into gold?"

"That's woman's work," he scoffed.

"Can you perform a small bit of wizardry, perhaps?"

"Madam, I never dabble in *small* wizardries."

"A large one, then?"

He considered it and said, "I'm afraid there's not enough room in here."

"I quite understand the difficulty."

It was the kind of bantering that had bounced through this loft years ago—the same kind of foolery that Maxwell and Elgin still shared during lighter moments, though it never occurred to Maxwell to wonder why this mood returned so easily when Glori was beside him. It was simply *there,* and he eased into it as naturally as he would his carpet slippers.

Glori could all but see Maxwell here as a boy, laughing with his cousins—sneezing. She supposed he would look like his uncle Neville in another thirty years.

"Why so deep in thought?" Maxwell said. "Surely you're not doubting my wizardry."

"*Never* that. I was only thinking that you'll probably look like your uncle someday, with a paunch and all."

Maxwell's stomach muscles hardened as he lifted his head to turn and stare incredulously at Glori. "With a *what*?" he demanded.

"I wondered if you'd look like—"

"With a *potbelly*?"

"That's not what I said."

"But that's what you meant. You meant I'd have a potbelly."

"Well, not *today,* for heaven's sake! Not for years and years!" She was in the process of pulling off a glove to wipe a speck of something from her eye.

"How did you ever come by that extraordinary thought?"

"I was wondering what you were like as a boy."

"And that made you think about me with a potbelly?"

"A paunch."

"It's the same thing," he grumbled, refilling the indentation his head had left in the straw, stomach muscles relaxing.

"I suppose we can say it's the same thing so that we can lay your wretched abdomen to rest," Glori said patiently, the way she might have spoken to one of her students back in East Wallow. "I was just thinking that it must have been grand to have had so much family about when you were growing up. I only wanted to know what it was like."

"Well, my cousins were ordinary enough, while I was tall and gangly with the rudiments of a potbelly," he informed her with a gleam in his eye. "In this very loft, between poker games, we spent endless hours racing anything that moved, lying about our manly exploits and contemplating Nelly Cooper's opulent, ornamental . . . " He held his arms in a circle over his chest to fill in what his words left out. Then he hastily added, "Of course, we didn't mention Nelly Cooper, or any naughty bits, when Cousin Jane was about."

After a moment Glori asked, "Who was Nelly Cooper?"

Privately Maxwell thought of Nelly as the poor man's Bella Saunders. To Glori he said, "She worked in the taproom of the White Ram in Sheepscombe when I was but a green lad, before venturing up to London."

"Maxwell, when you go back to London this time, how long will you stay?"

"I don't know. Nothing is certain because I'm looking about for another situation. When I find something I'm suited for, I'll take it.

"It's awful that you feel you must leave the diplomatic

service because of what has happened. It simply isn't fair!"

"I won't belabor you with the fact that life isn't fair. Life is simply life. Perhaps I'll find something I like as well as the service." After he sneezed again he turned to Glori and said, "What would you like to do? Other than teach, as we already have an instructor at our school here."

"I don't know, I haven't really thought about it."

"Do you miss your students?"

"I was saved from missing them too much when I took up tutoring Daphne's parrot. He was an ardent student—keen to learn but rather slow. Once he learned a thing, however, he seemed to retain it. He could still recite a Bible verse he'd learned years ago." Glori had been particularly impressed with that aspect of the bird's ability.

Maxwell didn't see any reason to tell Glori what he thought of Daphne's bird. He just said, "I'm not aware of any provisions to educate the local poultry."

"What about your home near Stratford? Perhaps when we remove there, I might teach the very young children in that school."

"Until I can arrange something else, I had planned on you staying here, unless you truly dislike it. As far as the Stratford property is concerned, I don't expect the tenants to be leaving. In fact, I rarely see the place and have no plans to return."

"Were you so unhappy there?"

"Not at all. I simply have a great many other things to do."

Maxwell's answer had come like a dismissive flip of the hand. Glori touched his arm. His hand covered hers. Idly he traced the delicate bones that lay beneath his fingers. Whatever the thoughts were that took him so far away, he kept them to himself.

Soon enough he gave her hand a brisk pat and said, "Glori?"

"Mmmm?" Her eyes were closed. She wished he hadn't stopped doing what he'd been doing to the back of her hand.

"Are you falling asleep?"

"Mmmm."

"I'm thinking of going into Chipping Campden tomorrow to get a new watch stem. Would you like to come along?"

"Yes."

"It's an old wool market town. We can look around a bit if you like. On another day we might go to Chedworth and see what's left of an ancient Roman villa. Besides the Roman baths in Bath, the old boys had sumptuous homes all through the Cotswolds."

"Nice."

"We won't get back until quite late, so you'll want to take Lucy along."

"We don't have to worry about that sort of propriety any longer."

"You're right. Wouldn't you think I'd remember a thing like that? Have you ever thought of calling me Max? Most of my friends do."

"Maxwell . . . Max . . ." Glori rolled the names over in careful thought. "I'm not at all certain that you *are* a Max, but I'm awfully glad we're friends."

"It does make things more tolerable, don't you think?" Though it was a rhetorical question, Glori made an affirmative humming sound before Maxwell added, "By the bye, there's an old church in Fairford that's worth having a look at. Spectacular windows."

It didn't take a mathematician to tell Glori that it would be impossible for him to take her to see those places and still leave for London in a day or two, though she wasn't inclined to point that out. Yet of all the places they might go, and of all the museums she wanted to see, there wasn't anyplace Glori would rather be at this moment than right where she was, with Maxwell.

Feeling well disposed toward the man at her side, she said, "You were right. I should have told you I was tired."

"Yes, you should have. You were awfully foolish."

"You could at least say that it's turned out well enough, so it doesn't really matter."

"Well, I won't say it." Then he said, "Listen to that."

"I don't hear anything."

"That's what I mean. The rain has stopped."

"So it has." Actually, she'd been aware that the rain had quit some time ago.

Maxwell layered his hands beneath his head and said, "I suppose we should dig ourselves out of here."

"It will be dreadfully muddy if we leave too soon."

"You might want to write to your parents again."

Smiling into the gloom, she said, "Yes, I might."

After a while he asked, "Glori, how long has it been?"

"Been? Oh." She counted on her fingers. "Six days. Six days since Daphne's horrid ball."

"Amazing." Then he shifted around on his lumpy bed and said, "I wonder if we've missed luncheon."

"Oh, my!" Glori struggled to sit up again, then looked around for her hairnet and tried combing her tangled hair with her fingers. "I've got to do something about the straw in my hair before anyone sees me."

"Now, *that's* the wizardry for me," Maxwell confided, wagging one eyebrow. "I'm awfully good at straw into *hair*."

Glori groaned. "That is a rather poor jest."

"That's because I'm a rather poor jester. I'm ever so much better as a wizard," he said, and removed his leg from her exploding hoops.

The gaiety died the moment Maxwell saw the scuffed baggage sitting in the front hall. Something that sounded like "damn" squeezed through his pinched lips.

"Damn?"

Maxwell shook his head when he looked at Glori. She

still wore bits of straw on her clothes, and he thought she looked like a rag doll with the stuffing coming out. He tucked a few disheveled strands of hair behind her ears and supposed her hat was ruined. With a tired smile he said, "Glori, my girl, because *I* say damn, doesn't mean that *you* can say it."

"What is the problem?"

"I can't really explain it."

"Come now, Max," a deep voice echoed. "Surely you haven't forgotten who *those* bags belong to."

Glori looked around to see a man coming toward them. Tall, with a mustache, he looked very much like Maxwell except that his chin seemed weaker. Leaning negligently against the newel post, his stance conveyed a certain arrogance. Neither he nor Maxwell smiled.

"What brings you back just now?" Maxwell asked.

"I've been booted out of university again," the man replied. "Those blokes have no appreciation of what it takes for a man like myself to have a good time. I've even run through this quarter's allowance. Can you spare a few quid?"

Maxwell wasn't amused. "Does anyone else know you're home?"

"Only the staff and they don't really count, do they. But your fabled charm is slipping, Max. Do introduce me to . . . the lady."

"Glori," Maxwell said stiffly, a muscle jumping along his jaw, "this in my cousin Randy. He's an accomplished scholar when the mood strikes him—which hasn't been recently, judging from his appearance here today." To his cousin he said, "This is Glorianna, my wife. You'll have to excuse her before she catches cold in her damp clothes." Then he all but propelled Glori past Randy and up the first few stairs.

Randy couldn't have been more surprised as he looked from Glori's retreating form to Maxwell's stern face. "This is a joke, isn't it? You're surely knee-deep in some game, but for the life of me I can't imagine what it might be."

"There is no game. Glori and I were married Saturday last, from the home of her sister in London." But Maxwell wasn't about to tell him how that marriage had come about.

Randy came to his own conclusion. "Got her preggers, did you? For shame." When Maxwell simply ignored him to ascend the stairs, Randy took hold of his sleeve. He picked off a piece of straw and spun it between his thumb and finger. "Did you find a roll in the hay so much more sporting than your bed? Did you let the stable boys watch?"

There was a tense moment when Maxwell quietly warned, "You'd be wise to watch your tongue where Glori is concerned. If I have to remind you again, it won't be as gently." Randy released his sleeve, and Maxwell continued up the stairs.

And it was none too gently that Maxwell removed his dusty clothes, which took the brunt of his anger when he pitched them into a pile on the floor. The urge he'd had to lay his prodigal cousin out cold on the slate floor was almost too strong to resist, but he did his best to avoid another bout like the last one. A gentleman simply didn't lower himself to such undignified displays of temper. Besides, the last round had upset his aunt quite badly, though neither she nor Neville had known what the fight had been about.

It had blown up last January when Maxwell discovered that Randy had in his possession all manner of trinkets that obviously were not his own, and Maxwell wanted to know why. As Randy had come out on the short end of the ensuing discussion, he was obliged to confess all and swear that he would return to the path of goodness and virtue. But Randy hadn't reformed, and Maxwell knew it because Daphne had caught him stealing since then.

If Maxwell could find any consolation in the present

situation, it was that Glori wasn't in the style of the high flyers to which Randy was attracted, so that she, at least, would be left in peace.

Down in the front hall Randy had been left staring after Maxwell's back until he was lost to sight at the top of the stairs. A malevolent smile thinned his lips as he twirled the bit of straw he still held, thinking that he owed Maxwell *something* for the insults he had suffered when a few little things had fallen out of his luggage. It hadn't been any of Maxwell's business. Now Randy decided that he would just listen and watch and wait. He'd be the most congenial fellow that Westbourne Hall had ever seen. When the right opportunity presented itself, he'd know what to do.

It had started raining before dawn and looked like it would continue all day, so Maxwell abandoned plans to visit the Roman ruins and tried to think of something else that would be educational for a young lady. Actually, it wasn't a good day to go anywhere, but he needed to get away from Randy. He decided on a closed-carriage ride south to see a mill where blocks of rubber from South America were painstakingly cut into narrow strips, glued end to end, then woven around with silken threads to make elastic. With Glori bundled up against the weather, they left early, returned late, and had a rather glum time of it, though it was no fault of the elastic-wrapping machines.

During their outing Maxwell had really tried to be entertaining, and Glori let him think he had been. Resentfully she thought about what a fine time she and Maxwell had been having before Randy arrived to disrupt everything. She wished he hadn't come home at all. Then she remembered that Westbourne Hall was Randy's home, not hers. A sense of helplessness overwhelmed her, and she wanted very much to be closer to Maxwell to ease that awful feeling. Yet how could she say, "Maxwell, hold me, I'm frightened"? Clasping one neatly gloved hand over the other, she huddled inside her woolen cloak and turned toward the window as tears gathered behind her eyes.

"Glori, what's the matter?"

She only shook her head.

"Glori," Maxwell repeated, turning her around, "I didn't mean to be such a bore." Her eyes swam with tears, and he thought she was the saddest girl he'd ever seen. Sadder even than Cousin Jane had been the day some unidentified individual had tossed her new sunbonnet to the pigs. Maxwell pulled an unresisting Glori into his arms. Her little straw hat, minus the pink ribbons, scratched his cheek. Tightening his arms around her, he murmured, "Please don't cry, Glori. Whatever it is I shall try to mend it." She slid her arms inside his coat and sobbed.

Not knowing what else to do, Maxwell simply held her. Her wrap was cumbersome, but her body gradually grew warm against his. He had never known quite what to do with a woman when she cried, and was at an even greater loss with a crying girl in his arms. In his desperation he tried to remember how long his cousin Jane had cried over her trampled sunbonnet.

At last Glori's tears slowed and ended in a final shuddering sigh. Even so she made no effort to pull away from the arms that held her. Maxwell's voice nudged her softly when he said, "Glori, we're almost home." Then he waited for her to move of her own accord, which she finally did, and he hunted through his pockets to find her a clean handkerchief. "Are you recovered now?"

She sniffed daintily and said, "I think so, but my nose turns red when I cry, and I just hate it."

"I like your red nose, it gives you a bit of color. Tell me why you were crying."

She tried to think of some witty retort, but she couldn't and gave way to another sigh. "I was merely feeling sorry for myself," she said. "I was angry because Randy arrived when we were having such a fine time and spoiled it all, and when you leave for London it's going to be dreadful!" The tears threatened to return, but she blinked them back.

Maxwell sighed, too, running a calloused thumb over her tear-dampened cheeks. "Perhaps I can stay until you're more comfortable at the Hall. Would it really matter so much?"

"Yes!"

The instant that one word was out, Glori felt the warmth of a blush and found it easier to look out the window again. Hearing Maxwell chuckle, she swatted at him.

"That's better," he said.

If Glori had been watching, she would have seen him smile for the first time since Randy's return.

It was a few uneventful days later that a horseman appeared in the distance on the far side of the shallow stream where Maxwell's horse was drinking. It would have done Maxwell no good to pretend he hadn't seen his cousin coming. He knew he'd be followed if he rode off.

Randy came splashing in and called, "Max! You've been the devil himself to find." With a friendly smile he explained, "You have a guest. An old chum of yours, he says. One Royce Dobson from the foreign office. He's been warming the sofa in the blue salon for over an hour. Glori has served him coffee and cakes and is entertaining him with tales of the Cotswolds. She doesn't seem to mind being buried in this sheep-infested countryside."

Maxwell's thank-you was polite enough, and he spurred his mount homeward. Randy rode at his side throwing compliments before him like rose petals, destroying his peace and quiet. Maxwell's thoughts took another direction.

That direction was Glori. He had missed the girl while

he'd been attempting to keep away from the Hall and
Randy. He hadn't expected to miss her. It wasn't even
anything he'd thought about until he found himself wondering what she was doing and wishing they were doing
it together. Every so often Randy's voice intruded with
a remark about how ticklish the upstairs maid was, the
cockfight he'd been to, or the athletic abilities of an amo-
rous opera dancer he'd met someplace or other.

For crissakes, if he would only shut up!

When Maxwell came into the blue salon, Glori left
the gentlemen to themselves, for she knew that Royce
Dobson was there on official business. Before he arrived
she had been in the breakfast room, restoring a flower arrangement on the satinwood sideboard. Now she
returned there to finish the task, though she did so with
a heavy heart. While she removed tired blossoms and
discarded wilted ferns, she wondered if Maxwell would
emerge from that conference and tell her that he would
be leaving. Leaving when they were just getting to be
more like . . . like what? Husband and wife? It might
be so during the daytime, perhaps, but not at night. The
flower stem she held got snipped far too short.

Swallowing with more determination than the act usually required, Glori forced herself to define what it was
that she wanted from this union with Maxwell. She knew
that there were many couples who went to their marriage
beds with far less to recommend themselves than she and
Maxwell had. She and Maxwell were already friends.
More than friends, actually, but they were running out of
time together. If something didn't happen soon to make
him notice that she was a woman, not a reincarnation of
his Long-Lost Cousin Jane, he might go away and never
come back to her. What she didn't know was how she
could change the course of events.

In the blue salon there was a hurried farewell so that
Dobson could catch the train back to London, but he'd

left Maxwell with a lot to think about. The offer of a
position with the British embassy in Canada had been
a good one, a grand opportunity, though it meant that
he'd have to be away from England for a long time. A
week ago he would have snapped it up. Now, since he'd
gotten to know Glori better, it was far more complicated.
What he did would affect her, too, so he wanted time to
explain everything before he told anyone else or sent his
letter of acceptance.

But the opportunity for that private conversation was
not easy to come by. When Glori and Maxwell said good
night, she was as ignorant as ever of his intentions to
accept the Canadian offer. In fact, she was still unaware
that such an offer had even been made. Of course, Maxwell knew that Glori's room would certainly be private,
but that was out of the question. He remembered all too
well that being in her room at night had badly distorted
his perceptions of her, of himself, and the entire world.
He'd gotten some awfully peculiar ideas, then felt like
a raving idiot the next day. It was enough to convince
him to stay out of Glori's room after dark.

Tomorrow, Maxwell thought, would surely offer them
the chance to be alone—though not in the morning. He'd
told his uncle that he would deliver a horse in the morning. Perhaps they would be able to slip away in the afternoon.

In another bedchamber Neville buttoned his nightshirt
while Maud tied her nightcap. Thus occupied, they began
to consider a suitable wedding gift for their nephew and
his wife. Neville fell asleep before they could think of
quite the right thing. Maud lay awake for a while longer,
fretting because she couldn't recall where she'd put her
garnet earrings.

Everyone seemed to be at a loss for an answer of some
sort. Everyone except Randy. He'd finally figured out
how to get even with Maxwell for the fuss he'd made
over a few pieces of jewelry that weren't even his.

CHAPTER SEVEN

" . . . but it is *so* good for the grass," Maud said while sorting through her new embroidery silks, the morning sun revealing the subtle differences in shade, tint, and hue.

"What is?" asked her husband, looking up from his correspondence.

"The rain." She leaned toward him and whispered, "It's my *knees*, you see. It rained last night and my knees are stiff and I'm staying at home this morning."

"Oh, I see," Neville whispered back.

Having discreetly explained the difficulty involving those intimate portions of her anatomy, Maud leaned back and went on to say, "Glorianna has offered to visit the Sibley cottage for me—Cora Sibley hasn't been doing well. So the rain is a nuisance, but it is good for the grass. The sheep do clip it terribly short."

Neville said, "Maxwell is on an errand for me, so he can't take Glori about. Does she know where the Sibley place is?"

"No, she doesn't, so Randolph has offered to drive her there."

"It's nice to see him taking an interest in the family," Neville said, and put aside his letters to join his wife on the sofa with the crocodile legs. "Now, about your knees, my love. What would make them better?"

"I've given up mustard plasters. Warm dry weather is the very best treatment, I should think."

With a seductive gleam in his eyes Neville leaned closer and murmured, "I can't control the rain, though I can warm your knees."

"How do you propose to do it?" Maud asked with a sparkle of her own. "We don't have a lap dog."

"I propose to warm your knees in bed, woman! I'd carry you upstairs this minute if I could still do it."

"You old coot, you'd ruin your back!"

"The merest technicality."

"Neville, you are *so* romantic. May I ask what was in the post to bring on this fit of passion?"

"I wasn't actually reading the mail. I was thinking about Maxwell and Glori and wondering what the devil is wrong. Though she's as thin as a Maypole, she's a delightful young thing, and you can see they like each other, yet . . " Neville searched unsuccessfully for the answer. "When I was that age, I couldn't stay away from you. I still can't." Smiling mischievously, he took hold of his wife's hand and pulled her up as he stood. Skeins of colorful floss rolled to the floor. "I think we should find someplace less public to continue this. Unless, of course . . ." He looked thoughtfully at the crocodile sofa.

"Neville, it's broad daylight! What will everyone say?"

"We won't know, love, we'll have our door closed. Besides, all the children are away for a while." His last words were muffled against his wife's neck.

Maud slid her arms around her husband's waist and sighed contentedly, the familiar scratchy tweed of his favorite jacket beneath her cheek. "We are a most unfashionable pair."

"True, but it's said that people who keep to the country like we do don't know any better."

They climbed the stairs more slowly than they had so many years before, but their destination was the same.

Out in the yard Randy helped Glori into the dogcart. Before tucking her skirts inside, he handed her several loaves of warm bread wrapped up in a clean cloth. Today Glori had dressed for the damp chill by tying a scarf over her head and wearing her woolen cloak, but it still felt good to hug the warm bread.

For this venture Randy had dressed in a tan suit with a double-breasted reffer jacket. His folded collar was well starched and his string tie arranged with careful negligence. He'd worn his billycock hat, too, the brim tilted at a rakish angle over his left eye. Yes, Randy was at his gallant best, having decided to charm Maxwell's wife away from him. He didn't think it would be too difficult, as his cousin seemed to neglect his bride shamefully. And a neglected wife, Randy had found, was most responsive to the simplest flattery.

"Are you comfortable?" he asked when they were both seated.

"Quite," Glori answered, and the cart began to roll. "Thank you for driving me. Your mother dearly wanted this bread delivered, and you know that Maxwell isn't able to take me out this morning."

"There's no need to thank me, Glori. I've been looking forward to being with you." He lowered his voice and added, "It's awfully good of you to make this call. You must be a very kind-hearted woman."

"Oh, kind enough," she quipped, uncomfortable with Randy's style of flattery.

"There isn't much to do around here, as you will learn soon enough," Randy said as they joggled along. "I'm overjoyed to find that I'll have you for company while everyone else is busy playing farmer."

"You don't care for country life, I see. Perhaps you'd

rather tell me what languages you study when you are at university."

Randy looked sharply at Glori. Was she playing the coquette? Though unsure, he still smiled his warmest. "I haven't been working on languages lately. Instead, I've been assembling the broken pieces and describing the details on an old Roman crock. The shards were unearthed about a hundred years ago, then forgotten in the musty cellars of the university. I've discovered more about the supplies and preparations for a feast to the god Mars than you can imagine."

"How perfectly fascinating! Tell me what you've found."

Randy saw Glori's continued interest in his studies as a thinly disguised interest in himself and slowed the horse from a trot to a walk. "Oh, there were brass pots and serving bowls, bags of nuts, fruit . . . and jars of honey," he said softly, staring at Glori's mouth. "They were wonderfully keen on . . . honey."

Moving the bundle of bread between them, Glori looked straight ahead and said, "Perhaps we should pick up the pace before the horse stops altogether."

Randy smiled and obliged. He supposed Glori didn't want to appear overly eager. Besides, they had the ride back to the Hall to discuss that supply list in greater, more *intimate* detail. When it was time to return, however, one of the Sibley children needed a ride to the Hall to help in the kitchen. Sibley himself insisted that Cook was waiting for the boy, and Glori was quick to assure him that it would be no trouble to take the tyke along.

It was impossible for Randy to know if he was being gulled, but he knew he'd look like a fool if he refused to take the little brat with them. So he complied, confident that he'd get his knees between Glori's skinny legs soon enough. For now he would simply be good company. He did such a good job of it that Glori supposed she had mistaken his earlier remarks.

It was well into afternoon by the time Maxwell returned to the Hall. There had been trouble with the delivery of the horse. The creature didn't care to be relocated and was still thumping the stall walls when Maxwell left. They'd had a devil of a time getting him into the barn. Maxwell intended to discuss the problem with his uncle and then find a place to be alone with Glori. But by the time he left his uncle, a neighbor had come to call on the ladies of the house, and after that Randy was always hanging about Glori—fetching, complimenting, ridiculous.

At supper Randy managed to put himself next to Glori again, which kept Maxwell at a distance because he'd had quite enough of his cousin's company. Actually, Maxwell was bloody well ticked off. With the fish course came the realization that he probably wouldn't be able to see Glori alone unless he got her away from the house. He thought they might slip out right after breakfast the next morning, before anyone could trail after them.

But early the next morning a messenger was at the Hall asking for Maxwell. He was needed to fetch the disagreeable horse because it wouldn't let anyone near and was now kicking down the stall. There was a thought of sending one of the grooms, but Maxwell knew that it was his responsibility to see to the problem himself. The animal had worked itself into such a lather that it might hurt someone. For the first time he wished he had just gone to Glori's room last night and talked to her there. He could have stood at the door and kept his remarks as brief as possible. Surely it wouldn't have taken all that long to tell her that he was going to Canada.

So Maxwell had gone to collect the errant horse long before Glori came down to breakfast. She had begun to think he had forgotten that she was in the house. She didn't know how she was going to make him notice that she was a woman if he didn't even remember that she was there. Still, she had to think of *something*. It was like juggling frogs again.

As soon as she could politely excuse herself from the breakfast table where Maud and Neville lingered over their kidney and eggs, Glori went to the sewing room and cut the cloth she had left on the big table. After tacking front to back and the sleeves to the rest, she decided that her work there was finished. With a basket in hand she went downstairs and hurried across the neatly grazed lawn to the folly to begin the actual sewing. Lucy had said the place was rarely used, and that suited Glori perfectly, as someone came into the sewing room often enough to make her uncomfortable.

The folly, constructed entirely of creamy Italian marble, trimmed a rise to the west of the Hall, away from the farm buildings. Eight ionic-crowned columns supported the arches that formed a vaulted ceiling beneath a domed roof that was topped by a small cupola. Sunshine splashed through the tracery windows that filled the spaces between the columns, lighting the Westbourne crest that had been set in the floor in seven shades of marble. The whole design was distinctly original and appeared incongruous among the rough stone buildings of the estate, like an eccentric grand dame who had descended upon her less sophisticated kin.

Composing herself on a marble bench where the light would fall across her work, Glori began her stitching. Aware of nothing save the sun that warmed her fingers, she hadn't noticed that she'd been followed until she heard a soft scuff on the marble stairs.

"I believe you dropped this on your way out, Glori-anna." Maud presented a pincushion, then flicked a lacy handkerchief over another dusty marble bench and seated herself upon it. "I was going to send someone out with the thing, but it's too beautiful a day for me to stay indoors."

"Thank you," said Glori. "I would hate to lose your

pins." And she would hate to have Maud see what she was making.

Even though Glori tried to keep the delicate cloth folded in a small pile, the older woman couldn't help but notice the amount of stuff at hand. She said, "Glorianna, there seems to be so much fabric. Is it going to be such a large waist?"

"Oh, large enough, but not too large." Glori kept her eyes on her sewing.

"I must say, the manner in which that lace inset has been placed across the bodice is quite cleverly done. You've managed well with the scrap that was left, though it's too bad there wasn't enough for the sleeves, too. It came from Milton's in Stratford-on-Avon, but that was so long ago—I don't suppose they would have any left. May I have a closer look at what you have done?"

"Actually, there isn't a great deal to see. I wouldn't like to trouble you with it."

"It's no trouble at all, Glorianna. I suspect you're far too modest with your accomplishments. Do let me have a look," Maud coaxed. Glori capitulated as she couldn't very well refuse.

Admiring the way it was all fitting together, Maud held the garment up. The bottom of it dropped to the floor. Looking at it in some confusion she said, "Glorianna, this is the longest waist I have ever seen."

Glori stared up at the domed marble ceiling when she said, "Yes, it is."

"It might do for a nightdress."

"Yes, it might."

"One can see right through it from your nose to your toes, Glorianna."

"Yes, one can."

"My goodness! I believe you might be trying to seduce my nephew!"

"I believe you might be right," came Glori's feeble reply.

"Well, I should hope so! I'd begun to think the pair of you had lost your wits." Maud piled the fabric into Glori's arms and said, "Do carry on, Glorianna. Just don't tell anyone I said so." She started back toward the house then, the faintest of smiles tugging at her mouth.

Early that morning a rooster's abrasive crowing had scrapped through Randy's brain. He hadn't slept well since. When he finally got up and looked out at the unpleasantly bright day, he decided that he would just go back to bed, but then he saw Glori hurrying across the lawn toward the folly. Instantly alert, he decided to take the long way around to that stone monstrosity and surprise her there. They had played cat and mouse long enough. With this in mind he kept watch out the window while he dressed. Before he had his shoes tied, he saw his mother cross the lawn in Glori's wake and decided that it wouldn't be an opportune time to pursue the girl after all, but he could be patient when he had to. These little obstacles were part of the game that made his life worth living. He'd simply have to devise another plan.

Fifteen minutes later, though perhaps it was twenty, Randy entered Maxwell's room. He looked through his drawers, sat in his chair, and waited for his cousin's wife.

Glori was singing softly when she returned to her room. After pulling the bell cord to call her maid, she placed the sewing basket in a corner and opened the wardrobe to find another dress to put on. The one she'd worn to the folly had to have a fair amount of dust brushed from it. Hearing the door open, Glori said, "Lucy, will you please help . . . " but when she looked up there was no one at the passage door.

Turning toward the door that joined her room to Maxwell's, she thought for a second that it was the man himself who stood there. Her smile withered before it bloomed when she realized it was Randy. She stepped back, only to be stopped by the half-open wardrobe door pressing between her shoulder blades.

"I say, no need to become alarmed, little cousin," the intruder drawled, moving farther into the room. "I'm looking for Max and thought he might be here."

"Randy, this is most improper! You'll have to look elsewhere for Maxwell!"

Randy produced his best boyish smile and said, "I've just remembered that Max is gone from home, so there's no reason to look for him at all."

"Randy, Lucy will be coming—"

"Oh, I shouldn't worry too much about Lucy. I don't think she can be here in anything less than an hour, if she hurries, and I doubt that she will. When I saw her in the passage a while ago, I seem to have given the woman the idea that you wanted her to get something from the village. She thought it must be new ribbons for a hat and nipped off to find them for you."

Randy was the personification of innocence while he explained how he had tricked the maid into leaving the house. Glori's scalp tightened and a shiver ran down her back as annoyance gave way to fear.

"We could use this time to become better acquainted," Randy suggested with a sly grin. "One can hardly come to know one's cousin very well over the dinner table."

"There isn't anything for you to know."

His voice was oily smooth. "We're going to be *very* good friends."

"I don't think that's possible."

He said, "Don't play games with me, Glori," and seized her by the hair, pulling her against him. When she tried to push him away, he held her tightly to his chest, trapping her arms between them.

Her heart contracted into a suffocating knot—she tried to scream but couldn't. He found it amusing when she attempted to twist free. Kicking at him through her skirts was useless, so she bit his arm.

He swore and threw her down, and her spectacles went skidding across the floor. He climbed over her hoops to straddle her hips, pinning her arms beneath his knees so she couldn't scratch him with fingers that curled into claws. Wiping his sticky palms on his thighs, he made a sad face. "Poor Glori, what big eyes you have!" Then he smiled wolfishly and said, "I know Max doesn't visit your bed, because the maid who makes up your rooms tells me anything I want to know." Once again Glori's clothing hampered her movements when she tried to hit Randy in the back with her knees. Her writhing only excited him all the more, and he laughed at her.

Grinding his body against hers, he said, "Max may be a fool, but I don't intend to leave you ignorant of what you've been missing. You see, I owe him a *favor*, and this is the perfect way to return it." Randy was in no hurry at all as he began to undo the magenta buttons that ran down the front of Glori's gray dress. But when he bent forward to press his wet mouth against her throat, Glori pulled an arm free and hit him in the face with her elbow. A bloody nose accompanied his deafening roar.

She managed to scramble away when he pressed his hands to his face. But her freedom was brief, for he caught her skirts and dragged her back, cocking his arm to send his fist into her face—she shut her eyes and turned away, raising her hands to ward off the blow.

Then Randy gasped as a hand lifted him by the throat, hauled him to the door, and pitched him into the hall. Maxwell had arrived, and he was furious—dangerously so. He slammed the door and sent the bolt home.

"Glori?" His voice cracked as he hurried to her side, and his stomach churned when he knelt there and saw her tear-stained face and gaping dress spattered with blood.

He was afraid to take hold of her lest he compound the damage already done. Frantic now he said, "Glori, tell me how to help you!"

Her response was slow. She even blinked slowly. Licking her lips, she wanted to tell him that she hadn't been badly hurt, only badly frightened, but she couldn't. She could only breathe in and out and try not to cry.

His arms were braced on either side of her shoulders as he bent over her and said, "Be very still and I'll fetch my aunt to care for you."

She clutched at his lapel and shook her head. After a moment she whispered, "I'm not really hurt."

"But you're all—"

"I hit Randy in the nose."

Maxwell's body sagged in relief, and he choked out, "Good for you, old girl." He touched his forehead to hers and thought she felt as cold as she had when he'd picked her up from the floor at her sister's ball. It wasn't something he liked to remember. Daphne had used Glori in her blackmail scheme out of spite, and Maxwell was certain that Randy's assault had come about for a similar reason—but it was Glori who repeatedly paid the price.

Not so long ago Maxwell thought he hated Daphne more than he'd ever hated anyone. That was before he discovered Randy astride Glori, ready to bury his fist in her face.

Glori sniffled; Maxwell carefully lifted her from the floor and laid her on the bed. She winced when her head met the pillow.

"I'm so damned sorry about this, Glori. It's my fault that—"

She raised a silencing fingertip to his lips. He pressed a soft kiss there. His mustache felt as silky as she thought it would. Then she rubbed that finger over the worry line that creased his forehead. In a trembling voice that was half laugh, half tears, she said, "Maxwell, you have no idea how monotonous my life was before I met you."

"Glori . . . " He shut his eyes and swallowed hard, his head drooping. He couldn't remember the last time he'd cried, but tears were close now. Whatever he tried to say was lost to an emotion he couldn't control. Through a shaky smile he said, "It seems to be my destiny to pick you up from one floor or another. I don't object to the work, you understand, but if you could manage to be less dramatic about it in the future, I would be very much in your debt."

"I shall try," Glori assured him, her smile as wobbly as his. When Maxwell straightened up, Glori tried to pull the front of her dress together, but he made a more efficient job of it.

Someone rattled the doorknob. Glori froze.

"Mrs. Rutherford, please open this door!" It was Lucy.

Maxwell smoothed back Glori's hair, attempted one more overworked reassuring smile, then admitted the maid.

Lucy carried an assortment of ribbons that she had just brought down from the sewing room, not the village store. Horrified when she saw her mistress looking so battered, she dropped everything and rushed to her. After dampening a cloth, she began to wipe Glori's pale face to assess the damage.

Standing at the foot of the bed, Maxwell looked rather off-color himself. Solemnly he said, "The blood you see isn't Glori's. It's Randy's. Glori is terribly shaken and bruised, and I expect she has a wicked bump on the back of her head, but she says that's all there is to worry about." He couldn't bear to voice his fears about the effect this attack might have on her sensibilities. After a long silence he said, "Lucy, if you would take care of this yourself, I would appreciate it." He laid a finger on the side of his nose to let her know that he'd like the incident kept quiet. Lucy's reply was an indignant snort. Still, Maxwell knew that he could depend upon her.

When Glori's hands began to tremble, Maxwell became alarmed, even though he knew it was the result of the shock she had just suffered. Lucy assured him that what the girl needed now was a dose of laudanum and sleep, and told Maxwell to stay with her until she got back with the medicine. When she returned, she pointed out that Maxwell wanted tidying up himself. He agreed, but there was something he had to attend to first.

He stopped in his room for only a moment before he went in search of his cousin. Without knocking, Maxwell walked into Randy's room to find him laying across his bed, with a blood-soaked handkerchief pinched under his throbbing nose.

"I have a few things on my mind," Maxwell announced in a deadly monotone.

"Just look what that little bitch of yours did! She bit me and broke my damn nose!" came Randy's nasally whine. "God, even my teeth ache!"

Maxwell didn't doubt that his teeth ached badly. And his nose did look broken, and the flesh at the inner corners of his eyes was turning purple.

Randy said, "Glori asked me into her room—she said she wanted me to get something down from a shelf—then she climbed all over me!"

"Liar!"

"I had to protect myself!"

"Liar!"

"It's the truth, I swear it!"

Maxwell took hold of his protesting relative's shirt and yanked him off the bed to bounce him against the wall. Randy turned painfully pale.

"If you go anywhere near Glori again, you'll wish you were dead! Do you understand?" Maxwell shook him so violently that his nose began to bleed again. "There will be no part of your rotten body unbroken! Do you understand?" Another messy shaking followed.

Smiling contemptuously, Randy met his cousin eye to

eye and said, "Too bad you weren't first, Max. She has the body of a lizard, but the soul of a whore who likes it rough."

Before Randy saw it coming, Maxwell grabbed him by the collar, twisted it over his hand and drove him up the wall until his toes hardly touched the floor. Dangling there, Randy clawed at the fist that dug into his throat. He hiked his knee—Maxwell tightened his grip and the knee dropped. Maxwell felt a horrible satisfaction at watching Randy's face darken for want of air.

"You'd better get out of this house and stay out while Glori is here," Maxwell panted. "I'll give you two days to heal and enough money to leave."

Randy's chest heaved as he fought for breath. "You can't make me leave my own home!" he rasped. "This is going to be *my* house someday. Mine! And then I'll throw you out!"

"Someday is not today! If you touch Glori again, you'll wish you had solid-brass balls! Two days," Maxwell repeated, and let go of Randy, who crumpled to the floor. Dropping the promised bank notes beside him, Maxwell departed as quietly as he had arrived.

Back in his own room Maxwell didn't even notice the sting of the soap in the scratches as he washed his hands. He just kept scrubbing and wondered if he would ever feel clean again after touching Randy. He'd come close to killing the bastard—tightening his collar until everything putrid was choked out of him. It would have been easy, but he hadn't done it. He wondered if he should have.

Maxwell walked to the connecting door and stood there for a moment before he opened it, then quietly went in and sat on the edge of Glori's bed as she slept. She felt warmer to the touch now, her color was better. Lucy was in a nearby chair with her mending. They agreed that between them Glori wouldn't be left alone while Randy was still at the Hall.

When the family began to gather in the drawing room before supper that evening, Lucy sent word that Glori would not be joining them owing to the headache. Neville leaned toward Maxwell and told him that, being a married man, he'd just have to get used to it.

A troubled Maud announced that Randy wouldn't be among their numbers either, as he wasn't feeling well. She said she had gone to see if he was ill, only to find that he had a nose like a pomegranate. She said that Randy had told her he'd run into a door, but she didn't believe him. Remembering the fights that her two boys had had in the past, Maud looked questioningly at the scratches on Maxwell's hands. Maxwell didn't explain the marks, but he was honestly able to say that he wasn't responsible for the condition of Randy's nose.

The next day Lucy suggested that Glori's clothes might be altered. That would keep the two of them together without requiring awkward explanations. Glori welcomed the idea, as she didn't feel overly sociable. Maud joined them for tea while they pinned and stitched, coaxing Glori to have another pudding or tart, blessedly unaware of the girl's encounter with her son. Any sign of uneasiness on Glori's part was attributed to her thinness being so obvious while the fittings were being made.

As vigilant as the queen's guard, Maxwell escorted Glori from her bedchamber to the blue salon before meals and returned with her afterward, inspecting her room for anyone who might be lurking there, since Randy hadn't been joining the family at table. At night the doors from both bedchambers to the passage were secured, while the door connecting the two rooms was left open so that Maxwell could hear Glori if she cried out. She wondered what would happen if she simply called to him, though she didn't try it.

But he knew when she had nightmares. When she tossed and turned in her sleep, he was there, talking softly to push the menacing visions away, assuring her that she was safe, holding her until she slept peacefully again. Only then did he return to his own bed.

When the two days for healing were up, Randy was still at the Hall. Early in the morning of the third day he decided to join some friends in Paris and left in time to catch the early train out of Little Woolston. Maxwell hadn't been sure he would go until he had actually gone.

Each time Randy appeared, his parents hoped he had outgrown his wild ways, only to realize, once again, that no such thing had happened. Each time he departed, they hoped he would stay out of trouble, knowing that he probably wouldn't. When Randy left this time, his parents kept extra busy and visited Daisy and her pups earlier than usual.

That's why Maxwell and Glori were alone over breakfast—except for the staff, who seemed to be everywhere. To be *truly* alone Maxwell considered taking Glori outside until she said, "Would it be possible for you to take me shopping today? I'd like to purchase some lace. Though, if you're busy . . . "

"I'm not that busy," he assured her. "How soon can you be ready to embark upon this expedition?"

"Half an hour?"

"Perfect. Chipping Campden should have a bit of lace."

"Actually, the lace I need to match came from Milton's in Stratford-on-Avon. Though, if you would rather not—"

"Stratford is a lovely place, Glori. I think you'll enjoy it, though we can't dawdle."

A review of Bradford's train schedule told them that the next train left too late. So they could take the carriage or wait until another day. They decided to take the carriage.

Maxwell was eager to do *something* to make amends for what Glori had suffered. If she wanted lace from

Milton's, she'd have lace from Milton's, though he had the feeling that what she'd like most was a chance to get away after being trapped in the same house with Randy for the past few days.

Intending to drive himself, Maxwell had the light carriage and pair brought around. The horses were fresh and eager to go as Glori settled into the tufted horsehair seat. Her walking dress had been brushed clean of dust and straw, and the new ribbons on her hat fluttered in the breeze when they left the house at a smart clip. Maud and Neville waved them off. A peacock turned to face them when they passed, shaking his spectacularly fanned tail feathers to let them know that he was not a bird to be ignored. At the end of a long driveway they turned north onto a road where neat stone fences bordered rolling fields. A flock of Suffolk sheep with white wool and black faces took only brief notice of them, placidly returning to the job of being sheep.

It seemed like there was so much to say, yet neither was in a hurry to begin. It was Glori who finally said, "What would you have done if Randy hadn't left the house?"

"I would have taken you away."

"Where?"

"To my rooms in London, I suppose, if something had to be done quickly."

Glori smiled shyly. "I would have liked that."

"It's a rather small place," he said absently. "I never entertain there."

Casting her eyes to heaven, Glori wondered how she could have been foolish enough to think that Maxwell would have responded to her flirtations. Actually, he hadn't even noticed that she *had* been flirting. How mortifying!

But Maxwell's mind was elsewhere because time was running out. Dobson would be expecting a reply to the Canadian offer soon, and Glori still didn't know about it.

She deserved to know first. He would have liked more time, but he simply didn't have it.

"Glori," he began cautiously, "do you remember when I told you that I was looking out for another position?"

"Yes, I remember," she said uneasily.

"The thing is, I've been offered a plum—that of under secretary at the British embassy in Montreal, Canada."

"Canada!" she said, turning halfway round to stare at him. "That's so awfully far away! Is that what your friend came to talk to you about?"

"Yes, though I haven't given him an answer yet."

"Are you seriously considering it?"

"Yes."

"If you go, would I be going with you?"

After a deep breath he said, "No."

Glori took a deep breath and said nothing.

It had been Maxwell's intention to tell Glori that such an offer had been made and that he would be accepting it. It should have been simple enough. He could see, however, that she really was upset about it. Because she'd been so badly shaken up already, he decided to allow her a few hours to adjust to the idea that he *might* be going, before telling her that he *would* be going.

Oddly enough, the determining factor in Maxwell's decision to accept the offer had been Glori herself. For as fond as he had become of her, he didn't feel that he was taking very good care of her. His very presence seemed to bring her nothing but disaster. Her peace of mind, her very *life* had been threatened, all because of him. It seemed to him that the way he could best protect the poor girl was to stay away from her.

Glori had lost her usual enthusiasm. There were no bright smiles, no questions about the places they were passing. No pleasant chatter. Maxwell missed it. To cheer Glori he thought he could tell her about some really amusing things that had happened within the foreign office, but then he thought it wiser not to mention them right now. And there were a good many other stories that he knew Elgin would find terribly funny, but he wouldn't tell them to Glori.

The safest ground was Westbourne Hall and his life there. So he told Glori, in great detail, about the raft he and the neighbor lads had built when they were all about ten or twelve years old. After they had dragged it down to the brook, it sank, so they put rocks under it until it looked as if it were floating and then pretended they were rafting.

"Did you do things like that when you lived in Stratford?" Glori asked.

Maxwell took a long time before answering. "My pastimes there were less daring," he said. "Perhaps because I was so much younger. I had a friend named Percy, and we dug holes all over the place. My mother finally began to pick the spots for the holes and plant things in them." He shrugged. "I felt awfully proud of myself at the time."

Glori was teasing when she said, "Don't you feel awfully proud of yourself now?"

"Not particularly."

"Why?"

"Why do you ask so many questions." It was a statement, not a point of inquiry.

"I don't think I do."

"Well, you do!"

"Humbug!"

It became awfully quiet. Once Glori shivered, though she didn't look cold. Maxwell supposed she was thinking about Randy. After enough of the countryside had rolled by, he said, "I want to apologize for being so abrupt with you."

"You're forgiven."

Glori had put an end to the business as simply as that, and Maxwell breathed easier. He then went on to tell her about Stratford Trinity Church, the Knot Gar-

dens at the New Place, and the birthplace of William
Shakespeare—who, he reminded her, shouldn't be confused with Daphne's nasty bird.

Glori listened attentively to everything Maxwell said,
though once again she wondered why he was so terribly sensitive about anything associated with his boyhood
home.

Soon enough the limestone of the Cotswold Hills
gave way to the clay of the Avon River Valley, where
Stratford-on-Avon flourished. Maxwell repeated what
his father had told him about the settlement having sprung
to life in ancient times as a river-crossing market town.
"That," he said tutorially, "was long before the Romans
or the Saxons arrived to occupy the place. And trade,
not Shakespearian souvenirs, still supports Stratford."

They entered the bustling city in fine style from the
south by the Old Clopton bridge that crossed the wide
Avon. Leaving their equipage at a hostelry, Glori and
Maxwell first sought out Milton's Emporium in Chapel
Lane. It was easy to locate from the directions Maud
had provided, occupying the lower floor of a sixteenth-
century half-timbered building, flanked by a draper and
a tobacconist. Though Maxwell had removed his top
hat, both he and Glori still had to duck to enter the
doorway, and neither could stand up straight while they
were inside. It was obvious that the general population
of Queen Elizabeth's time had been considerably smaller
in stature than those of Queen Victoria's.

It hadn't really come as a surprise to Glori when she
couldn't match the lace Maud had given her. She did,
however, find another piece that was similar enough to use
with it. When she opened her purse to pay for it, Maxwell
was there before her. She found it strange to have a man
other than her father making purchases for her. Strange,
but rather pleasantly domestic.

The New Place was nearby, so they strolled through
the gardens there. Then Maxwell found a shoemaker that

sold ready-made shoes in addition to custom-made and guided Glori inside. She left wearing a pair of black half-boots of silk twill. Her scuffed button-ups were wrapped in brown paper and tied with string to carry home.

A huge wooden clock hung outside the narrow shop of a watchmaker, an establishment hardly wider than the door itself. Maxwell left his timepiece there to be repaired while he and Glori refreshed themselves at the Romeo and Juliet Tea Rooms. After they collected the watch, Glori stopped to look in the window of a millinery shop. There were little summery hats of colored straw, festooned with ribbons and net, but she declined Maxwell's invitation to pick one out. She said she wasn't in the mood for a hat just now, that she'd wait until another day, thank you.

What she wasn't in the mood for was looking into a mirror on this special day. She was agonizingly aware of the admiring glances cast in Maxwell's direction by other women. Some of them were wonderfully pretty, while she herself looked . . . like she looked.

Seeing the very tired expression Glori wore, Maxwell said they should begin their trip home, promising her that she could be a tourist again on another day. He was afraid that he'd be picking her up from the sidewalk if she did much more walking.

After claiming their carriage and horses, Maxwell drove Glori past Shakespeare's birthplace so she wouldn't miss it completely. Then he gave their route some serious thought and turned north, though they had arrived in Stratford from the south. He hadn't offered a reason, but Glori suspected where they were going.

Having left the main road for a smaller one, they soon turned onto an even less traveled lane. They came to a stop where the lane narrowed into a sun-dappled cart track offering a view of an orderly farm. The rambling house had a newly thatched roof. Maxwell devoured everything he saw. So much of it was the way he remembered it, but he had to search for the path that had once taken him to his friend Percy's house. Even less recognizable was the stick his mother had planted in one of those numerous holes. It had grown into a tall maple.

A child played in a bucket of water in the kitchen garden while a pair of women beat the dust from a mattress that had been thrown over the fence. A stack of boards lay on the ground near an empty wagon. Someone else's dog now slept in the sun by the side of the house, but the house was just the same. It had been essentially unchanged for three hundred years, and, Maxwell supposed, it wouldn't be much different three hundred years from now. A story and a half high, it boasted three great chimneys and a pegged-timber frame, filled with wattle and daub. They could see five dormer windows on the upper floor. A low stone wall surrounded a small front garden filled with climbing roses and early flowers.

"It's called the Willows," he said, without taking his eyes from the place. "I was born there."

Glori slipped her hand into his. "Have you missed it so very much?"

He curled his long fingers around hers and said, "Yes . . . yes, I have."

"Why have you stayed away so long?"

A sardonic smile tugged at one corner of his mouth. "You really do ask a lot of questions."

"Why?" she repeated softly.

CHAPTER EIGHT

M AXWELL gazed across the fields that surrounded his old home. A rabbit darted across the track to disappear into the tall grass beyond the ditch. Small white moths flitted through the weeds. Peewits chirruped. The air smelled of spring.

Glori waited.

Shuffling horses twitched their ears and rippled their dark hides to chase away the buzzing flies. Tails swished. Harnesses jingled as the animals became restless. Eight hooves stomped crescents in the dust.

And Glori waited.

Closing his eyes, Maxwell inhaled deeply and exhaled slowly, remembering. Whole minutes went by before he said, "I'd been such a brat before they left for Ceylon." By *they* he meant his parents. "I didn't want them to go, and I told my mother that I wouldn't love her anymore if she went away. But she just smiled and kissed me and said she would love me all the same, and that they would bring home a grand surprise. You already know they didn't return." Then he muttered, "It's a damned silly thing to tell anyone."

"Did Elgin think it was silly?"

"Elgin doesn't know. Actually, no one else does."

143

Glori nodded in recognition of that information and followed Maxwell's unbroken study of the farmland. "What you've told me sounds a great deal like something that happened to a little boy at the East Wallow school," she said. "When I announced that I would be going to visit my grandmother—she had been quite ill, you see—he told me that he wouldn't like me ever again if I went away. He wouldn't even speak to me for the rest of the day."

"And?"

"And when I returned we were pleased to see each other again, and things went on as usual."

"That's all fine and dandy because you came back to view it through the rosy light of hindsight. It won't wash if you try to tell me that you weren't cut up just a little by what the boy said to you."

"Oh, it didn't hurt me a bit. After all, he hadn't really behaved so awfully badly. He was only a worried child who liked me and didn't want me to leave him. In a way I suppose I was even flattered that he cared so much about whether or not I left."

"You make it sound so ridiculously simple."

"It truly was," Glori insisted. "Such behavior isn't at all unusual for a child who is frightened. And I truly do understand why you regret having said what you did, but it's perfectly awful that it's haunted you for so long. Why didn't you ever tell your aunt and uncle?"

He shrugged. "When I was younger, I didn't want anyone to know how bad I had been. When I got older, I didn't want anyone to know it still bothered me." He returned to his quiet contemplation of the unchanging scenery.

Yet some things weren't the same. After his secret had been hung out in the light, it didn't look quite the way he'd remembered it for so many years. He only wished the other beast that chewed on his conscience could be so easily pacified.

"You're awfully quiet," Glori said. "I truly believe anyone's mother would have—"

"It's more than that. The whole of it is more complicated, though I suppose it wouldn't make any more sense."

"Perhaps we can talk about it."

"Perhaps we can't."

Maxwell said nothing more on the subject. In fact, he thought he'd already said too much. He wondered why he'd ever brought Glori to see a place he himself had been avoiding for twenty-odd years. And he didn't know why he'd told her what a disagreeable creature he'd been when he was a boy.

"Do you know the people who live there now?" Glori asked.

"Hmm? Oh, the Morrisons. No, I've never met them, though I believe some of the staff might still be the same. My agent handles everything."

Glori wanted to drive over to see the place and meet the Morrisons, but she didn't suggest it. She knew that coming this far hadn't been easy for Maxwell. That's when he checked his watch, took up the reins, and turned the horses. At the first crossroad he headed for the Willows.

When they came clip-clopping into the yard, they saw draperies hanging on the clothesline to air. Leaving their carriage, they saw that furniture had been moved outside into the sun, where a woman inspected it for signs of insect damage. People that Maxwell had never seen before passed him with a rug he remembered very well. It looked like the Morrisons were moving out, but a wiry man carrying a board on his shoulder said that the family was only on holiday for a month. While they were gone, the whole house was being turned out for cleaning.

Then someone Maxwell did recognize came puffing up from the potting shed, calling out, "Hello, laddie! Ya look so much like your father that it might be himself with a new hat!"

It was Logan, the gardener, and he was as happy to see Maxwell as Maxwell was to see him. Logan was no less pleased to be introduced to Glori. The sturdy old fellow then explained that only he and his missus remained from the Rutherford days, and that she was now housekeeper as well as cook.

Unconcerned with the best parlor hospitality that would have been shown to the usual gentry, Logan ushered this pair into the kitchen to see Mrs. Logan, who was rolling out egg noodles on a floured board. Gray-haired and roly-poly, she delighted in seeing her favorite boy all grown up, and with a wife, too. As she had in the old days, she set out sweet mint tea and biscuits on the long maple table and bewailed the fact that she didn't have a single piece of Maxwell's favorite gingerbread in the place. And she fussed over Glori, saying how glad she was that Master Maxwell had brought his bride all this way to meet them, glad that he hadn't forgotten them after all these years.

Though everything was in a state of confusion, the Logans encouraged Maxwell to take his wife about the place, which he did, but he was awfully quiet the whole time. Still, he gave Glori a look at everything from the cellar to the attic—except the master bedchamber. Though that door had been open, he walked by.

Maxwell wanted to show Glori the grounds, too, but departure couldn't be put off any longer. He was afraid that they would need a cloudless sky to make use of what moonlight there was before they reached the Hall tonight. They had to find the Logans, thank them for their hospitality, and turn their horses south. But there, at the bottom of the stairs, twisting his tired felt hat, was old Logan. His cotton smock and cord pants had been brushed clean for this sojourn into the house proper.

"What is it?" Maxwell asked when he saw how disturbed the fellow was.

"I'm much afraid 'tis your carriage wheel, lad."

"The wheels were sound enough when I inspected that rig this morning."

"This morning, maybe, but no' this evenin'. I pulled the thing off myself and had a boy take it t' the wheelwright."

Maxwell scowled and said, "Perhaps I'd better have a look. Glori, you'll probably be more comfortable in the parlor."

Glori waited in the parlor.

The carriage was there in the yard for Maxwell to see, minus the right rear wheel. The cause of the problem had been the child who belonged to one of the newly hired cleaning women. Left unattended, the little girl had become bored with the bucket of water she had been playing in and moved on to other things. Those things were the tools in the box that had been left beside the pile of lumber in the yard. As the carriage was close by, she had used a key hole saw on three of the spokes before someone caught her.

With this news in his pocket Maxwell returned to the parlor. He was scowling worse than ever when he dropped himself onto a shrouded chair and drummed his fingers on the padded arm. When it seemed that he'd gotten the rhythm to his satisfaction, he said, "We are missing a wheel from our carriage. The wheelwright can't get it repaired until late tonight, and by then it will be much too late to leave here!" Pushing himself out of the chair, Maxwell stuffed his hands into his pockets to pace the entire length of the unobstructed floor, the furniture having been moved to one side to roll up a Chinese carpet that he had never seen before.

"Under the circumstances we cannot leave as planned. Is that all?" Glori said as Maxwell reached the fireplace and turned.

"I should think you've had enough sprung on you lately," he replied, pacing his way to the far end of the room.

Glori turned in her chair to follow his movements and said, "I must admit that it is inconvenient, but it isn't anything really bad. Surely we can stay here while the wheel is being fixed." Maxwell was on his return trip when Glori added, "If Randy returns to the Hall, he won't find us there. What if he only went to the train station, then returned home again?"

Maxwell's frustration fizzled when he looked at Glori. He knew that she'd been glad to see the last of Randy, but it had never occurred to him that she might fear his immediate return. He wanted to hold her close and tell her not to worry so, but he couldn't do such a thing in someone else's parlor. After a moment he just said, "I don't suppose it would make much difference if we remained here for the night. Before we left, Aunt Maud did suggest that we might want to stay in Stratford long enough to see a play. When we don't show up tonight, she'll think that's what we've done." Then he looked at Glori's tightly clasped hands and said, "I really don't think Randy will return to the Hall in the near future. I gave him good reason to stay away."

Glori heard such a hard edge to Maxwell's voice that she supposed Randy really would keep his distance.

They both looked around when Mrs. Logan cleared her throat. Standing at the parlor door holding her apron, the good woman said, "We're so sorry about the damage to your carriage, but we'll be happy to have you stay as long as need be." Addressing Glori she said, "I'm having things put to rights in the guest room this very minute, dearie. You look as if you need a rest."

So Glori rested soundly while her husband and Logan looked over the farm, reminiscing as they went.

When Glori awoke, Maxwell took her along the well-trodden paths of his youth. The walk ended at a wooden bridge that crossed an invitingly picturesque creek, the place where ancient willows grew. Sitting side by side, they dangled their feet over the water, tossing in pebbles. They counted fourteen regular minnows and one they called the whale. With that for inspiration, Glori sang a song about whaling. There followed songs about pirate raids and hurricanes and Saint Elmo's fire dancing along the yards. There were pumping songs and heave-hoing songs, and the lament of a sailor who had left a love in every port, which drew a reluctant grin from Maxwell.

And it was while she sat so demurely, all pink and ribbons, that Glori raised her thin soprano voice to relate a tale of cannibalism aboard a becalmed merchantman, which laid Maxwell flat on the bridge, laughing. It wasn't because there was anything humorous in the verse, but that the grisly thing had erupted from such an innocent mouth to the tune of "Gentle Shepherd Love Thy Lambs."

She wasn't expecting it, but it was the laugh Glori had wanted to hear before Maxwell went away. Instead of making her happy, it only served as a sad reminder that he would soon be leaving.

"Glori, by any chance was that the song you sang for the minister on Christmas Eve in East Wallow?" Maxwell asked.

"How did you guess?"

"Where did you ever learn such a thing?"

"There was an old sailor in East Wallow whose sight had gone so dim that he couldn't go to sea any longer. He lived with his nephew, who was the smithy. On nice days he sat in the sun outside the shop to tell stories and sing songs for the children."

Maxwell was still grinning when he said, "I wish I could have heard him."

Glori wished she could just lean her head on Maxwell's shoulder while they spoke of more tender things. And when he offered her his hand to help her up, he might not let it go. She would then tell him how very dear he was to her, and he would clasp her hands to his heart and confess his affection for her, as well.

None of those things happened.

Even so, they returned to the Willows companionably to sup upon roast mutton with noodles and carrots and a bottle of dandelion wine at a small table set before a crackling fire in the guest bedroom. The chill of the evening held back as long as the embers glowed in the grate, and those dancing flames seemed to consume Maxwell's interest.

Glori said, "You're thinking about your mother, aren't you?"

"Actually, I was thinking about my father, too."

"Same old ghosts?"

"Same old ghosts." He tossed his serviette onto the table and said, "I think I'll turn in now."

It was after he'd said a pleasant good night to Glori and sought his old room that Maxwell received another unwelcome surprise. His bedchamber was where it had always been. His old bedstead was where it had always stood. His old mattress was nowhere to be found. In fact, there wasn't any mattress at all.

Elbows on the table, thoughts in the air, Glori still lingered over her last cup of chamomile tea when Maxwell burst in. He didn't even say hello, he just closed the door and leaned against it.

"There is a problem," he said in slow distinct tones.

Glori lowered cup to saucer. "There is always a problem, it would seem. Have we lost another wheel?"

"No, we have lost a mattress," he said irritably, "not to mention all the niceties that go on top of it." He plowed his forehead with three rigid fingers.

Glori refrained from asking about either the mattress or the niceties, electing, instead, to wait for him to expand upon his brief but curious statement.

"I had expected to sleep in my old room," he explained. "That's out of the question unless I plan to sleep on the floor, which would prove embarrassing if the cleaning women find me there in the morning."

"Yes, I see what you mean."

"Now we'll both have to sleep in this room, because I can't very well expect anyone to prepare another bed at this hour. It would put the whole house in a pother."

"Of course it would," Glori replied sympathetically.

"And I can't sleep in your bed any more than you can sleep on the floor," Maxwell added.

"Well, perhaps we could share the bed."

"Don't be silly, Glori. It wouldn't work."

"Why not?"

"Because I'm a man, for crissakes, and you're a girl!"

"I am *not* a girl, Maxwell. I am—"

"Yes, I know, you're a wonderfully wise young lady. Now I'm going down to the kitchen to see if Mrs. Logan might still have some tea in her pot. While I'm about it, I'll ask her to send someone to help you with your clothes. You needn't wait up for me." With his hand on the door latch he looked back and said, "Leave the lamp burning." When he said good night, he closed the door more sharply than he had intended to.

Maxwell reached the kitchen to find Logan bent over a gardening book. At the sound of his steps the old fellow looked up and said, "Hello, lad!" He put down his pipe and stood respectfully, glancing at the row of small silent bells high up on the wall. "Is the bell wire t' your room broken? I'll get the plumber over here tomorrow t' patch it."

"The wire is sound enough as far as I know. I merely thought we might visit a bit more because I've been away for so long."

"Good, good," chimed Logan as he set out another chair. "The missus has gone t' see about somethin' for your wifey afore she goes t' bed." Dark eyes twinkling, he wheezed, "You just sit, lad, and I'll fetch us a drop o' beer. The womenfolk need never know."

Maxwell accepted both the seat and the beer, plus a

few refills of that foaming libation as the clock ticked away. There came an hour when he thought it was time to retire, only to wonder if Glori was asleep yet. Unbuttoning his jacket, he had another glass of beer.

Glori had been left to say good night to the heavy oaken door that closed firmly behind the man she had married. With nothing better to do she dawdled over her tea until it went cold, folded her serviette into the shape of a duck, then gathered some bread crumbs beside her plate and pinched them into a perfect little pyramid.

Before construction could begin on a miniature of the Great Sphinx or the Temple at Karnak, an apple-cheeked maid arrived. She managed a curtsy before she put down a can of hot water. Over her shoulder she carried a man's nightshirt and Mrs. Morrison's second-best nightgown, the latter having been endowed with a generous supply of lace-edged ruffles. Both garments were laid neatly on the bed. From the maid's pockets came a hairbrush, shaving things, toothbrushes, and a jar of tooth polish. These were placed on the small dressing table.

Glori was impressed with how thorough Maxwell had been with thoughts for her comfort until the girl said, "Mrs. Logan sent these and told me to help you out of your clothes. Would you like me to brush your hair, too, Mrs. Rutherford?"

Mrs. Rutherford sat before the dressing table while the girl removed the pins from hair, brushed it, and fashioned it into a long night-braid. When undressed to her drawers and chemise, Glori dismissed the girl, who then piled the dishes onto a tray, tossed Glori's dress over her shoulder, and carried everything away.

Standing on a colorful rag rug before the washstand, Glori finished undressing. Then she used a snowy washcloth and warm water with scented soap to bathe away the road dust. By the time she slipped the flannelette nightgown over her head, the maid was back with her

dress, well brushed, which she hung on a wall peg, as
the room had no wardrobe. It was clear to Glori that
Maxwell could have walked in as easily as the maid had.
But it would serve no purpose to move behind the folding
screen now, so she hopped into bed and pulled the covers
up under her chin. There was little else to to but stare at
the ceiling.

And wait.

She had begun to feel like she'd spent the whole day,
perhaps even her whole life, waiting for *something*. Now
she waited for the man who was her husband and wondered if *something* was about to happen. There was a
time when she had wondered if she might change from
a young lady to an old one without ever finding out what
that something was, exactly. When she considered the
disagreeable look on Maxwell's face when he'd left the
room, she thought lifetime ignorance might be a distinct
possibility.

Glori had found that a good many subjects of a personal nature had been covered in a book she had read
called *Dr. Samuel Ellsworth's Complete Home, Family, and Medical Cyclopedia*, with an extensive section
on Women's Complaints and Magnetic Corrections. But
waiting in bed for the arrival of one's espoused wasn't
among the subjects discussed in any of those discreetly
illustrated chapters. Even so, Dr. Ellsworth's *Cyclopedia*
was one of those publications that *right-thinking people*
insisted be kept under lock and key lest a lady or a child
be corrupted by it. Those *right thinkers* maintained that
tons of filth invaded sacred homes under the seemingly
innocent covers of medical books. Even the queen agreed
with them. But Glori's father hadn't been inclined to lock
that book away, so she simply took it from his book room
and read it.

When that hefty volume was finally returned to the
shelf, Glori wondered how anyone could be corrupted by
what she had just read, and why only ladies and children

needed to be saved from the possibility of corruption. Had men a greater resistance to sin than women? She decided that it was unlikely and suspected that the entire business had been thought up by some man who didn't want to be bothered by quite so much saving. There was, however, the baker's wife in Helmsley, who snickered about anything that sounded the least bit naughty. If ever there was a woman who needed saving, it was certainly she.

Snuggling farther into the soft bedding, Glori abandoned corruption to study the room she was in. The place smelled of freshly whitewashed plaster and the beeswax used to polish the furniture. Eight thick rafters crossed the ceiling. One mirrorlike window nestled in a gabled recess; the curtains had yet to be rehung. Against the wall, to her right, stood a dressing table with a small mirror and a bench that had a dark red velvet cushion.

A black enameled folding screen was zigzagged in the corner with greeting cards pasted to each of the four panels. There was a small table on each side of the bed, but only one with a lamp. And then there was the bed, of course, with tall plain posts. Though the furniture was old, it was in very good condition, and Glori wondered if the pieces belonged with the property or if they had been brought in by the Morrisons. When Maxwell returned, Glori thought, she would ask him.

Ah, yes, when Maxwell returned. An unnerving thought. Glori simply didn't know how one was supposed to go about waiting in bed for a man, especially when that man wouldn't be the least bit pleased about getting into bed. It became obvious to her that everything would be easier for both of them if she was asleep when he returned. With that end in mind she shifted around until every part of her was comfy, then shut her eyes and waited.

Sleep didn't come.

Neither did Maxwell.

It was too embarrassing. Glori got out of bed and moved the bench from the dressing table to the gabled window. If she sat there and put her knees up, she could pull the nightgown over her feet and stay a bit warmer. She would tell Maxwell that she was admiring the night sky. Then *he* could get in bed and go to sleep first, and then *she* could get in bed, and everything would be fine. She wondered which side of the bed he would prefer. Then she wondered if he might really sleep on the floor, instead. There were two pillows on the bed but only one comforter. He'd have to sleep in the bed.

Stifling a strained laugh, Glori pulled her nightgown closer around her legs and remembered a whispered conversation with her old friend, Caroline Barnstable, when they were about eleven. Caroline had confided that she had put her ear to the closed schoolroom door and happened to overhear their governess, the dour Miss Fernwood, telling the about-to-be-married older Barnstable sister that a lady must lie back in bed and think of England, or recite scriptures, or sing hymns very softly during those unavoidable episodes of her husband's insatiable carnal demands.

There followed a hushed discussion by the two girls as to what those carnal demands might be, what scriptures or hymns Miss Fernwood would recommend, and whether or not they should start learning any special ones right away, just to be prepared. Caroline decided against asking the formidable Miss Fernwood for that information and said she would ask her mother instead. The next day Caroline reported that her mother had been quite embarrassed by the entire subject, saying that *nice* girls didn't ask such questions. Everything, her mother assured her, would be explained to her by her husband on their wedding night.

To make matters even more confusing, Caroline had managed to smuggle out a curious item from her sister's trousseau. She'd hidden it under her coat. Away in a cor-

ner of the vast Barnstable gardens the two girls inspected
a white nightdress. Beautifully trimmed with French lace
and ribbons tied in love knots, it also had an odd placket,
closed by three mother-of-pearl buttons. When Caroline
held the nightdress against herself the placket reached
her thighs. This gave way to active speculation as there
were a limited number of uses such a placket could have.
The girls finally decided that the thing had been put on
the wrong side by mistake, having been intended for the
back instead of the front, and someone had run out of
buttons or it wouldn't have been so small.

When Glori approached her own mother to ask about
thoughts of England, scriptures, and hymns during moments of carnal insatiability, her mother had been greatly amused. She said Miss Fernwood was rather foolish
and assured Glori that when the time came for her to
be married, the two of them would have a cozy chat.
Unfortunately, the time had come but the chat hadn't.

Of course, Glori knew more than she did when she was
eleven, but not so very much more, which left her feeling
rather stupid at her age. She knew, for instance, that men
and women did *something* to make babies, which was
how one of the dairymaids got into trouble the previous year. The baker's wife still snickered about it, saying that the girl lacked dignity in any shape or form,
which caused Glori to wonder if the coupling process
was so awfully undignified. She hoped people weren't as
boisterous as cows, with all that bellowing and mooing.
Years before she had heard the noise from the barnyard
when the cow was being bred, but her father had forbidden her to go there.

So despite the fact that Glori had been raised in the
country, she lacked any great understanding of the mating
process. For all that the reproductive methods of flowers
had been a part of her youthful studies, such knowledge
really wasn't any help.

Then there was that *Cyclopedia* of Dr. Ellsworth's.

Though full of *words*, it lacked *information*. She had read his stern warnings against overindulging in *sanctified joy*, without ever finding out what it was. Gloomy predictions went on for page after page, warning of insanity, weak eyes, poor bladder control, hair loss, and endless irreparable injuries to one's constitution, if one partook too generously of that joy. In fact, the good doctor stated emphatically that twice a month was quite enough of whatever it was. Though, if desperate, once a week might be allowed. Once a month, however, was safest of all.

Glori wondered if Miss Fernwood had read Dr. Ellsworth's book, because she had surely left out a lot when she lectured Caroline Barnstable's older sister about the marriage bed. But Glori was certain that Maxwell would know what Miss Fernwood had omitted. After she asked him about the origins of the furniture in this room, she would ask him what the prim governess had left out. While considering the amazing diversity of Maxwell's knowledge, Glori fell asleep.

Maxwell made his way up the stairs, grinning foolishly, singing softly. He wasn't singing hymns. The lyrics were rollicking ones about a willing wench with flashing eyes and bouncing thighs. No one like Glori. Sooner than he wanted to he reached the door that had Glori on the other side of it. A faint strip of light showed beneath that door, assuring him that the lamp still burned. There would be no provokingly intimate shadows around her bed this time, and he wouldn't make a roaring ass of himself.

Quietly entering the room, he approached the bed to get a pillow to sleep on the floor, expecting to take whichever one Glori wasn't using, except Glori wasn't there. In his befuddled state he tried to remember if he'd left her somewhere else, but decided that she was supposed to be right there. And she must have been in bed at some time, because the covers were churned up. He looked under the bed. Then he looked around for something that would tell him if he was even in the right room. That's when he saw Glori, all huddled up on a bench near the window. He didn't know what she could possibly be doing there. The next thing he did was turn up the flame in the lamp, making the room just a little brighter.

For a while Maxwell just stared at his companion and wondered what to do with her. He had wondered the same thing before but still hadn't found an answer that would help him. A single braid hung over her shoulder. He hadn't thought her hair was that long.

Gently tapping the end of her nose, he said, "Glori, wake up." She wrinkled her nose and huddled into a smaller lump. He said, "You're cold, Glori. Climb into bed and I'll cover you." She still didn't move, so he bent over and gripped the sides of the bench, bringing his face close to hers. Taking a breath, he softly called, "Glorrriii, wake up!"

CHAPTER NINE

RUBBING sleepy eyes, Glori yawned and blinked and there was Maxwell. When he'd left the room a while ago, he'd looked so awfully stuffy. Now he looked . . . unstuffed. He had actually become a bit rumpled, with a lazy grin and a wisp of wavy dark hair that fell across his forehead. Glori smiled and buried her face against his neck, curling her fingers around his lapels. Though he smelled of tobacco smoke and onions and beer, she didn't particularly care.

He said, "Good God! Your nose is cold. And you're not supposed to cuddle like that, old chum, you're supposed to get up." All the while he scolded her, he was trying to undo her fingers from his coat. Her hands were as cold as her nose.

"You smell like beer," she said.

"That's no great surprise. I've had too much of it down in the kitchen with old Logan." He had formed his words with great care. "In case you haven't noticed, I'm regrettably intoxicated."

"Are you really?"

"Unquestionably. Will you please let go of my coat?"

"Are you often in this condition?"

"I haven't been in this condition since my first term at

159

university, which was a good many years ago. I usually have sense enough to stop before this happens."

"I'm glad to know that. Just go to bed and you'll be fine."

"I seriously doubt it, my girl, but that's beside the point. What in heaven's name possessed you to sleep on a cold bench when you've got a warm bed? Do you walk in your sleep?"

"I was looking at the stars."

"Without your spectacles?"

"It would be difficult to explain."

"Then I don't want to hear it. All I want to do is go to sleep, but I can't very well leave you sitting about. It wouldn't be gentlemanly, and I am, after all, a gentleman." Then he burped and pressed his hand to his mouth. "Excuse me."

Stifling a laugh, Glori said, "You're excused," and lifted her arms to him.

Maxwell shook his head. "Impossible. I can't carry you. I can hardly carry myself. We'd both be on the floor."

"The floor is much too hard and cold for comfort."

"Damn right it is," he grumped. "Fire's gone out, too. I don't think I'll sleep there after all."

Glori still hadn't lowered her arms, so Maxwell balanced as well as he could before he picked her up and walked carefully to the side of the bed. When he tried to put her down, he fell across the covers with her in his arms because she hadn't let go of him. At least she landed right side around with her head toward the pillows.

Tugging his arms out from beneath her, Maxwell hiccupped and said, "Madam, it seems that this time, at least, you have managed to procure my knight-errant services without being so damsely distressed. We are making progress, indeed, and for that I do offer my thanks, though I fear I've squashed you beyond repair."

Glori giggled. "Certainly not beyond repair."

With his face buried in the bedding, he said, "I'm gratified to hear it. Do get under the covers, if you please."

"I can't. You're lying on me. You simply must move."

"Must I?" he groaned.

"You must."

Ponderously, Maxwell rolled his bulk off the fragile body beneath his, vaguely aware that it was more womanly and less childlike than he had supposed. He then turned a quarter-way around to flop with his face in a pillow, an arm flung over the female at his side. In a muffled voice he asked, "Are you quite sure you're not squashed?"

"Quite sure."

He mumbled something else into the pillow.

Neither one of them moved. Glori wondered what was supposed to happen next, then decided that nothing would happen at all because Maxwell was asleep. After a little while she curiously, cautiously, reached out to skip her fingertips over the tendons and bones that ridged the back of his hand where it lay on the bed beside her.

"Roses," he mumbled this time.

Snatching her hand away, she said, "It's Mrs. Morrison's soap."

"Umm."

Glori didn't know what *umm* meant but thought she may as well turn out the light and go to sleep, too. When she reached toward the lamp, a steely arm suddenly hooked around her waist to drag her back, thumping her firmly against the male chest behind her.

"Don't touch the lamp!" Maxwell growled into her hair.

"Are you afraid of the dark?"

"I am now."

"I don't understand."

"Good!"

Glori pushed at the arm that locked around her, saying, "Maxwell, you have a remarkably strong grip."

A silly smile spread over his face, and he gave her a squeeze. "You have remarkably fine hips. I must be the only man in the world who knows you have any hips at all." That notion, swirling with the alcohol through his brain, pleased Maxwell. With a mighty yawn he nestled deeper into the soft bed, taking Glori with him.

Once again Glori thought he had gone to sleep. This mistake was made obvious when the hand that had been tucked around her waist crept slowly along her ribs until it bumped into a breast and stopped amid a tangle of flannelette ruffles.

Glori became very still. Stiff, in fact. That happened when she held her breath. She had waited and waited, and *something* had finally happened. Not a great deal, she didn't suppose, but it *was* something, or the *beginning* of something. She felt like warm honey inside, with the most curious urge to turn around and hold Maxwell, too. And she wanted to suggest that he take off his coat now that they were in bed, and his shoes, too. This was another topic that Dr. Samuel Ellsworth's *Cyclopedia* hadn't spent any ink upon.

There was one thing, however, that Glori finally did understand. The notions that swayed so provocatively through her mind were definitely some of those *impure thoughts* that Dr. Ellsworth had warned his readers against. The man's advice had been to busy one's self with good works and lofty thoughts to cast off the dangerous clamorings of one's body. Deciding that she'd much rather cast off Dr. Ellsworth, Glori sighed contentedly in her husband's arms.

Instantly alerted by that sigh, Maxwell said, "Glori, what's the matter?" Without waiting for an answer he mumbled a blaspheme and buried his hand in the bed linen again. "I'm sorry, love," he murmured against her ear. "I've tippled too long and made myself unforgivably drunk and I'm having one hell of a time remembering why I'm not supposed to be in your bed. And I hate this ridiculous nightgown." He gave the thing a shake. "Still I want you to know that no matter what condition I'm in, you need never be afraid of me." He pulled her closer and nuzzled her neck, acutely aware of the woman in his arms. His warm mouth brushed her cool skin when he repeated, "There's no reason to be afraid of me. Do you understand?"

She nodded yes, but he needed to hear her answer to know that he hadn't frightened her, to know that she wasn't crying. He moved back to allow more room, then took her by the shoulders and turned her around. Framing her pale face with his large hands, he studied her intently and repeated softly, "You needn't be frightened of me. Do you understand?"

Glori covered his hands with her own and tried to say, yes, I understand, but her answer was lost in his kiss.

Her mouth softened beneath his as she melted against him, an arm slipping around his back, wonderfully aware of the tightening of his body and the hunger of her own. His silky mustache licked her lips and the dark stubble of his beard rubbed her chin. Never ever had she been so attuned to anyone. Tingling all over, she wanted to climb under his shirt. If Dr. Ellsworth's *Cyclopedia* was to be believed, Glori supposed she was on her way to ruination right now. She decided that she would go well pleased with the trip and snuggled closer to her husband.

Her husband was glad that her nose had warmed up. While rubbing her back with long slow strokes, he wondered if he felt as good to her as she did to him. Smiling, eyes closed, he whispered, "I'm not going to apologize for what just happened."

"I should hope not," she whispered. "I think I like kissing."

"I like kissing *you*," he said. "I might even do it again when my head stops spinning."

"It's the beer."

"It might be you. You're soft."

"It's the nightgown."

"We could get rid of the thing and find out."

"It's the words of a man who wears his shoes to bed."

Holding fast to Glori, Maxwell pushed off his shoes, then rolled onto his back with her in his arms so as not to crush her. When he pulled her remarkable hips tightly against his aroused self, she looked startled. He just chuckled and said, "I'll hate myself in the morning, but we've got to get rid of this nightgown now." Taking a firm hold of Glori's ruffled and buttoned neckline, he intended to give it the treatment it so justly deserved.

"Maxwell, no!"

His grip held for a moment longer before his hands dropped away. He said, "You're right, we can't very well shred our hostess's nightclothes." Then he locked his hands firmly around her back and nuzzled her cheek.

Glori wasn't worried about the nightclothes. She had fastened onto the one revealing thing Maxwell had said, and asked, "Why would you hate yourself in the morning?"

Nibbling along her neck, he said, "Because I'd feel like a cad . . . for seducing you . . . when I'm supposed to be taking care of you." He kept nibbling right up to her ear and thought she squirmed delightfully.

"Would you *truly* hate yourself?" Glori persisted with difficulty as the nibbling continued.

"Not until tomorrow," he said, his voice growing huskier as he slid his hands farther down her back to massage her derriere.

But his words had cut Glori to the heart. By morning Maxwell would hate himself and her as well because of what they were about to do tonight. It became an effort not to cry. She wondered if this might be one of those occasions when Miss Fernwood might recommend reciting something. All she could think of was *The boy stood on the burning deck when all but him had fled* . . . which provided no solace whatsoever and she felt worse.

"We can't do this!" Glori wailed, wedging her elbows between her chest and Maxwell's.

Holding her tightly, Maxwell said, "Glori, don't be frightened. I won't forget that you've never done this before." He thought she was stalling for time because she was afraid of the intimacy that lay ahead of them.

And Glori was stalling, and she was a little frightened. She didn't know what to expect, but if they were on the brink of sanctified joy, it was going to be nothing more than sanctified regret by morning, and everything would be ruined when he hated her.

She was frantic to distract him when she said, "Maxwell . . . why . . . why are you still so troubled by your parents' disappearance?"

"What?"

"Why are you so—"

"For crissakes, Glori, not *now*! We are on the threshold of a Great Adventure! You are about to become a woman, and I am about to become rather queasy. We'd better not wait too long."

"Will you tell me, please?"

When Glori sounded like that, it was nearly his undoing. He didn't want her to be frightened about anything, and he felt even worse when he remembered finding Randy sitting on her, ready to . . .

Maxwell squeezed his eyes shut. He thought he'd better slow down, allow Glori more time. Giving her a reassuring hug, he rolled her onto the bed and held her beside him. Then his stomach rolled, and he reached up to loosen his tie.

Light as a butterfly, Glori's fragile hand settled protectively over Maxwell's strong one, and he could hardly stand it. *He* was supposed to be taking care of *her*, but somehow it had got to be the other way around. Easing his hand away from hers, he removed his tie and tossed it aside. Then he loosened his collar and reached around her to fiddle with his cuffs, and she waited. When he finally resigned himself to answering Glori's ill-timed question about his parents' disappearance, he found that he didn't know quite how to begin.

He finally said, "It was the monkey, if you must know. That's what made the whole thing so awful. My parents didn't simply disappear on some scenic drive. They disappeared while they were out looking at a bunch of yammering monkeys!"

Knowing that he didn't sound sensible, even to himself, Maxwell wished he'd never started to explain anything. But here he was, and there Glori was, so he forged on. "My mother was going to bring home something special, you see. I wanted a monkey. I had *begged* for a monkey. My mother and father died when they went out to look at monkeys. If I hadn't wanted the monkey, they wouldn't have gone off and been killed. There you have the beginning and end of it." A dismal silence followed.

"So you think their deaths were your fault," Glori said. "I suppose you've never told anyone about that, either."

"God, no!"

"A child who wants a pet is common enough, Maxwell, but—"

"Is this another homily about the simple life in East Wallow?" he demanded cynically.

"You needn't become waspish, I was only thinking that a boy who wants a puppy is quite common. How did you ever become so eager for a monkey?"

He shrugged. "Oh, picture books, I suppose, and stories. As I recall, I loved any story with a monkey in it."

"You must have been quite a fine reader for such a little boy."

"Actually, I wasn't a swift reader at all," he replied quite honestly. "My mother read the stories to me. And she told me about the monkey her aunt once had. His name was Timothy. He liked to wear fancy hats and eat ice cream, and he had his own little seat at table. Such things were all the fashion then."

"Your mother must have enjoyed Timothy a great deal."

Maxwell was able to smile when he said, "Yes, I believe she did, though she told me that he had bitten her on more than one occasion and threw things when the inclination overtook him."

Carefully picking her words, Glori said, "I suppose that if I ever wanted to have a monkey, and if I had a child who might be afraid of it, or even jealous of it, I would tell him lots of jolly tales about monkeys so that he would be glad when I brought it home."

Maxwell drew back and looked at Glori like she'd just grown hairy warts on her nose. "Are you suggesting that my mother had planned to bring home a monkey because *she* wanted one, and all those stories she told me were just to get me to like the little blighter before it arrived?"

"I'm only saying that if I planned to bring a monkey home and—"

"I *know* what you said!"

"Is there something wrong with it?"

"Everything's wrong with it. Do you really expect me to believe that's the way it happened?"

"I'm not expecting anything. I simply told you what I would do."

He closed his eyes and said, "I'm too inebriated to think about it. We should have done more Great Adventuring when we had the chance."

"Maxwell, I don't understand why you should hate yourself in the morning after this adventuring, but if you did you would hate me, too, and I simply couldn't stand it." Laying her hand on his arm, she lowered her voice and confessed, "I really don't want you to leave at all. You see, at first it wouldn't have mattered as much, but now it matters quite a lot." Nearly bursting with untried love, she exclaimed, "Oh, don't you see how well it's all coming about?"

She waited for some word, any word of mutual regard,

but he didn't say a thing. Glori elbowed his inert form and said, "Maxwell?"

His reply was a gentlemanly snore.

With a touch of envy Glori recalled the shy glances exchanged between one of the parlor maids and that young nice-looking footman at Westbourne Hall. She'd heard that they had been seen out walking, holding hands. Glori didn't suppose either one of them had ever read Dr. Samuel Ellsworth's *Cyclopedia* and decided that they were probably better off without it.

Sitting up, Glori lifted her knees and wondered what to do now. She didn't think Maxwell looked very comfortable for all that he had taken off his shoes and tie. And he had the covers tangled. Intending to make him a little more comfortable, she managed, with considerable difficulty, to lift one shoulder and pull away a sleeve of his suit coat, hoping that she wasn't dislocating his shoulder. Then she turned him over, peeling off his coat as she went, stopping before she rolled him right off the bed. Then she rolled him back so that she could pull his other sleeve away, entirely divesting him of the encumbering garment. That was as far as she could go without weighing the delicacy of it all against any additional comfort she might afford him.

Shivering from the cold but deciding to be brave, Glori removed Maxwell's elastic braces. When she undid his shirt buttons, the backs of her fingers brushed over silky, tickly body hair from collarbone to belly button. She had expected to encounter a woolen undershirt like the one her father wore and thought Maxwell was inviting a chill by dressing with so little caution. Tugging his shirttail out of his trousers was easy enough and removing his shirt proved to be a simpler job than separating him from his coat had been. Never, never, even in the country in the heat of summer, had Glori seen a man wearing so few clothes. Timidly she extended her hand, palm down, fingers splayed, to touch his chest. Fascinated, she combed her fingers up to one heavily muscled shoulder. He felt warm and fuzzy, smooth and hard. Nice. There was a vaccination scar on his left arm.

Taking a deep breath, Glori sat back on her heels and considered Maxwell's trousers, knowing very well that the only way to remove them would be to unbutton them. That's when she decided that he was comfortable enough the way he was and turned her attention to straightening out the covers.

Then Maxwell frowned and shifted awkwardly in his sleep, and Glori felt like the Great Beast for not doing whatever she could to ease his minor misery. Kneeling beside his half-naked self, flipping her long braid back over her shoulder, she tucked one cold, dainty fingertip beneath his waistband, thinking to free the top button with a flip of finger and thumb. It was such a snug fit, however, that she needed the fingers and thumbs of both hands to do the job. That's when she had the feeling she was being watched. Glancing up, she found that Maxwell had lifted droopy eyelids and was grinning at her. She felt like a clumsy pickpocket.

"I was merely trying to get your trousers off!" she announced.

His lazy grin broadened, and he layered his hands beneath his head.

"For heaven's sake, I was only trying to make you comfortable!"

He winked at her.

"I didn't intend to wake you up, but the wretched button was stuck!"

After deftly releasing that top button, Maxwell put his hands beneath his head again. He was still grinning.

Giving him the glowering look she reserved for unruly children, Glori deposited herself as close to her side of the bed as she possibly could, unable to take any of the covers with her. Maxwell only chuckled and caught her around the waist again, hauling her against his bare chest and hard belly. Groping behind him, he found an edge of the comforter and pulled it over both of them.

For as irritated as she had been, Glori found her new position too much to her liking to leave it. Resting her own arm over the one Maxwell had wrapped around her, she let her eyes drift shut. Two breaths later her eyes flashed open and she said, "Maxwell, exactly *when* did you wake up?"

"I won't tell you," he said with a sleepy smile.

"Well! I was only trying to—"

"Shhh."

"There's a nightshirt for you on—"

"For crissakes, Glori, go to sleep."

He was standing in front of the mirror, razor in hand, wrapped in a sheet that kept slipping. He had known the moment Glori awoke, but he didn't turn around. What could he possibly say to a female of her tender years that he shouldn't have been in bed with in the first place? Handling uncooperative dignitaries was something he had done on numerous occasions, with admirable skill. And he'd managed the occasionally rapacious wife without handling her at all. During one touchy situation he had even subdued a terrorist before he could throw a bomb, though it had been a very small bomb. Facing Glori, however, was another matter entirely.

Yet in that misty place between sleeping and waking, Maxwell had been blissfully content. Glori had lain in his arms then. They'd slept as snug as two spoons, his knees bent behind hers. They'd been wreathed in the faint scent of roses. As he came nearer to full consciousness, the thing he became most aware of was the pain in his head. The next thing he noticed was that the arm which lay beneath Glori had gone to sleep. It felt like wood, though he was able to drag it away without waking her.

He'd thought Glori looked so unbelievably, innocently young as she slept so trustingly at his side. The delicate pink blush in her cheeks had come from the warmth his body had given hers. She caused such an odd mixture of inexplicable tenderness and erotic longing in him that he'd felt more guilty than ever. He had to remind himself that she was only a girl, for crissake! He was supposed to be taking care of her until she was old enough to take care of herself. And he'd told her he was a gentleman to be trusted. He'd assured her that she needn't be afraid of him, even though he was stewed as a prune. After that he'd almost . . . He didn't want to think about it. Yes, he did, actually, but he knew he shouldn't.

"Good morning," Glori said when Maxwell put aside the razor to wipe the last of the shaving soap from his face.

"Not so loud, if you please," came his soft, staccato reply.

"So sorry," she whispered. "I quite forgot that you might have a delicate head this morning. Mulled wine and beer share similar properties, I believe." Sitting cross-legged with the covers tucked up high, Glori began to unbraid her hair.

Knowing that it couldn't be put off, Maxwell turned around ever so carefully and said, "Glori, last night I—"

"You said you wouldn't apologize. Please don't." As she worked her fingers through her hair, she looked at the bump one of her knees made under the covers, not at Maxwell.

"Dammit, Glori . . . " He couldn't finish. He turned back to the mirror and wiped his face again.

"What's happened to your clothes?" she asked softly, having become a master of distraction.

He didn't answer, turning only halfway around with a silencing finger across his lips.

"Oh, sorry again. I suppose you've sent everything off to be brushed and pressed."

Glori's hair was now undone, and she wanted to get up and find the chamber pot, but Maxwell was there, and she simply couldn't. And if she went parading about in her nightdress, it would surely be awkward for both of them. It didn't seem to occur to her that a man wearing a sheet might present any difficulty at all.

"Maxwell, come lie down until your clothes are returned. I shall attempt to be quiet."

Loathe as he was to get into any bed with Glori still in it, Maxwell accepted her invitation, clapping a pillow over his suffering head as soon as he was prone. Glori then slipped out from beneath the covers and hurried behind the folding screen, where she managed to dress without assistance before leaving the room. A few undone buttons and hooks were of little account this morning.

In less than an hour they were on their way back to Westbourne Hall, even though Glori suggested that they postpone their departure until Maxwell felt more the thing. Despite the restorative potion that Mrs. Logan had provided, the movement of the carriage and the bright sunshine caused him considerable suffering.

Glori, looking like a thin, drab mouse again, was considerately silent except for the time she said, "Maxwell, do you think it might be advisable to find an inn, a dark quiet inn, where we may rest a while?"

"Thank you for your kind thoughts, but it won't be necessary," he told her, determined to press on to the security of their separate bedrooms at Westbourne Hall. Trying to think about something other than his suffering, Maxwell concentrated on the Willows. His return hadn't been painful—at least, not like he thought it would be. Though the house had welcomed him *back*, though it hadn't welcomed him *home*, but it was all right because home was somewhere else now. He wanted to explain it to Glori, but he just didn't feel like talking.

When he glanced at her, she smiled at him and memories of what had happened the night before crowded out everything else. He wanted to keep anyone like Daphne or Randy from taking advantage of Glori, then he had done it himself. He had to take the matter of watching over the girl more seriously, and now he knew he couldn't do it from Canada. Yet he couldn't stay at Westbourne Hall because he seemed to lose his objectivity when he was too close to her. It would be unthinkable to have a repeat of last night.

"Damn!"

"I beg your pardon?" Glori was looking at him curiously.

"Nothing. It's nothing," he said impatiently.

"Of course not."

When they reached the Hall, a boy came running up from the stables to tend the horses. Maxwell assisted Glori from the carriage and stiffly escorted her into the house, where he told her that he would be going directly to bed and expected to remain there for weeks, perhaps months, until his head quit pounding.

Glori went upstairs, too, coming to her own bedchamber before Maxwell reached his. Because the door between their rooms hadn't been closed all the way, she heard him clearly when he entered his room. His steps took him across the bare oak floor, where he stopped and slid a drawer open to poke around in it. His footfalls became louder as he approached the connecting door, and Glori could only stare as it was closed with a chilling click. Once again she heard the sound of a key being fitted into a lock, turned, and removed. Footsteps receded. Though less distinct this time, she heard the drawer being opened again and the thud-clink that followed when the key landed inside. The drawer was slammed shut with a vengeance. She heard nothing after that and assumed Maxwell had quietly and carefully laid himself down upon his bed.

When she was at her sister's house in London, Glori had thought that being locked in was dreadful. She now found that being locked out was even worse. She was still looking at the door when Lucy entered, so she pretended that she had been standing there to take off her hat.

As maid helped mistress remove her dusty clothing, she talked about their house guest. It was that nice young man, that Mr. Elgin Farley, who had arrived that morning with a letter for Mr. Maxwell.

"I trust this intrusion is necessary," Maxwell grumbled from his bed, folding a pillow over his ears as Elgin viciously dragged a chair across the floor.

"I've brought you a letter. Simms said it was delivered a week ago."

"How did you get it?"

"I happened by your rooms to inquire after your whereabouts. Thought I'd best nip up here and see what's afoot. Brought the letter along. Amazed that you're still at the Hall, old man."

The pillow was still over Maxwell's head when he pleaded, "Be a good fellow and read the thing to me. But read it softly, if you please."

Paper tore, paper crackled. "It's from Dumbarton and Davidson," Elgin said after a moment's perusal. "They are in possession of an ironworks in Glasgow which makes decorative railings and such. They seem to think that you would be interested in a position they have to offer, and hope you'll grace their premises with your illustrious person to discuss it—at your convenience, of course."

"I'll probably accept it. If it's the Davidson I'm thinking of, he makes a remarkable bamboo fly-fishing rod."

"Let us not act with undue haste," Elgin warned. "One ought not make such a decision as this on the worth of a fishing pole. This letter doesn't say what D and D have in mind for you, though they do mention your fine reputation with the foreign office."

"Glasgow, you say?"

"Yes. Is it too close to London?"

"Not at all. It sounds perfect."

"You're bloody well off your rocker!" Elgin loudly informed his cringing friend. More softly he said, "Didn't you hear me say that there's no mention of what they will actually expect? You do have a certain position to uphold, you know, with connections that someone always wants to use."

"Perhaps there are ulterior motives involved, but let us hope, for now at least, that Messrs. Dumbarton and Davidson haven't a deceitful bone in their collective bodies."

"Your uncle won't like it. He'd probably pay you not to accept."

"It wouldn't surprise me. Will you look in on Glori whenever you're trotting through the neighborhood? I hate to leave her without any friends, but if I can know that you'll be popping in from time to time, I'll rest easier."

"You shouldn't be leaving her like this. She's really rather nice, you know."

"Yes, I know. Keep the Glasgow business under your hat for the time being, will you? That's a good chap. I want to tell Glori about it myself, before it's broadcast."

"Max, what if these fellows in Glasgow are simply after you because they're looking for political favors from your uncle?"

"Then they certainly will be disappointed."

"Something else will turn up in the diplomatic field if you'll just be patient. You're prostituting yourself to take a job like this."

"Perhaps we're all prostitutes of a sort. We simply sell different parts for different prices."

Even if she hadn't seen the hard set of his jaw, Glori would have known there was something wrong. It wasn't the common thing to find Maxwell loitering in the passage outside her chamber. He had been leaning against the wall but straightened as soon as she opened the door. Clasping her fingers tightly, she crossed the narrow strip of carpet to meet him. She even tried to smile when she said, "I suppose you're waiting here to tell me something of vast importance."

"Yes. I'll be leaving soon, and I want you to know before I tell the others at supper."

Tears filled Glori's eyes, but she blinked them back. "Are you going to Canada, then?"

"Scotland. Glasgow, actually. An ironworks there."

"When will you be going?"

"As soon as I can get packed."

Glori's smile wavered badly. "At least Scotland is closer than Canada."

"Yes, it is." Maxwell tried to smile, too. "Elgin will come by to see you every now and then."

"That will make everything nice and tidy, won't it!" she cried.

"Glori," he said softly, laying a gentle hand against her cheek, wiping away a tear with his thumb. "I'm doing the best I can for us. Please believe that."

"I'm trying to." She gave a loud, unladylike sniff.

He put a fresh handkerchief into her hand and pulled her roughly to him, hugging her fiercely. Her arms went around him while her head rested easily against his shoulder. He had only to turn his head to lay his cheek against her hair. "I'll send you a present from Glasgow," he said. "And you must get well and grow up into a fine lady and write to tell me how you're getting on here."

"I will," she said, holding tightly to him for what she feared would be the last time.

Supper was agony.

Maxwell left the next day, taking the early train north. But he hadn't written that letter to the barrister in London.

CHAPTER TEN

〜✳〜

THE morning had gone well. Quite well, in fact. It had taken him all of the past four weeks to prove that he wasn't just a name on a door, with a titled family, but he had done it. Because he'd known something of the men involved, Maxwell's advice regarding a particular investment had saved Dumbarton and Davidson from an expensive mistake. Such a success should have left him immensely satisfied, but it didn't.

Arms folded, face void of any readable expression, Maxwell leaned against a window frame in his richly appointed office crushing the heavy brown velvet draperies with his shoulder. Instead of seeing the blue, blue sky over the Cotswold Hills, there were the tall chimneys of the River Clyde Ironworks which spilled gray coal smoke and black soot over the city of Glasgow. Ugly as it was, Maxwell knew that all that grime meant that several thousand people had jobs and could feed their families. But his mind didn't linger on the dismal scene before him for he knew that the apple orchards were in blossom at Westbourne Hall. And he wondered what Glori would be doing at two o'clock on a Wednesday afternoon.

The fact that he could be distracted by such unproduc-

tive thoughts irritated him. A month ago, when he'd left
the Hall, he didn't have this annoying problem. A month
ago he only wanted to be off and away from everything
in his life that had tumbled so absurdly out of control,
and Glasgow seemed like the answer.

The first thing Maxwell had done when he reached his
destination was to find a hotel. He called at the offices
of Dumbarton and Davidson the following day, where
his reception by those gentlemen was hearty and open.
After a lengthy discussion they all agreed that he would
join the ranks of the ironworks to review and advise upon
foreign contracts and investments. Though the position
lacked the prestige of government service, the monetary
compensation was far more impressive.

At this first meeting the partners had said that they
looked forward to seeing Maxwell across the dinner
table. They readily admitted to the pleasure of having
a duke's nephew in their midst in a town so void of
nobility, for Glasgow had produced an industrial aris-
tocracy. Maxwell decided that he liked them both for
their blunt Scots honesty. A few days later he found
furnished rooms in Claremont Terrace and sent word
to his man Simms, in London, to pack up and present
himself at the new address.

With his employment and lodgings secured, Maxwell
went in search of the promised gift for Glori. After considering the merchandise displayed in one shop window
after another, he decided on a paisley shawl, a fitting gift
from Scotland as it had been woven in the mill town of
Paisley, across the river to the west of Glasgow. He'd
almost purchased a length of woolen goods instead,
because paisley shawls were commonly presented to
brides and Glori wasn't exactly a bride. But in the
end he thought the swirling patterns in dark reds and
ochers might keep her from looking quite so pale and
sent it anyway, including a second shawl for his aunt
lest anyone suppose there might be some poetic meaning

hidden in such a gift to Glori alone.

Thus, despite an unidentified restlessness, Maxwell thought he'd landed on his feet in clover, with the ragtag ends of his life all neatly tied up. The scandal that Daphne had threatened had been averted, Glori was safely tucked away at Westbourne Hall, and Maxwell found his new situation in Glasgow quite to his liking—though he had expected to find some added peace of mind along with his move. Instead of feeling peaceful he felt annoyed because thoughts of Glori kept popping into his head at the absolutely *worst* of times.

The Dumbartons' dinner party of the previous evening, for instance, had been painfully dull until it became apparent that the ravishing brunette seated to Maxwell's left was his for the picking, ready to drop into his lap like a juicy peach—an event for which she was as well seasoned as he was. Her name was Fiona Canfield and, like Bella Saunders, the young widow of a wealthy older man. And though Maxwell never discussed Glori, he made it known to Fiona that he was not a single man. It didn't matter. Thus, after dinner and the harp recital that followed, Maxwell was to be found escorting the lovely Fiona home through the chilly night in the lady's own closed carriage.

When they stopped in front of the widow Canfield's impressive residence in St. Vincent Street, the lady placed her gloved hand ever so lightly over Maxwell's and said, "Mr. Rutherford, perhaps you would like to come in for a wee drop of something to warm yourself? I'd like your opinion on a most remarkable collection of old ivory carvings."

"I'm afraid I know very little about any kind of carvings, Mrs. Canfield." His smile was deprecating. It wouldn't do at all for her to think that he would be able to advise her on investments in antiquities.

Fiona's soft laugh was impishly inviting. "You misunderstand. I already own the carvings and have no plans to sell. I found them secreted among my late husband's things. They had been shown only to his closest friends, and I believe you will find them quite interesting."

One eyebrow rose perceptibly when Maxwell decided that those carvings would undoubtedly prove to be of an exotic nature. A rakish grin tilted his mustache when he thought that Glori, who sang outrageous sea shanties, might even want to see them. Of course, if those carvings would ever be shown publicly, which he doubted, he and Glori couldn't view them together.

Indelicate objects of art such as nude statues would be shown during special hours set aside for ladies so that they wouldn't encounter the embarrassing presence of any men while they indulged their cultural curiosities. It must be remembered, however, that the statues would have draperies put on them to cover their nakedness. If it was an illustration or painting, however, leaves might be added of a size necessary to do the job tastefully.

With that bit of musing the damage was done. Thoughts of Glori caused Maxwell's burgeoning interest in the lovely Fiona to shrivel beyond resurrection. He simply couldn't continue the sort of flirtation they'd begun now that Glori was present, even in spirit. It seemed . . . indecent.

Lifting the lady's hand to his lips, he pressed a lingering kiss to her fingertips and said, "I'm terribly afraid that I'm coming down with a nasty cold, and I would loathe myself for eternity if you suffered for a moment because of it. Perhaps I may call upon you and your carvings at another time?"

"Yes, of course you may," she replied, properly affected by his concern for her well-being. As she sighed with regret, her creamy bosom rose and fell impressively.

That's when Maxwell decided that he must be getting soft in the brain, too.

Mrs. Canfield's liveried footman appeared in the circle of lamplight at the front entrance to open the carriage door and lower the step. Maxwell emerged into the cold night air to assist Fiona's descent. She touched her palm to his jaw and sighed again. With a swish of black moiré and a gentle smile, she entered the house. Maxwell returned to the carriage. The footman raised the step and closed the door, then gave a nod to the coachman, who then pulled away. Fiona had thoughtfully directed that her gentleman friend be delivered to his own address.

Maxwell could hardly believe he'd let her go. Despite the puritanical attitudes of most Glaswegians toward entertainment in general, the city did have its compensations—but not the way he was going about them. Now he'd have to wait a week or so to recover from the cold he didn't have before he could call on Fiona without looking addled. He never considered that he may have refused Fiona's kindly offer to warm his hands in the privacy of her home due to any feeling of fidelity toward Glori. If it had been suggested, he would have laughed it off.

Maxwell pushed himself away from the window and crossed the thick Persian carpet to his desk, leaving behind the crushed velvet draperies, the smoking chimneys, and visions of Fiona Canfield's heaving bosom. Giving a tug to the knees of his striped trousers and a flip to the tails of his black coat, he seated himself in a leather chair on casters and pulled himself closer to the desk. Then he stretched out his arms to gain more elbow room in the sleeves and began to riffle through an assortment of reports and letters waiting for his attention—letters that weren't nearly as interesting to him as Glori's were. There had been two from her since he'd left Westbourne Hall, two reinforcements that confirmed his conviction that he had done the right thing in leaving her with his family.

Glori, he told himself once again, is doing just fine, just the way things are.

According to her last communiqué, she was fattening up, which made her dresses snug, and that meant picking out some of the tucks that Lucy had put in. Glori and his aunt Maud sent their thanks for the beautiful paisley shawls. Glori's parents had come from East Wallow for a brief visit. Squire Huntington's granddaughter would be spending the summer in the neighborhood. Maxwell thought he remembered her: wild-haired like a gypsy, but a quiet little thing.

Elgin had written to assure him that all was well and that Glori was riding now. She had a good seat and a gentle hand, Elgin had said, and Elgin ought to know.

His aunt sent a few lines saying that the flower gardens looked lovely, that his uncle and the dogs were in fine fettle, and that they were having the windows at the Hall reglazed. As a postscript she added, "Glorianna is learning to dance remarkably well. Elgin is teaching her to waltz."

Yes, Maxwell could see that Glori was doing quite well without him, yet he wasn't completely gratified by that fact. Once again he told himself that she was now safe from attack by anyone with a grudge to settle. Then he admitted that she was now safe from himself, as well. Rubbing a finger across his forehead, he conceded that since their night together at the Willows he had become his own worst problem. Glori was no beauty, yet there was something about her . . .

But she was so awfully young.

Pushing aside his paperwork, Maxwell laid down a clean sheet of stationery, fitted a new steel nib to his pen, and commenced a letter to Glori in practiced copperplate. He said he was glad that she and his aunt liked the shawls. He explained that Robert Davidson—of Dumbarton and Davidson—had invited him to join a fishing holiday that was in the planning, and he had accepted with great pleasure. And he told her about the ancient canoe that had been found in the bank of the River Clyde when workmen were digging to put in another dock.

He mentioned having met a French chemist named

Pasteur, who was working on his germ theory at a Glasgow hospital, and he described the fine statue that commemorated the visit of Queen Victoria and Prince Albert to the city in '49.

After a careful study of what he'd written, Maxwell included a description of the horse-drawn omnibuses, which were decorated with the owners' tartans. He'd heard it was back in '32 or '33 that there had been an explosion of one of the steam-powered transports, which put them out of favor with the public.

Despite all that, Maxwell still wondered if his letters were sufficiently informative and educational. He wondered if Glori had attended the theater in Stratford and if it was Elgin who had taken her there. And he wondered how she would feel with the extra weight she had put on, curled up in his arms at night, her hips against his belly.

Ink spattered across the page when he threw down his pen. Such thoughts occurred all too often. Glori is hardly more than a child! he reminded himself sternly. Someone he had sworn to care for. Taking up a file on pig iron, he studied the facts and figures until they displaced all thoughts of anything or anyone else. Even the plans to write that letter to his friend the barrister seemed to slip to the farthest dusty shelf in the back of his mind.

A stoneware bowl of ginger beer sat fermenting on the cottage hearth. Nearby a little girl in a carefully patched dress jabbered to her rag doll. Cora Sibley, recovering after a difficult confinement, sat at the rough table peeling potatoes. Holding the new baby, Glori occupied the rocking chair amid this scene of humble domestic splendor.

"I dunno what we woulda done without yer help from up ta the Hall when I was down," Mrs. Sibley said for the umpteenth time. She had given Glori her thanks in ample doses, for what she said was true. The Sibleys had needed assistance. But it was the custom that the family at the Hall should help with the needs of the tenant farmers in such circumstances.

Glori herself felt uncomfortable accepting such gratitude when her visits were prompted as much by her own delight in playing with the new baby as by any sense of duty she felt toward a needy family. It was only good manners, however, to accept such tributes graciously, and she did so by saying, "We're all truly pleased that you're well again, Mrs. Sibley," then led the conversation, such as it was, to the activities of the eight older Sibley children.

Into this came the sounds of a horse and cart in the lane outside the cottage. Elgin had delivered Glori half an hour ago—now it was almost two o'clock and he had arrived to collect her. She stood and thanked Mrs. Sibley for the cider, gently transferring the sleeping infant from her own arms to the outstretched arms of his mother without causing him to stir. The little one's stubby eyelashes made a pale fringe against baby-fair skin, while his tiny pink mouth sucked contentedly at a dreamed meal. Smiling affectionately, Glori brushed her lips over his downy head. Before slipping into her cloak, she laid a small bundle of baby clothes on the table, along with some treats for the other children.

In the lane outside the Sibleys' cottage Elgin stood beside the dogcart in his tweeds and knee stockings. When the heavy cottage door creaked open, he looked up. Glori stepped outside, pausing to tie the ribbons of a new hat beneath her chin. Actually, it was more of a bonnet than a hat, intended to protect her face from the sun. To Elgin's eye Glori looked marvelous, and he was convinced that Maxwell lacked a proper appreciation of the woman he'd left behind.

As Glori approached, Elgin smiled broadly and said, "It seemed like time was standing still. Would you have minded awfully if I had charged in and carried you off?

I've only a week left before I must leave, you know. If I don't show up for my sister's coming out, me mum will set the hounds loose." During this monologue Elgin had assisted Glori into the cart, impatiently stuffing in her skirts.

Glori's smile was even merrier than Elgin's as she watched him dash around the cart to gain his own seat beside her. "You are an impetuous devil!" she chided. "At this rate you'll wear yourself out before the week is finished."

"Take pity on a besotted fool and show a little kindness, my girl."

"Do you think this condition of yours is such foolishness, then?"

"Absolutely, but I wouldn't have it cured for the world." Elgin took the reins in hand, giving them a flick to set the horse in motion. "This is the best piece of luck I've had since I was born a British gentleman," he happily announced. "Who would have believed that I, who have survived an impressive number of London Seasons, would become so hopelessly enamored of a female who had been stashed away in the wilds of the Cotswolds."

"We are hardly in the wilds, my good man, but let us come to the point. Are you actually saying that you are in love?"

Elgin's eyes twinkled when he said, "Oh, yes, I do believe I'm that far gone. But it must remain our secret for a while longer. A chap doesn't want to look like an idiot for letting everything out of the bag prematurely. And there's still the family to contend with."

"Then it shall remain our little secret, except, of course, for Maxwell. It does seem like it's time to tell him. My correspondence is rather flat, I'm afraid, but this would liven it up."

"Glori, I'd rather you didn't tell Max anything just yet. I know you've waited, but wait a little longer, pleeease."

The request was followed by one of Elgin's most endearing smiles.

Glori's eyebrows arched in surprise. "Surely you don't suppose for a moment that he'd object to—"

"No, no, of course not," Elgin interrupted, waving aside Glori's suspicions, "I don't think the old boy would give a piddling hoot. Nothing like that."

The cartwheels rolled down the rutted lane and through a long silence before he said, "I suppose my reluctance to confide all in Max is a matter of excessive pride, really. After the needling I've given him on one occasion or another about his problems . . . Well, I'd just rather not let him know about the muddle I'm in at the moment."

Glori gave a resigned sigh. "Would you prefer to tell him yourself when you think the time is right?"

"Yes, I rather think so. Do you mind terribly?"

Glori said she really didn't mind that much because Maxwell was probably quite accustomed to her flat letters by now. Elgin told her that he'd gladly kiss the hem of her garment for keeping silent, but there might be someone watching.

He thought that Cupid had a perverse sense of humor. Here he was, a grown man and a British gentleman, but he couldn't go off sweethearting with the love of his life. While the British cowman might slip away with his milkmaid for a little cuddling and canoodling beneath the apple blossoms, he himself must use great caution when so much as holding hands with his wench.

Yes, forbidden fruit was sweeter, and Elgin fairly drooled to get it into his mouth. But his restraint wasn't a matter of being moral and he knew it. He had never claimed to have morals in any greater abundance than the next fellow. What he did have were more rules. Rules that reached up to London's drawing rooms and out to every blasted moor and moat. Rules saying that society's folk must be respectably chaste. Well, its nubile females at least. If so inclined anyone else had only to avoid getting caught at whatever naughty business they might be enjoying and still be respectable. But he had to admit that he did not know people who were proper to the core and seemed to take joy in every miserable moment of it. Elgin supposed they were rather like the Indian Holy Men who reclined on beds of nails.

His wool-gathering ceased when the cart rolled up before Huntington Manor. At the same instant the front door was thrown open and the young lady standing there raised her hand in greeting. Elgin's glum expression brightened and he whispered, "Iris."

Iris smiled shyly from beneath a wide-brimmed hat of leghorn straw that covered a head of unruly black curls. A rushed and ruffled dress of delphinium blue was almost hidden beneath a Prussian-blue cloak trimmed with lighter braid and tassels. She looked like she'd just sprung from the fairy world when she skipped down the steps. Elgin jumped from the cart to meet her.

Standing on tiptoe, Iris said softly, "I have yet to tell grandfather that you would like to speak with him. He's in such a black mood, you see, that I'm afraid anything you have to say will suffer for it."

Elgin looked down into his love's troubled blue eyes and asked, "Has he said anything in particular about me?"

"Nothing, though he knows you're a friend to Maxwell, so he finds your presence unobjectionable. Still, you must know that the family has intentions of securing a title for me."

"Ye gods! You can't mean they want to paste you up with Randy Rutherford!"

"Heavens, no! Grandfather calls him a loose screw, but there are others."

Elgin grinned affectionately and gave one ebony curl a playful tug. "To the devil with the others!"

From the cart Glori warned, "You have a week left, Mr. Farley. Are you going to spend it in Squire Huntington's drive? The entire household must be watching from the windows!"

Glori's prodding was enough to set her friends in motion, and the three of them drove off to a lovely ruin situated in a pasture dotted with sheep. Finding a stone to sit on that was sheltered from the spring wind, Glori made herself comfortable with her drawing box. While she sketched, her friends wandered about the place hand in hand, talking. Or they sat on their own stone, hand in hand, planning. Or, still holding hands, they strolled over to see how Glori was getting on.

"That's a fine bunch of sheep you've drawn," Elgin remarked.

"Those aren't sheep," Glori informed him patiently. "Those are stones from that crumbled wall." With her pencil she directed his attention to the pile of masonry across from them.

"Oh, quite so. Sorry, old girl. If, however, you would consider putting legs on the little fellows they might pass for sheep. Sheep, after all, are ever so much more difficult to draw than stones and would be a greater credit to you as the sort of artist who longs to go about the countryside drawing things."

Iris and Elgin strolled away while Glori added black noses and legs to all the stone sheep.

With regard to the general behavior of this trio, there had never been a time when they were out of respectable sight of one another. Still, their conduct was unquestionably risky. Elgin—knowing very well what was allowed a gentleman in the company of an unmarried lady—had no business doing what he was doing. The lady herself only scoffed and said that if anyone discovered the game they were playing, it would hardly matter to her. If it was supposed that she had been compromised by all this hand holding, she hoped her grandfather might insist that Elgin do the decent thing and marry her. But it was nothing more than a daydream, because Elgin hadn't a title, even a little one, and her grandfather was completely in accord with her parents' intention to see her married into the nobility.

And it was to ensure the success of this plan that Iris had been sent into the country with such haste. Her family didn't want anyone to find out that she had developed a rebellious streak that was quite unlike the usually docile young lady. The whole of her twenty-one years had been spent trying to please everyone, for it was the easiest path to follow when one was born the twelfth of fifteen children. Iris had been the good child, who, until now, had never given anyone a moment of trouble.

But all that goodness came to an end when Iris learned that her parents had been quietly grooming her to be the wife of the Marquis of Bumpstead and took it into her head to revolt, which hadn't been as easy as one might suppose, for she had a strong habit of obedience. It was no surprise that she was completely ignored when she said, "I do thank you for the trouble you've taken, but I must decline the honor." Her father decided that their Dear Little Iris had simply been overwhelmed by her good fortune and her brain temporarily addled by the wonder of it all.

So Iris was packed off to the country to the home of her grandfather and Great-Aunt Prudence, where her disagreeable behavior could be hidden away from the Marquis until she came to her senses. In fact, Iris was deported so quickly that her clothes had to be sent on a few days later. Her maid wasn't with her, either, for her family feared that the girl might carry tales back to town to the servants' grapevine, and then all their plans and efforts would come to naught.

Now that Iris was under her grandfather's roof in the country, it was supposed that she would come to understand what she was missing in town and learn to submit to wiser counsel. The old gentleman was pleased enough to see Iris become friends with the bride of Maxwell Rutherford, for his sister Prudence had pronounced Glorianna perfectly refined. Besides, it was supposed that the young ladies might discuss matters of a domestic nature rather than balls and dresses and young men.

When Maxwell's friend, Elgin Farley, arrived with Glori one afternoon, Squire Huntington decided that his granddaughter might benefit from a bit of carefully chaperoned genteel male company so that she wouldn't be so damnably awkward in the company of men. The squire knew the Marquis of Bumpstead to be a man of mature years, who found the company of stammering young ladies singularly boring. For this reason Iris had been allowed to walk through the gardens of the manor on the arm of Mr. Farley, which certainly warmed Iris's heart toward matrimony, but not to the Marquis of Bumpstead. By the third day of strolling among the roses, Iris had determined that she would rather wed Elgin Farley. She just didn't know if they would have to run off to Scotland to make that dream a reality. Elgin, for his part, preferred a more conventional matrimonial but didn't know if it would be possible.

As the respectably married chaperon, Glori knew she should have forbidden the very behavior she was promoting between her friends. She surely wouldn't have acted so irresponsibly a few months ago. A few months ago, however, she hadn't met Maxwell Rutherford and felt the trials and tribulations of unrequited love. It made her much more sympathetic toward the plight of Iris and Elgin.

The Great Deception had begun one afternoon during a meeting of the Gloucestershire Ladies Relief Society, which had collected material to roll bandages for British soldiers in foreign lands. During a private moment Iris had said that she and Elgin desperately wanted to be alone together after days and days of properly chaste walks through the rock gardens of Huntington Manor. Throwing caution to the dogs, Glori said that she would give

Cupid an assist—though at the time she hadn't known how. That evening she even confided the dilemma to Aunt Maud, who also thought Elgin and Iris would make an ideal couple. But Maud only warned Glori against doing anything that might create more problems than solutions. It was a surprise, then, when Maud came to the assistance of the young lovers the next day.

As chance would have it, Glori and Maud were invited to Huntington Manor to take refreshment with Iris and her great-aunt Prudence—Prudence Chumbly being the squire's sister, and, with her husband, a permanent resident at the manor. After refreshments were served in the ladies' parlor, their attention was directed to the pressed-flower arrangement that the venerable Mrs. Chumbly had assembled from last summer's wild plants. She had carefully laid each freshly cut specimen between sheets of blotting paper to dry, weighting them with books. Now arranged within a gilt frame, the flowers were positioned before the fireplace on an easel.

With a faint tink Glori fitted her teacup to its saucer and set it aside before she left her chair to inspect the piece more closely. "It is quite lovely," she said. "I do admire the way you've placed the ferns among the Queen Anne's lace. I think my mother would like it, too. She is a watercolorist."

"Have you followed in your mother's footsteps?" Prudence asked hopefully.

"No, though I've spent many pleasant hours drawing while my mother painted." Glori returned to her seat then, her skirts hiding all but the back of the spindly little rosewood chair on which she sat.

Dear lady that she was, Prudence Chumbly was quick to encourage Glori's creative inclinations by assuring her young guest that the Cotswolds offered much in the way of lovely vistas to inspire any artist.

That's when Aunt Maud grandly announced, "Prudence is absolutely right, Glorianna. You simply must begin drawing again. Tomorrow she and I will take you down the lanes and across the fields until you find something to interest you. As I was a notable whip in my youth, I shall drive." Turning to Iris she added, "You must come along, of course. Glorianna will need younger, stronger company in case we should become mired."

Horrified at the thought of racketing around the countryside and getting stuck there, Prudence extracted a handkerchief with tatted lace from the sleeve of her cambric dress and pressed it to her pleasingly plump cheeks. "Dearie me," she said, "there must be someone better suited to take the young ladies out and about."

"Well, there *is* Elgin Farley," Maud offered rather vaguely. "But, no, I don't believe he is much interested in drawing." She then tactically abandoned the subject of Elgin Farley's possible escort services to remark upon the weather.

"Oh, *do* ask Mr. Farley to take the girls out," Prudence begged. "I think he's such a nice, clever young man, and he wouldn't have to draw, you know, but merely drive them . . . here and there." She fluttered her handkerchief here and there to indicate how it might be done.

"My dear Prudence. As it is of such concern to you, I shall suggest it to the young man myself," Maud promised.

Dear Prudence looked relieved and poured them all more tea. Iris agreed to go along, of course, telling her great-aunt Pru that she would bring back any unusual flowers for pressing. Glori simply said thank you. Maud simply prayed that her intervention wouldn't turn into a scandal disguised as art.

So it was that Elgin had been persuaded to take Glori and Iris out for a drawing party. And it was he who had suggested the isolated ruin as their destination, making sure that there was a basket packed with lemonade, biscuits, and cheese for midday bait.

A few days later there was a second afternoon of sketching when Elgin took them to Jones's Mill. From rugs spread on the riverbank opposite the mill, the three of them idled away the afternoon, watching as drays arrived with sacks of grain and left with sacks of flour. With all the exactness she could manage Glori copied the old building before her with its angles and shadows and splashing waterwheel and wished that Maxwell had looked at her the way Elgin looked at Iris.

Two mornings later there was a small package on the breakfast table for Glori, from her parents. She'd been sent a lovely pearl brooch that had belonged to her grandmother. Glori explained that it was her birthday, and Maud scolded her for not telling them sooner so that they could have planned something special. Even so she did very well arranging a birthday dinner for that evening. The Huntingtons were invited, naturally, which gave Elgin and Iris a few more precious hours together.

It was obvious to anyone who cared to notice that Iris Huntington had swept Elgin Farley into a basket and daintily stepped in after him. Aunt Maud had been pleased with the romance that was unfolding before her very eyes, but even she hadn't expected the pair of them to burst into flames when their fingers touched over the walnut tort. After the guests had gone, Maud exclaimed, "I believe I could hear the angels plucking their harps when those two looked at each other!"

Glori said she thought it had been one of the footmen below stairs playing a mouth organ.

In early July, when Maxwell had been away from Westbourne Hall for nearly two months and Elgin had been gone for about two weeks, Glori spread out her drawings and carefully chose one for Maxwell. Not wanting to confuse the man with questionable impressions of stone sheep, or the study of chickens that she had done most recently, she decided on the picture of the old mill—the waterwheel being easily identifiable. In case there might be any doubt as to which site it was, she inscribed "Jones's Mill" at the bottom of the page. After folding it carefully, she tucked it into the envelope with her letter to him.

In that letter she said, "We all simply adore Elgin and are glad to learn that he and his family removed from London after his sister's coming out. The country is a far better place to be when there is yet another outbreak of cholera in town. When Elgin was here at the Hall he was both charming companion and informed guide while selecting the scenic views for my drawings. I would never have found such interesting places without him." She took care not to mention Iris's part in their outings, thinking that it was the safest way to keep from giving away Elgin's affair of the heart with that young lady. It was, after all, Elgin's news to tell.

Glori went on to explain that the mystery of the homesick horse had been solved. Uncle Neville had discovered that the animal had developed a strong attachment to the marmalade cat that took a nap each day in his stall. So the horse has been delivered once again, with the cat, who rode along in a hamper to ensure its attendance. More bits and pieces of news followed, ending with an account of the pig delousing. Like the others, this letter was signed "Your obedient Glorianna," which had caused Maxwell to choke so badly that his eyes watered the first time he'd read it. He could imagine Glori as many things, but obedient wasn't among them.

On nice days Glori could still be found bent over her drawings, though there was no longer a need to invent sketching expeditions so that Elgin and Iris could be together. She continued drawing because she enjoyed it. With time heavy on her hands Iris brought out her needlework and kept Glori company, entertaining her with stories of the months she had spent in Paris, perfecting her French accent and studying the flute.

One afternoon Glori and Iris sat in the rick yard, lamenting their missing men, while Glori drew the mushroom-shaped staddle stones upon which hay could be stacked above the damp ground. Iris sewed a tea cozy. On another day Glori sketched a team of work horses with elder flowers tucked into their bridles to keep the bluebottle flies away from their eyes. Iris stitched her initials onto a jabot. But Glori wanted to be alone the day she made a sketch of the barn loft where she and Maxwell had sought refuge from the storm.

Much to Maud's satisfaction Glori's health continued to improve and more of the tucks that had been put in her dresses had to be picked out. Lucy let out the corset laces again. As Glori was no longer made tired by negotiating stairs, Maud took her along to inspect the wine cellar and attics. Everyone considered Glori's progress remarkable.

Maxwell was ready to leave on his fishing trip when he glanced at the hall table and noticed that the post had arrived. On top of the other envelopes lay one that bore Glori's fine script. "Tell the coachman to wait," he said to Simms as he put aside his hat and coat. Taking the entire stack of mail, he went to his sitting room, where he dropped himself into a big chair near the front window. With the toe of one polished boot he hooked the footstool closer.

He slit open the vellum envelope bearing the Westbourne crest, extracted a folded sheet of heavy paper, and spread it out. Years had passed since he'd seen Jones's Mill, and he hadn't realized the place had fallen into such poor condition. The waterwheel had all but collapsed, and the roof sagged something awful. "What a shame," he said, then went on to Glori's narrative.

He had already noticed that her letters were more like entries in a journal, written over a period of days. He could see where the ink was different or the handwriting had altered slightly from sitting to sitting. There was nothing of remarkable content, only that certain something that he found as appealing as Glori herself.

Today he learned that it was Elgin who had taken her to the mill and other places as well, so that she could spend an occasional afternoon drawing. Maxwell could see that Elgin had been doing his best to make sure Glori didn't become too lonesome. After all, that's what he had asked his friend to do, wasn't it? Then why wasn't he pleased when Elgin was doing exactly what he had asked of him?

Next he opened a thin letter from Elgin himself. It was brief. Elgin's letters usually were. Scanning it, Maxwell read of his friend's departure from London right after his sister's coming out . . . a problem with a new tailor over buttons . . . Glori's birthday party . . . a friend of theirs had left for Boston . . . Nipper Yarmouth had taken a mistress and his wife found out.

What was that?

Going back several lines, Maxwell read that Glori had had a birthday party. Elgin said it was amazing how little she knew of the world for a lady of twenty and two. He turned the page to the light. There was no mistake. Elgin had clearly said twenty-two, not seventeen, as Glori's new age. How could that be? Maxwell was positive that Glori had been sixteen when they met, nearly *half* his own age, but how did he know that? His memory rumbled and mumbled and told him that Daphne had said so, but when? After Glori fainted, that's when. He was certain that Daphne had said it was the sort of thing that sixteen-year-old girls do.

Maxwell tossed Elgin's letter aside, asking himself how he could have been so blind. There was a vast difference between sixteen and twenty-one. Then he reasoned that sickly young women of any age would probably look very much alike. He next wondered how he could have been so thoughtless. He hadn't even asked Glori when her birthday would be. Under the circumstances it was something he should have known. That, however, was of little importance when some other things began to rattle through his brain. Now, at twenty-two, Glori was a woman, not a girl. And Elgin was a man, not a boy.

In an instant Maxwell had another of Elgin's letters dug out of the desk drawer, and he flopped back into his chair with it. Phrases like "Glori has a good seat" and "Glori is in fine looks" took on an entirely different meaning. With a sarcastic edge to his thoughts he wondered if Elgin had noticed Glori's long eyelashes, too.

That's when Maxwell gave serious consideration to those dancing lessons. Tapping that single page against his knee, he decided that he didn't like the idea of Elgin holding Glori to teach her anything. He thought of the night at the Willows when he had slept with Glori in his arms. She'd felt . . . nice.

"Nice, hell! I almost tore that damned flannel tent off her skinny little body," he muttered to the empty room, tightly wadding Elgin's letter to bounce it off the far wall.

Angry now, he kept thinking about all the time his best friend must have spent taking Glori out to draw her pictures. Just Elgin and Glori. Alone. Day after day. Week after week. They were even living in the same house! It looked to him like Elgin might be interested in Glori as much more than a friend. Worse yet, he wondered if Glori might have become attracted to Elgin. Stranger things had happened—just look at the horse and the marmalade cat!

Maxwell's stormy mood became thunderous. He was sure that this questionable association was bound to cause gossip, and he had to protect Glori from that sort of thing until she was wise enough in the ways of the world to watch out for herself. At least, that's the reason he gave himself for his sudden concern over what had been going on at Westbourne Hall.

Pacing the floor now, Maxwell decided that there was nothing else to do but send for Glori. It was for her own good, and he'd tell her so. He had to keep her out of trouble, and that meant keeping her away from Elgin. Maxwell thought of Glori as *his*. His *what* had not been at all clear. The word *wife* was never considered. But then the word *jealous* hadn't entered his mind, either.

The rug was saved from being worn through to the warp by the entry of Simms, who reminded him that his sporting companions were waiting. While Simms followed with his rods and winches, Maxwell collected his hat and coat, then went out to the carriage and climbed in with the rest of his baggage.

Wishing he'd had enough time to see to it before departing, Maxwell resolved to command Glori's presence in Glasgow as soon as he could. He thought he might find an opportunity to send notice that she begin preparations at once so that she would be ready to travel by the time he got back to Glasgow. Poor humor marked the commencement of his fishing holiday to the remote rivers of Scotland.

Without a hint of the things that plagued Maxwell, Glori led an active but peaceful country life. Summer days at Westbourne Hall were strung together like pearls on a silken cord, so it was a shock to them all when a messenger arrived with word that Randy was dead.

CHAPTER ELEVEN

"I came as soon as I heard the news." Elgin's voice was hushed when he joined Glori in the morning room, which, like the other public rooms, had been generously swagged in black crepe. He placed a chair opposite Glori and took her hands, chafing them between his own. The last time he'd seen her, she had been all peaches and cream and looked rather dashing. Today she looked pasty again.

"How are you all holding up?" he asked when he released her hands.

"Well enough, I think." Then Glori touched Elgin's sleeve and said, "Please, don't worry so. I'm not as fragile as everyone thinks I am." He looked doubtful. She said, "Aunt Maud and Uncle Neville haven't been receiving since the news of Randy's accident reached us yesterday. It's sad enough for them to lose their son without the circumstances of that loss being so difficult to bear."

"The news went through the clubs in London like wildfire before I learned of it in Kent," Elgin told her. "I think the whole town knew of it as soon as the official channels did—perhaps even sooner. A rather sordid business, what?"

The subject of Randy Rutherford's departure from this world was so delicate in nature that Glori didn't know if she could get through the telling of it. With her hands clasped on her lap, she was busy matching up her thumbnails. She said, "According to those who were there the night it happened, Randy had become involved in an argument with another man. Both of them had been drinking a great deal and . . . well . . . "

"We needn't go into the awful details," Elgin said gently. "I've heard enough to give me a fair idea of what happened."

"But we must go into it. Anything you heard may or may not have been accurate, so Uncle Neville will probably feel compelled to explain it all because you're so close to the family. I would spare him the additional distress of that explanation if I could, for Aunt Maud fears he might have an attack of asthma."

Elgin, too, would spare the Rutherfords any additional suffering, but he was awfully uneasy about the subject matter Glori wanted to discuss. That's why he got up and returned his chair to the place it had occupied on the far side the room and stayed there with it. After he straightened his tie and cleared his throat, he said, "Seeing that you insist upon discussing this, I'll tell you something of what I know." He paused, picking his words with care. "It appears as though Randy and this other chap had argued over a woman. It also appears that this woman was employed at the establishment where Randy met his end."

Elgin was trying to get through it as tactfully as he could. What he'd actually heard was that the fatal difference of opinion had been over which one of the two drunks would be enjoying the woman's services that evening, and that Randy didn't have his trousers on at the time. "It's also my understanding that it was Randy who had challenged the other fellow to a duel," Elgin continued cautiously.

"Yes, and everyone thought it was a joke until the pair of them went up to the roof."

Glad that he was no longer sitting knee to knee with his best friend's wife to discuss the shabby events at a house of ill repute, Elgin began to feel that the end of his travail was near. He said, "I heard that as soon as the pair of them reached the roof, the other bloke pulled out a pistol and shot Randy in the, ah, *limb*, which caused him to fall from the roof, killing him. Is that correct?"

"I was told it was a bullet to the shoulder that sent him over the edge, but I suppose it matters little, for the end was the same." Abandoning her thumbnails to look over the tops of her spectacles at Elgin, she said, "The young man who came with the message also said that Randy didn't have a weapon, so it was rather foolish of him to challenge anyone to a duel. Perhaps he was only trying to frighten the other man away."

"Perhaps," said Elgin, concluding the matter with great relief. "When will Max be here?"

A weary sigh was followed by, "I don't know. Uncle Neville's steward has sent two messages to Glasgow—one to Maxwell's office and another to his lodgings. We haven't had a reply as yet."

Elgin crossed the room and held out his hand to Glori. "Perhaps you should find your bed and rest. I'll be right here if anyone needs me."

She shook her head. "I'm afraid I can't leave just yet. I've told Aunt Maud that I would meet with the trades-people. Then mourning jewelry has to be ordered, and someone will be arriving with frocks for me, and there's the minister to talk to about the service."

"I can explain the needs of the family to the minister, and I'll decide what to do with the jeweler when he gets here. When your clothes are delivered, I'll send Lucy up with them," Elgin assured her.

Glori then added, "Someone from a printing shop is also on the way. It's to be a private funeral, but I'm not at all sure of what to tell him about the invitations. Aunt Maud told me that the man would know. Neither she nor Uncle Neville cares to see anyone about anything unless it's absolutely necessary."

"I'm familiar with the invitations, Glori. Who will be meeting the coffin at Dover?"

"The steward might have to do that, too, as Uncle Neville doesn't want to leave Aunt Maud just now."

"When?"

"The day after tomorrow, I believe."

"Perhaps I can help with that as well. For the moment there's nothing else to be done. You can rest."

Glori gave her friend a fatigued smile and left everything to him for the next few hours. Her own chamber was a welcome sight when she reached it, for she was desperately tired. Raw guilt had kept sleep away the night before.

Without calling for her maid, Glori slumped across her bed and pulled one edge of the counterpane over her shoulders. Shutting her eyes, she tried to think about new kittens and cuddly puppies and tried not to think about how much she had hated Randy Rutherford. She hadn't simply hated him, though. One day not too long ago she had actually wished him dead, and now he was. He was dead and in her heart of hearts she wasn't sorry, because now he could never hurt her again. But while his death provided a release from her own terrible fear of his return, it caused suffering to his parents, whom she had come to love, and *that* racked Glori with guilt. Pulling the cover more tightly around herself, wishing Maxwell was there to hold her, she cried herself to sleep.

The day of the funeral was better suited to clouds and drizzle, yet the sun burned brightly in a clear blue sky. The procession had traveled from the church to the Rutherford cemetery, with the superintendent of the duke's woods at the head of the family's principal tenants.

They rode two abreast, dressed in black with black silk hatbands and gloves.

The undertaker came next, followed by two mutes carrying black draped staffs. Six attendants were followed by two more mutes with staffs. All were mounted.

A man on foot bore an escutcheon with a large plume of black feathers and the Westbourne coat of arms. Behind him came Randy's horse, caparisoned in black, lead by a groom.

The hearse, emblazoned with the family crest, had been brought from the estate in Herefordshire. It was drawn by six black horses and driven by His Grace's coachman. On each side were four pages on foot, bearing staffs tipped with silver.

Behind that were three mourning coaches with six horses each, and four mourning coaches with four horses each, decorated with plumes and shields. Two pages walked beside each one of these coaches, the first of which carried the family and minister, then dignitaries and close friends. The coaches of the family solicitor and the physician came next, followed by stewards from the family properties. The coach with the upper male servants of the Hall went ahead of the coach that carried the upper female servants.

Bringing up the rear were other clergymen and gentlemen of the neighborhood on horseback. An odd collection of villagers followed on foot. All were in deep mourning.

Maxwell tried to catch up with the procession as soon as he reached home, but from a vantage point on a rise near the cemetery he could see people coming back down the hill. The service was over. It was easy to pick out his aunt and uncle from among the others. Close beside them were Elgin and Glori. He wished he could have been here to help them and to ease the responsibilities that had undoubtedly fallen upon the slender shoulders of his wife. But he supposed it was Elgin who had once again provided what she needed—what they all needed.

The night before, on the mail train that steamed south out of Glasgow, Maxwell's thoughts had been with his aunt and uncle. As he came closer to home, however, his thoughts included Glori more often, and he took her letters from his valise to read them again. He went over each one carefully but could find no hint of what her feelings might be for Elgin or anyone else. Still, if she had declared a flaming passion for himself, he would have thought she was ready to be kept in some nice peaceful place where she couldn't hurt herself. After all, he hadn't set out to inspire any affection in her. He had only wanted to be her friend—and marry her, of course.

A flash of silver harness trim caught Maxwell's eye—the first of the mourners had reached the dusty lane to claim their horses and begin the migration to Westbourne Hall for the funeral dinner. Turning his mount, Maxwell rode back across the fields toward home. He, too, had come as soon as he'd heard the news. It simply hadn't been soon enough.

Bypassing the dining tent that had been erected on the east lawn, Maxwell cantered onto the drive and past the front of the house, where all the draperies had been drawn and the door knocker covered with a black wreath. In the yard he swung down from the saddle and tossed the reins to the same boy who had hurriedly saddled the horse for him when he arrived home such a short while ago. Gaining entry to the house through a rear door, he asked that Their Graces be informed that he would await their pleasure in their own sitting room. Then time passed very slowly for Maxwell as he wandered about, looking at family photographs and poking at the fireplace tools with the toe of his shoe.

When the passage door opened, his aunt Maud entered, still veiled. In seconds they were in each other's arms.

"I'm sorry it took so long to get here." His words were muffled against her hat.

Releasing her nephew after a loving squeeze, Maud accepted his assistance with the removal of her cloak. "Glori has read your letters to us, so we knew of your fishing trip," she said. "Then, after the news of Randolph's accident had been sent to you in Glasgow, we received a reply from Mr. Dumbarton telling us that someone had been dispatched to find you. After that your man Simms sent the same notice. That electric telegraph is a remarkable invention, don't you agree? So much information flying all about the country so swiftly."

Reading the extent of his aunt's distress in her running monologue, Maxwell quietly laid her wrap across the back of a chair and simply listened.

"The Mountrockhams have sent their regrets saying that they have both been confined to the house with some temporary indisposition, though they assure me that it isn't of a serious nature. Glorianna's parent's cannot be here, either, I'm sorry to say. Her father dislocated his knee, and he requires a great deal of care."

Maud removed her gloves and hat and placed them on a small round table beside a tall vase of fresh flowers. Sharing that space was a picture of Randy that had been taken at the seaside the summer before. He was smiling then, his dark hair brushed by the wind. When Maud picked it up, Maxwell could see that the protective glass was smudged by a mother's fingertip that had traced and retraced the features she knew so well, a face she would never see again except within a frame or a dream.

"We had always hoped that Randolph's wildness would pass, yet we knew it might never happen," Maud said. After a moment she took a deep restorative breath and pushed away the impossible pain. Returning the photograph to the table, she drew on happier memories. Her reddened eyes were filled with tears when she said, "He had such chubby cheeks when he was a baby. Do you remember? He sang so sweetly . . . and I loved him so much." She tried to smile, but her chin only wobbled.

Maxwell said, "I think Randy loved you, too."

"I'm not certain that he ever understood what it meant to love or be loved," Maud replied sadly. "I'm very much afraid that we failed him."

"I don't believe it. If anything, Randy failed himself. Even so, I think he loved you as much as he was able to love anyone."

"I suppose we shall have to make do with that, won't we?" Tucking a few strands of hair beneath the black lace cap she had worn under her hat, Maud said, "Come now, Maxwell, we cannot stand about like this." She took her place on the sofa and patted the cushion. Maxwell joined her there. She said, "Glorianna, Elgin, and your cousins have everything in hand downstairs, so you needn't rush off. Your uncle will be here shortly—he's still talking to a few of the MPs who came down for the funeral." Then she nervously smoothed her hands over her skirt and said, "Maxwell, how much do you know about what happened to Randolph?"

"Only what I'd been able to find in the papers, a few lines about him having taken a fatal fall while visiting friends in Paris."

"Mercifully your uncle has enough friends in the right places to prevent the whole horrid story from bursting out in print like the pox."

"Then I won't ask you to repeat it for my benefit. I'll just ask Glori, if you don't mind."

"Mind? I'd be grateful."

When the door opened again, Neville entered. Maxwell had always seen him as a tall, impressive figure. Now he slouched and moved like the tired old man he had become. They shared a swift, intense embrace. Maxwell's apologies were repeated, the same assurances given. Family news filled their conversation after that, with particular attention to Cousin Jane in India, who had recently produced twins. Her eldest, a boy of five years, had just been sent back to a boarding school in England.

It was over an hour later that Maud said, "My dear Maxwell, we've kept you too long as it is. You must see to your wife now. Your uncle and I will manage quite nicely—everyone forgives an old woman her desire for solitude." Maud was almost pushing her nephew off the sofa as she said, "You know, I was afraid that Glorianna might take on too much during this crisis, but I needn't have worried. Elgin has been at her side constantly to see that she doesn't overdo. What a remarkable friend he has been, and they do get on so well. Now go."

Maxwell went. But the news that Elgin had been hovering over Glori so attentively only added some very unpleasant thoughts to the ones he already had.

"Max! It's jolly good to see you again! I was told that you'd be passing this way if I waited long enough." Elgin had been leaning against the balustrade at the top of the stairs when Maxwell came down the passage.

Grasping the offered hand, Maxwell met the candid, smiling face of his old friend. His suspicions faded in the light of such a welcome and he said, "Hello, Farley. I'm told that you've been a pillar of strength about the place, for which I must thank you."

"We all do what we can. How are your aunt and uncle doing after the fact?"

"Well enough, considering. You know better than anyone else how difficult this is for them."

Elgin stuffed his hands into his pockets, which abused the seams terribly. "Glori has been a blessing, you know. And at this very moment your cousin Peter is in the dining tent making a host of himself—doing the family proud. When you put on the nose bag with that fellow, you'd best have your studs polished. The thing is, old chap, I didn't wait about like this just to see your beaming face again. I'd like to talk to you without a gaggle of people about us."

As the housekeeping staff was trying to see to the bedchambers, Maxwell supposed that he and Elgin could have their talk in one of the downstairs rooms, but they found people wandering all over the house. When they went onto the terrace, they discovered some ladies seated there whom neither of them had ever seen before. After apologizing for the intrusion, the two gentlemen headed for the topiary garden. The fourth Westbourne had taken a fancy to shrubberies clipped into the shapes of mythical beasts.

"How many people are there staying at the Hall?" Maxwell asked as they crossed the lawn.

"I'm not sure, but they're stuffed up the chimneys and stacked in the cellars. Any number of the overflow has been similarly stored at Huntington Manor."

"How good of the squire to make the recesses of his home available to us." When he saw that they were now away from everyone else, Maxwell said, "I hope you're about to explain why we need this privacy."

Elgin stopped on the grassy path and reached into his inside coat pocket to produce a fat envelope. He said, "I have the feeling that this isn't something you would want your aunt and uncle to find out about. One of Randy's chums from the Paris enterprise, a fellow named Bogborough, gave it to me. He had accompanied the coffin across the channel to Dover, where I was waiting. He had been on the lookout for you, actually. Said he'd met you a long time ago and only gave this into my keeping after I swore that I would see it safely delivered."

"What's inside?" Maxwell asked as he slipped the packet into his own pocket and started them walking again.

"He said it contained everything Randy had left behind in Paris, except for his clothes and such, and someone else was packing up those. The envelope was sealed as you saw it when he gave it to me. Feels like lumpy letters."

"Or lumpy bills."

With the business of the envelope out of the way, they turned back toward the house. After a dozen paces in thoughtful silence Elgin said, "Max, has anyone enlightened you with the details of Randy's dramatic demise?"

"It's something I had intended to ask Glori about."

"Perhaps it would be better if you didn't. It was a new turn to the old screw, but the old boy lost his touch. He unbuttoned his britches and his brains plopped out. This time he tripped on 'em, fell off a roof, and broke his silly neck."

"Ah, yes, Randy was ever a man of mystery and charm."

An accounting of the accident followed, including the more risqué points that Glori had been denied. Elgin concluded by saying, "Randy was a fool among fools. A gentleman, at home or abroad, would never appear on a public roof without being properly dressed."

"He's done a great many queer things."

"Well, he won't do this one again. Have you got used to the change yet?"

"By change do you mean succeeding my cousin as heir to the title?"

"That's the one, old chap, or should I call you Your Lordship now? Your uncle must have some minor title that you'll be using."

"I don't even want to think about a title, especially one that had been Randy's. I feel as though I'm walking in someone else's shoes, and they pinch with every step I take—the whole thing makes me damned uncomfortable."

"Uncomfortable enough to send you back to Scotland?"

"No, I won't be going back. I told Davidson that before I left. Simms is packing everything in Glasgow."

Elgin grinned. "You certainly were in a flap to go there last spring. What did Glori say when you told her you'd be staying home?"

"I haven't told her yet. When you get back to the dining tent, will you tell her that I'll be with her as soon as I can get rid of my traveling clothes?"

"Glori isn't out there."

"Oh?"

"No. I sent her inside right after your aunt and uncle took to yonder castle—thought she might have seen you then. The thing is, I didn't think any more of this fuss and bother would be good for her. She was looking peaked."

"In that case I'll just go upstairs and tell her that I'm home."

"She already knows."

"Oh . . . I see."

Maxwell said the proper things to Elgin before they parted company, but that's about all he was capable of doing. It was terribly unsettling to have another man sending his wife off to bed, especially when that man had spent more time with her than he had himself. But none of it was as bad as learning that Glori had known he was home but hadn't cared enough to see him. She'd spent weeks—nay, *months* —in Elgin's company and now avoided her husband! That was more than Maxwell could overlook with good grace, and he went in search of her to tell her what he thought of such shabby treatment. Upon reaching Glori's chamber door, he knocked once and boldly entered, only to be told by a startled Lucy that her mistress had changed her dress and gone outside.

"Where outside?"

Lucy didn't know.

Quietly angry, Maxwell offered a brisk "Thank you" and took the most direct route to the rose garden, then the cutting garden, and scanned the kitchen vegetable patch without success. He was determined to find Glori and ask what her sentiments were toward Elgin. There would be no more wondering about who was doing what with whom!

Then he remembered that beyond the farthest row of herbs was the path that led to the greenhouse, and he followed it to its destination. Concerned only with his mission, he missed the sweet scent of basil warmed by the sun, the lacy stalks of dill, and the thick rows of mint. He didn't miss the woman who was visible through the dusty panes of the greenhouse windows. He was glad that he had finally run Glori to ground, and he intended to waste few words telling her what he thought of the way she had flitted off without saying so much as hello or good-bye. After all, she had known that he was home.

Rounding the corner, he stepped through the open door of the greenhouse and didn't say a thing. He had no idea who this woman was, either.

She hadn't seen him yet, but she obviously wasn't expecting to see anyone or she wouldn't have had her hair hanging down her back as though she were in her boudoir. This called for a quiet exit, as no gentleman would stand there and stare at a strange woman's unbound hair any more than he would stare at her ankles. It simply wasn't decent! Maxwell backed toward the door to make an undetected getaway and bumped into a rake, which fell to the floor with made an echoing *thunk*.

A muttered curse escaped his lips, and the woman spun around, her initial surprise followed by a promising smile of welcome.

He said, "I am dreadfully sorry—I hadn't realized you were here. Please excuse me."

He was already in retreat when the woman cried, "Maxwell, if you didn't know I was here, why did you come at all? And now that you're here, why are you going away?"

He halted abruptly. He didn't know the woman but knew that voice. Turning slowly, he studied the pretty oval face wearing spectacles and cautiously said, "Glori?"

"Yes!"

She was so happy to see her husband again that she almost threw herself into his arms, but his startled look held her back and the moment was lost; her excitement faded.

When Maxwell saw Glori's look of radiant welcome change to one of disappointment, he became even more confused. He supposed it was just as well that he hadn't recognized her right off, or he would have swept her into a shocking embrace, which probably wouldn't have been agreeable to her. After all, she really hadn't had much time to get to know him before he'd gone to Glasgow. He had no reason to be expecting hugs and kisses.

"Well, now, you *are* looking fine!" Maxwell said gaily, trying not to appear too forward.

"I'm feeling fine, indeed," Glori answered brightly.

After exchanging stiff smiles they proceeded to an equally stilted conversation, which confirmed how truly fine they both were. Though Maxwell was able to maintain an outward appearance of calm during this intercourse, his mind was turbulent. It seemed as though the Glori he had known had been swallowed up by a Glori he'd never seen before. Yet he was married to one of them, or *both* of them, which was such a terribly un-British arrangement.

"I'm glad you saw my note," Glori said when it had been firmly established that they were both unquestionably fine.

"Your note?"

"Yes," she said, pushing her spectacles up onto her nose with the back of her wrist. "When I learned that you were with your aunt and uncle, I left a note on your dresser telling you where to find me. Elgin—he is *such* a lamb—insisted that I rest, but I couldn't, so I came out here to get away from it all for a while."

"Umm," was Maxwell's unenthusiastic reply.

Leather soles scuffed the flagstones. Little bits of dried grass fell to the floor from the nest that a chirruping sparrow was building in the rafters. Glori fidgeted with her spade, for Maxwell simply couldn't keep from looking at her. He finally said, "Elgin told me that the past week has been especially difficult for you. I'm terribly sorry, Glori, I should have been here to help."

"Oh, Maxwell, you haven't caused any problems. It's only that I haven't slept very well lately." To keep the conversation from taking a maudlin turn, she pointed to the wooden flat with rows of green things coming up through the rich soil and said, "My mother sent me the seeds. They're going to be lilies when they grow up."

Maxwell stepped closer to inspect the little sprouts that resembled blades of grass and said, "Glori, it seems that you knew I had returned, yet you didn't come to see me. May I ask why?"

Glori pushed her spectacles lower down on her nose to look at Maxwell over the tops. "I thought you might like to be with your family for a little while."

"You're family, too," he reminded her. A grin rocked his mustache when he said, "Do you know that I came out here to rail at you for avoiding me?"

"I was not avoiding you!"

"I didn't know that until now; however, I do apologize for thinking such a thing." His expression became rather Puckish when he said, "Until now I didn't even know that your hair was quite so fair. Blond, really, and your eyes are like . . . amethysts. Cool and clear," he added softly, "with thick dark lashes. I do remember your lashes." He lifted the spectacles from Glori's nose and dropped them into his coat pocket, leaving her blinking.

Becoming more intrigued with his wife by the moment, Maxwell's voice was little more than a mellow rumble when he said, "How strange it is that we've been married since April, and now it's almost August, but this is the first time I've known the color of your eyes." His gaze never left hers as he traced the line of her eyebrow and continued the stroke down her cheek to the point of her chin.

Glori was finding it difficult to breathe when she said, "It's getting warm in here, isn't it?"

"*Awfully* warm," was his ragged reply.

Another sparrow swooped in through a broken windowpane with more grass in its beak and flew up to the rafters. After it hopped about for an hour, or it might have been a minute, Maxwell said, "Do you always take your hair down when you tend your plants?"

"No, though I have come out here on sunny days to let it dry after I've washed it. Do you think it was improper?"

"I've never had occasion to think about it at all. I simply wondered."

And he wondered if Glori would feel even softer now than she had before he left home, and he wondered how much of the change he saw in her was influenced by those complicated things that ladies wear under their dresses, and he wondered if his hand would still coast as easily from the swell of her hip to the dip of her waist when she lay beside him. But most wondrous of all was the bosom she had acquired, the kind the poets refer to as "A womanly breast upon whose cushioned ramparts the cares of the world are laid to rest"—along with the poet himself if he knows what he's about.

Maxwell closed his eyes and prayed that Glori couldn't guess what he'd been thinking—or notice the remarkable effect those thoughts had had upon him. With renewed dignity he stepped back and said, "Please, finish whatever you were doing when I interrupted you."

Glori stood motionless for a moment, then removed a length of blue ribbon from her pocket and gathered her hair to the back of her neck, where she tied it.

Maxwell stepped behind her, took the ribbon ends, and made a neat bow. Her hair smelled faintly sweet, like flowers—just the way he remembered it. His fingers brushed the back of her neck where her skin was smooth and warm—better than he remembered it.

"Thank you," she murmured when she felt him tug the bow loops into place. Not knowing quite what to do next, she moved away, to the potting table, where she made busywork of pulling on a pair of old gloves to transplant her seedlings.

Maxwell supposed that if Glori had turned toward him instead of turning away, she would have been in his arms and he would have relied on their combined instincts for the rest. Then he considered what might have happened if he had just asked her to turn around. That, in turn, caused him to speculate upon what might happen if he asked her to turn around now. He said, "You never did say why you took your hair down."

"All those hairpins poking me made my head itch."

"Umm."

As Glori assembled her spade and pots, Maxwell leaned against the potting table, crossing his arms to keep his cuffs out of harm's way. It reminded him of the day he'd gone up to see Glori in the sewing room, before he'd left for Glasgow. She had been just as busy then, but there had been less of a strain between them. Watching her now, he tried to determine when he had begun to care for her so much—or to think of her as a wife. More specifically, as *his* wife. Had it been during the hours he'd spent on a riverbank dapping for trout? He tried to remember, but he honestly couldn't. Then the green-eyed monster crept up on him again, and he wondered if Elgin had been out here with her while she potted and planted and left her hair down to dry. Shifting his stance, Maxwell crossed his arms a little tighter and told himself not to be so suspicious.

Though he had intended to confront Glori with the matter of Elgin's attentions, he found that he no longer wanted to do it. Such an action would present a whole new set of problems, and he didn't want any more problems. Besides, there might not have been anything going on at all.

Whatever he and Glori made of their life together would have to begin here and now. Slow and easy was the way they'd do it. After all, until very recently Maxwell hadn't really thought of himself as married, and he supposed Glori hadn't, either. They hadn't even been properly introduced. Joined together as unwilling strangers, they had never courted, he had never proposed, she had never accepted. . . .

That's when Maxwell decided to court his wife.

When Glori knocked over a pot, Maxwell easily reached out and caught the thing as it rolled off the edge of the table, then returned it to her with a smile. Glori smiled, too, and scraped the dirt back into the pot. After that simple act the space between them seemed less congested.

Someone had to say something, so Glori said, "Your cousin Peter wants to talk to you. He says he knows of a man who has a long overdue voucher of Randy's. This fellow was going to present it to Uncle Neville, but Peter asked him to wait until he could talk to you about it."

"Bless Peter for his good sense, which reminds me that I'd better turn myself into a host before the guests become too drunk to remember me. They might even begin to speculate unflatteringly upon our prolonged absence."

"Why should anyone care? They must know we're all exhausted."

Smoothing his mustache to hide his smile, Maxwell only said, "Perhaps you'll consider taking a rest when you finish with your lilies."

"Only if you return my spectacles. Otherwise I'll never find the house again."

"Oh, sorry."

Quickly producing the eyeglasses, Maxwell watched Glori's lips part when she tilted her face up to his. As he placed the wire frames on the bridge of her nose and fit the curved wire behind her ears, he wondered what one very small kiss would be like, or how it would feel to slide his fingers through her beautiful hair. But he only brushed the backs of his knuckles against her cheek before he hurried away.

Glori really hadn't wanted Maxwell to go, yet he'd gone just when it looked like he might stay. She thought she knew why. If ever there was a way to frighten a man off, she had done it by looking as unkempt as she did, with a soiled smock over her dress and her hair flying about like a witch. It was lowering to remember that just before Maxwell left for Scotland, he had told her to be a lady. Now he was home again and could see quite plainly that she wasn't a lady at all. And, to be honest with herself, she didn't expect things to improve very much.

While arranging the newly potted plants in the sun, Glori searched her mind for anything that could be salvaged after this disastrous visit with Maxwell. When getting out the watering can and filling it from the rain barrel, she decided that being a proper lady wasn't as important in the country as it was in the city. As she wet down the plants, she decided that what she needed to do was show her husband that life could go on quite happily in the country, despite her lack of refinements, and considered how she might go about providing such an illumination.

Covering the ground in hungry strides, Maxwell mulled over the proper way to conduct this courtship with his wife. It simply wouldn't do to sling her over his shoulder and carry her off to bed, though he'd thought of it while he was replacing her spectacles. The trouble was that by simply being close to her, his libido had tightened his trousers, and he had to get away before he embarrassed himself and her as well. It was nearly impossible to keep his hands off her as it was, for

Glori had a remarkable effect upon him. Fortunately, there was the business with his cousin Peter and his obligations as host as an excuse to leave her when he did. If he rushed things now, he might frighten her.

But before he began to court his wife in earnest, Maxwell thought he'd wait until things settled down at the Hall. He'd maintain a light friendly attitude until then. He'd pay her small attentions, of course, but do nothing to make her uneasy. After the company was gone, the two of them might go for long walks or leisurely drives. They could see the Roman ruins. Yet none of those activities sounded particularly romantic, and he wondered what courting couples really did find to do in the rural portions of the world.

When the time was right, Maxwell supposed he might take Glori to call on friends or go shopping, though everything they did would have to be in keeping with a household in mourning. Still, if all went as planned, they'd be holding hands within the week. In another month or two they might kiss, or something, and after that he could surely convince her that he cared for her in a husbandly way. His eyes crinkled at the corners when he smiled.

Silently blessing Cousin Peter for attending to family duties, Maxwell sought his room to shed his travel clothes. When he shrugged out of his jacket, the envelope that Elgin had presented glared at him from his inside pocket. Picking it out, he studied the thing, wishing he could see through the wrapping without soiling his hands on the contents. He conceded that there might well be letters inside, not bills. Perhaps this was a sampling of some incriminating correspondence that Randy had conducted, and, for a price, the rest of the letters would be relinquished. Or it might be from someone who was providing a catalog of everything Randy had stolen and, for a price, would keep silent.

Not overly eager to learn what other transgressions his departed cousin may have committed, Maxwell spun the offending packet onto his dresser. Like a curling stone it skimmed the polished surface and bumped against the note that Glori had left for him. She had folded it in half so it stood up like a little tent.

Pushing off his shoes with the elastic insets, Maxwell picked up Glori's note and propped himself up on the bed to read it. Her fine script read, "I shall be in the conservatory—perhaps you can join me there." In the lower right corner was her initial.

Balancing the folded note on one raised knee, he clasped his hands over his head and read Glori's words again. After that he simply looked at it. It seemed like the logical thing to do while planning the seduction of the woman who had written it. Happily enough, he knew that there were some restrictions he wouldn't be encumbered with during the courting process. He wouldn't have to ask for anyone's permission to go out and about with Glori, or have a chaperon in tow. It wouldn't matter where they went or how long they stayed. After all, she was already his wife—more or less. But mostly less, which was the problem. Though, the way he had it planned, it wouldn't be a problem much longer. In the meantime, there was that packet waiting on the dresser. He could see it sticking over the edge. Damn Randy anyway.

Maxwell swung his feet off the bed and padded across the room, where he traded Glori's folded note for the mystery package. Tearing it open, he spilled out an odd collection of papers and one gold ring. After looking inside, he tapped a corner and two more rings fell out. All three pieces of jewelry had had the stones removed.

Putting them aside, Maxwell began to sort through the papers. The first was a bill from a haberdasher in Paris for ten francs. The next was a playing card, the queen of hearts, embossed with the address of a female named Fifi. After that came a few vouchers for minor sums and more bills for larger amounts. Maxwell was finally left with a collection of untidy, unnumbered sheets that looked like a letter. He started reading the top and bottom lines of each page to put them in order. Before he was through he was reading every word with great interest, for in his hands was a rambling, disoriented, rather passionate letter.

To Glori.

The bile rose in his throat as he read on. There wasn't a question of showing this piece of tripe to anyone—especially Glori. Far from apologizing for anything he had done, Randy insisted that the only reason he had approached her was because he'd been driven to distraction by her flirtatious teasing. Through an eloquent use of drivel, he made it sound as though Glori herself had been to blame for the abuse she suffered at his hands. Randy even begged her to understand his mad moment of weakness as he had understood hers.

Whatever he claimed, Maxwell knew very well that the only thing Randy had been mad for was another chance to get under Glori's petticoats. On the last page of the badly scratched-over document he even professed his devotion to Glori and insisted that he would love no other.

After tossing the offensive rantings onto the cold fireplace grate, Maxwell found that the matchbox was empty. "Bloody hell," he muttered, retrieving the scrawled letter and wiping the soot off against the hearth rug. Then he looked around for someplace to hide it. There wasn't a spot that seemed to be safe from a maid with a feather duster or a stack of clothes to be put away. Without wasting any more time, he changed clothes and slipped the letter into the pocket of his new coat. Everything else of Randy's got stuffed back into the envelope and tossed into the drawer. Upon checking his reflection in the mirror for any telltale pocket bulge, Maxwell left his room.

A moment later he was back to search the drawer where he had just dropped Randy's envelope. After churning things around, he picked up a key and used it to unlock the door that joined his room and Glori's—the same door he had locked the night before he went to Scotland. Then he laid the key in the middle of her dressing table, closed the connecting door, and went outside.

CHAPTER TWELVE

WHILE the house was full, Neville appeared only at dinner, but Maud didn't join him even then. She said she found the situation difficult enough without the pitying glances from those who knew the disgraceful truth of Randy's passing. And just as bad were the strained expressions of sympathy from those who had felt the sting of Randy's rowdy ways. So Maud kept to her rooms, and Glori swayed beneath an additional measure of guilt because she felt like one of those questionably sympathetic people to whom Maud had unwittingly alluded.

While unaware that anything was pinching Glori's conscience, Maxwell found it quite agreeable to have her at his side. He thought she had managed everything amazingly well during the past week or so, even though she hadn't been trained from childhood in the art of household management in a place the size of Westbourne Hall. Of course, he helped her whenever he could—this was his home, after all, and he knew his way around it. This was his family, these were his friends. If he had a complaint at all it was that he and Glori never had a private moment.

Through it all Elgin was ever ready to assist Glori,

and she thanked him quite warmly for his efforts. On one hand Maxwell was glad that his old chum was doing his gentlemanly best during this time of trouble and woe. On the other hand he didn't want any help with the care and keeping of his wife, and he wished his old chum would go to hell.

It took a couple of days for the company to thin. Actually, only those awaiting connections to foreign ports still remained. As everyone had things to do now that supper was over, Maxwell said, "Glori, would you care to walk about the grounds? I don't think we'll be missed for a while." Glori accepted the invitation with an eager pleasure that fed his fantasies.

The stone porch held the heat of the sun, and Glori could feel it through the thin soles of her kid shoes when she stepped outside. The evening breeze cooled her face and played with a few wisps of hair that had escaped from the carefully coiled bun at the back of her head. With her paisley shawl draped loosely over her black dress, she slipped her hand into the crook of Maxwell's elbow and followed his lead down the steps and along the grassy verge of the drive. The western sky was silvery, fading to gray. A few sleepy birds warbled in the trees. When the breeze was just right, it carried the scent of night-blooming flowers.

Glori took a long deep breath and said, "I think it's going to rain."

Maxwell said, "Umm." After they walked a little farther, he pressed Glori's hand to his side and said, "It's good to be home again," and put a silent curse on her skirts that bumped and tangled around his ankles.

Glori asked Maxwell to tell her about fishing in Scotland, and he did so with splashing color, saying that he thought she would enjoy seeing it all someday. When he asked about her family, she told him that her father had slipped in the garden and turned his knee while he was inspecting snails.

Nothing of great importance followed, they simply enjoyed each other's undivided attention. When Maxwell stopped Glori to draw the paisley shawl up over her shoulders, a knowing smile took hold of him. He had looked at her on a number of occasions and wondered what to do with her. Now he knew.

"The shawl becomes you," he said. "I almost sent you something else instead. I'm glad I didn't." They started walking again.

Then came a whistling that could be heard long before they could see the whistler. Eventually Elgin Farley emerged from the shadows along the drive.

Suspecting that he had just seen Iris, Glori greeted him enthusiastically, longing to ask how he and his ladylove fared. But she had promised not to betray that confidence, so she asked nothing. Even so, she could have cuffed him when he only winked at her and smiled at Maxwell and continued on his way.

"What was all that about?" Maxwell wanted to know.

"Whatever do you mean?" came Glori's too innocent reply.

"All that smiling and winking. Is there anything I should know?"

"If there is it has nothing to do with you and me," she assured him.

Maxwell wasn't entirely convinced. He could tell that something was going on and knew that Glori wasn't telling him the whole of it. It made him uneasy.

Glori could feel Maxwell pulling away and determinedly wiggled her fingers a little tighter around his arm. She wasn't surprised that he was annoyed. It wasn't at all proper for a lady to have secrets with her husband's best friend. They returned to the house after that, and Glori spent the rest of the evening trying to figure out how to get things back to the way they were before Elgin went whistling past.

* * *

Distant thunder had awakened Glori quite early the next morning, and she lay there wondering if this might be as good a time as any to demonstrate to Maxwell that country life could be every bit as pleasant as life in London or Glasgow, minus a few refinements. With no one in attendance to ask awkward questions, she unbraided her hair and brushed it until it crackled. Then she put on the housecoat of ivory cambric trimmed with ecru lace that Maud had given her, only to take it off and put on the one she usually wore of pale blue piquet, printed with violets. She didn't want it to appear as though she had actually *planned* to look as attractive as she could. This was supposed to be the start of any ordinary day.

After finding that key on her dressing table several days ago, Glori knew that the door to Maxwell's room was unlocked, and knew that he wanted her to know it. This morning she would slip into his room to say good morning, then slip out again. She would say her piece and hope it was enough to set him thinking about how nice it would be to say hello to each other every morning. One cheery good morning, and she would be done. It wouldn't take more than a minute or two. Nothing could go wrong in only a minute or two.

After checking her buttons and smoothing her hair, Glori was finally ready and standing at the door. That's when she decided that she couldn't go prancing in there just to say hello. Maxwell might think there was something strange about it, and she didn't want to appear strange.

Ready to abandon her plan, Glori supposed she may as well get dressed and go downstairs to bid the last of the cousins farewell over an early breakfast. That's when it came to her that she could use her early morning call to remind Maxwell that his cousin was about to leave. There surely wouldn't be anything strange in that. Confidently, Glori raised her hand to the door.

Maxwell heard the knock, followed by the turn of a knob. It was beyond him to know what any sane person could possibly want so early in the morning. He wished Simms would get down here from Scotland to save him from these enthusiastic domestics who cut short his slumber. He'd been sleeping—or trying to sleep—next door to Glori for three nights now, and it wasn't getting any easier. They hadn't even gotten to hand holding yet, and he wondered if they ever would. Their walk the evening before had turned sour after that winking and smiling of Elgin's. Now he wished he had overlooked it.

Yet he needed some clear encouragement from Glori. He wasn't about to announce the degree of his regard for any woman if her affections lay elsewhere, even if the woman was his own wife. This courting business was wearing him out, and he'd hardly even started.

"Well, what is it?" he grumbled from beneath his pillow.

Through the muted light of the draped windows a soft voice called, "Good morning." She had come far enough into the room so that she could see him.

"Glori?" Wearing a sleepy smile and hooded eyes, Maxwell pushed the pillow aside and rolled over to look up at his wife, one bent knee tenting his covers. He liked the way her hair swished across her back when she moved—fair and silky, loose and shimmery. She wore a pretty but shapeless blue housecoat with little flowers all over. He guessed there would be a warm flannel nightdress beneath it. Beneath the warm flannel nightdress would be warm smooth Glori. A broader smile dimpled his beard-shadowed cheeks when he said, "I was just thinking about you."

"Humbug. You were sound asleep."

"You're right," he said. "I was *dreaming* about you." He raised a massive hand to cover a yawn, then rubbed his hairy chest. After that he wadded up his feather pillow and propped it beneath his head.

Glori tried not to look at Maxwell. After all, she had seen his chest before. But unlike that unexpected night at the Willows, for which they had made no preparations at all, Maxwell was now among his furnishings, and she had expected to find him in a proper nightshirt. A moment later her eyes grew larger and rounder when it occurred to her that he might never wear a nightshirt. If not, she wondered what he did wear. This wasn't going the way she had planned it.

Pulling the sheet up under his chin, he said, "I trust you'll forgive me for not standing when you entered the room."

"It's perfectly all right," she hastily assured him. "I just thought you might need reminding that the last of your cousins will be leaving this morning. I believe you said that you'd like to be there to say good-bye," and swiftly turned toward the door.

"Wait!"

Glori stopped and looked back at him. He was trying to think of something clever that would keep her there, but all he could say was, "We haven't had much time alone. It's impossible to talk when someone else is about."

"Is there something of a very private nature that you wish to discuss?"

He said, "Yes, in a way," and hunted through his sleep-stunted brain for something else to say.

"Has it anything to do with with Randy?"

"Randy? Yes, I suppose it does," he replied, glad of a direction for his thoughts. Actually, Maxwell had a lot on his mind that involved Randy, but little of it was fit for Glori's ears. Then it dawned on him that there must be something about Randy that still troubled Glori, or she wouldn't have mentioned him.

Sitting up, he watched with growing concern as Glori moved slowly to the chair with the cat-scratched upholstery. When seated, she arranged her housecoat over her knees, the toes of her Turkish-carpet slippers peeping out from beneath the folds of her flannel nightgown. Clasping her hands neatly on her lap, she matched up her thumbnails and prepared for whatever Maxwell had to say.

But Maxwell didn't know what to say. When he'd asked Glori to stay, he had supposed he could think of something to make her laugh, something to tease her about. He wanted it to be like it was that day when they had taken refuge in the barn loft. This reaction of hers frightened him. His heart felt like a fist, and a muscle jumped along his jaw. He hated to see that Randy could reach beyond the grave to hurt her. When he thought of Randy astride her, his mind screamed, *What else happened?*

"Ah, yes, about Randy," Maxwell began cautiously as he laid himself down again, thinking he might appear less aggressive that way. "One hardly knows where to dig in. It's all rather unpleasant, isn't it?"

"Yes," Glori agreed, still staring at her thumbs.

Plowing his fingers across his forehead, he said, "Randy and I didn't get on too well, especially after he'd hurt you. I think I wanted to kill him that day, but now he's saved me the trouble by doing it himself." When the expression on Glori's face became even more distressed, Maxwell felt sick with dread. Raising up on one elbow, he asked, "Glori, what's troubling you so? Did he treat you even worse than I'd thought?"

"No, it's not that, precisely."

"Then what is it, precisely?"

She didn't answer.

"I can't read your mind. Glori."

A great sigh raised her shoulders before they sagged. When she finally spoke, she said, "The trouble is that I feel so awfully guilty about Randy being dead because I'm rather glad he's gone."

"Why do you feel guilty? You didn't push the silly ass off that roof."

"I know, but I feel so wicked because I truly cannot regret his passing, even though it has made your aunt and uncle suffer so. I'm sorry he wasn't happier while he lived, yet I cannot be sorry that he won't be back. Ever. Is that what you wanted to say, too?"

"Hell, no!"

Then he rubbed a hand over his face and spoke more gently. "Glori, neither one of us needs to feel like a troll under a bridge because we don't have kindly thoughts about someone who never inspired such sentiments."

"I know, but once I wished he was dead and now he is and your aunt and uncle are *so* unhappy . . . " Her voice had dwindled away to nearly nothing, and she just shook her head.

Maxwell wanted to take her in his arms and tell her not to worry, but he didn't dare. Not yet. As simply as he could he just said, "Glori, I do understand. I feel perfectly wretched because I wasn't here when you all needed me. But what happened to Randy wasn't my fault or yours, either. You taught me a great deal about undeserved guilt."

"I?"

"Umm. We were in Stratford at the time—do you remember? Whether I wanted to hear it or not, you told me that the awful feelings I'd been dragging around since childhood had been badly misplaced. It took me a while to see it, but you were right. And though this business with Randy is different, it isn't so very different."

Glori shook her head.

"When I came home, it seemed like my aunt and uncle might be able to look right inside me and see how I really felt about the son they mourned—it was deuced uncomfortable, I can tell you that."

"I can see that it would be uncomfortable, however—"

"However, you feel like a hypocrite because of your

dislike for Randy despite your affection for his parents."

"How did you know?"

"I've lived with the situation longer than you have." Maxwell extended a comforting arm and said, "Come here and I'll explain it to you."

Glori didn't know quite what to do. Everything was going much too quickly, and her thoughts were badly agitated. She had only intended to say good morning and tell Maxwell that his cousin was about to leave. What if someone should come in and see them in bed? It would be too awful!

"Shall I come and get you?" Maxwell asked as he dropped his arm, rather amused by the look on Glori's face. "It should be easier this time without having to hoist you and your damned hoops up a ladder."

"No, I'll come to you," Glori said, hurriedly moving to sit primly on the end of Maxwell's bed, trying not to look at the way the sheet had slipped down his chest again. Though she was unable to resist a quick peek at his manly anatomy, she reminded herself that this was no time to have any of those *impure thoughts* which Dr. Ellsworth's *Cyclopedia* said would destroy her sinuses and ruin her nails.

"Don't sit alone when you're sad, Glori. I'm here whenever you need me." He didn't try to hide his smile when he said, "I'm even good for an assortment of other clever things."

"Like what?" she asked suspiciously.

"Well, I can breathe fire," he boastfully reminded her, trying to lighten her mood. To himself he said, Time. Give her a little more time. From some long neglected corner of his mind crept a refrain that went: *The boy stood on the burning deck when all but him had fled* . . .

Glori said, "It's all well and good to be amusing, but I feel as though I've been lying to your aunt and uncle because. . . . because . . . " Her words trailed away, and she swallowed hard.

Maxwell wasn't smiling when he said, "Glori, ever since I can remember I've loved my aunt and uncle. When Randy was young, I loved him, too. Then the older he got, the worse he got until I couldn't even *like* him anymore. So you see, I really do know how you feel." He extended a warm hand palm up; Glori laid her chilled hand upon it, and his fingers closed protectively. Maxwell had supposed that this moment would be rather romantic. Now he was just glad that Glori could trust him enough to be sitting here on his bed after what she had been through with Randy.

Idly rubbing his thumb over the plain gold band on her left hand, he said, "We both know that there are times when the truth is a noble, brave thing, but this isn't one of those times. There are other times when the truth is cruel or at least unkind, like now. You can't tell Maud and Neville about what Randy has done. Yet there's no need to feel guilty about your feelings toward him. He doesn't deserve the worry you've spent on him." Then Maxwell leaned forward and wiped Glori's damp cheek. "None of it matters," he whispered.

Her smile was thin, but it was enough to tell him that she understood, at least a little. And he thought about taking her in his arms and keeping her there until the hurt went away. He'd hold her tight and tell her that she was wonderful and beautiful and that he'd never leave her again. But he didn't want to frighten her with the intensity of his feelings, so he said, "I told you I'm a wizard. Do you have anything else on your mind that needs my expert attention?"

"Yes. You have one cousin left at the Hall, and he said he'd come up to say good-bye if he missed you at breakfast."

"Ah, me. I don't know whether I should laugh or cry, though I suppose I should be up and about while I decide. Would you like to leave before I leap naked from my bed?"

"Naked?" Glori squeaked.

"Naked as an egg." He grinned.

Glori disappeared into her own room.

After the door closed Maxwell swung himself out from under the covers. He hadn't wanted to get up. Mostly he hadn't wanted Glori to leave. He hurriedly shaved in cold water, then dressed quickly. When he opened the wardrobe to take out a coat, he realized that Randy's ramblings were still in the inside pocket of one of them. He decided to burn the letter now, before anyone found it. There were plenty of matches. While going from the wardrobe to the fireplace, he found himself reading the cursed thing one last time, like picking at a sore that just wouldn't heal, thinking that it was too bad his cousin couldn't have made his last letter of some use, of some comfort to his parents. He surely couldn't show this slanderous babble to them.

Or could he? What would it hurt if he simply softened the letter a bit?

As long as he could hear Glori moving about in her room, Maxwell knew that it wasn't time to go downstairs. From a box in his desk drawer he assembled his pen nibs and found one that looked like it matched what Randy had used. After that he took the letter to the window to be sure of the color of the ink. It was black. That's when he heard Glori's passage door open and close. Once again Randy's letter went into Maxwell's pocket, and he hurried down to breakfast.

Hours later, after the last of the Rutherford cousins had gone, Glori entered the estate room with a ledger that Maud had asked her to return. She was as startled to see Maxwell behind the desk as he was to see her come through the door. She also noticed his sheepish look as he slipped whatever he was writing into the top desk drawer. It seemed obvious to her that he must be conducting a secret correspondence, perhaps with some woman he'd left behind in London or Glasgow. Why else would he hide anything?

In the coldest, most dignified voice she could find she said, "Excuse me, Maxwell, I didn't mean to intrude." But a sense of betrayal aroused her, and she left the big book on a chair without staying long enough to put it away.

"Glori, wait!" Maxwell called to her trailing skirts as she swept from the room. Swiftly collecting the assorted pages of the letter, he stuffed them into his pocket again and took after her.

"What do you want?" she spat as she marched down the hall.

"I want to talk to you, what the hell do you think I want?" he spat back, easily keeping pace with her.

"I think you wanted to write a letter to someone, and you didn't want me to know about it!"

"You're right, I didn't want you to know about it."

Glori wheeled on him to demand, "Is she very pretty, this woman to whom you're writing your secret letter?"

"For crissakes, I'm writing a letter to Aunt Maud. I'll show it to you!"

Glori looked at him like he'd lost his mind and started walking again.

"I want you to see it!" he insisted, rather pleased to see Glori cared enough to resent even the possibility of another woman.

"I don't want to see it!"

"You're not going to cry again, are you?"

The look she gave him now was even more disgusted than the last one.

When they passed the open door of the unoccupied morning room, Maxwell ducked inside and pulled Glori in with him. The sound of the door being slammed shut echoed through the house. He steered her to a chair, turned her around, and sat her in it. As a preamble, he explained how he happened to be in possession of the letter in question. Then he dropped the wrinkled pages onto her lap and ordered, "Read on!"

Glori would have liked to throw the letter aside and walk disdainfully from the room, but in truth she was too curious to do so. She began to read, and what she read made her even more angry than she was before.

"Now you know why I didn't want you to see the thing," Maxwell said when she finished. "I had intended to send it up in smoke without anyone ever seeing it. Then I noticed that with a bit of fixing up, it could be passed off as a tolerable letter from Randy to me. Actually, I had planned to give my aunt and uncle only the last page and say that the rest was of a private nature. On that last page would be Randy's loving reference to his mother and other sociable things."

"You were actually doing something to deceive your aunt and uncle when I interrupted you?" Glori asked in amazement.

"Oh, for crissakes! I'm not trying to rob the Bank of England. All I'm trying to do is ease the suffering of two very nice people. It won't hurt anything or anyone for them to believe that Randy had something kind to say before he turned up his toes."

"How do you propose to salvage this?" Glori said, tapping her finger on the last page of Randy's letter.

"Look here," he said. "See where it says "love no other?" Perhaps the *no* can be made into *my* and we can put an *m* on the front of *other*. We might do something with a few of these other words, too."

"We?"

"Yes, if you wouldn't mind. Now that you've seen the awful thing, there's no reason for me to struggle with it alone. Though I've been able to match the ink and the pen, you can look at the page I've been practicing on and see that I'm having a devil of a time making strokes that resemble Randy's. Mine come out too even, like I've traced them. His are more fluid. Perhaps you might have a go at it."

After a perusal of Randy's scribbling, Glori said, "I think I can do it."

They left the morning room far more amiably than they had entered it. Maxwell was relieved to have averted a terrible misunderstanding with Glori, and Glori was most gratified to be included in Maxwell's plans. He'd made her his confidant, his partner, and she hugged the joy of it to her heart.

When seated behind the desk in the estate office where Maxwell had been practicing his forgery skills, Glori used a blank sheet of paper to practice drawing loops and lines. She wrote out a few words that looked like Randy's, then tried to see what she could do to change them. Because he'd been studying the letter for so long, Maxwell pointed out the places he thought changes might successfully be made. Glori concentrated on how those changes might be accomplished.

When Maxwell leaned over her shoulder to see how she was doing, his breath whispered against her neck and sent shivers down her spine. She thought it would be delightful if he would forget about the wretched letter and sweep her into a passionate embrace and smother her with kisses. After all, he was her husband.

But this only brought to mind the afflictions she would suffer from such abandon. Married or unmarried, the excitement of extreme passion was a debilitating evil to be guarded against, at least according to Dr. Ellsworth's *Cyclopedia*, though he assured his readers that virtuous women weren't afflicted with intemperate desire. Still, it seemed to Glori that moral and physical decay were her destiny, for her thoughts of Maxwell were anything but temperate. Supposing that Maxwell would be terribly shocked by her unladylike speculations, Glori moved a little farther away from his disturbing presence and began a renewed assault upon the paper before her.

Before Glori moved away, Maxwell saw the shiver his

nearness had caused her. He smiled and made a mental note on the progress of the seduction of his wife. Making love, however, was not to be one of this afternoon's diversions. Randy's letter was, and they set to it with a will.

"This business of twisting the truth has become a tangle," Glori soon realized. "Now we'll have to make up something to explain how it is that you've come by such a remarkable letter as this. You cannot simply say that you've had it for a while and just now got around to telling anyone. It would make you appear either stupid or unfeeling."

"I understand that," replied Maxwell as he knelt before the fireplace and set a match to the unwanted pages. They flamed and curled into fragile blackened leaves. When the last amber sparks died away, he used the fireplace shovel to flatten the charred remains into ash. When he stood again, he said, "I'll think of something."

When that one remaining page of Randy's letter was reworded and safely tucked away in Maxwell's pocket, they went out to see the horses as though nothing out of the ordinary had occurred.

When the funeral guests were gone, Maud came out of her rooms and threw herself into housecleaning. She began in the attics with a swarm of maids and soon progressed to the upper floors and the servants' quarters. Occasionally she invited Glori to see the contents of one old chest or another before it was pushed back under the eaves. Maxwell could only watch and wonder how long it would take for his aunt to wear herself out, though he supposed that everyone had to cope with grief in his own way. Neville spent a good deal of his time bringing the kennel records up to date and staring into space.

At his uncle's request Maxwell went over the account

books for the Hall, then spoke with the steward and the farmers themselves about needed repairs. That done, he rode across the fields and along the fence rows to be able to give his uncle a better assessment of the state of the estate. With the harvest under way this was no simple task, added to the fact that he wasn't used to spending long hours in the saddle and ached all over. Bone weary by the close of each day Maxwell suspected that he was being given these jobs to keep him home in case he took it into his head to return to Glasgow after all.

Glori and Maxwell saw each other while coming and going, but there never seemed to be a chance to simply talk. They met at meals, naturally, though the table wasn't the place to share little jokes or confidences. And Elgin was always there, as entertaining as ever when conversation slackened.

It was during such a lull that Elgin said, "Glori, what do you think about another afternoon of drawing? You look as if you could do with some fresh air." What Elgin wanted was another opportunity to whisper sweet nothings into the shell-like ear of Iris Huntington, who was always with them.

Unfortunately, Maxwell still didn't know of Elgin's attachment to the squire's granddaughter and wondered what Elgin was up to. When Glori smiled and said she'd arrange another drawing party as soon as she could, Maxwell suggested that Elgin join him for brandy in the library after the ladies retired and politely excused himself. They all supposed that the sobering effects of his new responsibilities had finally caught up with him.

It was quite late when Elgin entered the library. Maxwell made a gesture toward the sideboard. Elgin, curious to know what was on his old friend's mind, poured a glass of whatever it was from the nearest decanter and made himself comfortable in one of the high-backed chairs.

"I suspect something has been going on here while I've been in Scotland," Maxwell began, as he sat on the edge of his desk. "Something of a romantic nature, to be more exact."

Elgin slapped the arm of his chair and said, "What rotten luck! Did Glori tell you?"

"Give me credit for a bit of sense. I thought something was amiss before I ever left Glasgow."

Lifting his glass in salute, Elgin said, "You're more discerning than I've given you credit for. I hadn't thought anything had slipped out."

Maxwell began to pace. "It's not only what you've said, old boy, it's what you haven't said. And Glori has had nothing but praise for the way you managed those *sketching expeditions*."

Elgin looked pleased when he said, "Has she really? That was awfully sweet of her. She's a dear girl, you know. I told you that before you left for Scotland. If you recall, I said you shouldn't leave her."

"I don't need to be reminded of it. My untimely departure, however, has nothing to do with the way you've conducted this affair. It's a wonder someone hasn't caught you. Even if you didn't have a care for yourself, you might have remembered what could have happened to the lady's reputation!"

"You sure have gotten stiff-rumped since you've been respectably married."

"Husbands get that way!"

"I'll have to remember that."

"Have you considered her feelings?"

"Good God, Max, I know her better than you do. I'm *very* aware of her feelings."

"Don't be too sure. Have you forgotten that it's *my wife* who is involved in this?"

"Nothing would have happened at all if your wife hadn't been involved. How could I forget it?"

"Perhaps because I've made it so easy for you. I'll

have to do better in the future. Good night, Farley."

Alone now, Elgin set aside his drink, leaned back in his chair, and contemplated the astounding, sometimes confusing change in his old friend since his matrimonial. It wasn't the first time he'd seen this sort of thing happen, though he had to admit that Maxwell had never been particularly boisterous before he became so self-righteous. It was usually the wild ones who got to be so sanctimonious.

While Maxwell got ready for bed, he irritably wished that Elgin would go home. If Neville hadn't said that he was such a cheerful addition to the household, Maxwell would have suggested that Elgin leave long before this. But since his aunt and uncle had already lost Randy, he couldn't bring himself to deprive them of Elgin, too.

Pitching his shirt into the chair with the tattered upholstery, Maxwell remembered how eagerly Glori had welcomed Elgin's suggestion that they go out drawing again. It made him feel a little sick. Worse than that, it made him feel like an outsider in his own home. Didn't Glori know by now that he cared about her? Just because he hadn't wanted to marry her and then went anyway without her, it didn't mean he didn't care about her.

Feeling ill-used, he climbed into bed still trying to sort things out. On one hand he wanted Glori. On the other hand he wanted her to be happy. If having Elgin would make her happy, perhaps he should simply step aside and let them set up their love nest in some quiet corner of the world. He considered it for two or three minutes before he decided that he just wasn't that noble. Glori was his wife. He intended to be her husband.

Maxwell got out of bed and went directly to the connecting door. Then he went back and pulled on his trousers and entered Glori's darkened room. The first time he'd been in there, it had made him uneasy. Now it didn't bother him a bit. He belonged there. Besides, he'd gotten used to waking her up. He *liked* waking her up.

Arms folded across his bare chest, shoulder to the bed-post, Maxwell gazed into the shadows where his wife lay. His voice was a rumbly purr when he said, "Glori, I hope you're not asleep."

CHAPTER THIRTEEN

"GLORI?"

"Hmm?"

"How long will it take you to pack?"

She rolled onto her back and yawned.

"Pack," Maxwell repeated. "How long will it take?"

There was a groggy pause before she asked, "Why?"

"We're going to East Wallow. It's time I met your parents."

"In the middle of the night?"

"Don't you want to go?"

"Of course I want to go, but not at *this* hour, for heaven's sake. Actually, I wonder if we should even go at all."

"Won't your parents be at home?"

"They rarely go out into the world—the world usually comes to them. I only meant that this is simply a poor time to leave here."

"Do you mean to stay because of aunt and uncle? It's an admirable thought, of course, but I believe they might enjoy the solitude as much as we will."

"Maxwell, this is dreadfully complicated when I'm so sleepy. Is it that you wish to go to East Wallow to meet my parents or to give your aunt and uncle some quiet?"

"I want to go someplace where *we* can have some quiet. If we go to East Wallow, I can meet your parents as well. While we're about it, Aunt Maud and Uncle Neville can have all the quiet they want without feeling like they have to put on a cheerful face if they don't feel like it."

"Do you really think it would be all right if we go?"

"I really do. This might be the best time for it, actually, as Auntie is about to collapse from all this housecleaning, and she'll need a rest."

"How long would we be away?"

"About a week and a half, I should think, if we spend a week with your parents."

"Then I shall go, but not until morning," Glori mumbled through another yawn. Stretching, arching, sighing, she melted back into the bed.

Hardly daring to breathe, Maxwell could only stare into the shadows where his wife lay silky smooth and sleepy warm. A slow grin crept over him when he wondered what she would do if he just slipped beneath the covers with her. This time he wouldn't be wearing shoes. One hand dropped to the waistband of his trousers.

He tapped the button and sighed, knowing what scant progress he had made with this wooing business. Before he could proceed with the courting ritual, however, he had to put some distance between his wife and his best friend, and a visit to East Wallow did seem to be the most discreet way to achieve that end without obvious hostilities. It also occurred to Maxwell that with himself and Glori away, Elgin would surely quit the portals of Westbourne Hall for lack of companionship. Then, when he and Glori returned, they could get on with the various and pleasurable aspects of being husband and wife.

But when Glori moved beneath the covers, all Maxwell wanted was to be there holding her, pliant and soft against his own hard body, his hand sliding over the swell of her hip . . .

He shut his eyes tightly and concentrated on the cold floor beneath his bare feet, the mosquito bite on his knuckle, the ticking of the clock . . . sliding his hand over Glori's hip.

It was as plain as a pikestaff that he'd better get on with his plans.

"We can leave for East Wallow whenever you like," he said. "I don't suppose a few more hours will matter."

Glori rolled over but made no reply.

"We can leave in the morning, and Lucy will have more time to pack for the both of you."

"It's a small house. Perhaps it would be best to leave Lucy here."

"If you think you can manage without her, I'm agreeable."

Agreeable was a rather mild word, actually. Maxwell was overjoyed that there would be one less person underfoot. He wanted to be alone with Glori like they were now, except closer, and he wanted to tell her so. But he prayed for patience and started for his own room. Halfway there he stopped and looked wistfully back at the bed.

"Glori?"

"Yes?"

"Would you . . . that is . . . do you need more blankets or anything?"

"I have enough, but thank you for asking."

"Well, then . . . good night."

"Good night."

Alone, Glori punched her pillow and morosely wondered if her husband ever intended to share her bed. A little while ago when she awoke to the sound of his voice, she had assumed . . .

But she'd obviously been mistaken and felt rather silly. She felt even more foolish when she thought about the way she had shifted over to make room for him in the

bed. Then her dismals gave way to a secretive smile, for
she knew how few beds there were in that little house in
East Wallow.

When Maxwell awoke the next morning, he was a man
with a mission and soon had two portmanteaus and four
leather-covered, brass-studded trunks hauled down from
the attic. One portmanteau and three trunks were intended for Glori's use, while the other two pieces of baggage
were for his own things.

Maxwell told a footman who told an upstairs maid who
told his aunt's personal maid who woke Her Ladyship
and told her that travel plans were under way. Then
Her Ladyship sent word below stairs that young Lord
Rutherford and his lady would be leaving for Yorkshire
this day, so Cook left breakfast preparation to one of the
kitchen maids and went about the assembly of a basket
luncheon.

A whirlwind of activity began early in Glori's room
as well. She was awakened by thumping and bumping
sounds in the room next to hers. That was followed by
a turn of the knob and Maxwell saying:

"Good morning, I see that you're still abed. Thought
you might be." More thumping and bumping. "I've
brought you a few trunks."

Glori yawned and blinked and followed Maxwell's
blurry outline as he opened the draperies and lined up
the trunks in the middle of the room. Then he took
Glori's spectacles from the table, handed them to her,
and said that they had about two hours until they must
leave for the train station. Before he left he gave a tug
to the bell cord.

Glori had gotten as far as dangling her feet off the edge
of the bed when Lucy arrived, bursting with efficiency.
To save time Glori had breakfast in her room. Sluggishly
donning her robe, she chewed her toast and swallowed
it down with hot chocolate. Maud arrived then, already

dressed, having come to deliver a black silk parasol and ask what help Glori might need.

"I do have a problem, but I'm afraid it's beyond either of us at the moment," Glori said. "You see, my only traveling dress is of mulberry serge."

Arching one eyebrow, Maud opened the wardrobe to inspect this breach of etiquette. "Glorianna," she said, "this mulberry is almost black, and there are these Greek keys in black braid all along the edge—I've always considered Greek keys rather dignified—and there are black frogs and little black tassels, too. It will do well enough," she said, closing the wardrobe doors. "I doubt that the strangers you pass will know that you're supposed to be in deep mourning." Then she said that they would meet again downstairs and left.

Glori pushed aside her breakfast tray and joined Lucy to pack.

"Will you need your warm night things in Yorkshire?" Lucy wanted to know.

Glori said that indeed she would, so Lucy chose the thickest flannelette nightdress and a warm quilted house-coat. She did, however, lay aside the prettiest nightcap. After that she picked the nicest of the chemises and corset covers, too.

While Lucy packed black stockings, gray petticoats, and gray drawers to go under her mourning clothes, Glori collected little things: a brush and comb, hairpins, hair-nets, and curling rags. A nail file and chamois nail buff-er. An ivory toothbrush with soft white bristles. Jars of creams and a pot of tooth powder. She was almost out of her favorite lip salve—her mother would have the recipe for more.

Extra India rubber garters were set out, as were black gloves—both silk and kid. A spare corset lace and a buttonhook. Hair pins and scented face soap. Black ribbons. From the top left drawer of her dressing table came a stack of handkerchiefs edged in black. A small

vial of hartshorn intended for her purse, along with a
folding fan, a small sewing kit with tiny scissors, a little
mirror. Another pair of spectacles.

Two sets of nicely starched collars and cuffs, both
black, were laid flat on the bottom of one of the trunks
so they wouldn't become wrinkled.

Reaching into the wardrobe, Glori pushed aside a
mauve taffeta dinner dress and said, "Lucy, will you
help me?" She handed out two black day dresses, one
of sateen, the other of crepe. Lucy laid them on the
bed. To that assemblage Glori added her ever-practical
long-sleeved, plain blue dress. She would also have to
take two sizes of crinolines to go under the clothes she
was packing. Both sets of hoops were hanging at the
back of the wardrobe, with all the steel bands caught
up over one hook.

From the cupboard shelf Glori took her straw sunbonnet and black Sunday hat and laid them on the bed.
Lucy sent one of the younger maids into the attic for a
hatbox. It was then that Glori remembered her Balmoral
boots. She brought out her black button-up boots, too.
And her woolly slippers. She would have missed them.
Maud sent in a scarf.

While Glori was wondering if she should include her
Berlin-wool needlework, Maxwell was back again, asking what else he should take along as he was unfamiliar
with his destination. Glori smiled and said, "I'll be right
with you." She left as Lucy began to fill the portmanteau
with things that would be necessary for an overnight stop
along the way.

As Maxwell had brought so few of his things with
him from Scotland, he'd had to search his drawers and
cupboards to find enough clothing to be suitably dressed
for a visit with his in-laws.

After peering into his trunk, Glori said, "There isn't
a single drawing room in the whole of East Wallow, and
no one there dresses for dinner."

"Never?"

"Never."

"You're sure?"

"Quite."

Maxwell had his formal clothes removed and replaced by more tweeds and another pair of spats. And he put the black suit he would wear for the trip over a chair on the far side of the room so it wouldn't be packed by mistake.

Leaving her husband to contemplate the polish on his Wellingtons, Glori continued her own packing, filling only two of the three trunks. When the last hasp was snapped shut and the last key turned, Lucy pushed the baggage out into the hall and sent for a pair of footmen to remove it all.

With an eye to the clock Lucy put layer upon layer of clothes on her mistress as though she were dressing a doll. Then Glori's hair was unbraided, brushed, part ed down the middle, and coiled into a stylish bun. She didn't have to be told to raise her arms so that the skirt portion of her dress could be dropped over her head, or turn so Lucy would have better light to do up the small wire hooks at the back.

To make Glori's traveling dress a truly practical one, it had been equipped with a mechanical skirt lifter, an arrangement of small rings sewn inside the skirt, with cords that were tied at the bottom, then fitted through the rings to hoist the hem. Reaching through a placket at the top of the voluminous skirt, Lucy took hold of one bunch of cord ends and said, "Are you ready?"

Glori stood with her feet apart to keep her balance and said, "Quite ready."

Lucy pulled and the front of Glori's skirt went up like the venetian blinds on the library windows. The same procedure was followed to lift the back of the garment. To keep it all from falling down again Lucy tied the two clusters of cords into slip knots and tucked them back inside the skirt placket. Presumably the dress was now safely above the dirt of roads, muddy coaching yards, unkempt inns, and soot-covered railway platforms.

Glori then eased her arms into her dress bodice and fastened the frogs down the front while Lucy fitted the tiny hooks on the bottom edge of the bodice to eyes on the skirt to keep the top from riding up.

From an enameled box in the top right-hand drawer of her dressing table, Glori took a jet necklace and earrings set in silver. Jet, being black, was the only stone that Queen Victoria permitted at court these days, enhancing its popularity. After the jewelry was fastened, a small black hat with two curling feathers and a profusion of ribbons was perched on Glori's fair head and tied beneath her chin with a wide ribbon. After giving herself a final inspection in the mirror, Glori knocked at Maxwell's door to tell him she was ready to go, but he wasn't there.

A bright sun was well up in the sky by the time Maxwell stood watching two footmen strap the trunks to the roof of the Westbourne coach. When they stopped working to look out across the front lawn, Maxwell moved around the coach to see what had caught their interest. It was a wagon with two people in it, rattling along the sweep of drive where it emerged from the park. At closer range the upright passenger seated beside the youthful teamster proved to be Simms. The wagon was piled with Simms's own belongings as well as Maxwell's, the sum of everything that had traveled from London to Glasgow and now from Glasgow to the Cotswolds, including the fishing gear and garb.

"Simms, how devilish good it is to see you again!" Maxwell exclaimed, extending his hand in greeting as soon as his man had climbed down from the rough board seat. He was still holding fast to the valise that held his employer's valuables.

"As you might guess by the baggage, my wife and I are about to take a little trip," said Maxwell. "We're off to Yorkshire."

Simms did his best not to look harried by the prospect of another expedition just when he thought he could get some rest. Maxwell noted the fleeting expression and said, "No need to look so glum, old man, you'll be staying here to unpack. I would, however, like a few words with you about where things are to be put."

A gentleman's gentleman worth his salt followed his master's lead without saying that he already knew where everything was supposed to go.

Upon reaching the privacy of his bedchamber, Maxwell closed the passage door. In hushed tones he said, "Simms, I need you to do something for me."

Simms replied with a slight but dignified bow.

Drawing an envelope from the inside pocket of his frock coat, Maxwell said, "If asked, you need only say that you brought this letter to me today, along with some other mail. It came from Paris and was sent to me in London, then forwarded to my Glasgow address. You may want to add that it appeared to be in my cousin Randy's handwriting. That part is up to you."

"Is that all, sir?"

"That's all."

"If I may ask, when did this letter come into my keeping?"

"When? Oh, yes. It caught up to you about seven or eight days ago, I should think, which would explain why you brought it along instead of sending it ahead."

"Of course."

"Am I forgetting anything?" Maxwell asked.

"Not unless I'm supposed to know the content."

"You aren't."

"Then I can't suggest anything else at the moment."

"Thank you, Simms."

"My pleasure, sir."

Kneeling before the fireplace, Maxwell set a match to the wrinkled envelope in which he had kept the last page of Randy's letter. Once it caught flame, he stood, brushed off the knee of his trousers, tugged his cuffs back into place, and asked, "How have things been in Glasgow since I decamped?"

"The weather lacked a great deal toward being civil," Simms declared with a disdainful sniff. While listing the more interesting social events that Maxwell had missed, Simms took a bundle of letters from the valise he'd kept with him. He sorted through them and produced a lavender envelope. It was addressed in a fine hand and carried the scent of Fiona Canfield's distinctive perfume.

Maxwell slit it open and found it to be a letter of condolence upon the death of his cousin, nothing more. He'd have to write and thank the lady for her sympathy and let her know that he wouldn't be returning to Glasgow. Giving the tinted page a parting smile, he knelt before the fireplace and lit another match.

"Any more of these?" he inquired of his trusty servant when he stood and tugged at his cuffs.

"Only her calling card, sir."

"Send it after the letter, will you, old man?" Simms gave him a somber nod. Maxwell turned toward the door, missing the speculative smile that threatened that tired face.

Simms cleared his throat.

"Yes, what is it?"

"Your knee, sir. It wants dusting again."

"So it does. Thank you, Simms. And take yourself down to the kitchen before you unpack anything. You must be near starved."

Twenty minutes later the family was gathered on the front porch of Westbourne Hall. Elgin was among them now, freshly shaved with a nick on his chin. Mrs. Finney was there, along with Simms and Lucy and assorted members of the household staff.

Though this venture to East Wallow had been arranged with remarkable haste, neither Maud nor Neville was particularly surprised. They thought it was about time Maxwell took his marriage more seriously. Neville, however, thought they would be better off going to the seaside.

Now, as they were about to leave, Maud warned her loved ones to beware of pickpockets and the food sold by vendors at train stations.

Maxwell really hadn't been listening too closely, because he had something else on his mind. Reaching into his pocket, he produced the amended page of Randy's letter for the last time. He said, "I thought you might like to have this," and pressed it into his aunt's hand. When she looked down at it, he said, "You'll find the thing incomplete, I'm sorry to say. The rest of it was rather personal."

As Maud still looked rather puzzled by what she'd just been given, Maxwell added, "Simms brought along a stack of mail. It contained any number of things." Then he kissed his aunt's cheek, shook hands with his uncle, clapped Elgin on the shoulder with a bit more force than necessary, smiled at the lot of them, and hurried Glori with her cumbersome crinoline into the coach before his relatives could ask any difficult questions. He barely remembered not to ram his top hat into the ceiling of the coach. It seemed as though it took forever for the footman to lift the steps and close the door.

When they were well down the driveway, Maxwell turned around to look back at the house. Everyone was still on the porch; Randy's letter was ghostly white against his aunt's black dress. Slumping back into the seat, Maxwell closed his eyes and hoped the forgery wouldn't return to haunt him. All he had wanted to do was ease his aunt's sorrow. Now what he'd done seemed damned childish.

Glori reached out and squeezed Maxwell's hand. She

wanted to tell him not to worry so about that letter of Randy's. She wanted to tell him that she admired him for his good intentions, whatever might come of them. She wanted to tell him how much she cared but couldn't quite find the words.

Overwhelmingly glad that they were together, Maxwell wrapped his gloved hand around Glori's, lifting it to his lips before he tucked it close to his side. His breath came easier then, filled with the faint scent of wildflowers. Thank you, Glori, he thought, but didn't speak the words.

"You're welcome," she whispered.

When they arrived at Little Woolston Station, there was still time for Maxwell to purchase tickets and have their trunks and boxes waiting on the platform. After consulting the stationmaster's schedule, he asked the coachman to return in ten days' time to meet all the afternoon trains. The coachman stayed now to see that the trunks were taken up and personally set the luncheon basket in the train. Cook, he explained, had insisted upon it, and no one in their right mind argued with Cook. Maxwell considered that statement and agreed.

Thirty-six minutes later the train eased into the station, with great jets of steam hissing from it like a wounded dragon. Only a few others beside the Rutherfords waited to board. One was a small boy who was trying to hide a kitten under his jacket, but the tail kept poking out.

When they located the coach with their first-class compartment, Maxwell helped Glori up the steps. Inside, the high-backed seats were upholstered in blue velvet, though they weren't as soft as they looked. Cream-colored brocade draperies had thick fringe, satin cords, and long tassels. There were brass lamps with polished chimneys fixed to dark paneled walls. The ceiling was painted with cherubs holding garlands of flowers. What little floor there was had a medallion-patterned carpet.

Tapered crystal vases in brass sockets held fresh flowers. For the life of her, Glori couldn't remember anything about the train that had brought them to the Cotswolds on their wedding day.

Now, as then, Maxwell offered Glori a choice of seats. Once again she picked one facing forward, near the window on the shady side. He tucked her skirts out of the way and pulled out a little padded footrest from beneath her seat before seating himself. The coachman leaned inside to place the luncheon basket on the seat, touched his cap, and was gone.

When a double whistle blast cut the air, the train lurched forward, causing the flowers and the fringe on the draperies to tremble. Maxwell tossed his gloves into his upturned hat, unbuttoned his coat, and began an inventory of the luncheon basket. It was everything he expected it would be.

There was a jug of still-warm tea and fine cups from which to drink it. When they became hungry, there were linen serviettes to spread across their laps to catch the crumbs from dainty chicken sandwiches. And there were Maxwell's favorite roast beef sandwiches spread with Durham mustard on thickly sliced French bread. There was pigeon pie to eat from china plates with silver forks. Gingerbread and pickled eggs. Sliced apples wrapped in a cloth. Tea scones and raspberry tarts packed in a tin. In a glass jar there were small towels dampened with lemon water to wipe their hands.

For those who hadn't brought such a basket, the train had a dining coach. Maxwell thought it was awfully inconvenient. The only way one could reach it was to wait for the train to stop, then go along the platform to the dining coach and hope the food was worth it. Likewise, it was impossible to return to one's own seat until the train stopped again. From experience Maxwell much preferred the basket of food from home.

When they arrived at London's huge Paddington Station, Maxwell reminded Glori to keep a tight hold on her purse. Aside from that he had their belongings accounted for and transferred to a horse-drawn coach as soon as the crush would allow. When they were clattering toward their next destination, Glori said, "Maxwell, do you suppose there's enough time to shop before we start north? I would very much like to take a present to my parents."

"We can make the time, if you like."

Promptly lowering the window, Maxwell called out to the driver and directed him to detour though the West End shops, pleased to have some small service to perform for Glori. After all, that's what courting was about, wasn't it? And wasn't courting the reason they had commenced upon this pilgrimage to East Wallow?

Well, for courting and meeting Glori's parents, and Maxwell was looking forward to making their acquaintance. He was determined to get along with them so well that Glori would see that they were all just one happy family. Under such circumstances he was sure that she couldn't help but view him with greater affection. In fact, the idea of the *happy family* became an important part of Maxwell's courting plan.

But there were other things to think about now, for the store windows held a fascinating array of merchandise, and this was Glori's first opportunity to shop in London. Brief as that time would be, Maxwell wanted her to enjoy it.

Glori, however, wasn't looking in the windows. She was looking at what the fashionable ladies were wearing, and she didn't see a single one with a lifted skirt. Not wanting to risk being dressed so differently, she began to twist about awkwardly to find the placket in her skirt where the lifting cords were tied. Maxwell looked at her rather oddly and asked what she was doing as she found both knots and untied them. Before she went out the coach door, Maxwell gave her skirt a discreet tug here and there to make sure it hung properly.

The coachman followed their progress from store to store and stayed within hailing distance. At the end of it all Glori was in possession of a book on *The Propagation and Cultivation of the Oriental Lily* (with beautifully tinted illustrations), a small bundle of paintbrushes and sculpturing tools, and a dress length of printed cambric with lace to go with it. Last of all she had purchased a small porcelain doll in a ruffly dress that lay nestled in silver tissue. Showing it to Maxwell, she explained that it was a surprise for a young friend of hers.

While Glori had been shopping, Maxwell made a purchase of his own. It was a pamphlet on the habits of garden snails and other such things, which he kept in his pocket, out of sight. He intended to be informed when his father-in-law talked about his work with snails.

The afternoon was on the wane by the time they steamed north out of King's Cross Station. When they left the train at the little town of Cresswell, the bulk of their baggage went on to Thirsk without them. There was but one inn, though it served them well enough, providing a tolerable supper and two spartan bedchambers, with promises of hot tea and fresh biscuits for their basket the following morning.

The next day another train carried the Rutherfords in and out of other towns and other stations—the cathedral spires of the city of York came and went. Then the plains of York were left behind for the rolling landscape of the Yorkshire moors. With August upon them the heather was in bloom, carpeting the stark hills with tiny, fragrant, purplish blossoms.

But a traveler could find more than heather if he looked. The harsh land had green valleys tucked within its folds like precious gems. In such sheltered places cows got fat and sheep grew woolly. Small fields of corn ripened beneath cool blue skies. Dry stone fences meandered through the dells outlining patchwork quilts of land, taking an empty turn around a tree that had grown old and disappeared a century or two ago. Today the sun shown brightly on stands of towering elms, maples, pines, and gray stone buildings.

The land was fascinating, Maxwell couldn't deny that, yet he asked, "How did your parents ever come to live in East Wallow?"

Glori looked amused when she turned away from the window. "Papa won a house there in a card game, and the fellow refused to take it back. Papa said he told the man he'd much rather have his horse than his house, as he needed a horse, but the man declined. He said that the place had been left to him, but he couldn't sell it decently, so in losing it he saved himself the taxes."

"Surely a house, if it's sound, must be worth something."

"I suppose it was before the boardingschool closed. That was about forty years ago when someone set it on fire. Everyone says it had been a terrible place where the wealthy hid their unwanted children. The few shopkeepers who stayed in the village afterward did so because they also had sheep to support them."

"Yet your father decided to live in East Wallow?"

"Not until he needed a home for his bride. Fortunately, his grandfather had left him some stocks that paid a small but steady dividend, or finances would have been extremely difficult for them. As you know, a gentleman isn't schooled for much of anything except being a gentleman. Perhaps you recall my telling you that Papa is the black sheep of the family."

"Ah, yes. Instead of a proper marriage to a dowered young woman, he eloped with your mother, and I shall be eternally grateful that he did." A thought later he said, "By the bye, Glori, what do these parents of yours look like? If the neighbors are there when we arrive, I won't know one from the other."

"Oh, you'd know my father. I favor him a great deal, though his hair is darker than mine with a bit of gray.

He's quite tall, you know. Every bit as tall as you are, with a mustache and side whiskers. He has ruddy cheeks and his eyes are twinkly blue, and he smiles a great deal like your uncle Neville."

"You don't know how glad I am to hear it."

"And then there's the cane. I believe he's still using it since he slipped in the garden."

"One tall fair man with a cane."

"Named Jacob."

"And your mother?"

"Not quite as small as Daphne, and her hair is more auburn than red. Mum's eyes are hazelish and her skin is like alabaster. Her side of the family has wonderful skin, you see. She's quite pretty. Papa dotes on her shamefully."

"And her name is Ellen."

"Helen."

"Ah, yes, Helen."

Maxwell had grown pleasantly sleepy while he listened to Glori talk. Her hand rested on the seat between them, and he idly stroked the back of it with his finger. From the corner of his eye he noticed that the rise and fall of her bosom matched his stroke and his eyelids drooped seductively.

It was early afternoon when they arrived at Thirsk, a respectably sized marketplace of ancient lineage. Glori was relieved to find their trunks stacked inside the station, having entertained fears of them going all the way to Darlington or even Newcastle. Worse things had happened. Only last year Mrs. Cleveland, the apothecary's wife, left York with a supply of imported herbs, ginseng root, a half dozen pairs of scissors, select ribbons that matched snips of fabric given to her by the women of East Wallow, hooks and eyes, and a new Izod Patented Corset all packed in her bandbox, none of which were ever seen again.

Maxwell repeated the business of finding a coach and

getting everything loaded into it. Of course the coach-man knew the road to Scarborough very well, and his son remembered the north turn between Helmsley and Pickering that ended at East Wallow, having gone there recently.

Even if he'd been blindfolded, Maxwell would have known when they were nearing East Wallow because Glori became more animated. Before the narrow road tilted into a green valley, she pointed out the spot where a cow had been struck by lightning and the place where gypsies had camped.

When they came into East Wallow, the horses were slowed to a walk and the coachman yelled at a dog that lay sleeping in the road. Glori explained that the blacksmith shop was the fourth building down the road on the left, past the establishment which was the apoth-ecary, post office, and emporium all in one. A small stone church had stained-glass windows that glistened in the sun. While admiring that picturesque sight, Max-well missed the inn—a two-story affair with impres-sive chimneys, a newly painted sign, and an empty stable yard.

Several excited children ran out to stare at the equi-page that rolled into their hamlet, an event too great to be missed. When one small boy cried, " 'Tis our Miss Kendell coom home, she has!" they all ran ahead to the Kendells' house.

The driver followed the lead of the running, prancing children and unceremoniously banged on the roof of the coach with his whip handle to attract the attention of his passengers. He shouted, "This is the place, is it?"

"Oh, yes! Yes, it is!" Glori answered, eager to be out as the coach came to a halt before a place no bigger than the gatekeeper's lodge at Westbourne Hall.

Laughing, Maxwell threw his arms around her and said, "You can't just leap out, you know. Besides being dangerous, your parents will think you're running away from me!"

Glori's smile was pure tease. "We did try to arrange my escape once, didn't we?" When the carriage door was opened and the steps let down, she all but flew into the welcoming arms of her parents. They had heard the noise the children were making and come outside. For an extra coin from Maxwell's pocket the trunks were thumped and bumped inside and upstairs by the coachmen, who agreed to return in a sennight.

Once introductions had been made, they all went into the house to assemble in the best parlor, where Maxwell discovered the simplicity of Queen Anne furniture at its best. And he found that Mrs. Kendell fitted Glori's description very well. The petite dark-haired woman fairly bubbled with excitement over the arrival of her daughter and son-in-law. Kendell himself was more difficult to decipher. Maxwell thought it was because the man must be in some pain, as he still walked with a stick to take the weight off his right knee.

Steaming coffee and peach tarts, from their own hot-house peaches, were soon brought in by a shy young maid with a trace of flour on her chin. As the cups were filled and passed around, the Kendells made inquiry after the state of Lord and Lady Rutherford's health, offering their condolences for the recent bereavement. They tactfully omitted any reference to the scandalous departure of the deceased—a friend in London had kept them apprised of Randy's escapades after Glori married into the Rutherford family. Nor was any comment made on the fact that Maxwell would now inherit.

When the talk drifted to generalities, Glori set her cup aside and said, "I hope you'll excuse me, for I'm positively desperate to put off my traveling clothes." Naturally, everyone excused her. Mrs. Kendell went along to assist, as their only maid was helping Cook with the baking.

Sitting in thoughtful silence, Kendell watched his wife and daughter leave the room. When all that remained was their muffled laughter behind a closed upstairs door, he levered himself out of his chair and said to Maxwell, "Will you join me in the book room? I've got a decent bottle of Scotch in there, and we'll have fewer interruptions."

Maxwell said, "My pleasure," and followed his host out of the parlor and down the hall. It amused him that Glori had left out a bit when she described her father. The man was not only tall and fair but as big as a bull.

While going between parlor and book room Maxwell prepared himself for a *man-to-man* with Kendell, as he supposed the fellow would have something to say regarding *certain intimate considerations* toward Glori due to her recent poor health. After that was out of the way, Maxwell supposed that they might discuss the mess Parliament was in. Perhaps they'd talk about fishing in Scotland or even the strange disease that had been killing so many cattle. He tried to remember everything he'd read the night before about snails.

Kendell said, "Shut the door, if you please," and dropped himself into a big stuffed chair, using the head of his cane to pull the footstool closer so that he could elevate his injured knee. Nodding toward the sideboard, he said, "Help yourself."

"We had fine weather and a clear track all the way," Maxwell volunteered, pouring a drink he didn't actually want but felt obliged to take. "The moors are spectacular this time of year."

Kendell leaned back in his chair and said, "It's nice to have Glori home again. I wanted to bring her back with us when we were at Westbourne Hall, but her mother wouldn't hear of it. You were in Scotland at the time."

"I'm sorry to have missed you, but Glori was happy to have you there. Perhaps you can stay longer next time."

"There won't be a next time," Kendell said. "When you leave here, my daughter stays in East Wallow."

For a moment Maxwell was honestly speechless. Then he said, "That's ridiculous! She's my wife and I'll be taking her home!"

"Ha!" Kendell snorted. "From what little I could get out of Glori when we were at Westbourne Hall, I was left with the firm conviction that you hadn't really wanted to marry her. The wedding seems to have been some invention of Daphne's—God only knows why—but I won't have my daughter traded about like a sow! You may leave whenever you please, but Glori stays *here*." He aimed a meaty finger at the floor.

"For crissakes, Kendell, she won't want to stay here!"

"How can you be so sure? This is her home. She hadn't planned to marry you. Would you actually force her to leave because you have the right to do it?"

"I wouldn't force her to do *anything*! If she wants to stay, she'll stay!"

Kendell finally smiled. "My point exactly."

CHAPTER FOURTEEN

"I hope I'm not interrupting anything," came Glori's cheery voice when she found her father and husband in the book room. Maxwell was just leaving his chair. Her father was pushing the footstool with his cane. Both men assured Glori that her presence was most welcome.

"Papa, would you mind awfully if I took Maxwell for a walk through the village before supper? I expect he's had enough sitting during the past two days."

Before Papa could reply, Maxwell said, "I could do very well with a walk. In fact, I was just about to suggest something of that nature myself." He hoped he hadn't sounded too eager to get out of the house, but he was determined to keep anything from upsetting Glori during the time they would be visiting there.

Crossing the room to the chair where her father sat, Glori leaned over and kissed him on the forehead. "We shall see you at supper, Papa. It's *so* good to be home again."

Kendell smiled indulgently and said, "Though I hate to see you wearing black, I'm awfully glad you're here." Then he smiled ever so nicely at Maxwell, who smiled back as though his cheeks might cramp from the effort.

Maxwell didn't even look for his hat and gloves before

they left the house. Their walk through the village attracted a degree of attention that took Glori by surprise. Women she had known all her life came out of their homes to greet her with a curtsy. Men lowered their eyes and doffed their caps. The children, when they appeared, were instructed to do the same. But they all seemed to regard Maxwell with a mixture of awe and suspicion, falling back respectfully. It left Glori feeling awkward. Only the dog that plodded sluggishly out of the road behaved in any way familiar.

After a jog to the left and another to the right, they passed one vacant building before they came to the emporium. Pausing at the window, they looked over canning supplies, straw hats, and frying pans, then walked on. Behind them a door opened and closed, rattling the glass. Glori turned around at the sound and said, "Good evening, John."

On the step of the emporium with a key in his hand was John Cleveland, who looked up with a gentle smile. "Good evening," he replied. His greeting included Maxwell, but his attention was on Glori. "I heard you had returned, but I hadn't expected to find you here."

"We're out to see a bit of the place," Glori explained, then made the introductions and asked after the young man's family.

Young Mr. Cleveland was a courteous man, yet Maxwell had the feeling that he was defensive. People were sometimes like that in isolated communities, but this man didn't look as though he had lived an isolated life. Neither his dress nor his diction were that of a rustic. When enough polite words had been exchanged, they said their good-byes and went their own ways.

"John is the apothecary's son. He's been at university in Edinburgh," Glori explained to Maxwell when they began walking again. "We've known each other since we were babies because our mothers have been friends for so long."

"That might explain why he seemed to be rather protective of you."

"I suppose it might," Glori answered, letting the subject drop.

A little farther down the lane they came upon the blacksmith's shop, its double doors closed for the day. An empty wagon waited beside the building for a new hub. Glori pointed out the wooden bench against the wall where the old sailor had spent his days entertaining the village children. In the stillness she could hear echos of those old sailing songs and the laughter of the children she had known—the child she had been. She skimmed her hand along the rough stone horse trough, up the pump, and along the smooth iron pump handle, giving it a squeaky pull and push. From down the hill and across the fields came a gust of wind that carried the smell of new-mown hay so fresh she could taste it. Birds warbled night songs in the big trees across the road, and the westering sun dipped everything in butterscotch.

And Maxwell wondered how difficult it was going to be for his Glori to leave East Wallow again.

That's when she turned toward him and asked, "Would you like to see the school?"

"Is it the one where you taught?"

"It's the only one we have."

They hadn't gone very far in that direction when a scruffy little boy popped out from behind a garden wall to stand belligerently in front of Maxwell, his small fists balled for battle. Before the lad could get more than a few words out, an older girl ran up and clamped her hand over his mouth.

" 'e's joost foonnin' is our Robby," she said over his choked cries, looking quite embarrassed as she dragged the child up the path and into the cottage. An unseen hand snapped the door shut.

"What in heaven's name was that about?" Maxwell wondered, dark brows pinched over dark eyes.

Giving his arm a tug, Glori got them moving again. "Robby is the little boy I told you about who said he wouldn't like me anymore if I went to visit my grandmother. It would seem that he's even more upset now because I've moved away. He seems to think you're to blame."

"Is that what he was trying to say? I thought it was something about you being married to someone else."

Glori laughed softly. "I swear that you're my only husband. I think he meant that I might have married someone from here and not moved away."

"Is there someone in East Wallow whom you had intended to marry?" Maxwell wanted to see Glori's face when he asked his question, but he didn't want her to see his face. He was afraid that what he was feeling would show. "Glori?"

"Perhaps Robby thought I might have married John Cleveland. Children have such busy imaginations."

"Had *you* ever thought of marrying him?"

"Not really. We wouldn't have suited, you see, though he is wonderfully dear, and I hope we shall always be friends."

Maxwell made some remark about the value of old friends, while hoping that Glori wouldn't be seeing too much of this one.

When they came upon the little school, it had that deserted summer look. The yard and path had gone to weeds, for classes wouldn't start until the harvest was in. To assure herself that all was well, Glori wiped a clean circle on one dusty windowpane to peek inside. After a moment she turned away, a smudge on the tip of her nose.

Maxwell folded his arms and leaned a shoulder to the stone wall.

"Everything looks the same as it always has," Glori said thoughtfully. "I don't know if that makes me happy or sad."

Up went a questioning brow. "This lack of change, is it a bad thing?"

Clasping her fingers and biting her lip, Glori looked away to the heather-covered hills. "It isn't bad," she said, "it's just . . . it's just that I've always wanted to go somewhere and do something, because nothing ever changed here. But now I've gone and I've done and I've changed and I feel . . . odd."

Maxwell broke off a shaft of tall grass and began to strip the seeds. "A great deal has happened in the past few months. I'm not surprised that you feel a bit different."

"But this is where I've always lived, and I don't like feeling so awfully different, so left out."

"Give the good folk of East Wallow a few days to get used to you again. I don't suppose they've ever known another female who has gone off to convalesce from an inflammation of the lung and returned an apprentice duchess."

Glori smiled then. "I suppose you're right."

Tossing the shredded weed aside, Maxwell rubbed the smudge from the tip of Glori's nose with his thumb. When she looked presentable, he said, "Perhaps we should return to the house. Supper is probably on the table by now."

"If so there won't be anything left when we get there. While I was changing clothes, Mum told me that Cecil Nottingham is staying with us again. He's a parson-geologist from the British Museum and has proven himself an able trencherman."

"Is he visiting in the capacity of trencherman, parson, or geologist?"

"The last time he was here, it was to see our rune stone. He's here now as a fossilist. You see, this spring past—after I'd gone to London—Papa discovered the remains of an ichthyosaurus in the hills and wrote of his find to Mr. Nottingham. Unfortunately, Papa injured his knee before he could dig the thing out. When Mr. Nottingham arrived to see it, he hired some of the local men to help excavate when they weren't busy with their farms or flocks. That's why we're having supper so late. Mr. Nottingham won't be back until it's dark, because the dig site is almost as far as Whitby."

"You've never mentioned your father's propensity for poking about in fossil beds."

"Haven't I? He's done a great deal of it, though Daphne has a horror of anyone finding out. She says people will think Papa is rather strange when, in fact, he's really wonderfully clever. *You* don't think he's strange, do you?"

"Because he shovels up the moors to find old stone bones? Certainly not. It suits the office of a gentleman quite nicely, actually. Look what Charles Darwin managed to accomplish, though now that I think about it, he was another parson-geologist."

The evening meal was served soon after Glori and Maxwell returned to the house—traditional country fare that was all the better for the Irish crystal, Dresden china, and Georgian silver that graced the table. Like the stock certificates, these family treasures had been left to Jacob Kendell by his grandfather.

Predictably, supper conversation centered on progress with the ichthyosaurus and how well articulated the crocodilelike sea creature lay, the blackened fossil even darker than the gray clay in which it was found. And it was gratifyingly complete, with nary a vertibra missing from its fishlike spine, nor any of the bones disturbed in the fore and aft paddles that resembled those of a turtle. Kendell and Nottingham debated its age and gave various opinions of how it came to be there. Maxwell listened while Kendell explained that there were still those who insisted that such fossils had never been living things at all, but nothing more than rocks that God had made into interesting shapes for the amusement of men.

"Anyone who examines them closely can see that they

had once been alive," Kendell said. "These ichthyosaurus bones look good enough to put into the soup pot! But as to whether or not the thing ever lived in an underground sea and was trapped there, I really can't say, but I'll be glad when I can get about and find another."

Maxwell said, "The limitations caused by your injury must be terribly bothersome to you, Kendell. It's fortunate that you have your interest in snails to occupy you closer to home. They're fascinating creatures. I understand that—"

"Fascinating? Snails *fascinating*?" demanded Kendell incredulously. "I've been trying to figure out how to get rid of the damn things for years because they've been chewing up my wife's flowers! How in hell do you think I twisted my knee? I slipped on one of the slimy little buggers after I'd got it with a shovel, that's how!"

"Umm," replied Maxwell, returning to his meal.

Helen Kendell stared daggers at her husband. Glori was none too pleased with her father, either.

Attempting to save the evening from ruin, Mrs. Kendell promptly asked Maxwell about his stay in Scotland. He told her a little about the decorative pieces that the River Clyde Ironworks produced and repeated one of the more amusing Scottish anecdotes he had included in his letters to Glori. When the lady asked him if his business was concluded there, he glanced at Glori and his expression softened. "Yes," he said. "Everything is quite finished in Glasgow."

Time after time Cecil Nottingham speared his fork through a piece of beef, a bit of Yorkshire pudding, some beans, piled on a morsel of potato, and downed it while discussing the possibility of a plesiosaurus site in the same layer as the ichthyosaurus, for it wasn't unusual to find them similarly situated in these layers from the Liassic period. The after-dinner conversation continued in the parlor over coffee, reviewing the laborious progress of the dig in great detail.

All of it rattled past Glori, for her thoughts were else-where. She had expected that she and Maxwell would become closer while they were in this smaller house with fewer people and less happening to keep them apart. Instead, she could feel him withdrawing from everyone, herself included. It was easy enough to understand after the way her father had behaved at table, for she was aware of Maxwell's aversion to scenes. The evening had become intolerable, and she had to do something about it.

As soon as there was the slightest pause in the con-versation, Glori lifted her chin and calmly said, "I trust you will excuse us, for we are fatigued to the bone and must retire."

Maxwell had been studying the tips of his shoes, so no one saw his look of surprise that promptly became a grin which he disguised as a yawn and covered with a negligent hand to smooth his mustache.

Neither Glori's announcement nor Maxwell's yawn pleased Kendell.

Standing, Maxwell said good night. He thought about yawning again, but decided not to overdo it. Only a few minutes ago he'd been dreading to learn what the sleep-ing arrangements would be like. Now he was eager to find out.

He held the chamber stick aloft as they ascended the stairs, leaving Glori with her hands free to lift her skirt and hold the balustrade. As soon as they were within the confines of her old bedroom, her serene exterior crum-pled, and she turned a troubled face to Maxwell.

"I'm so terribly sorry about the horrid reception you've had in East Wallow, and what happened at table was worst of all. I just can't imagine what got into Papa!"

Maxwell quickly put the candle aside and wrapped Glori in his arms, holding her close. Hesitantly her fin-gers curled into the fabric of his coat, which sent a shud-der through him. He had begun to think that whatever could go wrong would go wrong, but all that was behind them now. He said, "The old boy might be a bit crusty, but it isn't the end of the world." When Glori cuddled a little closer, he held her all the tighter and rested his cheek on the crown of her head. "Due to the circumstances of our marriage, your parent doesn't think of me as a part of your life, you see, but something like another twisted knee that must be tolerated until it goes away."

"But he was so rude!" Glori wailed. "I suspect Mum will speak quite sharply when they close their door tonight."

Such a possibility struck Maxwell as awfully humorous. Smiling, he eased his hold and lifted Glori's chin, intending to say something to make her laugh. But when he looked into those shadowy amethyst eyes, his smile faded while his pulse quickened. He desperately wanted the woman he held, and she was already his wife! His soft, warm wife. With hips. And they were alone. Erotic images assaulted his mind to be swept along by an incredible surge of tenderness. He had to swallow hard to rid himself of the lump in his throat.

"Glori," he whispered, "we shall muddle through this, I promise. Just remember that I . . . that is, we . . . " Flickering candlelight painted distracting shadows around the room when his lips brushed hers in a gentle query, drawing an ardent reply. That reply sent his well-laid courting plans up in smoke.

Drawing breath again, they both looked rather stunned. Smiling shyly, Glori slid her arms beneath his coat and around his waist to lean against him in trusting contentment. His shirt was smooth, and his body was warm. His heart beat as wildly as her own. There didn't seem to be enough words in the world to express how she felt, yet one spoken word might have broken the spell.

The waiting was over.

With impatient fingers Maxwell probed Glori's hair for the pins that held it coiled and littered the floor with them. After drawing her hair aside, he eased his hands over the back of her dress to the topmost hook and set it free, then the next and the next. By the time he reached the last of the little fasteners, he was trying to keep his hands from shaking. He strummed his thumb down the corset laces that lay beneath her corset cover and asked, "Shall I help you with these as well?"

She shook her head no.

Yet neither of them seemed inclined to move until Maxwell took a deep breath and pushed himself away. He picked up the long flannel nightgown that had been laid across the bed and handed it to Glori.

Blushing, she took it and fled behind the folding screen, nearly tipping it over when she caught it with her skirt. But instead of undressing, she merely clutched the gown in cold hands and felt much like she did that night she tried to go out Daphne's window on a rope of knotted bedding and draperies. When she looked down at the ground, she had been too frightened to do what she was supposed to do.

Now she wished she had a door to run through or wings to fly away. She simply *couldn't* put on a piece of flannel and march out there where Maxwell was. A proper lady was supposed to be in her best nightclothes, tucked up in the marriage bed to await her husband—who would then explain what happened next.

Fortunately, reason returned and she knew that she couldn't stay where she was forever. If Maxwell came looking for her, she'd be more embarrassed than frightened. Besides, the final decision to marry him had been her own, and she had come to love him dearly. She intended to be his wife in fact as well as name. It was that intention, however, which caused her considerable anxiety, for she still didn't know exactly what being a wife entailed, but she knew she wasn't going to find out if she stayed where she was.

After Glori disappeared behind the folding screen,

Maxwell impatiently shed his coat, his waistcoat, then his tie. Glancing at the washstand, he wondered if he'd have time to shave, and decided that he wouldn't.

He pushed the elastic braces off his shoulders and let them hang, then pulled his shirttails free and began to undo the buttons. Just looking at the screen that concealed Glori caused his virile imagination to smolder. When her dress and ruffled petticoat came over the top, he wondered how long he could keep breathing. A shirt button broke off in his hand, and he looked at it as if he'd never seen a button before. Both shirt and button were tossed aside.

To remove his shoes he sat on the edge of the rope-spring bed that groaned under his weight. A door opened. A door closed. He looked around the darkened room. There was nothing to see, yet footsteps crossed the floor.

In a harsh whisper he said, "Glori, who's walking around and where are they?"

Hanging her crinoline over the corner of the screen, she whispered, "I think it's Mr. Nottingham in the room next door."

"These walls must be paper thin!" Maxwell replied, listening to Nottingham's shoes hit the floor before he poured water into a basin and splashed about.

"Daphne and I always had to whisper when we had company so they couldn't hear us."

Nottingham clanked a glass and gargled.

To a muffled chorus of disgruntled mutterings, Maxwell left the creaking bed, found his shirt, and put it on. Then he found the lamp and lit it, affording the discovery of a chair, flowers painted on the wardrobe doors, and a daybed in the far corner. The presence of that narrow bed gave him cause to rejoice until he realized that it, too, creaked. While he stood there trying to figure out what to do about two grumbling beds on his honeymoon, Glori added her corset and stockings to the clothing that draped the folding screen.

From the room next door came the unmistakable groan from another web of rope-springs as Nottingham took to his own bed.

A chemise, then drawers joined the other clothes, and Maxwell knew that there wasn't anything left to be hung out. He never thought he'd be glad to see Glori in that shapeless nightgown, but he would be now.

Nottingham must have rolled over because his bed cried out again. Maxwell grabbed his coat.

"Is something the matter?" Glori quietly asked when she emerged wearing her flannel cocoon.

"We have a bit of a problem," Maxwell answered stiffly as he attended to his buttons.

"Are you getting dressed or undressed?"

"Dressed."

"Why?"

"Because I haven't a nightshirt."

"Shall I get one from Papa?"

"No, that won't help the problem, I'm afraid."

"What is the problem?"

"The problem is that we must whisper in here!"

Maxwell's reasoning was obviously lost on Glori. It wasn't going to be easy for him to explain things, either. When she raised a slender hand to brush a shock of dark hair from his forehead, he put his hands on her shoulders and held her at arm's length.

He was very quiet and equally serious when he said, "Glori, for all that we've been married for months, we are still quite *new* to each other."

"Yes, we are."

"When a man and a woman share a bed, they need a certain amount of privacy so that they can . . . well . . . be private."

"Of course."

"Especially when they've never shared a bed before."

"We've shared a bed at the Willows," Glori reminded him.

"We shared a bed, but we didn't share each other when we shared a bed." He could see that Glori didn't understand that, either.

Frustrated beyond belief, Maxwell took her by the hand, led her to the bed, and held up the covers. "Get in."

She did. The bed groaned loudly. Maxwell groaned softly.

Nottingham pounded on the wall and called out, "Are you chaps all right in there?"

"We're as right as rain!" Maxwell shouted back, raking his hands through his hair.

"That's what I mean!" he growled, pointing a loaded finger toward the offending voice. "We've hardly begun our honeymoon, and we're sharing our bed with a petrified parson from the British Museum!"

Glori simply stared as Maxwell took a few turns around the room and wondered when he would calm down. She wanted desperately to be held in his arms and kissed again. She was all set to find out about sanctified joy. But unless her husband stopped marching about and got into her bed she would never know.

Maxwell splashed cold water on his face and grabbed a towel. When he could finally return to the edge of Glori's bed, his voice was so soft that he could hardly hear it himself. He said, "Glori, do try to understand. Making love, especially for the first time, can be rather . . . well . . . "

"Yes?"

"Resonant."

"Resonant?"

"For crissakes, I'm trying to make you understand why we can't sleep in the same bed until we can be *alone*!" His patience was obviously wearing thin while his desire was obviously not.

"But if we don't do anything unnecessarily resonant, or any mooing—"

"Mooing?"

Pure devilment dimpled Glori's cheeks. "You see, when I was little and asked why the cows were so awfully noisy on occasion, Papa said that they were getting married and—"

The laugh started as a soft rumble that ended before Maxwell brought down the plaster, for the absurdity of their situation was too much for him to bear with much dignity.

Nottingham pounded on the wall and cried, "Enough! Enough, I say! It isn't decent!"

Stifling a laugh of her own Glori held up her arms, inviting Maxwell into her heather-scented bed, knowing that he wanted to be with her as badly as she wanted to be with him.

But he only shut his eyes and shook his head. When he looked at Glori again, he jabbed a thumb over his shoulder and whispered, "I'll be sleeping *there*. You'll be sleeping *here*. Don't touch the lamp!"

Removing his coat but leaving his shirt and trousers, Maxwell took to the daybed. It creaked abominably. It complained even worse when he shifted around to unfold the quilt and cover himself.

After twenty or thirty seconds of silence, Glori said, "Do you have a pillow?"

"No, but—"

"I'll bring you one."

"Glori, stay precisely where you are!"

"I'm only trying to make you more comfortable!"

"Believe me when I tell you that despite your good intentions, you would only make me more uncomfortable than I already am. Stay there!"

All was quiet again until she said, "Maxwell . . . "

"Hmm?"

"That bed you're sleeping in . . . it was Daphne's, you know. She liked being closer to the window."

Maxwell's bare feet hit the floor like thunder. Glori was expecting it, for she didn't think he'd care to sleep in Daphne's bed. When he came striding over, she was prepared with a welcoming smile. When he snatched a pillow and turned away, she asked, "What are you doing now?"

"I'm going to sleep on the floor!"

"You can't do that . . . a mouse might bite you!"

"Tonight I'd bite it back!"

Even the floor creaked.

Folding his pillow and pulling at his too-short quilt, Maxwell passionately wished that they'd never left Westbourne Hall. He could hardly wait to get back. There his only problem was Elgin Farley's annoying interest in his wife.

Earlier in the day, about the time the younger Rutherfords' train had been chugging into Thirsk, Maud was taking tea in her private sitting room. She had been reading that single page of Randy's letter again, smoothing it over her lap, tracing the scribbled words with her finger. Since receiving the letter the day before, she had memorized every word.

The page began with only part of a sentence that read, " . . . to tell you that I shall love my mother quite as well. I swear she's not so bad, I've known worse." After that followed a rambling account of something else—Maud supposed it must have been a boxing match. None of it made a great deal of sense, she could see that, but she knew that excessive drink did such things to people.

In a nearby chair Neville read through the papers that had been brought to him by courier from London. Even though he tried to apply himself to his work, his attention was constantly drawn to his wife and the letter on her lap. Neville tapped his papers into a neat pile and slid them into an envelope, then set them aside before leaving his chair.

"May I?" he asked, reaching for Randy's letter.

Maud handed it to him and took up her stitching.

Neville walked to the window, partly for the light, partly to hide his thoughts from his wife. He was aware that she thought Randy had been drinking when he'd written this piece. Perhaps he had been. Something had to account for the letter's appearance and content. Unlike his wife, however, Neville had had several encounters with their son when he'd been drinking. He invariably found the young man quarrelsome—far from saying anything sentimental. He couldn't imagine Randy being as effusive as this unless he'd been asking for money, which he hadn't.

Neville's gaze shifted back across the room to his wife while his mind raced to catch something that danced just beyond his grasp. There was that niggling feeling that the letter he held wasn't quite what it was supposed to be. Still the RR signed with a flourish at the bottom of the page was surely that of his son, so it had to be his letter. Yet . . .

Neville pushed the thoughts away. If having such a letter from Randy eased his wife's aching heart, then he was glad of it. When Neville had gotten into dangerous territory as a boy, his nanny used to tell him to let sleeping dogs lie. This letter, he decided, was just such a dog. Carefully laying the page on the table next to her teacup, Neville turned to his wife and said, "Maud?"

She looked up expectantly.

"Those tiny stitches must be tiring your eyes something awful. Perhaps you'll allow me to read to you for a while." Holding out his hand, he said, "Let us go down to the library and select something together, shall we?" Maud put aside her needlework, and Neville helped her to her feet. When he straightened her cap, his palm lingered against her cheek and he said, "I do love you, Maud."

She put her hand over his and said, "I love you, too."

There was an ink mark on her finger, and Neville took out his handkerchief to rub it away.

CHAPTER FIFTEEN

THE first thing he was aware of was her laugh; soft, almost musical, floating on the air to blow in his ear and tease his dreams. Still half asleep, he smiled and reached for her and barked his knuckles on a leg of the dressing table. Thus Maxwell recalled that he was sleeping on the floor. Glori's voice was coming in through the open bedroom window.

His fingers hurt. He squeezed them—it didn't help. Everything hurt, actually, not just his fingers, and he slowly rolled over on the braided rug, displacing the extra blanket that Glori must have spread over him. He was glad he hadn't known when she'd done it, for he probably wouldn't have let her go.

Now, however, he had to get on with the day, so he got to his feet and pressed a broad hand to his lower back. He was glad there wasn't anyone to see his miserable state. He didn't want to think about spending another night like last night. Another day like yesterday wasn't to his liking, either. Between Jacob Kendell's antagonism and Cecil Nottingham's proximity, Maxwell thought his brain and body would become throbbing mutton before the week was done. Then there were the villagers, who watched him as though he might be another Bluebeard.

Scratching his bristly chin, he went to the window and pushed the lacy curtains aside to see if his wife was really out there.

She was.

A table had been carried out to the back lawn and spread with peaches. That's where Glori and her mother were sitting. Bits and pieces of their conversation reached the upstairs window as they dipped paintbrushes into a jar and applied whatever it was to the fruit. Maxwell remembered helping his mother and Cook with the same task when he was a boy and looked forward to offering his expertise to these ladies with the same job, but he didn't care to leave the window just yet. He simply wanted to look at Glori from where he was because he couldn't very well go outside and sit there and stare at her.

This was the first time he'd seen her with her hair caught up in loose curls on top of her head, pinned haphazardly to keep it out of her way. A few fair curls had escaped the pins to hang in appealing disarray, and he thought she was beautiful. He liked to think that her glow had something to do with what had happened last night—or what had *almost* happened last night. As agonizing as it had been, it still made him smile. He thought of gum arabic.

He'd just remembered that it was gum arabic his mother had used to preserve peaches. One layer of gum arabic followed by two coats of varnish over unblemished peaches would keep them for the winter. After the varnish dried it had been his job to pack the fruit in layers of sawdust in wooden boxes. The boxes were then stored on shelves in the cellar. And he remembered that one day in the middle of winter, he had crept into that cellar and taken one of those peaches, peeled the hard covering off like a rind, and sunk his teeth into the sweet juicy flesh—which reminded him of Glori.

He thought he'd better think of something else.

Scanning the area around that outside worktable, he looked for the necessary boxes. After he shaved and made himself generally presentable, he intended to find out where those boxes were kept and make certain that the sawdust was dry.

That's when Jacob Kendell came upon the scene, full of smiles. He bent over to kiss Glori on the forehead, then his wife on the cheek. In one hand he had his cane. In the other he carried a box with sawdust. Maxwell left the window knowing that there was no place for him among that closed set.

With little in the way of enthusiasm, Maxwell eventually went outside to bid good morning to his wife and her parents. He told them that he'd just had breakfast and could do with some exercise, so he was going to take another walk around the village.

"Oh, do stay for just a little while longer," Glori implored. "We'll have coffee soon, with peach—"

"Let the man go," said Kendell as he inspected the coated fruit. "He's just said he has things to do. He'll be back for tea, I expect."

It would have been so easy for Maxwell to tell his father-in-law to go to hell, but he didn't. He had only to keep the peace for a matter of days. Stepping closer to Glori, he repeated, "We shall muddle through. I won't be so very far away, you know."

"Yes, I know," she replied, though she was obviously disappointed. When she looked up at him, he dropped the lightest of butterfly kisses on the tip of her nose. She blushed, he grinned. Kendell scowled. His wife kicked him in the leg under the table.

For company Maxwell had the Kendell's terrier dog, which walked and pranced along beside him, stopping now and then at a familiar gate post, racing to catch up. Together they walked down the lanes and around the church, going inside to have a better look at the stained-glass windows. The dog, named Dog, waited outside the emporium when Maxwell went in to make the purchase of a handful of peppermint sweets and nightshirt. That striped garment was too wide, too short, and the only one available. It had also been around since the inn had seen more traffic. The men in East Wallow didn't buy nightshirts, Maxwell was told. They had mothers or wives or sisters who made them. Before the transaction was complete, Maxwell was glad that young Cleveland hadn't been the one behind the counter. Buying a nightshirt from a stranger wasn't difficult at all. Buying a nightshirt from a man who wanted to be the one sleeping with his wife might have been devilishly uncomfortable. He supposed it would have been even worse for Cleveland.

When Maxwell left the emporium, the position of the sun told him that it wasn't yet the hour for tea, so he and Dog had to find something else to occupy their time. That something else was the blacksmith shop. The big doors were open now, the fire glowing. A horse was being fitted with an offside hind shoe, and Maxwell leaned a shoulder to the doorjamb to watch. When the broad-shouldered smithy in the leather apron looked up, he said, "Good day, m' lord. It's soomthin' ya are wantin', is it?"

"No, thank you, I'm just looking about and content to watch you for a bit, if I may. The name's Rutherford, and I'm staying with the Kendells."

"Aye . . . the Rutherford of Westbourne Hall and the next duke at that, ya are. We knew all aboot ya here, bein' Miss Glori's hoosban' an' all." The man then turned to his forge, and a boy of about seven or eight years sprang to the huge bellows, his steady pulls providing the additional oxygen that changed the coals from red to white hot. When the color was right, the burly smith used long tongs to bury the horseshoe among the hottest coals until the iron was softened. The hammering, cooling, and fitting of the shoe continued without further comment until the thing was cooled and nailed to the horse's horny foot.

When the file was brought out to trim the hoof, Maxwell said, "I understand that your uncle, a seafaring man, used to stay here with you. My wife has spoken fondly of him."

The smithy grinned and said, "And a salty old fellow he was," and went on to relate some tales of the old man's sailing days that had never reached Glori's tender ears. On this improbable note the rest of the morning was spent, with Maxwell and the mutt returning to the Kendell cottage just in time for tea, which was taken in ominous silence.

While Glori and her mother finished the peaches, Maxwell spent the afternoon with Dog, the two of them poking about the fields and through the orchards they hadn't seen that morning. Supper that night was actually improved by Cecil Nottingham's presence. There was scant opportunity for petty remarks when the man was worried about running behind schedule. His workers would be gone to the Friday Fair in Helmsley, just when he needed them the most.

"If you can use my help, I'm glad to offer it," said Maxwell, seeing a way out of his present confinement and taking it.

"It won't be easy work," Nottingham warned, "but you appear to be set up well enough to manage—I suppose you've gone to a gymnasium. But I'll knock you up in the morning, if you like," to which Maxwell agreed.

When Glori went to bed, Maxwell deliberately lingered behind to talk with Nottingham about the dig. When he did retire, it was to find his new nightshirt on Glori's bed. Glori, bless her, had taken Daphne's daybed near the window.

While Maxwell was undressing, Nottingham pounded on the wall and called out, "Good night! Sleep tight!" Maxwell shook his head and slapped the wall in reply before climbing into his creaking bed, hoping that the noise hadn't awakened Glori. He then spent altogether too much time thinking about her silky hair and soft mouth and other agreeable things.

The next morning he was up and gone without Glori hearing him leave the room. She had hoped they might have breakfast together, but her romantic ideas would have to be trimmed even further to fit reality. Before anyone noticed, she made up the little bed she had slept in, unwilling to have even the maid know that she hadn't shared her husband's pillow.

Glori spent the day with her mother, compounding a supply of cosmetics. They made up a pomade for removing wrinkles by taking two ounces of onion juice, the same quantity of white lily, the same of honey, and one ounce of white wax. All of it went into a new tin pan on the stove. When the wax was melted, Glori removed it from the heat and stirred it with a wooden spoon until cool, then put it into small jars.

Hair coloring was made by boiling a mixture of mulberry leaves, walnut bark, and gallnuts in wine. Though any number of leaves, barks, and roots could be substituted, they all had to be used with a leaden comb. Glori recognized the preparation as the one that kept Cook's hair a glossy black beneath her white cap.

They began to mix a tooth powder of Peruvian bark, myrrh, chalk, Armenian bole, and powdered orrisroot until Helen Kendell noticed that the box marked Armenian bole was nearly empty, and they had to set the incomplete mixture aside. For the lad that helped in the stable, they made up a wart remover of burnt willow and strong vinegar.

That night, when Maxwell and Nottingham returned from the dig, they washed outside at the pump before coming into the house to take turns in the bathroom that Jacob Kendell had added to his house. Even after his warm soak, Maxwell was still limping. Upon inquiry

Glori learned that a rock had rolled onto his foot. At table she saw that his knuckles were badly skinned, and he had blisters on his hands. Still, he was smiling, though it was a tired smile.

"It's a grand beast, this ichthyosaurus," Maxwell said through cracked lips. "I hadn't realized they had so many sharp teeth. This specimen even has fossilized octopus remains in its stomach cavity. I thought it was unfortunate that its tail had been dislocated, but Nottingham says they're all like that."

Glori was glad that Maxwell had found something to make his week in the moors more tolerable. She thought about arranging a visit to the site but knew that such a jaunt would bring her father along and that would surely destroy any pleasure Maxwell might find in his work.

When Maxwell dragged his weary self up to the creaking bed that night, Glori dabbed his red face and lips with some of the sunburn wash her mother had made the summer before. There wasn't a twitch from him when she applied a soothing salve to his dry mouth. He was asleep before she had the bottle of healing wash recorked.

When Glori got into her little bed, she lay there twisting the satin ribbons on her night dress, wondering what had happened to the cozy week she and Maxwell were going to spend together. The week with walks and talks and sanctified joy.

Once again Maxwell and Nottingham left early in the morning. The ladies gathered rose petals to make rosewater. They finished in time to receive the apothecary's wife for tea. Later that day they went through the big chests in the attic and picked out some woolen blankets to be aired for use as the nights grew colder. Glori searched her mother's recipe book again and copied down the ingredients for the salve she had used on Maxwell's mouth. She supposed the housekeeper at Westbourne Hall could easily supply the white wax, beef marrow, and white pomatum, but she didn't know about the alkanet root.

After that she chatted with a group of children who had gathered around the front gate just in case she happened to come out. She petted the cat and scratched the dog and thought about what Maxwell was doing in the hills, hoping his blisters weren't getting any worse.

When Sunday morning came to East Wallow, Glori yawned and stretched and silently rejoiced. There had been no break-of-dawn departure for Maxwell. He was right there in the bed across the room, softly snoring. Once during the night she had gotten up to roll him over so that he'd stop making that awful noise. The distance back to her own little bed had been cold and lonely indeed.

Now there came a soft rapping on the door and the maid called, "Breakfast time, Miss Glori." The girl went on to Cecil Nottingham's chamber door to repeat the notice.

"Right-o!" trumpeted Nottingham on the other side of the wall.

That familiar voice struck a bell in Maxwell's head. Groggy, he sat up and muttered, "Damn."

Glori whispered, "Maxwell, there's no reason to rush. It's Sunday. We'll have breakfast soon and then go to church." She pushed herself up in bed and began to undo her hair.

Maxwell flopped back against his pillow thinking that he could give greater thanks for this day of rest if he didn't have to get out of bed at all.

In the room next door Cecil Nottingham left his squeaking bed to dress.

"The minister comes to East Wallow every other Sunday, and this is one of those Sundays," Glori said in a hushed voice when she left her bed for the dressing table. She combed her fingers through her hair, and it fell down her back in satiny waves before she picked up her brush.

Soon Nottingham's chamber door opened and closed, and he went stomping down the stairs. Then the front door opened and closed with a bang.

"Mr. Nottingham always goes out for a brisk walk on the mornings he isn't digging," said Glori, losing count of her brush strokes.

Maxwell seemed to come awake then, droopy-eyed but smiling. Throwing back the covers, he was across the floor and back to the groaning bed in less than half a minute with Glori in his arms. Looking more than a little pleased with herself, she had wrapped her arms around his neck and held on and that's how they fell on the bed. She still had her hairbrush—he tossed it to the floor. Then he sighed and she sighed and his fingers got tangled in the pretty ribbons on her gown.

"Is this your tent?" He meant her nightgown. She said yes, and he pulled the ribbons off with one impatient yank. When he undid the first few buttons to leave a line of nibbly kisses along her throat, she wasn't reciting scriptures. In fact, she found it impossible to think about anything else at all.

But Maxwell soon stopped his kissing to growl, "Glori, your father is knocking at our door. You'd better answer unless you want him in here with us."

Kendell knocked again and called, "Glori! Are you awake? We're having your favorite waffles for breakfast!"

Red-faced, Glori was not only awake but ready to bolt. "Yes, Papa," she answered weakly over Maxwell's shoulder, "I'm awake."

"Remember that Nottingham is here. If you don't hurry, you won't get anything!"

Maxwell chose not to comment upon that remark. It wouldn't have been gentlemanly. He only mumbled, "Glori, your father is a fiend," and rolled away from her. Then he said, "You get up first. I'm just going to lay here for a little while."

She got up first.

He lay there for a long while.

There were still plenty of waffles.

The Kendell pew in the village church was roomy enough for them all, with damask-covered cushions on the seats and well-oiled hinges on the little door.

When the last of the distant parishioners arrived with their baskets and bundles, the service began. Sitting at the end of the bench, Maxwell felt a light touch on his shoulder. The toucher proved to be a child in the pew beside theirs, a little girl in a straw hat who studied him through big blue eyes. Her father—Maxwell supposed it was her father—turned her toward the front of the church and sat her down. There was no one else, no woman in their pew. The man gave Maxwell an apologetic smile, then glanced at Glori. It was just a glance, no more than that, yet Maxwell had seen it before. That fleeting look of adoration had appeared on the face of John Cleveland. But this man was no green sprig in his father's shop. Whatever he did he did it well from the appearance he made. There was a solid maturity about him. There was the child at his side. And he remembered the porcelain doll that Glori had purchased for a special little friend.

It was the longest sermon Maxwell ever sat through.

The worshippers who remained inside the church after the service was over were those who had come a long way. Some of them had covered the distance on foot. As was the custom when home was so far removed, these people spread their tablecloths on the bare benches and laid out their cheeses, meat pies, and fresh bread for their midday meal. It was also a time to socialize before they began the journey home.

When they went outside, Glori and Maxwell were greeted warmly by family friends. Then the minister arrived and scolded them ever so gently for not having been married here in East Wallow. The child with the big blue eyes came over and tried to lean on Glori's skirts. Glori swung the little one up in her arms and made them all known to one another. In this way Maxwell was introduced to Alexander Holden, gentleman, and his daughter, Emily. Emily said how do you do and, with a pronounced lisp, told them that she was four years old, holding up the requisite fingers so that Maxwell would understand how old she really was.

Kendell let it be known that Holden was a widower who had land farther down the valley. "Not the size of Westbourne Hall, you understand, but respectable enough." Then Kendell addressed Holden and said, "You'll come to dinner, of course."

Holden's eyes were drawn to Glori for a moment before he politely declined, saying that his sister would be waiting for them at home.

"But Glori has a present for Emily," Kendell said, loud enough for the child to hear. And, hearing that, the little girl begged to go and of course the father relented.

So they sat down eight to dinner; the five regulars, two Holdens—with the child seated in a tall chair that had been brought down from the attic—and the minister, a quiet sort who often took his Sunday meal with them. Wherever the dinner conversation started, it always seemed to drift back to the affairs of East Wallow and things that didn't include Maxwell.

After dinner, in the parlor, Glori gave Emily her doll. Maxwell couldn't help but see the strong attachment she felt for the child. It seemed odd that Glori had never mentioned her. Would it have been too difficult for her to speak of this little girl and her father?

Through the muted conversation over coffee cups came a small clear voice that lisped, "Papa wath going to go to London to thee Mith Glori and buy me a dolly, but he didn't go. Ith thith the thame dolly?"

Holden said, "This is a different doll, Emily, but it's just as nice as the one I was going to buy for you." Then he asked to see it more closely and admired its pretty dress.

Another man might have scolded the child for the innocent but revealing remark, but Holden hadn't and Maxwell had to admire him for it. Helen Kendell easily changed the subject by trotting out the fossil excavation again, which set Nottingham off and running on his favorite subject.

Eventually Holden consulted his watch and announced that he and his daughter had to leave. He collected the tired child and gave his thanks for the Kendells' hospitality and Emily's doll, shaking hands all around. When he reached Maxwell, he paused, an eyebrow lifting a fraction in question, his expression intense. Maxwell's response was imperceptible to everyone but the man who had questioned him. It had taken very little for the fellow to ask if Maxwell would love and care for Glori. By the slight lowering of his eyelids Maxwell gave his assurance that it would be so.

But that exchange didn't tell Maxwell what Glori's sentiments were now that she had seen Alexander Holden again. This man from her past would willingly be a part of her future if she gave him the chance.

When the dinner guests were gone, Glori found the house almost suffocating. "I think this might be a fine time to explore the hills," she said to Maxwell. "Would you like to go?"

"Do you feel up to it?"

"If I get tired, I'll turn around."

Of course Maxwell knew better, remembering the time they had ended up in the barn loft to rest because Glori hadn't told him how tired she had become, but right now they both had to get out of the house. Glori changed from her Sunday clothes into plainer stuff and her comfortable button-up shoes more quickly than Maxwell thought possible.

*　　*　　*

It had been a climb to which Glori was no longer accustomed, though Dog was happy to have her company again no matter how slowly she went. When they reached the crest of the heather-covered hill, Maxwell spread out her heavy cloak, and she gave him a tired smile as she sank to her knees on the shiny black lining. Brittle plants crackled softly beneath her. She untied her hat and the wind pulled at her hair, catching it around her spectacles. Then she laid down and looked up to watch the gulls row across a sea-blue sky with snow-white wings, bound for the North Sea to the east. Insects hopped and buzzed among the blossoms and bracken; the sun was warm on her face. Glori's eyelids drifted shut as she inhaled deeply of the spicy-sweet air, trying to soak up enough of the feel and sound and smell of the day to last her through the winter. Maxwell had tossed his tweed hat next to Glori's bonnet and laid himself down to share her view of the world. Dog went off to chase butterflies.

In a drowsy voice she said, "It's difficult to believe that in a few months a freezing wind will come screaming across these moorlands."

Maxwell reached beyond the edge of Glori's cloak to break off a sprig of heather and brushed it across her lips.

Glori rubbed her mouth to stop the tickling, then removed her spectacles so that she could see Maxwell properly. Reaching out, she touched the tiny mole on his left cheek and said, "A penny for your thoughts."

He cocked one eyebrow and said, "A penny, indeed. I daresay they're worth a good deal more than that."

"A shilling then, but it's my final offer. My credit is quite good."

"You may have only a few of my less profound thoughts for a shilling on tick, madam." But after staring across the green valley for a minute or two, Maxwell became more serious. He said, "I was thinking that your father is a tough nut to crack. Though he hasn't gone as far as a bun fight at teatime, he's hardly civil."

"It's true, I'm sorry to say. I don't know what to suggest, either."

Maxwell shrugged and said, "At least the weather has been decent. We've got the entire ichthyosaurus wrapped in plaster bandages, you know, ready to haul out. Nottingham has arranged for a wagon to be brought to the site tomorrow morning. Did I tell you that he's invited me to come to the museum to help prepare it? Or at least examine its progress."

"Will you go?"

"I'm rather looking forward to it, actually. Would you like to come with me?"

"I'd love to! Have you any more thoughts left for my shilling?"

It was a long moment before he said, "I was just thinking that tomorrow we'll have to pack." He looked at Glori then, waiting for her to say something about going home, but she said nothing. Even so, he didn't think she would stay in East Wallow no matter what her father had said. If she planned to stay here, she wouldn't have said she wanted to go to the British Museum with him.

But now there was Alexander Holden to consider, for there wasn't a doubt in Maxwell's mind that Glori would have married the man one day if Daphne hadn't come up with a plan of her own. It made him wonder if there were any slumbering affections that might have been awakened in Glori's tender heart when she saw him again. What if she wanted to see more of him to be certain of her feelings? Her father had certainly encouraged it.

Picking apart a twiggy piece of heather, Glori said, "A week here just isn't enough time to get to know everyone again."

Maxwell hardly moved when he asked, "How much longer do you want to stay?"

"Oh . . . perhaps a month."

"A month!"

He didn't want to be away from Glori for that long, especially with this Holden fellow about. Yet he knew he couldn't stay in East Wallow much longer without a head-on collision with Jacob Kendell. Nor did he care to be away from his aunt and uncle for such an extended period—not right now.

"Maxwell?"

"I was just thinking that a month is an awfully long time."

"I suppose it is, especially with the way Papa has been acting, but next time it should be better."

"Next time?"

"Next time, when we might stay for a month. Now I just want to go home."

"Home? To Westbourne Hall?"

"Maxwell, it's still there, isn't it?"

"Of course!" he said, breathing easier.

"What are you thinking about now?" Glori asked when Maxwell developed a positively wicked grin.

"You don't want to know."

"I *do* want to know."

"It'll cost you another shilling."

"Oh, all right!"

He moved with a sensuous grace when he rolled onto his side and propped himself up on one elbow. A gust of wind lifted the dark hair that fell across his forehead. His dusky, bronze-flecked eyes were twinkling when he said, "I was wondering if we'd get caught if we made love right here in the heather. Don't look so shocked—you did ask, you know. But I expect every family in the village has a spyglass to look for stray sheep and cows, and we'd be the talk of the county for generations to come."

Glori wagged her finger at him and said, "You're practically indecent."

He caught her hand in his and readily agreed. While his mind wandered among those delightful indecencies, Glori twined her fingers through his and fell into a light sleep. Ankles crossed, an arm angled beneath his head, Maxwell dozed beside her.

He awoke to a cooler breeze, a lowering sun, and a maddening tickle in his ear. A sleepy swat connected with a bit of heather in a feminine hand. Smiling, he pulled Glori into his arms, and she snuggled to him. Rubbing his face against her hair, he said, "I'll be glad when we're home again, though your father will be unhappy when you leave."

"I thought he would understand that I now have a life beyond East Wallow, but he doesn't."

"You'll always be his little girl, Glori. He must have been half mad with worry when he learned that Daphne had married you off to a complete stranger and he hadn't been there to save you."

"You're being quite generous when one considers that Papa has treated you rather shamefully."

"I can afford to be generous."

"Oh?"

"I have you," he said with unconcealed satisfaction, "but perhaps we'd best start back before I change my mind about suitable occupations for people lounging about in the heather."

Leaning on his cane, Jacob Kendell came close to apoplexy when he looked out the door and saw Maxwell and Glori coming across the yard. Her cloak was slung over his shoulder.

"Helen!" he roared.

Expecting to find that his bad knee had given way, she hurried into the hall and said, "Jacob, what is the matter?"

"Stand right here and look out the door, and you'll *see* what is the matter!"

After a moment she said, "I see that they must have been up in the hills. Glori has always loved walking in the hills when the heather is in bloom."

"No, look at Maxwell, that scoundrel. He's smiling! *Smiling*!"

Helen Kendell took her husband by the arm and aimed him toward his book room, saying, "I hope you noticed that Glori is smiling as well. I'm happy for them. Even Dog is smiling."

"Open your eyes! Her cloak is covered with bits of stuff. Don't you know what *that* means?"

"Indeed I do. As I recall we once came back looking like that ourselves, though it seems to me that we were covered with leaves instead of heather." Kendell dropped into his chair, and his wife sat on the arm. "It was while we were on our honeymoon in Germany. Have you forgotten?"

"For God's sake, woman, this is *different*!"

"Why, because Glori is your daughter?"

"Because she's my daughter, and I *know* what Maxwell is *thinking*!"

"There didn't seem to be anything wrong with it when you were thinking the same thing thirty years ago."

"Woman, there are times when you exasperate me!"

"Jacob," she said firmly, "they are in love no matter how they came to be married, and that's a fact. If you insist upon making life difficult for Maxwell, Glori won't want to come back here."

"If it hadn't been for Daphne's damned interference, Glori would have chosen someone else and stayed in East Wallow," Kendell stubbornly maintained.

"But she didn't choose someone else, even when she had the chance. Now she's happy with the way things are. Think how much nicer it would have been for us if your father had accepted your choice."

"My father was a fool until the day he died!"

Helen Kendell only smiled.

After a grumpy silence Kendell had to admit that his wife was right. One massive arm pulled her gently onto his lap, and he cuddled her close. Resting his chin on her head, he said, "You've made your point, my love. I shall mend my ways, though it won't be easy. Prepare yourself for the most amazing transformation East Wallow has seen since Bucky Hampton made an ass of himself at the May Day picnic."

Black suits and white shirts, black dresses and white aprons—Glori thought they looked like penguins lined up on the steps of Westbourne Hall. There stood Cook and her assistant, the baker and his assistant, half the kitchen maids, the pantry boy, the knife boy, both lamp boys, the downstairs maids, and several footmen. Ahead of them were Simms, Lucy, Neville's valet, Maud's maid, and Mrs. Finney. But the feeling of homecoming didn't wash over Glori until she saw Maud and Neville come out onto the porch. The last one out of the house was Elgin.

When they had ascended the steps, Maud held out her hands in welcome. She said she hoped their holiday had been pleasant and inquired after Glori's parents. Glori left out the disagreeable parts, saying only that her mother was fine and that her father's knee was much improved.

While passing into the house, Glori leaned closer to Elgin and quietly asked how things were going with Iris Huntington. Maxwell hadn't heard the question. He only saw Elgin's secretive smile in reply to Glori's whisperings.

Maxwell wasn't smiling. What he'd just seen hurt too much. He'd become so confident of Glori's singular regard—how could he have been so wrong? The old monster surfaced again, and he wondered how deep her feelings were for Elgin. Maxwell couldn't stand to think of it. Glori was his wife, and *this* time Elgin really would have to go. Today. And he didn't much care how he got rid of him.

CHAPTER SIXTEEN

⁓⚬⚬⚬⁓

THE welcoming party disbanded when Glori and Maxwell went upstairs. It was well over an hour later that the two of them left their respective chambers and came down again, having bathed away the soot and dust to trade their dark traveling costumes for somber mourning clothes.

The French windows in the blue salon stood open to the terrace this fine August afternoon, and it was on the terrace that they expected to find Aunt Maud and Uncle Neville, with Maud presiding over a pitcher of lemonade. The lemonade stood on the trolley, but Elgin was the only one about. He'd served himself and become engrossed in the progress of a line of ants gathered around some of the sweet liquid that had dribbled onto the flagstones. Maxwell recognized his chance to have a few words of plain speaking with Elgin, but not in front of Glori.

After a polite exchange of greetings, Maxwell turned to Glori and said, "I meant to send word to the kitchen to tell them that I'd like tomatoes at table tonight. Would you see to it? I'd consider it a favor."

"Tomatoes?"

"Please."

"While I was dressing, Lucy recited the menu for

tonight. Sliced tomatoes will be served. There will also be soup and a joint of beef, browned potatoes, with custard for—"

"Glori," Maxwell interrupted quietly, "I'd like a few private words with Elgin."

"Then why didn't you simply say so? I expect he has quite a lot to say to you, too."

Leaning a hip against the stone balustrade that edged the terrace, Maxwell folded his arms across his chest and watched as Glori went inside the house, her trailing black dress sweeping up a few fallen leaves as she went. When she was out of sight, he turned to Elgin and said, "I'm surprised to find that you're still here, old chum. I should think your own property would be suffering from neglect by now."

Elgin looked up, having already decided that Maxwell's stay with his in-laws must have soured his stomach, and said, "My pigs and cabbages do well enough with a good steward. I've got a bit of unfinished business here."

"I shouldn't wonder that your unfinished business wears skirts," came Maxwell's sardonic rejoinder.

"I shouldn't wonder that it's true," replied Elgin with an obliging grin.

Conversation was suspended when a trio of footmen chose that moment to deliver and arrange more chairs. Elgin regarded his irritable friend with patient indulgence and went back to watching the ants.

While furniture was being moved about, Maxwell looked away to the snowy-white chrysanthemum beds, where he turned his thoughts loose. For old times' sake it was going to be hard to tell Elgin to collect his things and leave Westbourne Hall, but allowing him to run tame with Glori would be inviting trouble. He'd been sorely tempted to call up a carriage and bundle Elgin into it with his clothes on his lap, but he thought it only proper that the fellow should hear of his own impending departure before the coachman and servants did. But when it came time for the deed to be done, it would be swift, with no dramatic good-byes. Elgin would simply vanish in a cloud of horse-drawn dust. Maxwell would then explain that a sudden emergency had called him away. And it would be true enough, for if Elgin stayed any longer, Maxwell would begin tearing valued parts from his manly body.

Just as the footmen departed, feminine voices could be heard coming their way through the blue salon, effectively robbing Maxwell of the opportunity to complete his remarks to Elgin. The two men expected Glori and Maud to join them; they got Iris and her aunt Prudence instead. Maxwell looked surprised. Iris looked charming. Elgin looked charmed. Aunt Prudence looked for her fan.

The gentlemen expressed words of welcome and held out chairs—there were now plenty to go around—assuring the ladies that Glori and Maud would soon be among them. Prudence found her fan at the end of the ribbon she had tied to it. Elgin found Iris the most fascinating woman he'd ever seen. Maxwell found Elgin, the eternal flirt, behaving like an idiot over Glori's friend—which suddenly explained why he'd been sticking so close to Westbourne Hall.

While Elgin was dividing his attention between Iris and her aunt, Glori returned to Maxwell's side. To their guests she said, "Good afternoon." To Maxwell she whispered, "Isn't it simply marvelous?"

"You have no idea how marvelous it really is. I was taken completely by surprise."

"Didn't you suspect?"

"What could I have suspected?"

"Surely you and Elgin must have said something important after I left you alone."

"There were interruptions," he said in an offhand way.

A rustling of black taffeta heralded Maud's arrival with Neville behind her. Instead of taking a chair, however,

Maud glided regally toward her neighbor. With jeweled hands outstretched she said, "My dear Prudence, it is *so* good to see you, but I'm afraid the terrace might be a trifle damp for me today. Do let us retire to the sitting room, where I shall show you my embroidered violets. The young people must brave the elements alone, I'm afraid."

"What a perfectly wonderful idea!" exclaimed Neville, quick to assist Prudence to her feet, even though the lady didn't appear at all willing to leave her chair. As he steered the two women in through the French window, Neville glanced at Elgin and Iris and smiled as only a conspirator can.

"Does everyone know about this Romeo and Juliet business except me?" Maxwell quietly demanded.

"I'm not certain how much the squire knows. He's been terribly uncooperative, you see, wanting Iris to marry a title and all that. He has allowed Elgin to call on Iris, but refuses to consider anything serious between them, though Elgin is confident that he can bring him around. As for Pru . . . " Glori shrugged. "Your aunt and uncle, however, have been ever so helpful."

"Why didn't you tell me?"

"I thought Elgin must have told you by now, though he was afraid you'd think he was ready for Bedlam."

"*I* was the one packing for Bedlam!"

"I fail to understand why."

"Good. Let's leave the lovebirds to the lemonade and go off to admire the topiary so that you can tell me what I've missed."

So they walked along the grassy avenue. With the enthusiasm of a matchmaker Glori explained that Iris—poor dear—had been banished to the country by her parents until she learned to behave herself, while Elgin—lucky fellow—thought Iris unexceptionable and loved her to distraction.

Maxwell was more than happy to say nothing at all.

*   *   *

It was much later the same afternoon that Neville paced the library floor. When Glori entered, he looked up and said, "Oh, hello there. You rather startled me, you know. I'd been expecting Maxwell. I've just sent someone to fetch him."

"That's what I've come to tell you," said Glori. "He went riding with Elgin as soon as Iris and Prudence Chumbly left."

Neville's shoulders sagged. "Ah, well, it can wait if it must."

"May I be of any help?"

"I'm afraid not, my dear. The problem lies with that letter Randy wrote to Maxwell, so it's Maxwell I need."

"Oh, dear."

"Oh, dear, indeed! Did you see it?"

"The letter? Yes," Glori answered cautiously. "What is the matter?"

"It's a fake! It's not what it appears to be!"

"Oh, my."

As Elgin had once done, Glori now picked a chair on the far side of the room to give herself an opportunity to school her thoughts before she turned around to face Neville again. She took as much time as she could to be seated, then smoothed her skirt and clasped her hands primly on her lap. Back straight and chin high she said, "As Maxwell and I have discussed that letter, I believe I can tell you whatever he would tell you about it."

"Well, now, that does make a difference." Neville squinted thoughtfully and, said, "Can you tell me if Maxwell ever thought there was anything suspicious about it?"

"Well, he never doubted that the letter he received was written by his cousin, if that's what you mean."

"I've discovered that it wasn't written by Randy—not all of it at any rate." Neville began to pace the floor again, hands clenched behind his back, waistcoat buttons straining. When he stopped pacing, he said, "After my wife handled the thing I noticed that her fingertip had ink on it, but not all of the words were smudged. Why this should be puzzled me. I should've left well enough alone, of course, but I didn't."

Heart thumping, palms damp, Glori sat very still. Neville was talking about the letter she herself had altered with the pen and ink Maxwell had provided.

"Today, after Maud had gone to lie down, my curiosity finally got the better of me," Neville continued. "I found the letter, dipped it in my water jug, and saw that some of the ink rinsed away. What was left was not the account of a fight my son had witnessed, but a fight he had taken part in. Some words of the original text had been changed to make it appear as though he had merely been watching the brawl. I suppose the rest of the letter is that deceptive as well."

"You didn't dip the entire page then?" Glori asked anxiously.

"No, just the bottom. Even so, I can't let my wife see it now. The change is much too obvious. Yet if I don't return it, she's bound to ask what's become of the thing. I wanted to know what was wrong, but I never wanted Maud to be hurt by what I discovered." He looked utterly miserable.

"My goodness," said Glori, her mind awhirl. "There's really no need to upset your wife or Maxwell with what you've found out. If we work quickly I think we can fix that letter ourselves."

Neville didn't look like a believer.

"Truly, it can be done. After all, it's been done before," she pointed out. Then she said, "I did see the letter, though it was a while ago, so I don't remember exactly what I . . . it said. If you tell me what to write, I'll replace all the missing words."

"The paper is badly wrinkled where it was wet," Neville reminded her.

"I'll iron it flat just like a handkerchief. If anyone sees me take the iron from the laundry room, I'll say that I want to press some flowers." She stood then, impatient to begin.

"We must keep absolutely silent about this," Neville told her gravely.

"You can be confident that I won't tell a soul."

Neville's troubled face softened. He reached into his pocket, removed the letter and handed it to Glori. "Thank you, my dear. Still, I do wonder why the thing had been tampered with at all."

Glori shrugged and smiled and took the letter. By a stroke of good luck she would be able to protect Maud from the sad truth and keep Maxwell's secret, for she loved him too much to let him find out that his good intentions weren't as well disguised as he had thought. When Glori had that letter in hand, she felt a twinge of regret in regard to Randy, but that twinge was no longer a guilty one. After the job was completed, she retired to her own room to write to her parents, telling them that the return to Westbourne Hall had been pleasant and uneventful.

Before Maud awoke from her afternoon's repose, Neville had Randy's letter back in her dressing table drawer, well ironed and nicely retouched. After that he took himself to his library, where he was joined by Maxwell and Elgin. Over a spot of brandy they discussed Elgin's intention to leave for his home in Kent the following morning and Neville's plans to go up to London.

"We could do with a change of scenery since the funeral," Neville was saying from the depths of his favorite chair. "We've talked of redoing the house in London for a while, you know, then last week came this letter from the butler to inform us that the roof is leaking. He's having it repaired, of course, but the paint in two bedchambers has been ruined. Maud will dig in and have the place put to rights in no time at all." When he looked at Elgin, his smile was almost hidden beneath his walrus mustache. "My wife is jolly good at that sort of thing, you know. Loves happy endings whether they're for houses or people."

Elgin's reply was the fatuous grin of a man in love as he raised his glass in salute.

Maxwell looked up from the book in his hand and said, "Good heavens, I haven't been *that* far away during the past few months. How could I have missed what's been going on at home?"

Elgin said, "Perhaps you've had something, or someone, more interesting on your mind," and gave his friend a playful leer. Maxwell produced a pained smile and returned to the book in his hand.

While taking part in the general conversation, Maxwell had been wandering about the library, pulling down this book or that, thumbing through and putting it back. A volume of poetry held his attention while Neville and Elgin were deep in a discussion of painters and carpenters.

That evening, after supper, they all gathered in the small sitting room, where, several nights before, Neville had begun reading aloud from *Barchester Towers*. He continued now with emphasis and expression that did Anthony Trollope credit.

Maxwell gave every appearance of attending to the plight of Mr. Harding, but his thoughts were on Glori and the fact that this would be their first night back in their own chambers without Cecil Nottingham on the other side of a paper-thin wall. He wasn't exactly watching her, yet he was aware that she was leaning a little forward in her chair with her Berlin-wool work on her lap. There was blue yarn in the needle she held. When Neville turned a page, Glori would look up over her spectacles. Sometimes she would smile at an amusing passage as the story progressed. Even so, Maxwell wondered what she was thinking, or if she was thinking about anything else at all.

As Glori took another little blue stitch, she thought that Neville could read the labels on cigar bands and make them entertaining. She supposed he could have made a life for himself on the stage—if he hadn't been a gentleman—and done very well for himself. Elgin was quite impressed with his recitation, and Maxwell had hardly moved since he'd sat in his chair and stretched out his legs. Once he'd recrossed his ankles, and twice he'd sipped his coffee, but other than that he'd hardly moved. Glori wondered if he even remembered that this would be their first night back in their own chambers without Cecil Nottingham on the other side of a paper-thin wall.

When Neville closed the book on this night's reading, he signaled the close of the evening as well. Everyone stood up, Aunt Maud covered a ladylike yawn, and they all moved into the hall to take up chamber sticks from the side table to light the way upstairs.

Neither Glori nor Maxwell said a word. When they reached her chamber door, he opened it, followed her in, lit her lamp, and turned it low, softly gilding the room in burnished gold. He barely touched his lips to hers before he went into his own room and shut the door—and he'd done it all without once looking at the bed.

Lucy was in and out at top efficiency. Tonight all was arranged properly, and Glori was soon tucked up against the pillows. She puffed the sleeves on the revealing lacy nightgown she'd made, smoothed back her hair, and waited. After a while she began to think about the time she and Maxwell had been stranded at the Willows for the night, and he'd gone down to the kitchen and drunk himself stupid. Now, after waiting for so long, Glori stared at the connecting door and wondered where he was.

On his own side of that door Maxwell sat ever so quietly in his big chair. The candle wouldn't last much longer and things weren't getting any better.

After a soft tap on the door it was slowly opened and Glori peeked around it, bare toes showing from beneath her housecoat. She said, "Maxwell, why are you sitting there? It's practically dark."

"I've hurt my back."

"The digging has caught up with you."

"But I wasn't digging in *here*. I simply leaned over to take off my shoes, and my back went sort of *twing*."

"I'll call Simms."

"Lord, no! He'll have a herd of surgeons in here poking at me, when all I want to do is lie down with as little fuss as possible."

Glori went to his bed and turned down the covers. When she came back she stood in front of his chair and said, "Well now, tell me where to pull or push, and we'll get you up."

Slowly extending his arms, he said, "Take hold of both wrists and lean back, but not too fast."

Glori did and Maxwell came up out of the chair, grimacing. When he was finally on his feet, he just stood there, waiting for things to stop hurting.

She said, "Stand very still and I'll undress you."

"Like hell you will!"

But once he was under the covers, he admitted that he was more comfortable in only his drawers. Fluffing his pillow, Glori asked if he might like a hot towel for his back. He declined, carefully rolling over to draw her down beside him.

"But your back—"

"Is much better when I'm lying down," he said, and assaulted the tickly place on her neck.

He pulled her closer, and she wrapped her arms around him. He said, "You are so soft," and she said, "Is this a good time for you to explain everything?"

There was a confused pause, but he shook it off in an instant as he sought the row of buttons on her housecoat that started at her throat and ended somewhere beyond his reach. Picking one button, he began to work it free. Nuzzling her ear, he murmured, "What would you like me to explain?"

She sighed contentedly and said, "About our wedding night and sanctified joy."

Now his entire body grew rigid. After a moment he said, "Glori, you're twenty-two years old. Don't you know *anything* about this?"

"Well, Dr. Ellsworth's *Cyclopedia* said—"

"You can jolly well forget that! What else?"

"Caroline Barnstable's governess said to lie still and think of Eng—"

"Oh, for crissakes!" He rolled onto his back, and she dashed off like a rabbit. His cry of "Glori, wait!" didn't even slow her down before the door slammed behind her.

For one giddy moment Maxwell had the urge to pound on the wall and shout, "Enough, I say! It isn't decent!" for he knew that Glori would remember Nottingham and the house in the East Wallow. But that urge, along with some others, went unexplored.

A good while later Maxwell was still wondering what he was supposed to tell Glori about their wedding night. He didn't know how to go about seducing a lady of her innocence because he'd never done it before. Was he supposed to begin with an anatomical lecture, or start with birds and bees? Was he supposed to tell her it won't hurt much? He really didn't know, but he surely didn't want to hurt her, especially not *that* way.

He'd heard tales of those unfortunate honeymoon encounters. There was an especially awful one with a young lady who had to be returned to her parents' home sedated, where she'd been kept in a quiet room ever since. The young man, so the story went, was left unable to perform ever again, withered and wasted by his imprudent excesses. Though the story had seemed questionable, there were a few who swore they knew who the unfortunate parties were. But now even the possibility that it *may* have been true chilled Maxwell to the bone.

His own introduction to the delights of the flesh at age sixteen had been at the hands of a female with considerable experience in the art. His subsequent associations had been conducted with gentlemanly discretion, with women who shared his pleasure in it all, knowing that it was a passing thing—though there were a few who had hoped to change his mind. There had never been a need to explain anything to any of them.

Still he had to say *something* to his wife.

Glori would have appreciated instantaneous sleep, but it was not to be. Angry, hurtful thoughts churned through her mind like beans set to boil. She had done her best to behave with proper honeymoon etiquette, while Maxwell had behaved insufferably. But eventually one loses track of time in a darkened room when sleep won't come, and Glori couldn't tell how long it was before she heard Maxwell moving around in his room.

A wedge of dull gray dawn had pushed around the draperies by the time Glori finally decided that Maxwell must have gone back to sleep. That's when he opened the door and came walking into her room, wearing his dressing gown and a determined set to his jaw. He sat down slowly and made himself uncomfortable in the only upholstered chair.

"Go away," she said, "I'm fast asleep."

"I can see that. I'm fagged half to death myself." He started to stretch out his legs but stopped, took a shallow breath, and shifted a bit. Then he clasped his hands, and after a moment of concentrated thumb tapping, he said, "I've come to apologize."

"I accept. Go away."

"Not until you hear what else I have to say."

She shied a pillow in his direction but missed.

Maxwell studied the pillow where it lay on the floor, then looked back at the bed whence it came and repeated,

"I'm not leaving until you hear me out. Then, if you like, I'll go."

"Oh, all right! Say your piece and be done with it!"

Knowing that there was only one way to get this over with, he said, "I made a mess of it. The truth is that I didn't know what to say to you. I still don't, actually. I should have thought that your mother, or even your sister might have . . . you know . . . put you wise to this sort of thing."

A sharp retort came to Glori's lips, but she didn't let it out. She was as embarrassed as he was.

A few more awkward moments passed before Maxwell said, "You're not going to make this easy for me, are you, Glori?"

"I don't know what you expect of me."

"A few words of encouragement would help. We have some soggy ground to cover before we're through."

More silent moments passed before Glori was convinced that Maxwell wasn't about to leave, so she made a big fuss about sitting up and adjusting her remaining pillow.

Maxwell refrained from making any remark. Neither did he cross his ankles nor drum his fingers. He just sat there with his head against the back of the chair, finally saying, "Glori, if you had it all to do over again, would you still marry me?"

"Is this the soggy ground we have to cover?"

"Yes."

"We're already married."

"Just give me a simple answer."

"Just give me a simple reason."

"Because I love you, dammit!"

She smiled then and hugged her knees. "I love you, too."

"You haven't answered my question. If it were entirely your doing, with no interfer—"

"Yes."

"I'm awfully glad to hear it. I'm also tired of sleeping alone."

"So am I," she said. "Come to bed, you must be getting cold."

"I'm too tired to explain anything about sanctified joy."

"It won't matter tonight. You can explain tomorrow."

"I hurt so bad I can hardly move," he told her.

"Then I won't bother you if you snore."

"I've got to get my nightshirt."

"You can leave it off."

"Are you sure?"

"Quite."

"Good."

When he didn't move, she said, "Maxwell, are you asleep?"

"I'm awake, I just can't get out of this damn chair!"

Leaving her comfy bed, Glori stood before him and pulled him up again. When he saw the shadowy outline of her naked, shapely self through the sheer fabric of her nightgown, his pulse beat faster and he forgot his pain. Her body called softly—his answered enthusiastically and he reached for her. But that movement sent a sharp stab through his back, and he dropped his arms groaning in frustration. Glori guessed it was the strained muscles in Maxwell's back that caused him to utter such a mournful sound. With the efficiency of a nanny, she took away his robe and got him into bed and under the covers. So as not to bounce his already unhappy body, she went around to her side of the bed and got in very carefully.

Much too fatigued to bother with a tactful approach, Maxwell rolled toward Glori and dragged her into his arms, his belly to her back, curling around her womanly body to hook one leg over hers. His top arm was tight around her rib cage, his hand beneath her breast. Snuggly.

"We're being remarkably civilized about this," he

mumbled against her hair. "We're either terribly British or terribly tired."

"I wasn't terribly civil at all. I heaved a pillow at you."

"It wasn't a particularly *dangerous* pillow, as pillows go, and as pillows go it went very well." He gave her a squeeze and said, "You needn't apologize."

She gave him a squeeze and said, "I hadn't planned to."

He managed a forlorn smile and said, "G'night love."

"Mmm," his love replied. His legs were cold and rough against hers, but his chest was warm and she wiggled a little closer to him. Soon his breathing deepened and his arm went limp.

She was still awake when his thumb began a slow and easy stroke.

"Glori . . . " he murmured against her hair.

"Hmm?"

"I'm not as tired as I thought I was. Perhaps there is a thing or two I could explain to you tonight."

"What about your back?"

"Forget about my back."

She turned around, and he pulled away the ribbon that tied her braid, combing his fingers through that silken rope. How many times had he imagined her in his arms like this? But in his fantasies she wasn't wearing a tent, not even a sheer, lacy tent. With a calloused fingertip he traced her lips, then soothed them with his mouth. There was a ready glow in his sleepy eyes when he slid his hand to her hip and rocked against her.

"First I shall demonstrate cuddling and kissing," he said. "We should then be able to figure out the rest quite easily. It isn't too awfully hard to understand, you know. We'll deal with the difficulties when we get to them, and I swear that I shall patiently explain anything you want to know."

"Explanations can be so complicated. Perhaps you could simp—"

* * *

Glori and Maxwell were the last ones down to breakfast, though they looked quite normal when they got there. And even though they were a mite late, they were still in time to bid farewell to Elgin when he left for home. Everyone assured him that the house would be open to him whenever he cared to return.

After Elgin's departure Neville and Maud settled down to look at magazine pictures of fashionable rooms for ideas to redecorate the house in London. Maud still found the illustrations terribly cluttered-looking with fussy things crowded together, leaving no room at all for her to move about without knocking tables over. The thought of redoing the London house was rapidly losing it's appeal, and she thought she might just have the painters in to fix the water-damaged bedrooms and leave the rest as it was.

While Maud lamented modern decor, Maxwell and Glori had the dogcart brought around, put the marmalade cat into the wicker dog basket, and took the creature back to the neighbor who had bought the lonesome horse. This was the third time the cat had had to be returned—it seemed to enjoy the ride.

That evening the four of them—Maud and Neville, Glori and Maxwell—played dominoes. When Maud said her knees were acting up again, everyone was willing to make an early night of it. The following morning Maxwell and Glori missed breakfast entirely.

When they did join the elder Rutherfords in the morning room, those worthies turned to them in greeting, and Glori turned bright pink. Maud put her face to her embroidery and smiled. Neville looked at the floor and announced that he and his wife would be leaving for London on the late train. Feeling like he'd just been caught with his hand in the sugar bowl, Maxwell smoothed his mustache and asked for more particulars about their departure.

"We are not at all ready to go traveling," Maud said with no enthusiasm, "but Neville is convinced that if we put off leaving, I won't want to go at all. I daresay he's right. Neville's man and my Bitsey will stay behind to pack properly. I can manage with one trunk for a few days, as we shall be living quietly."

Actually, it wasn't until the following day that Maud was ready to go, even with one trunk.

Alone in a house with thirty-odd servants in residence, Glori and Maxwell spent the last days of summer blissfully happy. August slipped into September as though the Cotswolds had been enchanted. The young Rutherfords rode and walked the grounds and called on their neighbors. They made love until dawn in her bed or his—neither Simms nor Lucy entered either room now without being called. Maxwell came to believe that their life was enchanted, too, and that nothing in the world could spoil it.

One sunny afternoon the carefree couple picnicked on a blanket by the pond in the swale beyond the folly where the sun made glittering shadows through the leaves and swans glided beneath the drooping branches of a willow. Lacy iridescent dragonflies darted and hovered above the water. Overhead a squirrel chittered in alarm when the marmalade cat wandered out of the bushes to sniff at the empty plates and jump into the picnic basket. Maxwell lured the cat away with a piece of chicken.

As they cleaned up after their feast, their conversation included that animal. Maxwell was of the opinion that the little fellow had found a wife without telling them because he'd heard that the new litter of kittens at the next farm north looked just like you-know-who. Maxwell then speculated upon which of their own children might have his darker coloring or Glori's fair hair and striking eyes. Then Glori listened while Maxwell explained that a child conceived on a sunny afternoon would have a sunny disposition, but he was unable to convince her that they should begin immediate production, right where they were, to gain the greatest benefit from current atmospheric conditions.

Despite Maxwell's efforts, Glori only smiled and said, "Humbug," so he cheerfully rolled her off the blanket and slung it over his shoulder before picking up the basket. Being a gentleman, he did offer Glori his hand as she scrambled to her feet, plus the choice of any bedroom she liked in which to continue their discussion, as long as she didn't take too much time to make up her mind. The sun, he reminded her, was slipping away, and he didn't want to have a crabby child.

Glori considered the possibilities as she picked her wide-awake hat out of the grass and put it on. Maxwell straightened the thing on her head before he kissed her soundly and took her hand for the amble home. The cat strutted along behind them, ears up, tail twitching, looking for another game to play.

Neither one of them suspected that their approach to the house had been observed by someone seated on the ornamental bench in the garden. That someone was Daphne, and she wasn't at all happy. Her dissatisfaction stemmed from the belief that she had been left holding the bag—or the perch, if you like—for something Glori had done. So Daphne had come all the way to the Cotswolds for revenge. It was unfortunate that her resentful absorption with Glori and Maxwell had kept her from noticing the cat.

CHAPTER SEVENTEEN

WHILE crossing the lawn, the marmalade cat scooted beneath Glori's wide hooped skirt to hide. Seconds later he dashed out for an attack upon Maxwell's ankle, then dived under Glori's skirt again. He popped out once more to pounce on a weed and popped back. As Glori and Maxwell went up the steps and into the house, they were laughing because the cat was still tripping along under her skirt. After they entered the house, the cat slipped away unnoticed. Graham appeared from below stairs to take the picnic things and inform them that guests had arrived.

"Good old Farley's back!"

"Not Mr. Farley, sir. I believe it was Sir Henry and Lady Mountrockham who arrived over an hour ago. Mrs. Finney has had their trunks taken to the Chinese bedchamber."

"Where might they be now?" asked Maxwell, covering his displeasure very well.

"I believe Lady Mountrockham has gone into the garden. Sir Henry is in the library, and the bird has been installed in the blue salon, though it doesn't appear to care for the arrangement."

"The *bird*? Might it be a disagreeable parrot?"

"It does seem to fit that description, sir. It has already bitten the maid who brought it a drink of water."

"Well, now, Graham, perhaps you can figure out how to tame the creature, though I suggest you wear a pair of sturdy leather gloves while you're about it."

"I'll do that, sir."

During this exchange, Glori said nothing. Like an android she turned away and numbly climbed the stairs. By the time she reached the next floor, Maxwell was beside her, though neither of them spoke until they were within her bedchamber with the door closed.

Leaning against the door, Maxwell said, "Daphne is up to no good—I just can't imagine what it might be." Glori didn't contradict him. "If Daphne's arrival had any marks of the family visit about it, I might make her welcome and thank her for delivering me unto matrimony, but she's never shown the slightest indication of sisterly interest."

"She wants something," Glori said in a dull voice. She'd been tugging at the ribbons on her hat until she'd turned the bow into a knot. Maxwell undid it for her and spun the hat onto the bed. She would have turned away then, but he caught her by the arm.

He said, "Glori, we'll get through this no matter what she does."

"You don't know what she wants."

"Do you know?"

You! Glori's heart cried. Daphne still wants you! But she said nothing.

Maxwell laid a roughened hand against her smooth cheek and said, "I have to go downstairs to say hello to Sir Henry. Would you like to come with me?"

"No, I still have grass sticking to my dress."

"Shall I send Lucy to you?"

Glori shook her head no.

"Your sister really can't hurt you if you don't let her get under your skin," Maxwell said, but Glori didn't agree.

"Just remember that you are the most beautiful, the most wonderful woman in the world and I love you. If Daphne asks anything you don't want to answer, just smile. It will drive her positively batty." Then he kissed her softly and closed the door quietly.

When she was alone, Glori sat down at her dressing table and rubbed her hands together in an effort to warm them. She was cold all over and didn't think she'd warm up until Daphne was gone. The thing that chilled her through and through was her belief that Daphne and Maxwell had once been more than friends. She thought they were about to celebrate the reunion of two old lovers: one of them her sister and the other her husband.

"Welcome to Westbourne Hall," said Maxwell when he strode into the library, which smelled of leather and beeswax and rum-soaked tobacco. Sir Henry looked up and put aside his newspaper and pipe, but before he could stand to return the greeting, Maxwell was there to shake his hand.

"Don't get up," said Maxwell. "Can I get you anything?"

"No, thank you. I'm quite all right as I am."

Maxwell dropped himself into another chair.

"Your staff didn't seem to be expecting us," said Sir Henry. "Did you receive the telegraph message saying that we would be coming?"

"I'm afraid it didn't reach us," said Maxwell, suspecting that Daphne had disposed of that message before it had ever been sent. No one could tell her not to come if no one knew she was coming.

"That is strange." Sir Henry retrieved his pipe and settled back in the chair to take a contemplative puff. "I hope our arrival hasn't inconvenienced you, old chap."

"I wasn't planning to go anywhere," Maxwell assured him amiably, for his objection wasn't to the man, but to the man's wife.

"The whole purpose of our trip down was to deliver Shakespeare, you know. I don't mind telling you that the move hasn't pleased the bird in the least." Sir Henry took a long pull on his pipe. "Shakespeare doesn't seem to care for trains."

"Would you mind terribly if I asked why you've brought the bird?"

"Daphne suddenly decided that it would be impossible to take Shakespeare aboard ship when we leave for Italy. Ambassador Elliot will leave his post at the end of this year, as you know, and Daphne insists that the bird should be left in Glorianna's care. And she would have it that she deliver the bird herself to be certain that it is properly looked after." Holding his hands up in a gesture of surrender, Sir Henry said. "You know what Daphne can be like once she makes up her mind about something."

Maxwell knew it very well, though he was greatly relieved to learn that Daphne's only reason for being here was because of her disagreeable bird. He supposed the woman now understood that there could never be anything of an intimate nature between them, but if it came up again, he would explain it clearly. He was, after all, a diplomat and silently ticked off a few of his more noteworthy diplomatic successes to remind himself of the fact.

Of course, he thought about the letter to his aunt Maud. He thought it had been diplomatically well done. For all that he had bent the truth right out of shape, he'd managed to provide her with something from Randy that made her feel like she had been loved after all. On the success of that accomplishment alone, Maxwell felt certain that he could manage anything, even Daphne. Having lulled himself into a false sense of peace and harmony, he was able to lean back and enjoy the company of his friend.

As Maxwell put such store in that revised letter of Randy's, it was just as well he didn't know that far away in London his aunt Maud had just slid it to the back of a drawer, behind her gloves and scarves. Every so often she needed to make certain it was still there, though she knew Randy hadn't really written it. A few days after Maxwell had given the thing to her, she had accidentally splashed a single drop of water on it from the flowers she was arranging. She had quickly wiped away the drip, but that's all it took to show her that someone had taken a great deal of trouble to conceal a very dirty word. The magnifying glass from the butterfly collection left her with no doubt that many of the words had been *enhanced*. Though the page had undoubtedly been her son's creation to begin with, those scribbled words of affection—such as they were—had never come from his pen.

Though it was no great surprise, that truth still carried a sharp disappointment with it. Yet there was an unexpected comfort that came with knowing that someone, someone who loved her, had gone to so much trouble in an attempt to ease her aching heart. It's true that Maud wondered who it had been, but she hadn't the least desire to know the answer. She simply went to her davenport, took out pen and ink, and touched up the incriminating word. And she decided that someday, when people no longer spoke of it, the letter would quietly disappear. No one would ever know that she knew it was a forgery. Neville would never find out that their son hadn't written those oddly sentimental lines. Her unknown friend would remain content with the success of the effort.

Before Maud left the room, she hurriedly brushed the lint from her black dress, straightened her cap, and tightened her garnet earrings—she had misplaced them months ago, then found them in Neville's stud box and didn't want to lose them again. When she was tidied up, she went downstairs to join her husband in welcoming their guest, a talented young pianist to whom they had been introduced at a private recital. That small musical entertainment had been arranged by a dear friend as a bit of diversion from their long silent days of mourning. Upon asking their hostess about the musician, they had learned that he was in need of a sponsor if he was to keep body and soul together and study, too. Before the evening was over, she and Neville had decided to offer that patronage and would discuss it with the young man this very day.

Back at Westbourne Hall, while Maxwell was entertaining Sir Henry in the library, Graham entered the blue salon with the bird-taming equipment. After removing his coat he put on the canvas apron he wore while polishing the silver. Then he donned the recommended leather gloves and slowly approached the bird, who was hunkered down on his perch with his eyes closed. From the tin he'd brought along Graham took a few shelled walnuts and dropped them into one of the small glass bowls attached to the bird's perch.

Shakespeare recognized the tonal quality of nuts hitting his bowl. Nuts were worth looking at, so he opened his beady little eyes and shrieked at the stranger mucking about with his food. Graham leaned away so the bird couldn't sink its beak into him.

Looking beautiful and serene, Daphne had just come in from the garden, and it was in response to the bird's cry of alarm that she entered the blue salon. But the bird was forgotten for the moment as her attention was drawn to the fine specimen of manhood that was employed at Westbourne Hall as a footman. She had noticed him in the hall when she and Sir Henry arrived. Now he was facing the angry bird, and she could openly admire the broad shoulders that filled his white shirt and the way the back strap of his waistcoat buckled snugly to accentuate his narrow waist. Hanging loosely around his firm buttocks were the ties of a canvas apron. Elastic garters, red ones, fastened just above the elbow to keep his shirtsleeves from slipping too low. The garters, Daphne noted, circled wonderfully thick arms, and she wondered what he did to promote such lovely muscles.

But her dear bird was still squawking, so Daphne smoothed the bodice of her dress and advanced crooning, "Kissy kissy kiss." The bird echoed her words, fluffed its feathers, and became calmer.

"I can see that you have a good deal to learn about caring for Shakespeare," said Daphne to the footman. "Have you ever tended a parrot before?"

"No, madam, I haven't," replied Graham respectfully, uncomfortably aware of the beautiful woman that now stood so close to him.

"What is your name?"

"Graham, madam."

"Well, then, Graham. You needn't be quite so cautious about *everything*." Daphne removed the tin from his upturned hand and drew a slow sinuous line from his wrist down his palm to the tip of his middle finger, where she took hold of the glove and tugged at it. "No one is going to bite you," she said softly. Daphne gazed up into Graham's dilated eyes and inched the glove away. Beads of perspiration formed on the young man's fevered brow. She dangled the glove by that one finger before dropping it, then sorted through the stuff in the tin to choose a piece of apple. Laying it in Graham's hand, she murmured, "Shakespeare has a passion for apples."

By staring deeply into Daphne's eyes, the flustered footman managed to keep from staring deeply into Daphne's cleavage. Being a healthy man with predictable responses to certain stimuli, Graham was in trouble. And he was glad to be wearing a long canvas apron. When Daphne nudged his arm, he gave the fruit to Shakespeare, and a semblance of peace was established between himself and the bird.

Before leaving the room, Daphne reminded Graham

that she had a great deal more to tell him about the care and keeping of exotic birds. Graham left shortly after Daphne did, putting his coat on over his apron. When he got back to the kitchen, he decided that he'd better polish some of the silver, beginning with the large tea tray.

Glori was still in her room, but she knew she couldn't stay there. As much as she disliked doing so, she would have to find Daphne and go through the formalities of making her welcome. She'd put it off for as long as she could by picking the grass from her dress very slowly, but the chore couldn't be postponed any longer. In Maud's absence she was, after all, the mistress of Westbourne Hall. Glori stood in front of her mirror and tried on smiles until she found one that fit and wore it downstairs.

An assortment of lady's magazines were fanned out on the baroque table in the small salon. The carpet was old Kidderminster and the walls pale green. The paintings were Dutch and the tapestry on the west wall from Poland. The furniture, at least some of it, was Queen Anne. It was a cozy place, at least Glori had always found it so, and she didn't like seeing her sister in it now, but there was nothing to be done about it. Crossing the threshold, she said, "Hello, Daphne."

Daphne looked up from the magazine on her lap and said, "My goodness, Glori, let me look at you! You do appear to a much better advantage than you did last spring, but do sit down, you needn't stand."

To have Daphne invite her to sit down as though she herself were a lady of great rank or the mistress of the house was like a sliver in Glori's finger. Yet to remain standing just because Daphne had told her to sit down would be childish, so Glori sat.

"You're not looking quite so yellowish, and you've filled out so nicely!" Daphne exclaimed. "Still, you must take care not to get any heavier than you are. Papa's side of the family does run to fat," she said, but she'd said it with such a sweet smile.

Glori merely thanked her for her kind words and said, "Maxwell and I weren't expecting you, or we would have been here when you arrived."

"Sir Henry and I made our plans rather suddenly, you see. When it became obvious that I couldn't take Shakespeare to Italy, I thought of you."

"How odd. You've taken that bird everywhere for years, yet now you want to leave it here."

"The voyage would be disagreeable, I'm afraid, so I've brought him here to be cared for. You'll do it, of course."

"Of course, though you could have sent the bird along with one of your servants more easily than making the trip yourself. It makes me wonder why you really came here."

"Good heavens! I've just told—"

"Oh, put a cork in it!"

"Glori, your language hasn't improved in the least! Perhaps I should have a few words with Maxwell about it."

"I doubt that he would be interested in anything you have to say."

Daphne's eyelids drooped seductively, and a faint smile thinned her tinted lips. "Oh, he'll be interested, but then he's always been interested," she said reminiscently. "Did he tell you that we spent a few days together while he was in Scotland? Oh, my, by the look on your face I can see that he didn't. Sir Henry thought I was taking the waters at Harrogate." Daphne looked awfully pleased with herself when she said, "You see, Glori, no matter what has happened, or how long we've been apart, Maxwell and I have always had a special place for each other."

"Good heavens, Daphne! Your husband is a guest in this house. You can't think that Maxwell would—"

Oh, wouldn't he? Daphne said by merely lifting her eyebrows and tilting her head.

Daphne left the room then, knowing that the elaborately tucked and ruffled back of her trailing day dress made a stunning impression. Though she moved languidly, Daphne's thoughts were busy ones. When planning this trip to Westbourne Hall, she had intended to take her revenge upon Glori for what she had done in London, but she hadn't known how at the time. Now it appeared that her sister had developed an attachment to Maxwell, so getting even with her would be easy. While she was at it, she thought she'd yank Maxwell's chain. After all, it was one thing to have him married to her sister—it was something else entirely to see him enjoying it.

Left alone in the small salon Glori tried to tell herself that even if Daphne and Maxwell had been together in Scotland, it was before he had come home again, before he had come to love her. Surely Daphne wouldn't matter to him now. Taking up the fallen magazine, Glori turned the pages without seeing what was pictured on them. She had to do something until it was time to change for dinner.

Predictably, Daphne sparkled at table that evening. She fluttered her eyelashes and regaled them all with the most entertaining anecdotes from the *better drawing rooms of London*. Prominent names dropped like jewels from her lips. Maxwell looked into his glass and wondered if her perfume would taint his wine.

To anyone with any fashion knowledge, Daphne's black taffeta gown was unmistakably Worth. Glori's black serge dinner costume had come from a warehouse in London that supplied ready-made clothing to meet the emergency needs of those ladies upon whom bereavement had unexpectedly descended. Though anyone could see that the simple lines complimented Glori's classic beauty, she could only see that Daphne's dress created a dramatic foil for her red hair, pale skin, and green eyes.

The single strand of pearls at her throat and pearl drops at her ears provided a most correct accent. Other than her wedding rings, Daphne would never be so tasteless as to wear diamonds in the country. Glori wore little jewelry, only her gold wedding band and the cloisonné locket and earrings that had belonged to Maxwell's mother.

While Daphne glowed brighter, Glori could feel herself wilting away.

A muscle twitched in Maxwell's jaw as he watched Daphne give Glori the sour end of another sweet remark. He didn't know whether he was more irritated with Daphne for doing it or with Glori for letting her get away with it.

At the conclusion of the meal Glori rose to take Daphne into the blue salon with Shakespeare so that the men could enjoy their traditional smoke and brandy alone. Maxwell, however, stood when his wife did, suggesting that they remove together.

The bird—having scattered the contents of his food bowl—squawked excitedly when the two couples entered his domain. Side-stepping from one end of the perch to the other, the bird called out, "Kissy kissy kiss!" Daphne went to pat her feathered friend affectionately and dragged away a few pieces of melon and an odd crust or two with the hem of her dress when she took a seat among the others. That seat, of course, was across from Maxwell so that he might fully appreciate the artfully posed sight she presented.

The talk was small, with Sir Henry asking about the sheep and crops. Shakespeare muttered and mumbled in the background, interjecting a new train whistle among the old barking dogs and rattling wheels. When the trolley baring the tea service was rolled into the room, the well-polished silver instantly caught the bird's attention. To Shakespeare a silver pot meant that it was time to perform, for Daphne often had the bird brought in when she had the ladies in to take tea. When a few kissy kisses and a Bible verse were nicely done, there would be an extra bit of apple for a reward, and Shakespeare did like apples.

Impatient for the expected treat, the bird began with, "Yea, though I walk through the shadow of the valley of death," but left out most of it before he got to the end. Still, he waited for the apple to hit the bowl. Nothing happened. So "Kissy kissy kiss" came out on an abrasive note to awaken someone, *anyone*, to the fact that payment was now due. Maxwell didn't know what the bird wanted, but he did notice that Daphne had become increasingly uneasy as the creature chattered on.

"I believe Shakespeare has taken a cold from being next to the windows," Daphne announced. "Do have someone take him into another room without a draft."

"I should think your bird must be lonesome," Maxwell replied, wondering why Daphne was so anxious to get her beloved pet out of the way. "It would surely be cruel to move him into solitary confinement."

Daphne continued to insist that the bird must go, while Maxwell continued to resist its going. Sir Henry smiled indulgently at the foolishness of it all and asked Glori about her recent visit to Yorkshire. While pouring herb tea into flowered china cups, she began by telling him about the heather-covered hills and ended with the fossil dig.

With everyone ignoring the sorry state of Shakespeare's food bowl, the bird decided that a greater effort was needed to get the much-deserved treat. Bobbing up and down, he commenced to sing, "Amazing grace, how sweet the sound that saved a wretch like me," yet the reward failed to appear at the end of it. With greater effort still he pranced from foot to foot and sang out, "The naked lady, painted bold, hid twenty lovers in her hold."

A dead silence preceded Maxwell's chuckle, which

became a howling laugh that offended good taste. Maxwell, you see, had recognized that thin soprano voice.

"It isn't amusing!" Daphne cried, springing up to stamp her little foot and point an accusing finger at Glori. "You taught Shakespeare that dreadful song just to embarrass me!"

"Is that why you've brought the bird here?" Maxwell asked, wiping his eyes.

"I could no longer trust the damn thing!" Daphne snapped without caution. "The cousin of the archbishop of Canterbury came to tea last week and *that's* what Shakespeare sang right after reciting John three-sixteen! She thought the bird had learned that awful song from *me*!"

Pivoting slowly, Maxwell looked inquisitively at Glori, who had the grace to blush.

Certain of finding victory among the ashes of defeat, Daphne tilted her head back so that she could look down her nose at Glori. "Go to your room! I shall take this up with your husband!"

Standing obediently, Glori poured a cup of lukewarm tea down Daphne's cleavage. "Would you like milk and sugar?" she asked politely.

Gasping, Daphne turned on Maxwell to demand, "Aren't you going to *do* something?"

Maxwell handed Daphne a serviette. She struck it aside and marched from the room. Glori apologized for being so clumsy, gave the bird a bit of biscuit, and returned to her chair to refill her teacup, but she no longer looked quite so faded. Unruffled by it all, Sir Henry apologized for his wife's outburst, said nothing about the spilled tea—though one couldn't be certain that he actually saw how the spill had occurred—and inquired after the productivity of fossil digging in Yorkshire. By the time the larger inmates of the blue salon concluded the evening, the smallest one had anchored itself to its perch and gone to sleep.

Upon blowing out the bedside candle that night, Maxwell layered his hands beneath his head and stared into the darkened canopy of Glori's bed. The direction of his thoughts hadn't been apparent until he rolled toward her and whispered, "Would you like milk and sugar?"

He could feel Glori bristle when she said, "I was about to offer her a second cup of tea!"

Maxwell gathered his indignant wife into his arms and said, "You won't be invited to the *better drawing rooms in London* if you keep that up, my girl."

"Would you mind awfully?"

"I should." He rubbed his cheek against her hair and said, "Good night, love."

Glori snuggled against him and hugged the arm that hugged her, relieved that he still hadn't shown any signs of falling victim to Daphne's seductive wiles. Yet from long experience Glori knew that Daphne never gave up until she got what she was after.

The case clock on the landing chimed the noon hour long before Daphne made her appearance the next day. There was no hint of a tear-reddened eye or wilted countenance. She emerged as though last night's affray had never occurred, looking like an exquisite doll in shades-of-gray lace. She even sought out her sister, finding her in the blue salon, where she kept Shakespeare company while perusing a collection of menus. Old habits lived on.

"How delightful you look today," said a smiling Daphne to a wary Glori. "I'm sorry I missed everyone at breakfast."

"Your husband was invited to see Squire Huntington's new microscope. He left quite a while ago."

"Is Maxwell with him?" Daphne inquired with exaggerated innocence.

"Maxwell has business in Chipping Campden. He'll be gone for the day."

"Oh, has he?" said Daphne. "But I mustn't disturb you while you're being so frightfully domestic. I only came to say good morning."

"I see," replied Glori.

Daphne smiled sweetly and left. Glori's smile was even sweeter because Maxwell hadn't really gone to Chipping Campden. He'd gone to Little Woolston.

With a light step Daphne set off down the hall to find a servant to arrange for a carriage to take her shopping in Chipping Campden. It was Graham, however, with whom she came face to face, and her plans changed instantly. It took less than a breath to see that even if she went in search of Maxwell, she might not find him. There would be some satisfaction in letting Glori think otherwise, of course, because she was still so angry with her, but why waste an afternoon looking for someone else when she had a perfectly perfect man at hand?

"Graham," she said, smiling up at him, "I simply cannot abide being in the house this afternoon. Would you please serve tea outside for me? Perhaps I shall sit quietly and read for a while."

"Certainly, madam. May I ask where you would like to have your tea served?"

"Where would you suggest?"

"At this time of year Her Ladyship has enjoyed both the rose garden and folly, madam."

"The folly, then. I shall expect you in half an hour."

As soon as Daphne had abandoned the room, Glori left as well, taking herself off to the conservatory, where she could potter among her flowers in undisturbed peace.

That's why she was nowhere around when the din went up in the blue salon. It seems that the marmalade cat had crept in to play with the bird. The squawking and snarling was so alarming that the maids wouldn't go in. It took Sir Henry's intervention to make the bird let go of the cat, who dashed out of the room leaving clumps of fur behind.

While Sir Henry was uprighting the bird's stand in front of the French windows, he chanced to notice someone walking across the lawn with a tea tray and a folding table. It was the handsome footman, and he was heading for the folly. A glance up the rise revealed a small woman with red hair and a gray dress entering that structure. Sir Henry looked back at the footman and shook his head. Leaning toward Shakespeare, he whispered, "The poor devil doesn't have a chance."

"Kissy kissy kiss," crooned Daphne before taking a nip at Graham's ear.

Graham, the poor devil, moaned and said, "We're going to get caught."

"Do you want to stop now?" she asked in a breathy voice while urging him on. It was monumentally obvious that he didn't.

Daphne had been saved from contact with the cold marble floor by the mass of fabric in her clothes. The display of her lacy underthings, with conveniently accessible drawers, was an added stimulant to the servant, who, until now, had only fantasized about such an encounter with one of the fragile ladies from the world above stairs. They were well matched in their appetites until Daphne stiffened and said, "Do you smell smoke?"

"I wouldn't be surprised," came Graham's labored reply.

She said, "*Pipe* smoke, you idiot!" and pushed the vigorous young man away to behold her husband standing at the door of the folly.

CHAPTER EIGHTEEN

APHNE generated a scream that clanged around the inside of the vaulted marble folly until it made Sir Henry cringe. Then, pressing the back of one dainty hand to her brow, she pointed an accusing finger at Graham and cried, "He attacked me!"

"Yes, and he did it rather well, from what I saw, but then, I arrived late," said Sir Henry.

By now Graham was on his feet trying to yank up his trousers. He gave it up in favor of flight and hobbled to the doorway opposite the one where Sir Henry stood, hoping to make his escape through the pasture, away from the house.

It was Sir Henry's booming "Stop where you are!" that brought Graham to a halt, for he thought he was about to be shot. Sir Henry gestured toward the other man's drooping unmentionables and said, "My God, man! Pull them up before you frighten the cows!"

The stammering red-faced Graham stepped outside, adjusted his clothing, *then* fled, having protected the sensibilities of the dairy herd.

Daphne, too, had taken the opportunity to rearrange her own garments, deciding not to say anything else until she could best decide how to manage her husband. She thought she might even have to throw herself on his mercy and say that she'd been seduced from the path of virtue by a silver-tongued devil and all that.

Propped against the stonework doorway, Sir Henry puffed at his pipe. When he spoke he said, "By the bye Daphne, I had intended to tell you something before we left London, but it slipped my mind. It's about Italy." After drawing on his pipe again, he took it from his mouth, peered into the bowl, and saw that it had gone out. Methodically he went through his pockets until he found his matches.

By this Daphne concluded that assistance was not to be forthcoming and got up from the floor unaided. Well aware of those things that were to her best advantage, she picked a bench where she could sit in the path of a sunbeam. It gave her a sort of halo. "Henry," she said sweetly, dabbing at her eyes, "what is it that you wish to say about Italy?"

"Hmm? Oh, yes, sorry." Sir Henry finished relighting his pipe, and after that he had to find the right pocket in which to put his matches. Then he puffed a few puffs and said, "Daphne, it's been obvious for some time that you've been having a great deal of trouble learning to speak Italian, though I know very well that you've been applying yourself diligently with that fine-looking language instructor who comes by twice a week when I'm out." He puffed some more.

Having reached the end of her tether, Daphne said, "Forget your ghastly pipe! What about Italy?"

"I'm taking someone along to translate for you."

"Who?" she asked hopefully, thinking of that talented instructor of hers.

"Why, Bella, of course. Speaks Italian like a native, along with French, Spanish—"

"Bella Saunders?" Daphne shrieked.

"Good heavens, you sound just like the bird when you do that. But, yes, Bella Saunders. She's going to be your companion—sleeping in our house, eating at our table. It wasn't easy to get her to agree to leave London."

"I detest that woman! If she goes, I won't!"

"Then I'll be forced to cut off your funds and credit, my love. No more Paris dresses or big houses with servants. Somehow I can't imagine your sister taking you in."

Tugging the bodice of her dress back into place, Daphne said, "It won't matter, I can easily find someone else!"

"I'm sure you can, but he'd better be a rich someone else. Perhaps he'll even set you up in a nice little place in St. John's Wood. You might even try to make new friends there, because society as you now know it will be closed to you." After he brushed a bit of ash from the sleeve of his tweedy jacket, Sir Henry went on to say, "I'm stuck with you, Daphne, because a divorce would put a period to my career. There is, however, a limit to how much I'll tolerate, career or no. If you return to London and behave yourself—for I have some knowledge of your dalliances—I'll continue to keep you in style. If I'm satisfied with your efforts, I'll take you to Italy. If not . . ." Shrugging eloquently, Sir Henry turned to leave.

Grim-faced Daphne took the sugar bowl from the tea tray and hurled it. It flew like a silver comet with a crystalline tail, and caught her husband square in the back, then clanked to the floor, where it spun in a wobbly circle.

Turning around, Sir Henry waited politely while the badly dented vessel completed its final revolutions. "There is one other little thing," he then said to his seething wife. "It has occurred to me that our visit has disrupted this household quite enough, so before coming out here, I directed your maid and my valet to pack our things. I'm afraid you must collect yourself as quickly as possible, for we have a train to catch." Tipping his hat, he excused himself to walk back to the house. With so little time until their departure, Sir Henry assumed that he'd be able to get his wife away from Westbourne Hall before she caused any further mischief.

It was a few hours later when Maxwell returned from Little Woolston. Prickles shivered up the back of his neck when he realized how quiet everything was. A face peeked from behind a curtain on the ground floor of the house. The stable boy who took his horse averted his eyes.

"What's going on here?"

"I can't rightly say, sir," answered the lad, scuffing a foot in the dirt.

Maxwell's stride was long and swift, taking him into the house through the nearest door. By the way Mrs. Finney appeared out of nowhere, it would seem that she had been waiting for him. Without even the briefest word of welcome she said, "May I have a few words with you in private, Mr. Rutherford?"

"Certainly." Maxwell removed his hat and gloves and delivered them into the keeping of a waiting maid. From behind a partially closed door he could hear muffled whisperings and someone saying shush. Something like fear made a knot in his chest and he quickly lead the way into the blue salon. Closing the door firmly he said, "Mrs. Finney, has anything happened to my wife?"

"Oh, my, there's no need to be alarmed, sir. Mrs. Rutherford is in the conservatory, where she has been for most of the afternoon."

The knot in Maxwell's chest loosened, and he motioned the woman into a chair before seating himself. In a much lighter mood now he said, "Perhaps you can tell me why the staff has been playing peekaboo."

"I can see that I will have to deal severely with a few who are forgetting their places and manners, but I suspect they're all curious to find out what your reaction will be to the day's events, Mr. Rutherford. Westbourne Hall has always been such a quiet place, except for the times when your cousin was at home."

"And now?"

"One hardly knows where to begin, except to say that Sir Henry and Lady Mountrockham have departed." Mrs. Finney looked as though she, too, would like to avert her eyes and scuff her foot. As housekeeper, she took any family embarrassment very personally.

While Mrs. Finney organized her thoughts to relate them with some propriety, Maxwell became more aware of the room itself. He even twisted around in his chair to have a better look. After giving it a good going over, he said, "I see that the perch is here but the bird is gone. Did it get away?"

"No, sir. It was taken away."

"By whom?"

"I'm not certain. I noticed its absence less than an hour ago, but when I told Mrs. Rutherford, she said that the bird had probably gone back home."

Preparing for a lengthy story, Maxwell slouched in his chair and stretched out his legs.

At the conclusion of a rather lurid report, with a point or two that needed clarification, Mrs. Finney said, "I do hope Mrs. Rutherford hasn't been too terribly disappointed by her sister's departure. Lady Mountrockham went to the conservatory to say good-bye, but Mrs. Rutherford didn't return with her to see the carriage off."

After digesting that tidbit, the lump slipped from Maxwell's chest and landed like a rock in his stomach. Thanking Mrs. Finney for her accounting of things, he excused himself and hurried to find his wife.

Upon entering that greenhouse, Maxwell offered a cheery "Hello" to Glori's kneeling figure.

"Hello," said she from the floor, where she was stacking flowerpots. Her voice wasn't cheery—she didn't even look at him.

"Is something the matter?"

"What could be the matter?"

Crossing his arms, Maxwell stood there for a long mute minute before he said, "I have the feeling that your sister set the fox among the chickens with her farewell address. What did she say?"

"Only that she is looking forward to seeing you in London next week. She was absolutely delighted that you're considering the possibility of traveling to the Continent after all."

During this recitation, Glori had stacked her pots so roughly that one cracked, but she kept on going. Maxwell came over and squatted among the pottery so that she was forced to look at him. The sunshine glinted off her fair hair, and her amethyst eyes swam with angry tears. His brow drew into furrows, and he said, "Glori, I think it's time for us to talk about this."

"I can scarcely credit that you actually want to talk about it. Most men keep their mistresses away from their wives!"

"What the devil are you talking about?"

Rising swiftly, she glowered down at him and said, "Daphne!"

"Oh, for crissakes!" He got to his feet and said, "What else did she say?"

"She has never made it a secret that the two of you were once lovers. I had long suspected it anyway!"

"Do I *look* like that kind of fool?"

"I prefer not to answer that," Glori replied airily. Walking proudly around him, she removed her gloves and dropped them onto the potting table. That's where Maxwell caught her. The very nearness of him pushed her hooped skirts so far under the workbench that she couldn't even turn around. That was fine with him.

"We're going to talk," he said over her shoulder. Leaving her then, he dumped some flower bulbs out of an apple crate and turned it over next to the stacked pots. Glori was invited to sit on it, which she did, folding her hands primly on her lap. Maxwell leaned against the edge of the table, crossed his arms, and scowled. Then he looked up at the bird nest in the rafters. There weren't any birds in it now. He looked out through the walls of streaky glass panels and across the gardens he knew so well.

When he returned his gaze to Glori, he took a long deep breath and let it go just as slowly before he said, "I haven't any plans to go to London or the Continent. Daphne is not my mistress. She never has been, she never will be. I don't want a mistress any more than I want you to take a lover. Am I making myself clear thus far?"

"Quite."

"Do you believe me?"

"Did Daphne visit you in Scotland?"

"No."

Glori sighed. "I suppose she was lying again."

"Do you know why your sister and her husband abandoned ship so unexpectedly this afternoon?"

"Well, they had already delivered the bird into my care."

"The bird is gone."

"Yes, I know, but perhaps it didn't want to stay, so Daphne—"

"Daphne didn't take the bird with her, and it didn't fly away. It appears that Graham made off with the wretched thing after Daphne left."

"Whatever for?"

"I'll come to that presently. Let's return to the reason your sister has left us. You may as well know from the beginning that the entire household is aware of what happened. In fact, the whole county may be hooting uproariously by now."

"Certainly not hooting!"

"Glori, this is serious. I've been told that Sir Henry caught his wife in a compromising position, in the folly, with Graham. At first there was only one maid watching the fellow take a tea tray out there to Daphne. By the time the debauch was over, there wasn't an unoccupied window on that side of the house. Sir Henry and Daphne bailed out soon after the grand event. He left a letter for me, though I have yet to read it."

Shifting his weight against the potting table, he said, "I can only deduce that since our love-worn footman had been deprived of Daphne's company, the next best thing was to have the bird that sounded just like her, so he pinched it, much to my everlasting joy. He probably guessed that he'd be sacked anyway—his belongings are gone. It's a frightful waste of a good footman, actually, and he's got nearly three months' pay coming at the end of this quarter."

There was genuine regret in Glori's voice when she said, "Poor Sir Henry."

"Poor Sir Henry, indeed! The brain fairy must have missed Daphne by a league. Though possessing a remarkable degree of cunning, she lacks the basic elements of common sense!"

Staring at her hands, Glori inspected her fingernails and lined up her thumbs. "Speaking of Daphne's cunning," she said, "just how did she *really* convince you to marry me? Surely other men have managed to escape such weak entrapments, especially with a lady who didn't appear healthy enough to be allowed to marry. You could have saved yourself on the grounds of my debility alone."

"I expect I would have married you even if they had carried you in on a shutter."

"I do hope you intend to explain yourself."

It was a few moments before he admitted the truth. "It was plain and simple blackmail, my love. Daphne had a slanderous piece of information, and I was willing to sacrifice myself, and you as well, to keep her from broadcasting it. She would have ruined the family if I hadn't cooperated. After what happened today, however, she's in no position to even hint at anything unsavory lest she herself should become suspect. Once a lady's reputation is sullied, society is more than willing to heap the sins of the world upon her. Which reminds me, I must write to my aunt and uncle before they hear of the folly in the folly from some other source."

"Maxwell, about this business of blackmail . . . had it anything to do with Randy?"

"Daphne told you?"

Glori shook her head no. "It's only that Randy popped up in scandalous places."

"That he did. In this instance the one and only had taken it upon himself to become a thief, you see. He was busy filling his pockets in someone else's house when Daphne caught him. To make it even worse he was dressed up as a housemaid, with a ruffled cap pulled low as a disguise. Given the size of him, he couldn't have been too hard to spot. It's true," Maxwell insisted when he saw the look on Glori's face. "On one occasion, when Randy had just returned from a house party, his valise toppled from the stack in the hall and burst open when it hit the floor. I was quite startled to see a dress fall out. Along with it there was a lacy apron in which he had wrapped some pieces of jewelry—watch fobs and ladies rings, things of that nature. He and I had quite a go-round over it. That's how I learned what he was up to in his apron and cap."

To her credit Glori did apologize for laughing. After that she became more serious and said, "You've explained how Daphne was able to blackmail you into marrying me. But you haven't said why she ever bothered to do it. It was an awful lot of trouble to take if there wasn't anything in it of benefit to her."

"It was a pay-back, I think. I'm afraid I set her back up at a poetry reading last spring, and she became a wee bit spiteful." Maxwell's explanations stopped there. He still wouldn't tell Glori that she looked so pathetic at the time that her sister had seen her as the ideal instrument for revenge. Intending to divert her from further questions, he said, "Do you have any regrets, madam wife, in regard to your enforced wedded state?"

With that Glori left her apple crate to stand before her husband. Sliding her hands inside his wool jacket she laid her head against his shoulder and hugged him hard. He draped his arms around her, and she cuddled closer. She heard his heartbeat quicken. He didn't see her smile.

She tiptoed her fingers up the bumps of his spine and said, "I shall never let Daphne bother me again. I should have known better this time. And you must stop thinking that you forced me to the altar, because you didn't."

"Are we speaking of the same altar?"

"Yes, indeed. You see, even before we were married I had come to like you, because despite what Daphne had done, you had been so terribly decent. Still, I had actually thought about walking right out of her house while everyone was gathered for the wedding ceremony. I could have done it, you know, but I decided to marry you because you were so nice . . . and you did say please."

Tightening his hold on her, Maxwell shifted a bit and blew at the wisps of Glori's hair that tickled his face. He found her agreeably warm right through their clothes, though he cursed her stiff lacing and the steel hoops that dug into his legs. Dark eyes twinkling, he said, "Surely niceness couldn't have been the *only* reason you married me."

"Well, I might have been *modestly* influenced by the fact that if I married you, I wouldn't be stuck in East Wallow for the rest of my life." Looking up at him then, she added, "You've seen East Wallow."

Maxwell twirled one end of his mustache and said, "I thought you married me because of my irresistible charm." Then he jiggled her and said, "Stop laughing, we have more talking to do."

But her mouth still quivered when she asked, "What else would you care to talk about?"

"What? Why . . . this fine table," he answered, giving it a smart slap. "The thing is well constructed of sound wood. It's been in the family for years, having begun its life in one of the barns as a harvest table. Generations of Cotswoldians have used the thing. It could affect the rest of our lives."

"Oh?"

"Haven't I ever told you that a child conceived in a greenhouse will seldom cry? Science has demonstrated, or is about to demonstrate, that such children are—Glori, stop that! I was only teasing you, actually. It was all in jest! Oh, for crissakes, Glori, not *now*!"

HISTORICAL ROMANCE –

—send in the coupon below—

To get your FREE historical romance and start saving, fill out the coupon below and mail it today. As soon as we receive it we'll send you your FREE book along with your first month's selections.